FALLING FOR DR DIMITRIOU

BY
ANNE FRASER

RETURN OF DR IRRESISTIBLE

BY
AMALIE BERLIN

Anne Fraser was born in Scotland, but brought up in South Africa. After she left school she returned to the birthplace of her parents, the remote Western Islands of Scotland. She left there to train as a nurse, before going on to university to study English Literature. After the birth of her first child she and her doctor husband travelled the world, working in rural Africa, Australia, and Northern Canada. Anne still works in the health sector. To relax, she enjoys spending time with her family, reading, walking, and travelling.

There's never been a day when there haven't been stories in **Amalie Berlin**'s head. When she was a child they were called daydreams, and she was supposed to stop having them and pay attention. Now when someone interrupts her daydreams to ask, 'What are you doing?' she delights in answering: 'I'm working!'

Amalie lives in Southern Ohio with her family and a passel of critters. When *not* working she reads, watches movies, geeks out over documentaries, and randomly decides to learn antiquated skills. In case of zombie apocalypse she'll still have bread, lacy underthings, granulated sugar, and always something new to read.

FALLING FOR DR DIMITRIOU

BY
ANNE FRASER

MILLS
BOON

Published in Great Britain 2014
by Mills & Boon, an imprint of Harlequin (UK) Limited,
Eton House, 18-24 Paradise Road, Richmond, Surrey, TW9 1SR

© 2014 Anne Fraser

ISBN: 978-0-263-90782-7

Harlequin (UK) Limited's policy is to use papers that are natural, renewable and recyclable products and made from wood grown in sustainable forests. The logging and manufacturing processes conform to the legal environmental regulations of the country of origin.

Printed and bound in Spain
by Blackprint CPI, Barcelona

Dear Reader

Many of you will know that I like to set my books in countries I love, and where I have spent time—and this one is no exception.

The Peloponnese is perhaps less well known than the Greek islands or Athens, but it has its own charm—stunning beaches, spectacular mountains (with very scary roads!), and around every corner a famous city, ruin, or legend.

I hope you enjoy spending time with Alexander and Katherine, each of them with their own secret, as they track down the source of a meningitis epidemic while trying not to fall in love.

Anne Fraser

Dedication

To Rachel and Stewart—my personal on-call doctors—
and to Megan Haslam, my supportive,
patient and all-round fabulous editor.

**These books are also available in eBook format
from www.millsandboon.co.uk**

PROLOGUE

IT WAS THAT moment before dawn, before the sky had begun to lighten and the moon seemed at its brightest, when Alexander saw her for the first time. On his way to the bay where he kept his boat, his attention was caught by a woman emerging like Aphrodite from the sea.

She paused, the waves lapping around her thighs, to squeeze the water from her tangled hair. As the sun rose, it bathed her in light adding to the mystical scene. He held his breath. He'd heard about her—in a village this size it would have been surprising if the arrival of a stranger wasn't commented on—and they hadn't exaggerated when they'd said she was beautiful.

The bay where she'd been swimming was below him, just beyond the wall that bordered the village square. If she looked up she would see him. But she didn't. She waded towards the shore, droplets clinging to her golden skin, her long hair still streaming with water. If the village hadn't been full of gossip about the woman who'd come to stay in the villa overlooking the bay, he could almost let himself believe that she was a mythical creature rising from the sea.

Almost. If he were a fanciful man. Which he wasn't.

CHAPTER ONE

Katherine placed her pen on the table and leaned back in her chair. She picked up her glass of water, took a long sip and grimaced. It was tepid. Although she'd only poured it a short while ago, the ice cubes had already melted in the relentless midday Greek sun.

As it had done throughout the morning, her gaze drifted to the bay almost immediately below her veranda. The man was back. Over the last few evenings he'd come down to the little bay around five and stayed there, working on his boat until the sun began to set. He always worked with intense concentration, scraping away paint and sanding, stopping every so often to step back and evaluate his progress. But today, Saturday, he'd been there since early morning.

He was wearing jeans rolled up above his ankles and a white T-shirt that emphasised his golden skin, broad shoulders and well-developed biceps. She couldn't make out the colour of his eyes, but he had dark hair, curling on his forehead and slightly over his neckline. Despite what he was wearing, she couldn't help thinking of a Greek warrior—although there was nothing but gentleness in the way he treated his boat.

Who was he? she wondered idly. If her friend Sally were

here she would have found out everything about him, down to his star sign. Unfortunately Katherine wasn't as gorgeous as Sally, to whom men responded like flies around a honey pot and who had always had some man on the go—at least until she'd met Tom. Now, insanely happily married to him, her friend had made it her mission in life to find someone for Katherine. So far her efforts had been in vain. Katherine had had her share of romances—well, two apart from Ben—but the only fizz in those had been when they'd fizzled out, and she'd given up on finding Mr Right a long time ago. Besides, men like the one she was watching were always attached to some beautiful woman.

He must have felt her eyes on him because he glanced up and looked directly at her. She scraped her chair back a little so that it was in the shadows, hoping that the dark glasses she was wearing meant he couldn't be sure she had been staring at him.

Not that she was at all interested in him, she told herself. It was just that he was a diversion from the work she was doing on her thesis—albeit a very pleasing-to-the-eye diversion.

Everything about Greece was a feast for the senses. It was exactly as her mother had described it—blindingly white beaches, grey-green mountains and a translucent sea that changed colour depending on the tide and the time of day. She could fully grasp, now, why her mother had spoken of the country of her birth so often and with such longing.

Katherine's heart squeezed. Was it already four weeks since Mum had died? It felt like only yesterday. The month had passed in a haze of grief and Katherine had worked even longer hours in an attempt to keep herself from thinking too much, until Tim, her boss, had pulled her aside and told her gently, but firmly, that she needed to take time off—especially as she hadn't had a holiday in years. Although she'd protested, he'd dug his heels in. Six weeks, he'd told her, and if he saw her in the office during that time, he'd call Security. One look at his face had told her he meant it.

Then when a work colleague had told her that the Greek parents of a friend of hers were going to America for the birth of their first grandchild and needed someone to stay in their home while they were away—someone who would care for their cherished cat and water the garden—Katherine knew it was serendipity; her thesis had been put to one side when Mum had been ill, and despite what Tim said about taking a complete rest, this would be the perfect time to finish it.

It would also be a chance to fulfil the promise she'd made to her mother.

The little whitewashed house was built on the edge of the village, tucked against the side of a mountain. It had a tiny open-plan kitchen and sitting room, with stone steps hewn out of the rock snaking up to the south-facing balcony that overlooked the bay. The main bedroom was downstairs, its door leading onto a small terrace that, in turn, led directly onto the beach. The garden was filled with pomegranate, fig and ancient, gnarled olive trees that provided much-needed shade. Masses of red bougainvillea, jasmine and honeysuckle clung to the wall, scenting the air.

The cat, Hercules, was no problem to look after. Most of the time he lay sunbathing on the patio and all she had to do was make sure he had plenty of water and feed him. She'd developed a fondness for him and he for her. He'd taken to sleeping on her bed and while she knew it was a habit she shouldn't encourage, there was something comforting about the sound of his purring and the warmth of his body curled up next to hers. And with that thought, her gaze strayed once more to the man working on the boat.

He'd resumed his paint scraping. He had to be hot down there where there was no shade. She wondered about offering him a drink. It would be the neighbourly, the polite thing to do. But she wasn't here to get to know the neighbours, she was here to see some of her mother's country and, while keeping her boss happy, to finish her thesis. Habits of a lifetime were too hard to break, though, and four days into her six-week holiday she hadn't actually seen very much of Greece, apart from a brief visit to the village her mother had lived as a child. Still, there was plenty of time and if she kept up this pace, her thesis would be ready to submit within the month and then she'd take time off to relax and sightsee.

However, the heat was making it difficult to concentrate. She should give herself a break and it wouldn't take her a moment to fetch him a drink. As it was likely he came from the village, he probably couldn't speak English very well anyway. That would definitely curtail any attempt to strike up a conversation.

Just as she stood to move towards the kitchen, a little girl, around five or six, appeared from around the corner of the cliff. She was wearing a pair of frayed denim shorts and a bright red T-shirt. Her long, blonde hair, tied up in a ponytail, bobbed as she skipped towards the man. A small spaniel, ears flapping, chased after her, barking excitedly.

'Baba!' she cried, squealing with delight, her arms waving like the blades of a windmill.

An unexpected and unwelcome pang of disappointment washed over Katherine. So he *was* married.

He stopped what he was doing and grinned, his teeth white against his skin.

'Crystal!' he said, holding his arms wide for the little girl to jump into them. Katherine could only make out enough of the rest of the conversation to know it was in Greek.

He placed the little girl down as a woman, slim with short blonde hair, loped towards them. This had to be the wife. She was carrying a wicker basket, which she laid on the sand, and said something to the man that made him grin.

The child, the cocker spaniel close on her heels, ran around in circles, her laughter ringing through the still air.

There was something about the small family, their utter enjoyment of each other, the tableau they made, that looked so perfect it made Katherine's heart contract. This was what family life should be—might have been—but would likely never be. At least, not for her.

Which wasn't to say that she didn't love the life she did have. It was interesting, totally absorbing and worthwhile. Public health wasn't regarded as the sexiest speciality, but in terms of saving lives most other doctors agreed it was public-health doctors and preventive medicine that made the greatest difference. One only had to think about the Broad Street pump, for example. No one had been able to stop the spread of cholera that had raged through London in the 1800s until they'd found its source.

When she next looked up the woman had gone but the detritus of a picnic still remained on the blanket. The man was leaning against a rock, his long legs stretched out in front of him, the child, dwarfed by his size, snuggled into his side, gazing up at him with a rapt expression on her face as he read to her from a story book.

It was no use, she couldn't concentrate out here. Gathering up her papers, she went back inside. She'd work for another hour before stopping for lunch. Perhaps then she'd explore the village properly. Apart from the short trip to Mum's village—and what a disappointment that had turned out to be—she'd been too absorbed in her thesis to do more than go for a swim or a walk along the beach before breakfast and last thing at night. Besides, she needed to stock up on more provisions.

She'd been to the shop on the village square once to buy some tomatoes and milk and had had to endure the undisguised curiosity of the shopkeeper and her customers and she regretted not having learnt Greek properly when she'd had the chance to do so. Her mother had been a native Greek speaker but she had never spoken it at home and consequently Katherine knew little of the language.

However, she hated the way some tourists expected the locals to speak English, regardless of what country they found themselves in, and had made sure she'd learnt enough to ask for what she needed—at the very least, to say please, thank you and to greet people. In the store, she'd managed to ask for what she wanted through a combination of hand signals and her few words of Greek—the latter causing no small amount of amusement.

She glanced at her papers and pushed them away with a sigh. The warm family scene she'd witnessed had unsettled her, bringing back the familiar ache of loneliness and longing. Since her concentration was ruined, she may as well go to the village now. A quick freshen-up and then she'd be good to go. Walking into her bedroom, she hesitated. She crossed over to her bedside drawer and removed the photograph album she always kept with her. She flicked through the pages until she found a couple of photos of

Poppy when she was six—around the same age as the little girl in the bay.

This particular one had been taken on the beach—Brighton, if she remembered correctly. Poppy was kneeling in the sand, a bucket and spade next to her, a deep frown knotting her forehead as she sculpted what looked like a very wobbly sandcastle. She was in a bright one-piece costume, her hair tied up in bunches on either side of her head. Another, taken the same day, was of Poppy in Liz's arms, the remains of an ice cream still evident on her face, her head thrown back as if she'd been snapped right in the middle of a fit of giggles. Katherine could see the gap in the front of her mouth where her baby teeth had fallen out, yet to be replaced with permanent ones. She appeared happy, blissfully so. As happy as the child she'd seen earlier.

She closed the album, unable to bear looking further. Hadn't she told herself that it was useless to dwell on what might have been? Work. That was what always stopped her dwelling on the past. The trip to the village could wait.

Immersed in her writing, Katherine was startled by a small voice behind her.

'Yiássas.'

Katherine spun around in her chair. She hadn't heard anyone coming up the rock steps but she instantly recognised the little girl from the bay. 'Oh, hello.' What was she doing here? And on her own? 'You gave me a bit of a fright,' she added in English.

The child giggled. 'I did, didn't I? I saw you earlier when I was with Baba. You were on the balcony.' She pointed to it. 'I don't think you have any friends so I thought you might want a visitor. Me!' Her English was almost perfect, although heavily accented.

Katherine laughed but it didn't sound quite as carefree as she hoped. 'Some adults like their own company.' She gestured to the papers in front of her. 'Besides, I have lots of work to do while I'm here.'

The girl studied her doubtfully for a few moments. 'But you wouldn't mind if I come and see you sometimes?'

What could she say to that? 'No, of course not. But I'm afraid you wouldn't find me very good company. I'm not used to entertaining little girls.'

The child looked astounded. 'But you must have been a little girl once! Before you got old.'

This time Katherine's laugh was wholehearted. 'Exactly. I'm old. No fun. Should you be here? Your family might be worried about you.'

The child's eyes widened. 'Why?'

'Well, because you're very small still and most of the time parents like to know where their children are and what they're up to.' She winced inwardly, aware of the irony of what she'd said.

'But they do know where I am, silly. I'm in the village! Hello, Hercules.' The girl knelt and stroked the cat. Suddenly pandemonium broke out. It seemed her spaniel had come to look for her. He ran into the room and spotting the cat made a beeline for it. With a furious yowl Hercules leapt up and onto Katherine's desk, scattering her papers, pens and pencils onto the floor. She grabbed and held on to the struggling cat as the dog jumped up against her legs, barking excitedly.

'Kato! Galen! Kato!' A stern male voice cut through the chaos. It was the child's father—the boat man. God, how many other people and animals were going to appear uninvited in her living room?

The spaniel obediently ran over to the man and lay down at his feet, tail wagging and panting happily. Now the father's censorious gaze rested on his little girl. After speaking a few words in Greek, he turned to Katherine. 'I apologise for my daughter's intrusion. She knows she shouldn't wander off without letting me know first. I didn't notice she'd gone until I saw her footprints headed this way.' His English was impeccable with only a trace of an attractive accent. 'Please, let us help you gather your papers.'

Close up he was overwhelmingly good-looking, with thick-lashed sepia eyes, a straight nose, curving sensual mouth and sharp cheekbones. Katherine felt another stab of envy for the blonde-haired woman. She lowered the still protesting Hercules to the floor. With a final malevolent glance at the spaniel, he disappeared outside.

'Please, there's no need...'

But he was already picking up some of the strewn papers. 'It's the least we can do.'

Katherine darted forward and placed a hand on his arm. To her dismay, her fingertips tingled where they touched his warm skin and she quickly snatched it away. 'I'd rather you didn't—they might get even more muddled up.'

He straightened and studied her for a moment from beneath dark brows. He was so close she could smell his soap and almost feel waves of energy pulsating from him. Every nerve cell in her body seemed to be on alert, each small hair on her body standing to attention. Dear God, that she should be reacting like this to a married man! What the hell was wrong with her? She needed to get a grip. 'Accidents happen, there is no need for you to do anything, thank you,' she said. Thankfully her voice sounded normal.

'Yes, Baba! Accidents happen!' the little girl piped up in English.

His response to his daughter, although spoken softly in Greek, had her lowering her head again, but when he turned back to Katherine a smile lighted his eyes and played around the corners of his mouth. He raked a hand through his hair. 'Again I must apologise for my daughter. I'm afraid Crystal is too used to going in and out of all the villagers' homes here and doesn't quite understand that some people prefer to offer invitations.'

Crystal looked so woebegone that Katherine found herself smiling back at them. 'It's fine—I needed a break. So now I'm having one—a little earlier than planned, but that's okay.'

'In which case we'll leave you to enjoy it in peace.' He glanced at her ringless fingers. 'Miss…?'

'Burns. Katherine Burns.'

'Katherine.' The way he rolled her name around his mouth made it sound exotic. 'And I am Alexander Dimitriou. I've noticed you watching from your balcony.'

'Excuse me! I wasn't watching you! I was working on my laptop and you just happened to be directly in my line of sight whenever I lifted my head.' The arrogance of the man! To take it for granted that she'd been watching him— even if she had.

When he grinned she realised she'd let him know that she had noticed him. The way he was looking at her was disturbing. It was simply not right for a married man to look at a woman who wasn't his wife that way.

'Perhaps,' he continued, 'you'll consider joining my family one day for lunch, to make up for disrupting your day?'

She wasn't here to hang around divine-looking Greek men—particularly married ones! 'Thank you,' she responded tersely. 'I did say to Crystal that she could come and visit me again some time,' she added as she walked father and daughter outside, 'but perhaps you should remind her to let you know before she does?'

She stood on the balcony, watching as they ambled hand in hand across the beach towards the village square, Crystal chattering and swinging on her father's arm. Even from this distance she could hear his laughter. With a sigh she turned around and went back inside.

Later that evening, after Crystal was in bed, Alexander's thoughts returned to Katherine, as they had over the last few days—ever since the morning he'd seen her come out of the water. It was just his luck that the villa she was staying in overlooked the bay where he was working on his boat.

He couldn't help glancing her way as she sat on her balcony, her head bent over her laptop as she typed, pausing only to push stray locks from her eyes—and to watch him.

And she *had* been watching him. He'd looked up more than once to catch her looking in his direction. She'd caused quite a stir in the village, arriving here by herself. The villagers, his grandmother and cousin Helen included, continued to be fascinated by this woman who'd landed in their midst and who kept herself to herself, seldom venturing from her temporary home unless it was to have a quick dip in the sea or shop for groceries at the village store. They couldn't understand anyone coming on holiday by themselves and had speculated wildly about her.

To their disappointment she hadn't stopped for a coffee or a glass of wine in the village square or to try some of

Maria's—the owner of only taverna in the village—home-cooked food so there had been no opportunity to find out more about her. Helen especially would have loved to know more about her—his cousin was always on at him to start dating again.

But, despite the fact Katherine was undeniably gorgeous, he wasn't interested in long-term relationships and he had the distinct impression that Miss Burns didn't do short-term ones.

However, there was something about this particular woman that drew him. Perhaps, he thought, because he recognised the same sadness in her that was in him. All the more reason, then, for him to keep his distance.

CHAPTER TWO

THE NEXT MORNING, having decided to work inside and out of sight, Katherine only managed to resist for a couple of hours before finding herself drawn like a magnet to the balcony.

Gazing down at the beach, she saw that Alexander, stripped to the waist, his golden skin glistening with a sheen of perspiration, was back working on his boat again. Dragging her gaze away from him, she closed her eyes for a moment and listened to the sound of the waves licking the shore. The sweet smell of oranges from a nearby orchard wafted on the breeze. Being here in Greece was like a balm for her soul.

A sharp curse brought her attention back to the bay.

Alexander had dropped his paint-scraper. He studied his hand for a moment and shook his head. He looked around as if searching for a bandage, but apparently finding only his T-shirt, bent to pick it up, and wound it around his palm.

She could hardly leave him bleeding—especially when, prepared as always, she'd brought a small first-aid kit with her and it was unlikely there would be a doctor available on a Sunday in such a small village.

The blood had pretty much soaked through his temporary bandage by the time she reached him but, undaunted, he had carried on working, keeping his left hand—the damaged one—elevated in some kind of optimistic hope of stemming the bleeding.

'*Kalíméra!*' Katherine called out, not wanting to surprise him. When he looked up, she pointed to his hand and lifted the first-aid kit she carried. 'Can I help?'

'It's okay, I'll manage,' he replied. When he smiled, her heart gave a queer little flutter. 'But thank you.'

'At least let me look at it. Judging by the amount of blood, you've cut it pretty badly.'

His smile grew wider. 'If you insist,' he said, holding out his injured hand.

She drew closer to him and began unwrapping his makeshift bandage. As she gently tugged the remaining bit of cloth aside and her fingers encountered the warmth of his work-roughened palm, she felt the same frisson of electricity course through her body as she had the day before. Bloody typical; the first time she could remember meeting someone whom she found instantly attractive he had to be married—and a father to boot.

'It's deep,' she said, examining the wound, 'and needs stitches. Is there a surgery open today?'

'Most of them are open for emergencies only on a Sunday. I'm not sure this constitutes one.'

'I think it does.' Katherine said, aware that her tone sounded schoolmistress prim. 'I'm a doctor, so I do know what I'm talking about.'

His eyebrows shot up. 'Are you really? The villagers had you down as a writer. A GP, I take it?'

Katherine shook her head. 'No. Epidemiology. Research. I'm in public health.'

'But not on holiday? You seemed pretty immersed in paperwork yesterday.'

'My thesis. For my PhD.'

'Brains too.' He grinned. 'So can't you stitch my hand?'

'Unfortunately, no. I could if I had a suturing kit with me but I don't. Anyway, you'll likely need a tetanus shot unless you've had one recently. Have you?'

'No.'

For some reason, the way he was looking at her made her think that he was laughing at her. 'Then one of the emergency surgeries it will have to be,' she said firmly. 'I'll clean and bandage the cut in the meantime. Is there someone who can give you a lift?'

'No need—it's within walking distance. Anyway, this little scratch is not going to kill me.'

'Possibly not but it could make you very sick indeed.' She thought for a moment. 'I strongly advise you to find out whether the doctor is willing to see you. I'll phone him if you like. As one doctor to another, he might be persuaded to see you.'

He was no longer disguising his amusement. 'Actually, that would be a bit embarrassing seeing as I'm the doctor and it's my practice—one of them anyway.'

'You're a doctor?' She couldn't keep the surprise out of her voice. She felt more than slightly foolish, standing before him with her little plastic medical kit. If he was a GP he was probably more qualified than she to assess the damage to his hand. Now she knew the reason for his secret amusement. 'You might have mentioned this before,' she continued through gritted teeth.

Alexander shrugged. 'I was going to, I promise. Eventually.' That smile again. 'I suppose I was enjoying the personal attention—it's nice to be on the receiving end for a change.'

'You really should have said straight away,' she reiterated, struggling to control the annoyance that was rapidly replacing her embarrassment. 'However, you can hardly suture your hand yourself.' Although right this minute she was half-minded to let him try.

'I could give it a go,' he replied, 'but you're right, it would be easier and neater if you did it. The practice I have here is really little more than a consulting room I use when the older villagers need to see a doctor and aren't unwell enough to warrant a trip to my practice. But it's reasonably well equipped. You could stitch it there.'

'In that case, lead the way.'

His consulting room had obviously once been a fisherman's cottage, with the front door leading directly onto the village square. There were only two rooms leading off the small hall and he opened the door to the one on the left. It was furnished with an examination couch, a stainless-steel trolley, a sink and most of what she'd expect to find in a small rural surgery. The one surprise was a deep armchair covered with a throw. He followed her gaze and grimaced. 'I know that doesn't really belong, but my older patients like to feel more at home when they come to see me here.'

Not really the most sanitary of arrangements, but she kept her own counsel. It wasn't up to her to tell him how to run his practice.

He opened a cupboard and placed some local anaesthetic and a syringe on the desk, along with a disposable suture tray. He perched on the couch and rested his hand, palm up, on his leg.

He definitely has the physique of a gladiator, she

thought, her gaze lingering on his chest for a moment too long. She shifted her gaze and found him looking at her, one eyebrow raised and a small smile playing on his lips. As heat rushed to her cheeks she turned away, wishing she'd left him to deal with his hand himself.

She washed her hands and slipped on a pair of disposable gloves, acutely conscious of his teasing appraisal as she filled the syringe with the local anaesthetic. Studiously avoiding looking at his naked chest, she gently lifted up his hand and, after swabbing the skin, injected into the wound. He didn't even flinch as she did so. 'I'll wait a few minutes for it to take effect.'

'So what brings you here?' he asked. 'It isn't one of the usual tourists spots.'

'I was kindly offered the use of the Dukases' villa through a colleague who is a friend of their daughter in exchange for taking care of Hercules and the garden. My mother was from Greece and I've always wanted to see the country where she was born.'

'She was from here?'

'From Ītylo. This was the closest I could get to there.'

'It's your first time in the Peloponnese?'

'My first time in Greece,' Katherine admitted.

'And your mother didn't come with you?'

'No. She passed away recently.' To her dismay, her voice hitched. She swallowed the lump in her throat before continuing. 'She always wanted the two of us to visit Greece together, but her health prevented her from travelling. She had multiple sclerosis.'

'I'm sorry.' Two simple words, but the way he said it, she knew he really meant it.

She lightly prodded his palm with her fingertips. 'How does that feel?'

'Numb. Go ahead.'

Opening up the suture pack, she picked up the needle. Why did he have to be nice as well as gorgeous?

'I hope you're planning to see some of the Peloponnese while you're here. Olympia? Delphi? Athens and the Acropolis for sure. The city of Mycenae, perhaps?'

Katherine laughed. 'They're all on my list. But I want to finish my thesis first.'

He raised his head and frowned slightly. 'So no holiday for a while, then? That's not good. Everyone needs to take time out to relax.'

'I do relax. Often.' Not that often—but as often as she wanted to. 'Anyway I find work relaxing.'

'Mmm,' he said, as if he didn't believe her. Or approve. 'Work can be a way to avoid dealing with the unbearable. Not good for the psyche if it goes on too long. You need to take time to grieve,' he suggested gently.

She stiffened. Who was he to tell her what was good for her and what she needed? How he chose to live his life was up to him, just as it was up to her how she lived.

'I must apologise again for yesterday,' he continued, when she didn't reply, 'You were obviously working so I hope we didn't set you back too much. My daughter's been dying to meet you since you arrived. I'm afraid her curiosity about you got the better of her.'

Katherine inserted a stitch and tied it off. 'Your daughter is charming and very pretty.'

'Yes, she is. She takes after her mother.'

'I take it the beautiful woman on the beach yesterday is your wife?' she said, inserting another l stitch.

When she heard his sharp intake of breath she stopped. 'I'm sorry. Did that hurt? Didn't I use enough local?'

His expression was taut, but he shook his head. 'I can't

feel a thing. The woman you saw is Helen, my cousin. My wife died.'

Katherine was appalled. 'I'm so sorry. How awful for you and your daughter. To lose her mother when so young.' She winced inwardly at her choice of words.

'Yes,' he said abruptly. 'It was.'

So he knew loss too. She bent her head again and didn't raise it until she'd added the final stitch and the wound was closed. When had his wife died? Crystal had to be, what? Four? Five? Therefore it had to be within that time frame. Judging by the bleakness in his eyes, the loss was still raw. In which case he might as well be married. And why the hell were her thoughts continuing along this route?

She gave herself a mental shake and placed a small square dressing on top and finished with a bandage, pleased that her work was still as neat as it had been when she'd sutured on a regular basis.

'What about tetanus?' she asked. 'I'm assuming you have some in stock here?'

'Suppose I'd better let you give me that too. It's been over five years since I last had one.' He went to the small drugs fridge and looked inside. 'Hell,' he said after examining the contents. 'I'm out. Never mind, I'll get it when I go back to my other surgery tomorrow.'

'It could be too late by then—as I'm sure you know. No, since it seems that you are my patient, at least for the moment, I'm going to have to insist you get one today.'

He eyed her. 'That would mean a trip to Pýrgos—almost an hour from here. Unfortunately, Helen has taken my car to take Crystal to play with a friend and won't be back until tonight. Tomorrow it will have to be.'

She hesitated, but only for a moment. 'In that case, I'll drive you.'

'Something tells me you're not going to back down on this.'

She smiled. 'And you'd be right.' She arched an eyebrow. 'You might want to fetch a clean shirt. Why don't you do that while I get my car keys?'

But it seemed as if she'd offered him a lift without the means to carry it through. Not wanting to drive down from Athens —she'd heard about the Peloponnese roads, especially the one that ran between here and the Greek capital—she'd taken a circuitous route; first an early morning flight, followed by a ferry and then two buses to the rental company In hindsight it would have been quicker and probably far less stressful to have flown into Athens.

And now she had a puncture. Thankfully the car did have a spare wheel. She jacked it up and found the wrench to loosen the bolts but they wouldn't budge. No doubt they had rusted.

'Problems?'

She whirled around to find Alexander standing behind her. He had showered and changed into light-coloured cotton trousers and a white short-sleeved shirt.

'Puncture. I'm just changing the wheel. As soon as I get a chance, I'm going to exchange this heap for something better.'

The car the company had given her had more dents and bashes in it than a rally car after a crash. She would have insisted on a newer, more pristine model, but the company had said it was the only one they had available.

His lips twitched. He walked around the car, shaking his head. 'They palmed this off on you?'

'Yes, well, I was tired.' She resented the fact that he

thought she'd let herself be taken advantage of—even if she had.

'Which company did you rent this from?'

She told him.

'In that case, they have a branch in Katákolo, which isn't too far from where we're going.'

'Will it be open on a Sunday?'

'The cruise ships all offer day trips to Olympia from there. Like most places that cater for tourists, everything will be open. Once I've been jagged to your satisfaction I'll make sure they exchange it for something better.'

'I'm perfectly able to manage to sort it out myself.' Did all Greek men think women were helpless?

He drew back a little, holding up his hands. 'Hey. You're helping me. And it's not far from where we're going.'

She was instantly ashamed of herself. He'd done nothing to warrant her snapping at him. It was hardly his fault that he made her feel like a schoolgirl with her first crush.

'I'm sorry. It's just that I'm a bit hot.' She sought a better reason to excuse her behaviour, but apart from telling him that he found his company unsettling she couldn't think of one. 'In the meantime, I still have to change the wheel.' She picked up a rock and hit the wrench. Nothing. No movement. Not even a centimetre.

He crouched down next to her, the muscles of his thighs straining against the material of his trousers. 'Let me do it.'

'I can manage. At least I would if the things weren't stuck.'

He took the wrench from her. 'It just needs a little strength.'

'You shouldn't. Not with your hand recently sutured.'

He ignored her and within moments the nuts were off

the wheel. He took the flat tyre off and silently she passed him the spare.

'I probably loosened them.' He looked up at her and grinned. 'I'm sure you did.' He lifted the new wheel into position and replaced the bolts.

'Thank you,' she said. 'I can take it from here.'

He stood back and watched as she lowered the car to the ground.

'I'll just tighten the bolts again,' he said, 'then we'll be good to go. Would you like me to drive?'

'No, thank you.'

Despite the open windows the car was hot; unsurprisingly, the air-conditioning didn't work either. Katherine gripped the steering-wheel, trying not to flinch whenever a car overtook her, the vehicle often swerving back in just in time to avoid being smashed into by another coming in the opposite direction. Perhaps she should have taken Alexander up on his offer to drive? But if he drove the same way as his countrymen did, being a passenger would be ten times worse. She preferred being in control.

Eventually the countryside gave way to denser traffic and by the time Alexander directed her to a parking spot in front of the surgery she was a nervous wreck, her hands were damp and she knew her hair was plastered to her scalp. She was beginning to appreciate why the car the company had given her was badly dented.

He looked relieved as he undid his seat belt. 'This won't take long but why don't you go for a walk while you're waiting?'

'If you're going to be quick I might as well come in with you.' She was curious to see how the medical services in Greece worked.

While Alexander greeted the receptionist, Katherine took a seat in the small waiting room next to an elderly woman with a bandage on her knee and clutching a walking stick. Alexander turned to her and said something in Greek that made her laugh.

'Mrs Kalfas is waiting for her husband to collect her,' he explained to Katherine, 'so I can go straight in. I won't be long.'

A few moments after Alexander disappeared from sight, a man in his early to mid-twenties, staggered in and, after saying a few words to the receptionist, almost fell into one of the empty chairs. He was good-looking with dark curly hair, a full mouth and olive skin, but his jeans and checked shirt were stained and crumpled as if he'd picked them up off the bedroom floor, too ill to care. His cheeks were flushed and his eyes, when he managed to open them briefly, glittered with fever. Perhaps she should have gone for that walk. All doctors knew that hospitals and GP waiting rooms were bad news for the healthy.

Mrs Kalfas tried to strike up a conversation with him, but he appeared to have little interest in whatever she was saying. Warning bells started to clamour in Katherine's head as she studied him covertly from under her eyelids. Now she wondered if his eyes were closed because the light was annoying him—and the way he kept pressing his hand to the back of his neck as if it were sore alarmed her too. He really didn't look well at all. The receptionist should have let the doctors know that he was here.

Katherine was about to suggest it when he gave a loud moan and slid to the floor. Instantly she was on her feet and, crouching by his side, feeling for his pulse. It was there but weak and rapid. She glanced around but annoyingly there was no sign of the receptionist. Mrs Kalfas was staring, horrified.

'I need some help here,' Katherine called out. 'Alexander!'

The door behind which he'd vanished was flung open and Alexander, followed by a short, balding, overweight man with a stethoscope wrapped around his neck, rushed over and knelt by Katherine's side.

'What happened?' Alexander asked.

'He came in a few minutes ago. I was just about to suggest he be taken through when he collapsed. He's been rubbing his neck as if it's painful or stiff. We should consider meningitis.'

Alexander and his colleague exchanged a few words in rapid Greek and the other doctor hurried away.

The man on the floor groaned softly. The receptionist reappeared and came to stand next to Mrs Kalfas, placing a comforting arm around the older woman. Alexander said something to the younger woman and she hurried back to her desk and picked up the phone.

'It could be a number of things but to be on the safe side Carlos—Dr Stavrou—is going to get a line so we can start him on IV antibiotics,' Alexander told Katherine. 'Diane is phoning for an ambulance.'

Carlos returned and ripped open a pack and handed Alexander a venflon. He quickly inserted it into a vein and, taking the bag of saline from his colleague, attached one end of the tube to the needle. When Katherine held out her hand for the bag of saline, Alexander passed it to her and she held it up so that the fluid could flow unimpeded. In the meantime, Alexander had injected antibiotics straight into one of the stricken patient's veins.

As Katherine placed an oxygen mask over his face, she

was vaguely aware that the receptionist had returned and along with Mrs Kalfas was watching intently. Alexander whirled around and spoke rapidly to the receptionist. He translated her reply for Katherine.

'Diane says the ambulance will be here shortly. She's agreed to take Mrs Kalfas home instead of making her wait for her husband. Seeing she's had a bit of a fright, I think it's better.'

Katherine was impressed with the way he'd considered the old woman, even in the midst of an emergency. Their patient was still unconscious but apart from keeping an eye on his airway there was little more they could do until the ambulance arrived. They couldn't risk taking him in a car in case he arrested.

'You have a defib to hand?' she asked.

'Naturally.'

She wondered what had caused the man to collapse. A number of possibilities ran through her head, meningitis being one, but without further tests it was impossible to know. All they could do now was stabilise him until they got him to hospital.

Diane picked up her handbag and helped the old lady out. Soon after, the ambulance arrived and the paramedics took over. They spoke to Alexander before quickly loading the patient into the ambulance.

'Should one of us go with him?' Katherine asked.

'No need. Carlos wants to go. He's his patient.'

The ambulance doors were slammed shut and it drove away, sirens screaming.

'Are you all right?' Alexander asked.

'Perfectly. Could you make sure they test him for meningitis?'

'Bit of a leap, isn't it? Carlos said Stefan—the patient—

is not only accident prone but there's a few bugs doing the rounds. Besides, I didn't see any signs of a rash.'

'Trust me. Communicable diseases are my area of expertise and that young man has all the signs—sensitivity to light, fever, neck pain. The rash could appear at any time.' Alexander studied her for a moment. 'It couldn't hurt to do a lumbar puncture. I'll phone the hospital and make sure they do all the tests. At least he's been started on IV antibiotics. In the meantime, I'm afraid we're going to have to wait here until Carlos returns. Is that okay?'

'Sure.' She smiled at him. 'You can show me around while we wait.'

The practice was as well equipped as any Katherine had seen. In addition to four consulting rooms, one for each of the doctors, one for the nurses and one for their physio, there was an X-ray room and a sleek, spotlessly clean treatment room. All the equipment was modern and up to date.

'You appear to be almost as well set up as a small hospital,' Katherine said, impressed.

'We never know what we're going to get, so we like to be prepared for the worst. We have, as you can imagine, a fair share of road traffic accidents on these roads and sometimes people bring the casualties here as it's closer than the hospital.' Not quite the small family practice she'd imagined.

'We don't do much more than stabilise them and send them on,' Alexander continued, 'but it can make the difference between survival and death.'

'You have advanced life-support training, then?'

'Yes. We all do. It also helps that I used to be a surgeon.' He picked up the phone. 'Would you excuse me while I phone the hospital?' he said. 'I need to tell them to watch out for meningitis, as you suggested, and Carlos was telling me earlier that one of my patients was admitted there last night. I'd like to find out how he's doing.'

'Be my guest,' Katherine replied. As she waited for him to finish the call she studied him covertly from under her lashes. The more she learned about him the more he intrigued her. So he used to be a surgeon. What, then, had brought him to what, despite the expensive and up-to-date equipment, was still essentially a rural family practice? Had he come back here because of his wife? And how had she died? Had she been a road traffic victim?

While he'd been talking on the phone, Alexander's expression had darkened. He ended the phone call and sat lost in thought for a while. It was almost as if he'd forgotten she was there.

'Something wrong?' she asked.

'The patient Carlos was telling me about has been transferred to a hospital in Athens. The hospital doctor who admitted him yesterday sent him there this morning, but he's left to go fishing and can't be reached. None of the staff on duty today can tell me anything.' He leaned back in his chair. 'I'll speak to him tomorrow and find out why he felt a transfer was necessary.' He shook his head as if to clear it. 'But I have spoken to the doctor on call today about Stéfan. She's promised to do a lumbar puncture on him.'

'Good,' Katherine said.

'So what is your thesis on?' Alexander asked.

'As I said, communicable diseases. Mainly African ones.'

'What stage of your training are you?'

She raised an eyebrow. 'Consultant. Have been for four years. I'm thinking of applying for a professor's post. Hence the doctorate.'

He whistled between his teeth. 'You're a consultant! You don't look old enough.'

'I'm thirty-four.'

They chatted for a while about her work and different infectious diseases Alexander had come across in Greece. Caught up in discussing her passion, she was surprised when she heard footsteps and Carlos came in. She'd no idea so much time had passed.

'How is our patient?' Alexander asked in English, after formally introducing her to his partner.

'His blood pressure had come up by the time I left him in the care of the emergency team at the hospital. They'll let me know how he is as soon as they've done all the tests.'

'Will you let me know when they do?'

'Of course.'

Alexander pushed away from the desk and stood. He smiled at Katherine. 'In that case, let's go and swap that car of yours.'

The car rental company did have another car for her, but it wouldn't be available until later that afternoon.

Katherine turned to Alexander. 'I'm sure you want to get home. Isn't there another rental company in the area?'

'I suspect you'll find the same thing there. The cruise ships come in in the morning and a lot of the passengers—those who don't want to take the bus tour to Olympia—hire a car for the day. They tend to bring them back around four.'

'Damn. That's three hours away.'

'We could have lunch,' he suggested. 'Or, if you're not hungry, we can go to Olympia ourselves. It's years since I've been and it's less than thirty minutes from here. By the time we get back, Costa here should have a car for you.'

He smiled. 'You're in Greece now. You'll find life a lot easier if you accept that here time works in a different zone.'

She hid a sigh. She should be getting back to her thesis. By taking the morning off she risked falling behind the schedule she'd mapped out for herself.

Whoa—what was she thinking? Had she completely lost it? He was right. What was the hurry anyway? It was Sunday and an interesting, *single* hunk was wanting to spend time with her.

'I would love to see Olympia,' she said. And she would. It was near the top of her list of places to visit. It would also be less intense, less like a date, than having lunch.

'Good. That's settled, then.' He opened the passenger door for Katherine. She looked at him and arched an eyebrow.

'I think it will be less stressful—and safer for us all— if I drive,' he said. 'I know the roads better.'

She hesitated, then broke into a smile. 'To be honest, if I never have to drive that heap of scrap again it would be too soon. So be my guest. Knock yourself out.'

It wasn't long before she was regretting her decision—and her words. As far as she was concerned, Alexander drove just like every other Greek driver.

'When I said knock yourself out,' she hissed, 'I didn't mean literally.'

He laughed. 'Don't worry. I promise you driving this way is safer.'

Nevertheless, she was hugely relieved when they arrived still in one piece. Alexander found a space in the crowded car park.

'There are two parts to the site—the ruins of the ancient city and the museum. I suggest we start off in the museum, which is air-conditioned.' He glanced at her appraisingly and his lips twitched. She was wearing navy trousers and a white cotton blouse with a Peter Pan collar, which, she had to admit, while neat and professional were almost unbearably hot. 'It'll be cooler by the time we're finished. If I remember correctly, there is very little shade in the ruins.'

She wandered around the exhibits, trying to concentrate but not really able to. She was too acutely aware of the similarity between the physiques of the naked statues and the man close by.

When they'd finished in the museum they walked across to the ruins. Although it was cooler than it had been earlier, it was still hot and almost immediately she felt a trickle of perspiration gather between her breasts. Alexander, on the other hand, looked as fresh and as cool as he'd done since they'd left the village.

As he pointed out the temples of Zeus and Hera, Katherine began to relax. Perhaps it was because, away from the statues, she could concentrate on what Alexander was saying. He knew a great deal about Greek history and was an easy and informative guide and soon she was caught up in his stories about what life must have been like during the Ottoman era.

When they'd finished admiring the bouleuterion, where the statue of Zeus had once stood, he led her across to the track where the athletes had competed. 'Did you know they competed in the nude?'

Instantly an image of Alexander naked leaped into her head and blood rushed to her cheeks. She hoped he would think it was the heat that was making her flush but when she saw the amusement in his eyes she knew he was perfectly aware what she'd been thinking.

It was nuts. After Ben she'd only ever had one other significant long-term relationship—with Steven, one of her colleagues. When that had ended, after he'd been offered a job in the States, she'd been surprisingly relieved. Since then, although she'd been asked out many times and Sally had tried to fix her up with several of the unattached men she or Tom knew, and she'd gone out with two or three of them, no one had appealed enough to make her want to see them again beyond a couple of dates.

Relationships, she'd decided, were overrated. Many women were single and very happy—as was she. She could eat when she liked, go where she pleased without having to consult anyone, holiday where it suited her and work all weekend and every weekend if she wanted to. Until her mother's death, she had rarely been lonely—she hadn't lied to Crystal when she'd told her she preferred being on her own, but that didn't mean she didn't miss physical contact. That didn't mean she didn't miss sex.

She felt her flush deepen. But sex without strings had never been her cup of tea.

God! She'd thought more about sex over these last two days than she had in months. But it was hard *not* to think about it around all these nude statues. Perhaps it hadn't been such a good idea choosing to come here instead of lunch. Lunch might have been the safer option after all.

A replacement car still wasn't available when they returned to the rental company.

'Really!' Katherine muttered. 'It's almost six.' Unlike Alexander, she needed to cool off, preferably with an ice-cold shower. And to do that she needed to get home—and out of Alexander's company.

'He promises he'll have one by seven. If not, he'll give you his own car.' Alexander grinned. 'I did warn you about Greek timing.'

'But aren't you in a hurry to get back?' she asked, dismayed. 'I mean, you've given up the best part of your day to help me out. You must have other stuff you'd rather be doing. And I should get back to my thesis.'

'Nope. I'm in no rush. As I said, I'm not expecting my cousin and Crystal home until later. And surely you can give yourself a few more hours off?' The laughter in his eyes dimmed momentarily. 'Trust me, sometimes work should take a back seat.'

It was all right for him, he clearly found it easy to relax. But to spend more time in his company, blushing and getting tongue-tied, was too embarrassing. Still, she couldn't very well make him take a taxi all the way back home—even if it was an appealing thought. Maybe *she* should get a taxi home? Now she was being ridiculous! She was behaving like someone with sunstroke. She almost sighed with relief. Perhaps that was it? She clearly wasn't herself. She realised he was watching her curiously. What had he been saying? Oh, yes—something about dinner.

'In that case, dinner would be lovely,' she replied, pulling herself together. 'Do you have somewhere in mind?'

'As a matter of fact I do. It's down by the shore. They sell the best seafood this side of Greece.' He tilted his head. 'You do like seafood, don't you?'

'I love it.'

'Good. We can wave goodbye to the cruise ships and more or less have the place to ourselves. We'll leave the car here. It's not far.'

They walked along the deserted main street. Without the hordes of visitors and now that the shopkeepers had brought in their stands that had been filled with tourist souvenirs, maps and guides, the town had a completely different feel to it. It was as if it were a town of two identities—the one belonging to the tourists, and this typically Greek sleepy one.

The restaurant was situated at the end of a quiet cul-de-sac and it didn't look very prepossessing from the rear, where the entrance was situated. Understated was the word Katherine would use to describe the interior with its striped blue and white table runners and unlit candles rammed into empty wine bottles. But when they were guided to a table on the veranda by the *maître d'*, the view took Katherine's breath away. White sands and a blue, blue sea glittered as if some ancient god had scattered diamonds onto its surface. Alexander pulled out a chair for her beneath the shade of a tree and she sank happily into it.

When Alexander chose the lobster, freshly caught that morning, she decided to have it too. And since he was determined to drive they ordered a glass of chilled white wine for her and a fruit juice for himself.

They chatted easily about Greece and the recent blow to its economy and Alexander suggested various other places she might want to visit. Then he asked which medical school she'd studied at and she'd told him Edinburgh. Surprisingly, it turned out that it had been one of his choices but in the end he'd decided on Bart's.

'What made you decide to study in England?' she asked.

'I was brought up there. My mother was from Kent.' That explained his excellent English.

'So you have a Greek father and an English mother. I'm the opposite. How did your parents meet?'

'My mother met my father when she was working in a taverna while she was backpacking around Greece. It was supposed to be her gap year but in the end she never made it to university. Not long after she and my father started dating, they married. They moved to an apartment in Athens and after a couple of years they had me, then my younger brother. But she always pined for England. My father lectured in archaeology so he applied for a post at the British Museum and when he was accepted, we upped and left. I was five at the time.

'My father always missed Greece, though, so we came back as a family whenever we could, particularly to see my grandmother—my father's mother—and all the other family—aunts and uncles and cousins. Greece has always felt like home to me. Dad died when he was in his early forties. My grandfather died shortly after he did and, as my father's eldest son, I inherited the villa I live in now, as well as the land around it. It's been in our family for generations. Naturally my grandmother still lives in the family home.'

Katherine wanted to ask about his wife, but judging by his terse response in the village consulting room earlier that was a no-go area. 'And where's your mother now?' she asked instead, leaning back as their waiter placed their drinks in front of them.

'Still in England,' Alexander continued, when their waiter had left. 'She hasn't been back since my father died. I don't think she can bear to come anymore. She lives close to my brother in Somerset.'

'Doesn't she miss her grandchild?'

'Of course. However, Mother's life is in England—it's where her friends and my brother and his family are. We visit her often and, of course, there's video chat.' He took a sip of his drink. 'That's enough about me. What about you? Is there someone waiting for you in the UK?'

'No. No one.'

He looked surprised. 'Divorced, then? I'm assuming no children otherwise they'd be with you.'

She hesitated. 'Not divorced. Never married.' She swallowed. 'And no children.'

'Brothers and sisters? Your dad?'

'My dad passed away when I was fifteen. And no brothers or sisters.'

'So an only child. Being on your own must have made your mother's death even harder to handle, then,' he said softly.

The sympathy in his voice brought a lump to her throat. But she didn't want him to feel sorry for her.

'As I told Crystal, I like my own company. I have loads of friends in the UK when—if—I feel the need to socialise.'

'No one who could come with you? We Greeks find it difficult to imagine being on our own. As you've probably noticed, we like to surround ourselves with family.'

'Plenty of people offered to come,' she said quickly. 'But this trip was something I needed to do alone.'

He said nothing, just looked at her with his warm, brown eyes.

'I wish I could have come with Mum before she died, though. She always hoped to return to Greece, with Dad and me, to show me her country, but sadly it never happened,' she found herself explaining, to fill the silence.

'Because of her MS?'

'Yes. Mostly.'

But even before her mother's diagnosis the trip had been talked about but never actually planned. Her parents' restaurant had taken all their energy, money and time. At first it had seemed to be going from strength to strength, but then the unimaginable had happened. Dad had died and without him Mum had become a shadow of herself and had talked less and less about returning to Greece.

It had only been later that she'd realised that her father's death and struggling with a failing business hadn't been the only reasons Mum had been listless. She'd hidden her symptoms from her daughter until the evening she'd collapsed. And that had been the beginning of a new nightmare.

'What do you do when you're not working?' he asked, when she didn't expand.

'I kind of work all the time,' she admitted 'It's honestly my favourite thing to do.'

He frowned as if he didn't believe her. But it was true. She loved her work and found it totally absorbing. Given the choice of a night out or settling down to some research with a glass of wine in one hand, the research won hands down.

Their food arrived and was set before them. Katherine reached for the bowl of lemon quarters at the same as Alexander. As their fingers touched she felt a frisson of electricity course through her body. She drew back too quickly and flushed.

He lifted up the dish, his expression enigmatic. 'You first.'

'Thank you.'

'So why public health?' he asked, seeming genuinely interested.

'I thought I wanted to do general medicine but I spent six months in Infectious Diseases as part of my rotation and loved it—particularly when it came to diagnosing the more obscure infections. It was like solving a cryptic crossword puzzle. You had to work out what it could be by deciphering the clues, and that meant finding out as much as you could about your patient—where they, or their families, had been recently, for example. Sometimes it was ob-

vious if they'd just come from Africa—then you'd start by
think of malaria—or typhoid or if they'd been on a walking
holiday in a place where there were lots of sheep, making
Lyme disease a possibility. It was the patients who made
the job so fascinating. When you'd found out as much as
you could, you had to decide what tests and investigations
to do, ruling diseases out one by one until the only one left
was almost certainly the right answer.'

She rested her fork on the side of her plate. 'Of course,
it wasn't always a good outcome. Sometimes by the time
you found out what the patient had it was too late. And what
was the point in diagnosing someone with malaria if you
couldn't stop them getting it in the first place? I became
really interested in prevention and that's when I moved into
public health.' She stopped suddenly. 'Sorry. I didn't mean
to go on. But when I get talking about work…'

'Hey, I'm a doctor, I like talking shop.'

'Why did you decide to come back to Greece?' she
asked.

Something she couldn't read flickered behind his eyes.
'I wanted to spend more time with my daughter,' he said
shortly. 'But we were talking about you. How did your
parents meet?' It seemed he was equally determined to
turn the conversation back to her.

'Mum met Dad when he was in the armed forces. He
was stationed in Cyprus and she was visiting friends there.
They fell in love and he left the army and they moved back
to Scotland. He tried one job after another, trying to find
something he enjoyed or at least was good at. Eventually
he gave up trying to find the ideal job and started working
for a building company. We weren't well off—not poor but
not well off. We lived in a small house bordering an estate
where there was a lot of crime. When I was eight my father

became unwell. He didn't know what was it was—except that it was affecting his lungs. He was pretty bad before Mum persuaded him to see his GP.' She paused. 'That's when I began to think of becoming a doctor.'

He leaned forward. 'Go on.'

'We used to go, as a family, to his doctor's appointments. We did everything as a family.' Sadness washed over her. 'First there were the visits to the GP, but when he couldn't work out what was going on, he referred Dad to the hospital. I was fascinated. Everything about the hospital intrigued me: the way the doctors used to rush about seeming so important; the way the nurses always seemed to know what they were doing; the smells; the sounds—all the stuff that normally puts people off I found exciting.

'Of course, I was too young to understand that the reason we were there was because there was something seriously wrong with my father. His physician was a kind woman. I remember her well. She had these horn-rimmed glasses and she used to look at me over the top of them. When she saw how interested I was, she let me listen to my father's chest with her stethoscope. I remember hearing the dub-dub of his heartbeat and marvelling that this thing, this muscle, no larger than his fist, was what was keeping him—what was keeping me and everyone else—alive.

'I was always smart at school. It came easy to me to get top marks and when I saw how proud it made my parents, I worked even harder. My school teachers told my parents that they had high hopes for me. When I told Mum and Dad—I was twelve—that I wanted to be a doctor they were thrilled. But they knew that it would be difficult if I went to the high school in our area. It had a reputation for being rough and disruptive. They saved every penny they could so they could send me to private school.

'My father had received a payment from the building company when he left—by this time he'd been diagnosed with emphysema from years of breathing in building dust—but I knew he'd been planning to use the money for a down payment on a mortgage to buy a little restaurant—Dad would be the manager, Mum the head cook—and I didn't want them to use their life savings on me, not if they didn't have to.

'I persuaded them to let me apply to one of the top private schools. My teacher had told them that the school awarded scholarships to children with potential but not the funds to go to the school. She also warned them that it was very competitive. But I knew I could do it—and I did.'

'I am beginning to suspect that you're not in the habit of letting obstacles get in your way.'

Suddenly she was horrified. She wasn't usually so garrulous and certainly not when it came to talking about herself. Over the years she'd become adept at steering the conversation away from herself and onto the other person. Now she was acutely conscious of having monopolised the conversation, and when she thought about it she realised she'd made herself out to be a paragon of virtue when nothing could be further from the truth. Perhaps it was the wine. Or the way he listened to her as if she were the most fascinating person he'd ever met. Her heart thumped. Perhaps this was the way he was with everyone. She suspected it was. In which case he'd be an excellent family doctor.

'So how long have you been back in Greece?' she asked when their waiter left them, after replenishing their water glasses. She really wanted to know more about *him*.

'Just over two years.' His gaze dropped to his glass. He twirled his water, the ice cubes tinkling against the side. 'Not long after I lost my wife. I worked at St George's in

London—As I mentioned earlier, I trained as surgeon before going into general practice—but my wife, Sophia, wasn't really a city girl, so we bought a house in a nearby suburb and I commuted from there. And when I was on call, I slept at the hospital.' A shadow crossed his face. 'In retrospect, that was a mistake,' he murmured, so softly she couldn't be sure she'd heard him correctly. 'Why did you change to general practice?'

His expression darkened. 'I gave surgery up when I decided to return to Greece.'

It wasn't really an answer and she had the distinct feeling he was keeping as much back from her as he was telling her. Had he really been content to give up the challenges and adrenaline rush of surgery to return to Greece to be a GP? But bereavement often caused people to change their lives.

'Was your wife Greek?'

'Yes.'

'Did she work while you were in the UK?' she asked. How had she felt about leaving her country and going to a much colder, much greyer London? But, then, she had been with the man she'd loved and who had loved her. No doubt she hadn't cared.

'She was a musician,' he replied. 'She always wanted to play in an orchestra. She gave that up when we moved to England and taught piano instead.'

'Crystal must miss her terribly.'

'We both do. I see her mother in Crystal every day.' He swallowed and averted his gaze from hers for a few moments. 'What about you?' he asked, eventually. 'Don't you want children?'

He was looking at her again with that same intense expression in his eyes.

'Don't most women? But...' She dropped her head and fiddled with her butter knife, searching for the right words. 'It wasn't meant to be,' she finished lamely. Her heart thumped uncomfortably against her ribs. *Keep the conversation on neutral territory,* she told herself. 'I enjoyed the trip to Olympia. You know a lot about Greek archaeology and history,' she said.

He slid her a thoughtful look as if he knew she was deliberately changing the subject.

'My father was an archaeologist and my wife shared his passion,' he said. 'What chance do you think I wouldn't be? I doubt there is an archaeological site in Greece I haven't been to. Every holiday, when we returned here, that's what we did. I think my wife thought it was her mission in life to educate me.' His face clouded and Katherine knew he was thinking of his wife again. He had loved her very much, that much was clear.

What would it be like—the thought almost came out of nowhere—to be loved like that? To know that there was one person in the world who treasured you above all else? That there was someone you could turn to in your darkest moments, share your deepest secrets and fears with?

It was unlikely she'd ever know.

Katherine sank back into the leather seat of her replacement car, grateful she didn't have to drive back to the villa on dark, twisting roads. Alexander switched on the radio, and the soothing notes of a Brahms concerto softly filled the silence that had sprung up between them since they'd left the restaurant. The lights of the dashboard and the occasional passing vehicle revealed a man absorbed with his own thoughts, his forehead knotted, his eyes bleak. He turned the volume up a little more.

'You like this?' she asked. 'It's one of my favourites.'

He glanced at her. 'It is? My wife used to play it all the time. I haven't listened to it for a while…' He looked away, his mouth set in a grim line.

His wife was like a ghostly presence in the car.

Katherine closed her eyes. Deliberately shifting her focus from Alexander, she wondered how Stéfan was faring. If it was meningitis, he could very well be struggling for his life at this moment. She hoped she was wrong and he just had an infection that would be quickly cleared up with antibiotics.

Becoming aware they had entered the village, she sat straighter in her seat.

Tension seeped between them as he brought the car to a standstill outside her villa. They unclipped their seat belts and climbed out of the car.

As he handed her the keys, their fingers touched. She looked up at him from beneath her lashes, wondering if he had felt the electricity too. Would he ask to come in? Or if he could see her again?

Instead, his voice was as neutral as his words. 'I enjoyed today. Thank you, Katherine.'

Disappointment washed over her. But what had she expected? It was clear he was still grieving for his wife.

'I did too. Good night…'

'Good night, Katherine.'

She winced inwardly as she heard the finality in his tone. Hercules, purring loudly, curved his body around her legs as she opened the front door.

He was some comfort at least.

As the door closed behind her, Alexander thrust his hands deeper into his pockets and, before turning for the short walk home across the square, cursed himself for the fool he was.

Throughout the day he had been aware of the rising of desire he felt for this strait-laced, reserved, intelligent and beautiful woman. But hearing the melody Sophia had played so often had reminded him that Katherine would be leaving too. Even if she hadn't he had only ashes to give her.

No, his first instincts had been correct. It wouldn't be right to become entangled with this hurting woman.

CHAPTER THREE

'Yia-Yia says you must come to our house.'

Katherine started. She hadn't been aware of Crystal coming in. Now here she was again, as bold as brass in her sitting room, as if she had every right to be there. But, then, Katherine conceded silently, she had extended what had amounted to an open invitation.

'Excuse me?'

'Yia-Yia says you helped Baba with his hand so she wants you to come to dinner. She says it's not good for someone to be alone all the time.'

'Yia-Yia? Your grandmother?' When Crystal nodded, she added, 'Does your father know you're here?'

The little girl hitched her shoulders and flopped her arms to her side, her hands bumping against her legs. 'I did tell him.' Her sigh was dramatic. 'He's working on his boat again. He also wants you to come.'

Katherine wasn't sure she believed Crystal. She didn't want to impose herself on Alexander's family—particularly if he'd be there. He'd come to the villa the evening after they'd been to Olympia to tell her that her diagnosis had been correct. Stéfan did indeed have meningitis and was in Intensive Care. But Alexander hoped that, because of her alerting them to look out for meningitis, Stéfan would recover.

She hadn't seen Alexander since then but, to her dismay, she'd found herself thinking about him—a lot—during the week and knew she was in real danger of developing a crush on him. An unreciprocated crush, clearly, and someone like him was bound to pick up sooner or later the effect he was having on her. The ending of their evening together had indicated, more than words could, that he wasn't interested in pursuing a relationship with her. No, if the invitation had been extended by him, it had been out of politeness—from one colleague to another.

In which case it would be better not to encourage Crystal to visit too much.

Katherine managed a smile. 'I'm very busy, Crystal, so...' she picked up her pen pointedly '...would you thank your grandmother very much for her kind invitation but tell her I won't be able to make it?'

But instead of taking the hint, Crystal came to stand next to her. 'What are you doing?' she asked.

'It's a paper I'd like to finish before I go back to work.'

'Like homework?'

'Exactly.' Trying to ignore the child next to her, Katherine made a few more notes on the page. But it was clear Crystal had no intention of leaving any time soon.

She suppressed a sigh and put her pen down. 'Would you like some orange juice?'

'Yes, please.'

When she got up to fetch it, both Hercules and Crystal followed her into the small kitchen.

'I told Baba that Yia-Yia and me thought you must be lonely all by yourself and he agreed. So it's good I can keep you company sometimes.'

As Katherine crouched down to give Hercules some food she felt her cheeks grow hot. It was bad enough, mortifying enough, that Alexander had said that, but for him, his six-year-old and his grandmother to be discussing her was too much. Was that what this dinner invitation was about? A let's-keep-the-solitary-woman-company-for-at-least-one-night-so-that-we-don't-have-to-worry-about-her-being-on-her-own? She swore silently.

It made it more important than ever that she stay away from him; she absolutely refused to be the object of sympathy.

'You can tell your father, as I've already told him, I'm perfectly happy being on my own. I'm not in the least bit lonely.' Why was she justifying herself to a child? If she *did* feel a little bereft at times, it was only to be expected after losing Mum so recently. She handed Crystal the glass of juice.

'I could paint your toenails if you like,' Crystal said. She held up a plastic bag. 'Look. I got three different colours for my birthday from Cousin Helen. Baba says I'm too young to be wearing nail polish.' Her mouth drooped. 'Helen shouldn't have given it to me if I couldn't wear it. What was she thinking?'

The last phrase sounded so much like something her friend Sally would have said, it made Katherine smile.

'If you let me do your nails, it'll make you even more beautiful,' Crystal continued plaintively, and apparently without the tiniest hint of guile.

Katherine knew when she was beaten. 'Okay,' she said.

A smile of delight spread across Crystal's face. 'Can I? Really?'

'Yes, but *only* my toes. I don't wear varnish on my fingernails. A doctor has to keep their fingernails short.' She held up her hands and wiggled them.

'Okay. You sit on the couch and put your feet on this

chair,' Crystal instructed, lugging one of the kitchen chairs over.

Wondering whether she'd made a mistake by agreeing to the child's demands, Katherine slid her feet out of her sandals and placed them on the vinyl-covered seat. 'Like this?'

Crystal nodded. She opened the popper of her little plastic bag and very carefully placed three pots of nail varnish on the table. 'What colour would you like?'

Katherine studied the pots of varnish for a moment. One was deep purple and completely out of the question, even if she intended to remove the polish at the first opportunity, the second was deep red and the third a pale, coral pink.

She pointed to the pink one. 'That one.'

'But I like the red.' Crystal pouted.

Katherine bit down on a smile. 'Okay. Red it is.'

She leaned against the back of the couch and closed her eyes. Crystal's little hands were like feathers on her feet and, to her surprise, Katherine found it very soothing.

'There. Done. Look!' Crystal said eventually. She stood back to admire her work. 'I told you it would be pretty.'

Katherine peered down at her toes. It was as if someone had taken a machete to them, lopping them off somewhere below the metatarsals. There had to more nail polish on her skin and the seat of the chair than on her nails. But Crystal looked so pleased with herself that Katherine quickly hid her dismay. 'Mmm. Quite a difference.'

Crystal tugged her hand. 'Come on, let's show Baba.'

'I don't think your father—'

But Crystal was pulling her to her feet. 'Helen wouldn't let me do hers, but when she sees yours, she will.'

'Crystal! I said ten minutes!' Alexander's voice came from below the balcony.

'Coming, Baba. In a minute.'

'Now, Crystal!'

Keeping her toes spread as far apart as possible, Katherine hobbled over to the balcony and looked down. Alexander was wiping grease-stained hands on a rag. His T-shirt clung damply to his chest and his hair was tousled. Yet he still managed to look like a Greek god.

'Hi, Katherine.' His teeth flashed. 'Sorry I'm calling up, but my feet are sandy, my hands grubby and I need a dip in the sea before I'm fit for company. You are coming to dinner, aren't you?'

Crystal bumped against her as she climbed excitedly onto the rung of the balcony. 'She says not to dinner, Baba, but can she come for a visit? She is much more beautiful now! You have to see her.'

Katherine was about to protest when his eyes locked on hers. 'The part I can see of her already looks pretty good.' For a long moment the world seemed to disappear until there were just the two of them. 'Why not dinner?' he asked, breaking the spell.

'Because I've work to do and, anyway, I don't like to intrude on your family.'

'I assume you take time off to eat?'

'Yes, you have to eat!' his daughter echoed.

'My grandmother will be disappointed if you don't. She's already started preparing her best dishes.'

Alexander's family appeared determined to adopt her. She winced at her choice of words and sought desperately for an acceptable excuse. Apart from the effect Alexander had on her, every time she looked at Crystal she was painfully reminded of what she'd lost.

'Yes, *lahanodolmádes* and *patátes yemistés*,' Crystal added. 'Oh, and *baklavás* for afters! What else, Baba?'

'Crystal, could you please stop interrupting everyone?'

He looked at Katherine again. 'Stay for dinner at least and then you can leave.'

It seemed that she had no choice but to allow herself to be dragged out of the house—it would be churlish to continue refusing not only Alexander's pleas but those of his daughter too. And to be honest, her mouth had started to water when Crystal had been listing the menu. It was a long time since she'd tasted home-cooked Greek food like her mother used to make.

'Yes, then. I'd love to.'

Crystal, victorious, clenched her fist and stabbed her folded elbow backwards. 'Yes-s-s! I'll see you at home, Baba. I'll bring her.'

'Not *her*, Crystal. Dr Burns.'

'Katherine is fine,' Katherine said.

He grinned at her. 'You did bring this on yourself, you know, by being so mysterious and elusive.'

Mysterious? Was that how he saw it? That she was the elusive one? She couldn't help smiling back.

'And you did tell Crystal she could visit. My daughter appears to find you irresistible.'

Her heart plummeted. She preferred *him* to find her irresistible.

The pint-sized tyrant wouldn't even let her stop to put on her sandals, saying severely that she would spoil it all if she tried to put them on too soon.

Alexander's home was set back from the village square and up a steep, narrow path. It was several times larger than hers, with shuttered windows, a cobbled driveway and paths and lush, established grounds. He must have a wonderful view from the wide balconies of his clifftop home.

It took a while for Katherine's eyes to adjust to the dim interior after the bright light and blinding white beach outside. The house was cool, probably because it was shuttered against the heat of the day, although now the shutters were spread wide, allowing a breeze to penetrate the rooms. Despite Crystal hurrying her along, Katherine managed to catch glimpses of her surroundings: engraved, dark wood furniture; colourful striped rugs on polished terracotta tiles; and montages of family photographs, old and new, on white, rough-plastered walls. Crystal swept her into the kitchen where Katherine's senses were assailed with the aromas of garlic, herbs and browning meat.

A plump white-haired woman, bent over the pots steaming on an enormous traditional stove, lifted her head. She smiled warmly at Katherine and addressed her rapidly in Greek.

'Yia-Yia welcomes you and says she's happy you are here, visiting our home,' Crystal translated. 'Please sit at the table.' Without allowing Katherine time to reply, she turned to her grandmother and spoke in Greek, pointing excitedly to Katherine's toes. The older woman leant over and exclaimed. Katherine didn't need to understand any Greek to gather she was praising her great-granddaughter's efforts. Crystal's face said it all.

She had barely sat down before a plate of spanakopita was set down in front of her. Crystal's great-grandmother turned back to her stove, muttering happily.

'Aren't you glad you came?' Crystal said triumphantly. 'Look how pleased she is!'

If the child hadn't been so young, Katherine would have suspected her of engineering the whole situation.

'What's your great-grandmother's name?' Katherine asked.

'Yia-Yia, silly.'

Katherine took a bite of the miniature spinach and

feta pie. She flapped a hand in front of her mouth. 'Hot. *Thermo.* Hot. But wonderful,' she added hastily. Two pairs of dark brown eyes studied her 'No, I mean what should *I* call her?'

'The same as everyone. Yia-Yia. She knows your name. Baba told her. I'm just going to get him!' Crystal said, flying out of the door.

Yia-Yia beckoned Katherine over to where she was working and pointed at the leaves of pastry she had laid out on a baking tray. She brought her fingers to her lips and made a smacking sound. It was clear she was showing Katherine what she was making for supper and that it would be delicious. Katherine could only smile and nod in response.

She was almost relieved when Crystal returned, dragging Alexander in her wake. His hair glistened almost black from his shower and he had changed into a bitter-chocolate T-shirt and cotton jeans. 'Show Baba your toes,' Crystal ordered.

Grimacing to herself, Katherine did as she was asked. She saw the leap of laughter in Alexander's eyes as he dutifully studied her feet. 'Very beautiful,' he said to Katherine, before murmuring so his daughter couldn't hear. 'Do you actually have toes at the ends of those feet? Or should I get the suture kit out again?'

Katherine spluttered with laughter, just managing to turn it into a cough at the last moment. But suddenly Alexander was whooping with laughter and she was too. She couldn't remember the last time she'd laughed like that. Yia-Yia and Crystal looked puzzled for a moment then they were whooping too, Yia-Yia's deep brown eyes almost disappearing in her chubby face.

'What's so funny?' Crystal asked, when everyone stopped laughing.

Alexander tweaked her nose. 'If you don't know, why did you join in?'

'I couldn't help it.' She was hopping from foot to foot. 'I just liked hearing you laugh, Baba.'

The atmosphere in the room changed subtly and the light in Alexander's eyes disappeared, replaced by something Katherine couldn't read.

'If you'll excuse me,' he apologised, 'a neighbour is complaining of a tight chest. It's nothing that staying off cigarettes wouldn't help, but his wife is always happier if I look in on him. I'll be back in a little while.' He turned to his grandmother and spoke to her. She nodded, unsmiling.

'Can I come, Baba?' his daughter asked.

'Of course. You know I always like to have my little helper with me. As long as you stay out of the way and as quiet as a mouse.' He caught Katherine's eye and raised an eyebrow. 'My daughter as quiet as a mouse? Who am I kidding?' he murmured, his lips curving into a smile.

Crystal was out of the door almost before he'd finished speaking.

Once again, Katherine was left alone with Yia-Yia. There was an awkward silence for a moment before the older woman beckoned Katherine to come forward. With a series of hand gestures and nods of the head, she indicated to Katherine that she wanted her help to finish preparing the meal.

'I'm sorry, I can't cook,' Katherine protested. There had never been a need to learn. When her mother had been alive and Katherine had been living at home they'd always eaten at the restaurant. And when she'd moved out and into her first flat she'd taken her main meal at the hospital or had eaten simple salads or pasta for supper. Then, when Mum had become too unwell to be on her own and Katherine had moved back home to look after her, she had fetched Greek delicacies from a nearby restaurant—their own having been sold a couple of years earlier—in an attempt to tempt Mum's failing appetite.

But almost before she'd finished speaking she was being passed a bowl of minced lamb and handed bunches of pungent-smelling herbs. Either Yia-Yia didn't understand what she was saying, or it had never crossed her mind that not all women liked cooking.

In the end it was one of the most peaceful and relaxing hours Katherine could remember spending for a long time. With Crystal's grandmother coaxing her along, while keeping a watchful eye on what she was doing, Katherine stuffed vine leaves and baked rich syrupy cakes. Every now and again the old woman would cluck her tongue and shake her head. At other times she'd nod, murmur something in Greek, and smile approvingly.

When dinner had been prepared to her satisfaction, and Alexander and Crystal still hadn't returned, Yia-Yia took her hand and led her outside to a bench in the garden. For the next ten minutes they sat in peaceful silence as the sun sank in the sky.

After a little while Yia-Yia gestured that they should go back inside. By the time Alexander and Crystal returned, a spread that could have fed eight had been laid out on the dining-room table.

Alexander's dark eyes swept over Katherine and he grinned, making her heart skip a beat. 'Somehow I never quite saw you as being domesticated,' he said.

Catching sight of her reflection in the large mirror on the wall, Katherine realised she was still wearing the flowery apron Grandmother had insisted she put on. Added to her bare feet and splotchy nail polish, she must look ridiculous. Her hair was a mess and clinging to her flushed cheeks. And was that a smudge of flour? Liking to appear neat and tidy at all times, tailored dresses with tights and decent shoes or smart trousers and blouses were what she usually wore. Two weeks in Greece and her colleagues would hardly recognise her. *She* barely recognised herself.

But, oddly, she rather liked the look of the woman in the mirror.

She seemed different from the last time he'd seen her, Alexander thought, studying Katherine from the corner of his eye. But if possible she was even more beautiful. Her blonde hair, bleached white-gold from the sun, had come loose from her plait and damp tendrils curled around her cheeks. A tiny wisp of hair clung to the corner of her mouth and he curled his hands inside the pockets of his jeans to stop himself from reaching out to tug it away. His grandmother's apron and the smudge of flour on her nose only added, somehow, to her allure. But those feet! As he'd said, it looked as if someone had bludgeoned her toes with a hammer.

It had been Yia-Yia and Crystal's idea to invite her for dinner. He'd tried to dissuade them, but his grandmother had insisted that not to, after Katherine had helped him, was not the Greek way. He'd had no choice but to agree. And, whatever he'd told himself, he was glad that she was here.

There was something about Katherine that drew him and despite everything he'd told himself he hadn't been able to stop thinking about her. He wasn't sure what to make of her. Her blue eyes were the colour of the sea at its deepest—more so when sadness overtook her. Was it only the loss of her mother that was causing that look in her eyes? She intrigued him. One minute she'd be the cool professional, like when they'd helped the young man who'd collapsed, the next she'd be blushing at something he'd said or refusing to hold his gaze, ill at ease in his company. And then over dinner she'd seemed to relax. At least until he'd asked her about her private life.

When Helen had found out they'd met and she'd sutured Alexander's hand and they'd spent the day together, her curiosity had known no bounds. That Katherine was also doctor tickled her.

'Perhaps she's like you,' she'd said. 'Maybe she has lost her lover and is here to mend her broken heart.' Helen liked to spin stories, usually romantic ones, about people. 'Yes, it has to be a broken love affair, I'm sure of it.' She'd slid him a mischievous look. 'Perhaps together you can mend your broken hearts.'

Despite himself, he'd laughed. 'You know I'm not interested in getting married again.'

'It's been two years, Alexander. A man like you isn't meant to be on his own. Grandmother won't be around for ever. I have my own life in Athens and as much as I love you both, I can't keep making trips down here every weekend, especially when it means leaving Nico on his own. And once we get married…' She shrugged. 'I won't be able to come so often. Crystal needs a mother. Someone who can be there for her all the time.'

'Crystal has me,' he'd replied tersely. 'No one can ever take Sophia's place.'

Helen was instantly contrite. 'Of course not.' Then she'd smiled again. It was hard for his cousin to stay serious for long. 'Anyway, who's saying anything about marriage?'

Typical Greek women. Always trying to matchmake.

'She is good at cooking,' his grandmother said to him in Greek, drawing him back to the present. 'For an Englishwoman. But she is too skinny. She should eat more.'

He grinned at the older woman. If she had her way they'd all eventually have to join a slimming club. 'I think she looks fine.'

'At least she dresses like a good Greek woman. No shorts up to her bottom like your cousin.'

Under the apron, Katherine was wearing a pair of light cotton trousers and a white blouse, neatly buttoned almost to the neck. No wonder his grandmother approved.

Katherine was looking at him enquiringly and he realised they had been speaking in Greek and excluding her.

'My grandmother says you are a good cook.'

'It's been fun—and informative,' Katherine admitted with a wry smile.

'But why does she seem so sad?' his grandmother continued. 'What does she have to be sad about? She is here in Greece, working in my kitchen, making food, and about to eat a fine meal.'

'Her mother died not so long ago,' he replied.

His grandmother's face softened in distress. She pulled Katherine into her arms and patted her on the back. 'Poor girl,' she said. A bewildered Katherine stared at him over her shoulder and he had to fight not to laugh.

He sobered. 'I told my grandmother that your mother died recently. She is saying she is sorry.'

Katherine gently extricated herself from his grandmother's arms. 'Tell her thank you, but I'm all right.'

'And what about a husband?' Yia-Yia continued. 'Where is he? Has she left him in England?' She clicked her tongue. 'A woman shouldn't leave her husband. Where is her ring?'

'She's not married, Grandmother.'

'And why not? She is old not to be married! Is she one of those modern women who think they don't need husbands? Or is she divorced?' Her mouth turned down at the corners. Grandmother didn't approve of divorce.

'I don't think she's ever been married, Yia-Yia.'

She looked relieved. 'Good. Perhaps she will fall in love with you. Would you like that? I think you like her, no?'

Katherine was watching him, waiting for him to translate, but he was damned if he was going to tell her how interested his grandmother was in her marital status—and her suitability as a partner for him.

'Grandmother is saying she is happy to have you here in her kitchen. She hopes you will come often.'

'Tell her it's lovely to be here.'

To his relief, the business of serving them all dinner prevented further comments from his grandmother. Crystal insisted on sitting next to Katherine, her body pressed so tightly against her Katherine had to find it difficult to eat. Yet she said nothing. She laid down her knife so that she could eat with one hand. Crystal was a friendly child but he'd never known her to form an attachment quite as quickly. It wasn't as if she wasn't surrounded by love.

'So you don't work on weekends?' Katherine asked him. They had taken their coffee onto the balcony. She'd offered to help clear away but his grandmother wouldn't hear of it, insisting it was Crystal's job. Or at least that was what Alexander had told Katherine. Grandmother would have been only too delighted to keep their guest in her kitchen while she cooked some more.

'Carlos—my partner, who you met briefly—and I take turns and we have a colleague who fills in the rest of the time. He retired early so he could spend more time on his thirty-footer, but he likes to keep his hand in.'

'What news about Stéfan?'

'He's still in Intensive Care.'

'But he is going to be okay?'

'I don't know.' He rubbed the back of his neck. 'He's on a ventilator. They think it's a rare type of bacterial meningitis that he has. They're still doing tests.' He stood. 'I'm sorry, but you're going to have to excuse me. It's time for Crystal's bedtime and she likes me to read her a story.'

'Of course. I should get back anyway and do some more work before I turn in.' Her cheeks had flushed. 'Please say good night to Crystal and thank your grandmother for me. I had very pleasant evening.'

'You'll come again?' he asked. She was easy company and he found being with her restful. Actually, who was he kidding? He just liked being with her.

'I don't want to keep intruding,' she said, the colour in her cheeks deepening.

'You're not. Trust me.'

She gave him the ghost of a smile and left.

He watched her pick her way down the steps and into the square. He'd found it difficult to concentrate on his paperwork the last few days. His thoughts kept straying back to her, distracting him. Yes, he thought. She was a distraction—a very enjoyable one—but that was all she would ever be.

CHAPTER FOUR

THE FOLLOWING MORNING, just after dawn had lightened the sky and Katherine had taken her coffee out to the balcony, she noticed that Alexander was back working on his boat. In which case she would work inside, at least until she was sure he'd gone. She'd already had more to do with him than was wise. Relationships, particularly brief flings with attractive Greek doctors still grieving for their wives, had no place on her agenda.

But even as she reminded herself of that, she wondered if she could make an exception. It would be so good to feel someone's arms around her again. Good to have company, good to have someone to share walks and trips with, and who better than a man she would never see again once she'd left here?

She shook her head to chase the thoughts away. She suspected he found her attractive, but that wasn't the same thing as wanting even a casual relationship with her. And just how casual did she want it to be? Unbidden, she imagined him naked, tanned body against white sheets, his hands exploring every inch of her.

She retreated back inside and determinedly fired up her computer. Work. That was what kept her sane. Her paper was what she should be concentrating on.

She edited all day, acutely aware that her attention kept wandering back to Alexander. Just before supper she heard the excited voice of Crystal and, unable to resist a peek, peered out at the bay. He was there again, but this time in the water with his daughter.

She watched as he raised Crystal above his head before tossing her in the air and catching her just before she hit the water. The little girl shrieked with pleasure and wrapped her arms around her father's neck. A few minutes later Alexander, Crystal balanced on his shoulders, waded out of the water, his swimming shorts clinging to narrow hips and lean but muscular thighs.

It wasn't just that she found him sexy as hell. She liked the way he was with his child—clearly she was the centre of his universe and that was the way it should be: a child's happiness should always be paramount. Her chest tightened. What would he think if he knew her secret? Not that she was ever to going to share it with him.

She went into the kitchen and made herself a Greek salad with some of local goat cheese and olives, along with plump, ripe tomatoes she'd bought from the village store. Telling herself it was far too beautiful an evening to eat inside, she took her plate out to the lower veranda. Alexander and Crystal had disappeared, no doubt having gone home to have their evening meal. As the sun sank below the horizon, she sighed. Despite everything she'd told herself, their absence made her feel lonelier than ever.

Alexander excused himself from the game of cards he had been playing and, taking his beer, walked over to the small wall surrounding the village square. Crystal was riding her bike around the fountain in the centre in hot pursuit of the neighbour's boy, her little legs pedalling as fast as they could so she could catch up with him.

Alexander smiled as he watched her. He'd made the right decision, coming back. Crystal was thriving, his grandmother was delighted to have her close by and he was…well, content. As long as his daughter was happy he was too—or as much as he had any right to expect. Sometimes he wondered whether Crystal even remembered Sophia. She spoke of her mother periodically, asking if she were still in heaven and telling him that she knew Mama was watching her from the sky. Occasionally he would show Crystal video footage he'd taken of them on the too-rare occasions he'd taken leave and they'd come here. His daughter would lean forward and watch with shining eyes.

What would Sophia think if she knew he was back in Greece? How would she feel about him giving up his job in London? Would she be pleased that he'd finally, even when it was too late, realised what was important? Would she approve of the way he was bringing up their child? God, he still missed her and, God, he still felt so damned guilty.

He sipped his cold beer and gazed out over the sea. It was then he noticed Katherine. She'd just emerged from the water, her long legs emphasised by the black one-piece costume she was wearing. She dried off then wrapped the towel around her and sat with her back to him, knees pulled up to her chest, staring out at the same sea he was.

Under her prim exterior and natural reserve, there was a loneliness, an aura of something so vulnerable about her he found himself, for the first time since Sophia's death, wanting to know another woman better. But what did he have to offer? He wouldn't, couldn't, get married again. No one could ever match up to Sophia.

He took another gulp of his drink and turned away. Why

had the possibility of getting married again even crossed his mind? The moonlight was making him fanciful. His life was complicated—and full—enough.

Crystal whizzed by him on her bike and waved. Right there was everything that mattered. He glanced at his watch. It was time to get his daughter to bed.

CHAPTER FIVE

As HAD BECOME a habit, Katherine was sitting outside his house on the bench with Grandmother, after spending a couple of hours cooking with her in the kitchen. She'd closed her eyes to savour the sensation of the breeze on her face, but when Grandmother poked her in her ribs with her elbow she opened them to see that Alexander was coming across the square towards them.

Katherine's heart leaped. Frightened of what he would read in her eyes, she lowered her lids until she was sure she could look at him calmly. She could deal with her developing crush on him as long as he never suspected.

'Hello, you two.' He bent and kissed his grandmother on her cheek and said something to her in Greek that made her laugh. Although Katherine's Greek was improving, when the Greeks spoke to each other it was usually too fast for her to follow.

Alexander grinned at Katherine. 'I've just asked her what she's thinking of, sitting down when dinner's due. She says now she has you to help her, sometimes she can take time off to enjoy the Greek sunshine.'

Nevertheless, the old woman got to her feet and retreated back inside, leaving her space on the bench for Alexander. He took a seat next to Katherine and, like she'd been doing earlier, turned his face up to the sun and closed his eyes. 'My grandmother is right. We all need to sit in the sun more often,' he murmured.

His usual vitality seemed to have deserted him and he looked tired.

'Is everything all right?' she asked.

'No, not really. Stéfan—the man with meningitis—died last night.'

'I'm so sorry. I really hoped he would be okay.'

He opened his eyes and turned to face Katherine. 'So did I, but once he developed multi-organ failure…' He paused. 'We've asked for a post-mortem but, according to the pathologist, it might be another week before they can do it. They have a bit of a backlog as his colleague is off on leave.' He rubbed the back of his neck and frowned. 'I was speaking to one of my colleagues in the area today and he tells me he's had a case too—a couple of days ago, a teenager. He's been admitted to a hospital in Athens.'

Katherine's antenna went on red alert. 'Two cases in a week? Doesn't that strike you as odd?'

'He isn't sure his patient has meningitis. He's going to call me as soon as he has the results of the lumbar puncture. But I'd be surprised if they both have it. As far as I'm aware, meningitis normally affects similar age groups.'

'Usually, but not always. It depends on the strain.'

'We'll find out soon enough. They're giving his patient's family antibiotics prophylactically to be on the safe side.'

'Sensible,' Katherine murmured. However, if Alexander's colleague's patient did turn out to have meningitis, it could be the start of something. Something terrifying.

'Any others you're aware of?' she asked.

'I rang around a few of the practices in the area, but no one else has come across any. I've told them to let me know if they do. I'm hoping these two will turn out to be random, unrelated events—supposing David, the teenage boy, does have it and, as I said, that isn't at all certain.'

He could be right, but there was a way she could find out.

She heard Grandmother calling Alexander from inside and got to her feet. 'Sounds like you're wanted.'

'I thought you'd want to know about Stéfan,' he said, rising too 'After I check in with Yia-Yia, I'm going to see the family of one of my other patients who I admitted to hospital after I diagnosed her with a nasty chest infection.' He smiled wryly. 'It's one of the privileges, but also one of the responsibilities, of being in general practice in Greece. Any member of a family becomes unwell and the rest expect you to see them through it as well. And that usually involves late-night tea and cakes and much discussion.'

Although she was disappointed he was going, the care he took of his patients was one of the things she liked about him. Besides, she wanted to do some checking up of her own.

She hurried back to her house. It was after six in the UK but Tim was divorced and rarely left work until much later.

She dialled the number of the office and was pleased when he picked up straight away. After exchanging small talk for a few moments—yes, she was enjoying her break and, yes, she would be coming back to work as planned at the end of September—she repeated what Alexander had told her.

'I've got a feeling about this,' she said. 'Is there any chance you could speak to your opposite number in Athens and ask him if there have been any more cases reported? I realise I'm probably being over-cautious but it wouldn't hurt to find out.'

'I doubt there will be anyone still there at this time. Will the morning do?'

'It will have to. As I said, it's probably nothing but it's best to be on the safe side. Thanks, Tim.'

He called her back on her mobile just before nine the next morning and came straight to the point.

'You were right,' he said. 'I've spoken to my opposite number in Athens and he tells me there have been reports of ten cases in and around the southern Peloponnese, including the two you mentioned. One or two would mean nothing but ten! It certainly suggests there is something to be concerned about.'

Excitement surged through Katherine. Her instinct had been right! 'What ages?'

'It varies. From teenagers to young adults. As you'd expect, it is the youngest who are most seriously affected. One child—a lad of seventeen—is in Intensive Care in Athens and it's not looking good.'

'The boy in Intensive Care—what's his name?'

'David Panagaris.'

Was he the same lad Alexander had told her about? It seemed likely. Her heart was racing. This is what she was trained to do. 'I could look into it. Could you let the department in Athens know I'm here and would like to help?'

'Absolutely not,' Tim protested. 'You're on holiday. They must have someone local they can call on. It's not as if Greece doesn't have public health doctors of their own.'

'Of course they do, but I happen to be here and I'm an expert in the spread of infectious diseases. I'm probably the most up-to-date person in Europe at the moment and you and I both know it's all much more co-operative now than it used to be. Come on, Tim, you know it makes sense.'

There was a long pause at the end of the phone. 'I guess

it does makes sense,' Tim said reluctantly. 'But is your Greek good enough to ensure you ask the right questions and, more importantly, get the right answers?'

It wasn't. But Alexander's was. 'What about the Greek doctor I mentioned? The one who alerted me to the possibility of an outbreak? If he's prepared to take time out to help me, that would solve the problem of my not being fluent in Greek.' She wasn't really sure she wanted to work with Alexander. It was bad enough catching tantalising glimpses of him most days, without being thrust into his company all the time. But she wanted to do this and she couldn't without Alexander's help. 'I'll need to ask him, of course, but I've no doubt he'll say yes.'

'Okay,' Tim conceded. 'I'll suggest it to my colleague.' Katherine released a breath. 'What more info do you have?'

'In addition to the boy admitted to Intensive Care in Athens, there have been two deaths over the last ten days—your man and a woman tourist from France in her teens. Her family have already repatriated her body. No obvious links between the deceased as yet.'

Her excitement drained away. Three families had lost a loved one or were in danger of doing so. And if there was an epidemic, and there seemed little doubt that was what they could be dealing with, if they didn't locate all those who had come into contact with the sufferers and treat them, more people could die. In addition, they needed to find out where it was coming from so they could reach people before they became unwell.

'Could you give me the names and addresses of the patients? Plus the names of their family doctors, or the doctors who treated them?'

'I'll email them to you straight away.'

As soon as she disconnected, she phoned Alexander's surgery only to discover he wasn't expected in until later. She flung on some clothes and, without stopping for breakfast, set off across the square to Alexander's home, praying he'd be there and not out on a visit.

The sun was already blazing down and she was perspiring by the time she reached his door. She found Grandmother in the kitchen, making bread.

'Morning,' Katherine said in Greek. 'I need to speak to Alexander. Is he here?' She didn't have time for the usual pleasantries today.

Alexander's grandmother frowned, wiped her hands on a tea towel and shook her head. '*Nè*. At work.'

'Hello.' It was Crystal, looking sleepy in pyjamas and holding a teddy bear. She said something to her grandmother in Greek and went to stand next to Katherine, slipping her hand into hers. 'Yia-Yia says you're looking for Baba. She says he's gone to his consulting room in the village.' Grandmother had lifted a pot of tea and was holding it up. 'She wants to know if you'd like some tea. And some breakfast? She's just made some.'

'Please thank her for me and say I'd love to stay but I really need to see your father. It's urgent.'

The child relayed it back to to her grandmother, who looked disappointed she'd have no one to feed.

'Is something the matter?' Crystal asked.

'No.' Katherine crouched down and ruffled Crystal's hair. 'At least, nothing for you to worry about. I promise.'

Leaving the house, she headed back down the flight of steps and along the street to the rooms Alexander used as a surgery for the locals.

She tapped on the door of Alex's room and, without waiting for a reply, let herself in. He was sitting at the desk, his chair turned to face the window so that he had his back to her. He swivelled around to face her.

'I'm sorry,' he said. 'This isn't a good time.'

'I heard,' she said softly.

He frowned. 'Heard what?'

'About David Panagaris, that is the name of your colleague's patient, isn't it?' When Alexander nodded, she continued. 'I thought it must be him. I gather he's in Intensive Care. I'm sorry.' Without waiting to be asked, she took the seat opposite him.

'Poor bloody parents. Perhaps if they'd brought him in sooner—' He broke off. 'How did you know he'd deteriorated? He was only admitted to Intensive Care last night.'

'My boss phoned me—I phoned him first. Let me explain.'

Alexander said nothing but leaned forward, placing his folded hands on the desk. He looked even more bushed than he had yesterday. There were dark circles under his eyes and underneath the tan he was drawn and pale. She wondered if he'd been up all night.

'As you know, my thesis for my doctorate is on meningitis and other bacterial infections—its spread and containment. That sort of thing. Our unit is one of the biggest in Europe but we have strong ties with others units across the world. We share information on all matters of public health, especially on infectious diseases. Over the last few years increasing numbers of countries across the world have bought into this collaborative approach. It makes sense to pool our resources rather than compete with one another. Africa, for example, has much better information on the spread of malaria, and so on...'

He nodded impatiently.

'When you told me about your cases it rang alarm bells

so I phoned my boss and asked him to contact the public health department in Athens. Apparently, apart from Stéfan and David, there have been eight other cases all in, or around, this area, including another death—a young French girl' She held out her phone. 'My boss has emailed me a list with all their names.'

'Eight other cases?' Alexander looked instantly alert, all traces of his earlier tiredness having disappeared. 'So there is an epidemic?'

'It appears so. The thing is, I've offered to take the lead in looking into the situation. But I'm going to need help. My Greek isn't good enough for me to do it on my own.'

He narrowed his eyes. 'You want me to help?'

'Yes,' she said simply.

'Of course,' he said with no hesitation. 'I'll need to arrange for Dr Kanavakis—my retired colleague—to cover for me, but I don't think that will be a problem. When do we start?'

'Now.'

He raised his eyebrows. 'Let me make that phone call, then.'

When he'd finished he turned back to Katherine. 'Cover's sorted. Now, what else do you know about the cases?'

'Very little. I have the names and addresses of all the patients. Most live in the southern part of Greece. Two come from Nafplio or very nearby. The French girl was on holiday there.'

He leaned back in his chair. 'Hell, that isn't good. A lot of cruise ships come into Nafplio. That will make tracing contacts more difficult.'

She checked the names on her phone. While Alexander had been on the phone she'd downloaded them into a document. 'What else can you tell me about David?'

'His parents live in a village close to Messini. He'd been snuffly and lethargic for most of the morning. They thought it was a cold, but when he deteriorated they brought him in to see my colleague. Unfortunately, he was already showing signs of septicaemia. He was given intravenous antibiotics and they arranged for an immediate transfer to hospital, but he was already in a bad way.' He raked a hand through his hair. 'He's only young.'

He jumped up and started pacing. 'If we do have an epidemic on our hands, none of the children will be safe.' He stopped in front of her. 'Come on. Let's go to the hospital. I'll let his doctor know what's happening. We need to find where the victims have been and who they've been in contact with.' He paused. 'Unless we should split up? You go to see the relatives of the other cases while I go to the hospital?'

'No,' she said, putting her hand on his arm. 'As I said, I might be the expert and know the questions to ask, but you can speak Greek and you're a local doctor. They'll find it more comfortable to talk to you and they might tell you things they wouldn't tell me. You'll also be able to pick up better than I if they are leaving out information that might be important. But what we should do is make sure the health services in Athens have put all the local family practices on alert, as well as warning the general public. Doctors and parents are more likely to be vigilant if they know what to look out for.'

'I'll speak to them, of course. What is the name of your contact there?'

Even before he put the phone down she could see the conversation hadn't gone the way he wanted. His voice had risen towards the end and he appeared to be arguing with whoever was on the other end. A muscle twitched in his cheek.

'They say they've warned the hospitals and practices to watch out for cases of meningitis but they won't put out a full alert on the radio or in the press. They say that if they do, people will panic and rush to the hospitals. They say the medical services will collapse under the strain and it's too early to take the risk.'

'I could phone my boss and get him to put pressure on them,' Katherine suggested. 'Although I suspect they'd do the same in the UK.'

'Be my guest.' He gestured to the phone. 'I doubt it would do any good. They're unlikely to do anything more until there are more cases. They insist the ones we know about might just be random at the moment—a blip, not connected at all.'

'It is possible,' Katherine said thoughtfully. 'We've noted and recorded many cases of infectious diseases in the past that seemed to be part of an epidemic but that turned out not to be. I think we should talk to the Stéfan's parents before we do anything else. As soon as I get the French girl's parents' contact details I'll call them.'

'Fine with me,' he said, picking up his medical bag. 'And I hope to God you're right about these cases not being connected. Stéfan's family is from a village near Sparta. We could go to the hospital in Athens from there.' He took his mobile from his pocket. 'I'll phone Carlos and let him know what's happening.'

The road leading to Sparta was the worst Katherine had ever been on. Travelling through and over the mountains, it was narrow, with barely enough room for two cars to pass safely. In addition, every few miles the road almost spun back on itself through a number of hairpin bends. She could barely bring herself to look. On her side of the car, the road fell away sharply and there were no road barriers to prevent the car, should it have to swerve to avoid oncoming vehicles, toppling over the side. Incredibly, the road conditions didn't stop drivers from overtaking, whether they could see or not.

'What's Crystal up to today?' she asked, trying to unclench her fists.

'She's having a sleepover with a friend a little way up the coast. Her friend's mother is coming to fetch her.'

'Could you slow down?' Katherine yelped, after they took a particularly sharp bend that she'd thought they'd never make.

Alexander turned to face her and grinned.

'If I slow down, it will only encourage other drivers to try and overtake us. They don't care whether the road is empty or not.'

'Please keep your eyes on the road at least.'

Despite her terror and worry about what they would be facing soon, she couldn't help admire the scenery as they whizzed along. Little villages clung to the side of the mountain, the houses often appearing to spill almost onto the road. Small cafés with old men outside, puffing on pipes or playing board games flew by in a blur. To her consternation, Alexander would often take his hand off the steering-wheel to give them a friendly wave as they passed.

At other times, almost out of nowhere, they'd come upon small farm stalls selling flowers or tomatoes or other freshly grown produce from the roadside. At any other time she might have enjoyed the trip and promised herself that once this emergency was over she'd come back—with her own car, of course—and savour the journey.

As she relaxed a little, her thoughts returned to the task in hand. She unfolded the map she'd brought with her and circled each victim's location with her pen. All of them lived in the Peloponnese, apart from the French girl, who had been on holiday there. Nevertheless, it was still a huge area.

'Is there any facility or event you know of that links the victims?' she asked Alexander.

He waited until he'd slowed down to let an overtaking car coming in the opposite direction pass before he spoke. 'None that I can think of. I'd have to study the map. I don't really keep on top of social events these days.'

A short time later, to Katherine's relief, they turned off the mountain road and towards Sparta and the road became wider and straighter.

'The village is about thirty kilometres northwest of Sparta,' Alexander said. 'We should be there in about twenty minutes.'

Katherine's stomach churned. In a short while she'd be facing two very recently bereaved parents and she wasn't looking forward to it.

'What's Sparta like?' she asked, more to distract herself than out of any burning interest.

'Little of the original city remains. Most of the what you'll see as we pass through has been built on top of ancient Sparta.' He glanced at her. 'You know the stories of the Spartans?'

'Only that they were tough and didn't believe in creature comforts.'

'It's grimmer than that. Under a system known as the *agoge* Spartan boys were trained to be as physically tough as possible. They were taken from their families at the age of seven and made to live in barracks. They were deliberately underfed so they'd become adept at living off the land. The boy babies who weren't expected to make the grade were taken to the top of the mountain and left there to die.'

Katherine shuddered. 'Their poor mothers.'

'It was cruel. I can't imagine how they felt, having their sons ripped from their arms. I suspect some ran away with them, even though they risked death to save them.' He blinked. 'It's what Sophia would have done. She'd never let anything part her from her child.'

Katherine's heart lurched. What would he think if he knew what she'd done? She was glad he would never know.

'You should try to visit Mycenae, though,' he continued, apparently unaware of her reaction. 'It's almost intact. It's very close to Sparta—only a few kilometres at the most. It has a less bloody past.'

'Have you been there?' Her throat was so tight she could barely speak.

He glanced at her and smiled. 'Naturally.'

They turned off onto a minor road and continued. It was much flatter here, the land planted with olive trees and vines. But then they turned a corner, drove up a street so narrow it would be impossible for another car to pass, and into a small village square.

Now they were here, her anxiety about facing the be-reaved parents returned.

'Are you all right about doing this?' Alexander asked.

'Yes.' She would be. She had to think of the children whose lives they would save rather than the one who was lost.

They parked the car and asked directions from an older man sweeping the square. He laid aside his brush and gestured for them to follow him. It was just as well because although the village was small, it was unlikely they would have found their way to the house, tucked away as it was behind a crumbling wall and almost hidden down one of the maze-like streets.

The house itself, like many of the others in the village, seemed to be built into the rock face.

A woman in a navy-blue long-sleeved dress answered their knock and after Alexander explained who they were, stepped aside to let them in.

Stéfan's parents were sitting in a darkened room surrounded by family and friends. They clung to each other and Katherine winced at the grief she saw etched on their faces.

This, she thought, was why she was an academic. Facing other people's pain, when she found it impossible to deal with her own, was something she'd spent most of her adult life trying to avoid. But she couldn't afford to be squeamish—or the luxury of dwelling on her own discomfort. However much she hated to intrude on their grief, she knew it was necessary.

Alexander introduced them again and very gently explained why they were there. 'I know this is a very difficult time for you, but we need to ask you some questions.'

Mr Popalopadous nodded. His wife seemed incapable of speaking. 'Please,' he said, 'ask your questions. If we can stop this happening to someone else's child…'

Katherine sat down and took Mrs Popalopadous's hands in hers. 'We need to know Stéfan's last movements—where he'd been before he became unwell and who he'd been in contact with.'

She looked bewildered. 'He was a teacher in the local school, but during the holidays he takes—took his boat out or went to the taverna with his friends. None of them are sick.'

Katherine exchanged a look with Alexander. None of them were sick *yet*.

'Should we quarantine the village?' Alexander murmured to her.

She shook her head slightly. 'Not yet.' She knew there was no point in getting ahead of themselves. What they had to do was retrace Stéfan's movements going back at least a week to establish who had come into contact with him. After that they needed to get in touch with those people where possible and make sure they—and anyone who had spent more than a few hours in their company—were given antibiotics.

When Mrs Popalopadous started sobbing again, Katherine leaned forward. 'I know it's difficult, but can you think of anyone apart from his friends or his pupils he might have been in contact with?' She ignored the warning look Alexander gave her. She wasn't unsympathetic to Mrs Popalopadous's grief but what mattered most now was that no one else would die.

Mr Popalopadous answered for his wife. 'No. No one different.' He wrapped his arm around his wife's shoulders. 'Now, I'm afraid you must leave us. We have arrangements to make.'

His dignity in the face of his grief was humbling. But Katherine wanted to press him further. However, Alexander got to his feet and taking her by the elbow forced her to rise to hers too. He scribbled something on a piece of paper and handed it to the bereaved father. saying something in Greek Katherine couldn't follow.

His hand still on her elbow, Alexander ushered Katherine out of the house and to his car.

'I still had questions for them,' she protested.

'For God's sake, Katherine, they've just lost their child. They've told us all they can.'

'You can't be sure of that. It's the things they don't think that are important that might matter most.'

'I gave him my mobile number and asked him to call me, day or night, if anything else does come to mind. I also told them to go to their family doctor and make sure they, and anyone else who might have been in contact with Stéfan, gets antibiotics. I'll call the family doctor to make sure they do—although I'm sure he'll have it in hand,'

'It won't hurt to make sure.' Katherine replied.

After he'd made the call, Alexander turned to her. 'As I thought, he plans to see them later this afternoon. As you can imagine, he's pretty keen that we get on top of this.' He frowned. 'The most likely source of the infection is the high school.'

'But not the only possibility!'

'No, but isn't it better to go with the most likely and work our way out from there?'

He did have a point. 'Perhaps once we've interviewed the other families something will jump out. In the meantime, I'd better get onto my boss and tell him to make double sure that all the medical facilities in the area are on red alert.'

'Shouldn't we do that?' Alexander asked.

'It's more important that we try and locate the source of the outbreak. My boss will liaise with your public heath team in Athens, although we should probably introduce ourselves at some point.'

They got into the car and Alexander turned the key in the ignition. 'Okay. Next stop Athens.'

'How long will it take us to get there?'

'About two and half hours. Less if you stop interfering in the way I drive.'

Katherine gritted her teeth. 'Just get there as soon as you can.'

Happily, it was a far better road to Athens than the one they'd come on. While they were driving, Katherine phoned the French girl's parents. Luckily her French was considerably better than her Greek. But that didn't make the conversation any less painful. Claire's father held himself together long enough to tell Katherine that Claire had been on a short break with her boyfriend in Greece when she'd become unwell. It had all been very sudden—too sudden for the family to make it to her bedside in time. There had been a long pause in the conversation when Claire's father had lost control, but eventually he had, for long enough at any rate to tell her that their family doctor had treated the family and the boyfriend with antibiotics. Katherine repeated what she'd learned to Alexander and they'd sat in silence, each absorbed with their own thoughts. She wondered if Alexander was thinking, like she was, how devastating it was to lose someone you loved—especially when that person was young—like Claire—or Sophia. When, a while later, Katherine's stomach growled she realised she hadn't eaten since breakfast and Alexander would be in the same position.

'I don't know about you but I'm starving,' she admitted.

'Would you like to stop at one of the tavernas?' he asked.

'I'd prefer not to take too long over lunch. I'm keen to talk to David's family.'

'I know a place near here that does pastries and decent coffee. We could pick something up and get back on our way.'

She was pleased he was in just as much of a hurry to get to the hospital as she was. She didn't think she could have beared to have stopped at a café and had a proper lunch, especially when she'd learned that in Greece there was no such thing as fast food served in a restaurant. While most times she appreciated the care they put into their cooking, today wasn't one of them.

When they stopped, she bought some bread rolls and cheese while Alexander downed a couple of cups of espresso in quick succession. She didn't care for the heavy, thick Greek coffee so she bought some fresh orange juice to go with their picnic lunch instead.

She took a few moments to split open the rolls and fill them. Alexander pulled a penknife from his pocket and offered it to her, and she quickly sliced the tomatoes and added them to the cheese. Once she'd done that she handed one of the rolls to Alexander. When she next looked up it was gone. He had to have wolfed it down in a couple of bites.

'Should I get some more?' she asked, astonished.

'No, that will do me for the time being. Shall we get on?'

She wrapped her half-eaten sandwich in a napkin. 'Suits me. I can finish this in the car.'

After they'd been driving for a while she asked, 'How long before we get there?'

He glanced at his watch. 'Another hour.'

She did some calculations in her head. An hour to get there, a couple more at the hospital and then what? A three or a three-and-a-half-hour journey back. They'd be lucky to reach home before midnight and they still had the other families to see.

However, it seemed he was there before her. 'I phoned a colleague while you were in the ladies. He's agreed to contact the doctors on our list and ask the families some preliminary questions. He said he'd call me back as soon as he had some information for us.'

Although Katherine would have preferred to have made the calls herself, she knew that Alexander had made the right decision. Every minute could make a difference— a life-changing difference—for one patient and his, or her, family.

Finally they arrived in Athens. After the peace of the countryside Katherine found the noise of tooting horns and the fumes of the cars that crept along the roads nose to tail almost overwhelming. She craned her neck to see the Acropolis, which dominated the city. It was on her list of places to visit but, like the rest of her plans, it would have to wait.

She was glad Alexander was with her to negotiate his way around the hospital. Although her spoken Greek wasn't too bad now, reading it was a completely different matter and despite many of the signposts being in English, it was still a busy and confusing hospital.

They made their way to the intensive care unit and she listened as Alexander explained to the doctor why they were there. Then he asked for an update on the patient.

'David is holding his own,' he said. 'But the septicaemia means we might have to amputate his hand. We have a theatre on standby.'

Oh, no! The boy was so young to be facing such drastic surgery. His parents must be beside themselves. And indeed, it seemed that they were too distraught to speak to them. The doctor apologised and suggested they come back in the morning when David's condition might have stabilised and the parents be more willing to see them.

'It can't wait,' Katherine protested. 'We have to find out where he's been and who he came into contact with. His family are the only people who can tell us.'

Once more, Alexander took her by the arm and led her away and out of earshot of the doctor.

'For God's sake, Katherine. Their child may be about to go into Theatre. Could you talk to anyone if you were in their position? I'm not sure I could.'

She knew why he was saying that, but she also knew that in circumstances such as these they couldn't afford the luxury of waiting.

'I know it's a bad time, but we need information as quickly as possible.'

'It can wait.'

'No, it can't.' She held his gaze. 'No it can't,' she repeated more softly. 'If you won't talk to them, I'll have to.'

He rubbed a hand across the back of his neck in what, she was beginning to realise, was a habit of his when he was thinking.

'Look, why don't I try to find another, less distressed family member to talk to? There's bound to be at least one here at the hospital—if I'm not mistaken most of the extended family will have gathered by now.'

'Fair enough,' Katherine conceded. 'But if they can't help I'm going to have to insist on speaking to David's parents.'

He nodded and Katherine was left kicking her heels while Alexander went in search of the extended family. While she waited she opened up her laptop and started creating a database. Then she reviewed what they'd learned so far—which wasn't much. They still didn't know what the cases had in common or how they might have come into contact with the virus. It was almost two hours before Alexander reappeared. He looked tired and in need of a shave.

'They decided they had to take David to Theatre and they've just taken him through to Recovery. They had to amputate the fingers on his left hand. Thank God he's right-handed.'

'I'm sorry,' she said. 'But it could have been so much worse.' She waited a few moments. 'Did you find out anything that might help?'

'Not really. I found his aunt, who lives next door to her sister. According to her, apart from school, a party and a trip to the beach he's not been anywhere out of the usual.' He held out a piece of paper. 'She's given me the names of the other kids at the party. None of them are the other victims, though.'

'They might be yet,' she said. 'We need to make sure everyone on that list and their doctors are contacted.'

'I telephoned Diane while I was waiting to hear how David got on in Theatre. She promised to get onto it straight away.'

She was impressed. She'd been right. Alexander was the perfect person to help with the crises.

'What about the other GP? The one you called—has he got back to you?'

'He phoned a few minutes ago. He's spoken to all the doctors, who have agreed to do as we requested.'

Alexander stepped forward and brushed a lock of her hair away from her forehead. The unexpected and tender gesture made her heart tighten. 'We've done all we can for the moment,' he said gently. 'Let's go home. We can discuss what we're going to do next on the way.'

* * *

On the way back. Alexander pulled off the main road. Katherine looked at him, surprised. 'Where are we going?'

'Neither of us have eaten since the rolls we had for lunch. I don't know about you but my brain doesn't work unless it's kept fuelled.'

Katherine had to agree. Now that he'd mentioned food she realised she was ravenous.

A short while later he stopped at a small taverna with tables set out on a veranda upstairs. Despite the hour, and its location, it was thronged with people enjoying meals and drinks in the cool evening breeze of the mountains. Alexander led her over to a table away from the other diners. The view was spectacular. In the crevasses of the mountain hundreds of lights glittered a snaking path downwards towards the sea. When the waitress came Alexander raised his eyebrow in Katherine's direction.

'You order,' she said, reading his meaning. 'I don't care what I eat as long as it's filling.'

Alexander rattled off something in Greek so rapidly she couldn't follow. While he did so she studied him from under her lashes. His earlier tiredness seemed to have disappeared and his usual energy was back. Although she was exhausted, she felt it too. Perhaps it was the urgency of the situation, the need to find answers that was making them both restless.

'So, what next?' Alexander asked, after the waiter had placed their meals in front of them. He'd ordered moussaka and a Greek salad to share. She speared a chunk of tomato on her fork and popped into her mouth. Delicious.

'We should check in with Public Health in Athens and see if any more cases have been reported.' She laid her fork down, rummaged in her bag, pulled out her mini-laptop and fired it up. 'While you were in with David's parents I made some notes.' She moved it so he could see the screen.

'I've made a table. In the first column I've put the patient's name, the second has the date when they first came to the attention of the medical services and the third has a list of immediate family and friends and anyone else we know of who might have come into contact with them. It's not complete yet—there's bound to be names missing. Next to each name on the list is a column indicating whether they have been given prophylactic antibiotics. The last column is for places they have been in the last couple of weeks and will include swimming clubs, parties, et cetera. By creating a database I can sort the information any way I want. Sooner or later I'm hoping a common link will leap out. In the meantime, I've emailed a copy to my opposite number in Athens.'

Alexander looked impressed. 'You did all that? In, what? A couple of hours. Less.'

Warmth spread through her. Her reaction to him confused her. She couldn't remember a time when she'd felt more at ease in someone's company, yet at the same time her heart raced all the time she was with him.

'It's what I've been trained to do. If I were back at the hospital I'd have access to much more sophisticated programs to do it. On the other hand, entering the data myself helps me to understand it.'

He frowned. 'Is that what they've become? Data?'

'Of course they're not simply data,' Katherine retorted, stung. 'I'm a doctor but also a scientist. Trust me, this is the best way to approach this. Getting too close to individual patients can hinder a person when it comes to seeing patterns.' Hurt, she lowered her glass and pushed her half-eaten meal away. Her appetite had deserted her. 'Give me a moment, will you?' And without waiting for a reply, she stalked away.

Hearing footsteps behind her, Katherine turned. Somehow she wasn't surprised to find Alexander standing behind her.

'Aren't you cold?' he said softly.

'No. It's a perfect evening,' she murmured.

'May I join you?' he asked. When she nodded, he sat down next to her. She could smell his aftershave, almost feel the heat radiating from his body.

'I'm sorry,' he said. 'That was a stupid thing to say. I know you don't see the patients as data.' He grinned sheepishly. 'I'm perfectly aware that underneath the scientist façade beats a soft heart.' He placed a hand over hers. 'Will you forgive me?'

Her heart started pounding so hard she could barely breathe. What was it about him that made her feel that a whole world of possibility lay out there somewhere? She'd accepted that she would remain alone for the rest of her life, which, apart from the sorrow of her parents' deaths and a deep regret about the life she might have had had she made different choices, was a happy one. Then why did she feel she'd been fooling herself all this time?

'What are those lights out at sea?' she asked, to break the tension.

'It's the fishermen. A lot of them like to fish at night.'

'What about you? Is that what you use your boat for? I don't think I've ever seen you go out in it.'

He smiled. 'I've been waiting until I finished repainting it. But normally I go out in it whenever I can. Not just for fishing. I use it to island-hop sometimes. I like taking care of it. It belonged to my father once.' After a pause he continued, his voice soft and reflective. 'When I was a kid and we came to Greece on holiday I used to go out fishing at night with my uncle. Once he wouldn't take me—I forget the reason why. Perhaps he had other plans—but I wanted to go. There was a full moon and only a slight wind—perfect fishing weather. So I waited until everyone was asleep, then I crept out and launched my boat.'

She smiled, imagining the scene. 'Did you catch anything?'

'Tons. There were so many fish I forgot to think about where the boat was, and didn't notice it was drifting. When I looked up I couldn't see the lights on the shore any more.'

'What did you do?'

'I don't know what I was more scared of,' he said, 'being dragged out to the middle of the sea or my father's wrath when he found out I'd been out on my own. I knew the stars pretty well.' He pointed to the sky. 'I knew if I followed the right star it would guide me back to shore. Maybe not here exactly but to somewhere where I could walk or hitch a lift home.'

'And did you?'

'There was only one problem. When I realised I had lost sight of the shore, I jumped to my feet and lost an oar overboard.'

'That must have been a bit of a pain.'

He laughed. 'It was. I tried using the one oar, paddling from one side then the other, but I soon realised that, given the zig-zagging course I was making, it would take days, not hours, to reach the shore. I nearly gave up then. I could have stayed where I was. They would have sent out boats to find me once they discovered I was missing.'

'It's a big sea.'

'And even bigger when you're out there on your own.'

'Were you scared?'

'The thing was, except for the first scary moment, I wasn't. I knew my father would move heaven and earth to find me. I knew whether it took him the rest of his life, whether he had to spend every drachma he had to employ helicopters and search boats to find me, he would.'

'He must have loved you very much.'

'More than life itself.' He turned his head to look at her. 'A parent's love is the strongest love of all. It's only when you have a child yourself that you realise that.'

His words were like a knife straight to her heart. She clasped her hands together and squeezed. He couldn't know how much they hurt her.

'Is that what happened? Did he call the emergency services out?' She was relieved to find her voice sounded normal—cool even.

'No. Thank God he didn't have to. Despite my years in England, I was a Greek boy brought up on legends and myths about Greek heroes. There was no chance I was going to wait for him to come searching for me. I would have died rather than sit there waiting meekly for rescue.' Although he sounded indignant, she could hear the laughter in his voice.

'So, what *did* you do?'

'I decided to try and swim back.'

She laughed. 'You're kidding!'

'It was madness. I know that now, but back then it was all I could think of doing. However I couldn't leave the boat to float out to sea. It was my father's pride and joy. So I threw the fish back. It almost killed me. A whole night's work and the best catch I'd ever had! I jumped out of the boat and, keeping hold of the rope, I swam back to shore.'

'You could have drowned.'

'I knew as long as I kept hold of the boat, I'd be all right. And it worked. It took me a bloody long time but I made it into a small bay just as the sun was coming up. But I still had to get the damned boat back to its proper mooring. So I nicked one of the oars from a boat that was in the bay and rowed home. I've never rowed as fast in all my life. I was determined to get home before my father noticed I was gone.'

'And did you?'

He smiled ruefully. 'Now, that was the thing. I did. At least I thought I did. I crept into bed and a few moments later I heard my father get up. I was pretty pleased with myself, I can tell you. But later, when I went down to the boat again just to check there wasn't any evidence of my night-time excursion, the oar I had pinched was missing and there, in its place, was a brand-new one.' He sighed.

'He must have known what I was up to all along. I bet he was sitting on the wall all night, waiting for me to come home. When he knew I was safe he must have hurried back to bed, and then, when he was sure I was asleep, gone down to check on the boat. Of course, he would have seen instantly that one of the oars had come from another boat and so he made a new one. And you know...' he paused and looked out to sea '...he never once mentioned it. Not ever.'

They sat in silence for a while. 'It sounds as if you have always been surrounded by your family's love. No wonder Crystal is such a happy little girl.'

He looked into the distance. 'I've been lucky, I guess, in so many ways. But the gods like to even the score.' He could only be talking about his wife.

'What about you?' he continued. 'Did you have a happy childhood too?'

Perhaps it was his Greek upbringing that made him talk

like this? Most British men she knew would rather die a hundred deaths then talk about their feelings. Or perhaps it was the night—perhaps everyone found it easier to talk under the cover of darkness.

'Of course my parents loved me. It's just that I think I disappointed them.' The words were out before she knew it.

'Disappointed them? The dedicated, bursary-winning scholar? Did you go off the rails or something when you were a teenager?' He shook his head. 'No, I can't see it. I bet you were head girl.'

Going off the rails was one way of putting it. Off track for a while was perhaps closer to the truth.

She shook her head. 'I was never that popular. Far too studious and serious. I was a prefect, though.'

'There. I was right. And then you went to medical school and here you are about to submit your thesis for your doctorate and one of Europe's top specialists in the spread of infectious diseases. What is there not to be proud of?'

Judging by the teasing note in his voice, he couldn't have known how close to the bone he had come with his questions. She scrambled to her feet. 'I am getting a little cold. I think it's time we went on our way.'

Later that night, she lay in bed listening to the gentle rush of the waves on the shore and thinking about what Alexander had said. She'd tried so hard to make her parents proud, and to an extent she had. Her mother had told anyone who'd listen, sometimes complete strangers, that her daughter was a doctor. In fact, to hear her mother speak you'd think that her daughter was single-handedly responsible for the health of the nation. But what she had wanted most of all, a grandchild she could fuss over, Katherine hadn't given her.

Throwing the covers aside, she went out to the balcony. Alexander was making her think about stuff she didn't want to think about, like loss, and families—and love.

Love. What would it like to be loved by Alexander? It hit her then—she wasn't just attracted to him, she was falling in love with him.

Of all men, why did it have to be him? He was still in love with his wife, that much was obvious. And even if he wasn't, his life was here in Greece and she'd be returning to the UK to pick up hers. But worst of all, if he knew her secret he would despise her. He would never understand why she'd done what she had.

She returned to the sitting room and flicked through the playlist on her iPod. She inserted it into the speakers she had brought with her and as the sound of Brahms filled the room she sat on the sofa and closed her eyes.

What was it with him and this woman? Alexander thought as he stared at the stars from his bedroom window. Why couldn't he stop thinking about her? It wasn't as if he had any intention of having a relationship with her. No one would ever take Sophia's place. Katherine would be returning to the UK soon and he couldn't follow her, she was as much married to her work as he was—there were a hundred different reasons.

Yet he couldn't fool himself any longer that he wasn't strongly attracted to her. Perhaps because he saw his own sadness reflected in her eyes? Or was it because, despite her protestations, he suspected she was lonely and he knew only too well how that felt? It was only when she talked about her work that her reserve disappeared. Her eyes shone and she became more animated. He liked it that she felt passionately about what she did—in many ways she reminded him of the way he used to be. And look how that had turned out.

His mind shied away from the past and back to Katherine.

He liked everything about her—the way she looked, her sensitivity and reserve, the sudden smile that lit up her face, banishing the shadows in her eyes, the way she was with Crystal, slightly awkward but not talking down to her the way many adults did, how she was with Yia-Yia and the villagers: respectful, but not patronising.

When the realisation hit him it was like jumping into a pool of water from a height. Shock then exhilaration. He didn't just like her—he was falling in love with her.

As the plaintive notes of Brahms's Lullaby filtered through the still night air from the other side of the square he went outside and listened. It had been one of Sophia's favourites—something she'd played often. He closed his eyes as an image of Sophia rushed back, her head bent over the keys of the piano, her hair falling forward as her fingers flew over the keys, a smile of pure happiness on her lips. His chest tightened. Sophia. His love. How could he think, even for a moment, that there could ever be anyone else?

CHAPTER SIX

COMFORTED BY THE soothing strains of the music and knowing sleep would elude her, Katherine studied her database, entering the list of names Alexander had given her.

She stopped when she came to Stéfan's name. He had been the first patient to fall ill. Concentrating on him was key.

There was something about him that was tugging at her memory. What was it? Yes! She had it. The day he'd collapsed at the surgery, he'd been sporting a bandage on his right hand. And it hadn't been clean either. It had looked professional, though. Someone had bandaged his hand but not recently. Hercules leaped onto her lap and started purring. She stroked him absent-mindedly as she dialled Alexander's phone. Despite the late hour, he picked up immediately.

'The boy who died. Stéfan Popalopadous? Do you know how he hurt his hand? Did he have it dressed at your practice?' she asked, coming straight to the point.

Alexander mumbled a curse under his breath. 'Hello to you too. No, I don't know how Stéfan hurt his hand. Not without looking at his notes, which, of course, are at the practice. But something tells me that's where I'm going.'

'Would you like me to come with you?' she asked.

'No. That's okay. Keep your phone near you and I'll call you as soon as I have an answer.'

It was over an hour before he called back. She snatched up the phone. 'Yes? What have you found out?'

'He damaged his hand in a winch on his boat. Apparently he often takes people out for trips in the evenings after work. He was treated in Nafplio. He runs trips between there and all the major ports along the coast.'

'Then Nafplio is where we're going. Pick me up on the way.'

Nafplio was pretty, with elegant town houses with balconies that reminded her of Venice. Alexander told her a little of the town's history on the way. During the Ottoman era it had once been the capital of Greece and the Palamayde fortress, which dominated the town, had been a prison during the Greek War of Independence. Now the town was a stopover for some of the smaller cruise ships on their way around the Mediterranean as well as for yachts either in flotillas or in singles. That wasn't good: If one of the transient visitors had come into contact with their patient, who knew where they would be now? Was that how Claire had contracted the disease?

They phoned the doctor of the surgery where Stéfan's hand had been dressed, rousing him from his bed, and discovered that they'd been right. Stéfan had been treated there a couple of days before he'd turned up at Alexander's practice. He'd had a temperature, but it hadn't been raised enough to cause concern.

Now they had their first contact, they could be reasonably confident of tracing the others before they became sick.

Katherine and Alexander exchanged high-fives as soon

as they left the practice. 'You're some public health doctor,' he said.

She grinned back at him. 'I am, aren't I?'

Over the next week, Katherine and Alexander visited all the villages and towns where cases of meningitis had been reported, as well as those of all the contacts they'd traced. Now they knew about Stéfan, it was easier to trace the people he'd come into contact with and their contacts. David, the boy in Intensive Care, had been taken around the coast with a number of his friends as a birthday treat, and the other eight victims, most of whom were recovering, had also taken trips in Stéfan's boat in the days before Stéfan had become unwell. Finally Claire's parents confirmed that their daughter had posted a photo on her Facebook page of Stéfan and his boat shortly before she'd become ill.

Katherine and Alexander set up temporary clinics and spoke to the local nurses and medical staff, advising them what to look out for and what information to give their patients. There had been one new case, but as everyone was more vigilant, she had been admitted to hospital as soon as she'd started showing symptoms and was doing well.

The longer she worked with Alexander the more she admired him. He was good with the patients, kind and understanding with panicked villagers, and authoritative with those who needed to be persuaded to take the antibiotics. It was tiring work and they spent hours in the car, driving from village to village, but she treasured those times most of all. They spoke of their day, what they had to do next, but they also talked about the music they liked and places they wanted to visit.

However, she was aware he was holding back from her, as she was from him. Often it was on the tip of her tongue to tell him about Poppy but the time never seemed right, or, if she was honest, she was too frightened of his reaction. What would he think if, or when, she did tell him? Would he be shocked? Or would he understand? And why tell him anyway? As long as there were no new cases of meningitis she would be leaving at the end of September and so far he'd said nothing, done nothing to make her think he saw her as more than a friend and colleague— albeit one he was attracted to.

She'd caught him looking at her when she'd been sneaking looks in his direction. Unsure of what it meant, she'd dropped her eyes, her pulse racing, finding an excuse to turn away, to speak to someone else.

But apart from the looks, he'd never as much as taken her hand or kissed her good-night. She suspected he was still in love with his dead wife and that no woman would ever live up to her.

The thought of returning to the UK made her heart ache. To leave all this when she'd only just found it. To go back to a life that more than ever seemed colourless and grey. To leave Alexander, his grandmother and Crystal—most of all Alexander—was breaking her heart.

Perhaps it was being here in Greece? Perhaps it was just the magic spell the country had woven around her? Maybe when she returned to the UK she'd be able to see it for what it was: infatuation, brought on by too much sun and the joy of working with someone who cared about what he did as much as she.

But she knew she was fooling herself. She wasn't just falling in love with him—she loved him—totally, deeply and would love him for as long as she breathed. But, he didn't love her. Nothing and no one could replace his wife.

His life was here with his daughter and his family while hers was back in London.

And what if he suspected how she felt about him? That would be too humiliating. Maybe he'd already guessed?.

She threw down her book and started pacing. Perhaps he thought she visited his house as a means to get close to him. And going to the square every evening to share a meal or a beer with him. Wasn't that practically admitting she couldn't stay away from him? God, she'd done everything but drool whenever he was near. She'd virtually thrown herself at him. How could she have been so stupid?

Well, there was only one way to rectify that. She would keep her distance. She wouldn't visit Yia-Yia, she wouldn't go to the square. If anyone asked she would say she was behind with her thesis. That, as it happened, was perfectly true. Besides, what did she care if anyone—least of all him—thought she was making excuses? As long as they didn't think she was some desperate woman trying to snag the local widowed doctor while she was here.

But not to see him? Except in passing? To even think it tore her in two.

She should have known this kind of happiness couldn't last.

Alexander stood on the balcony, a glass of cold water in his hand, his thoughts straying, as they always did these days, to Katherine. He hadn't seen much of her since they'd stopped visiting the affected villages and he missed her. She used to come most evenings to the square but she hadn't been for a while. Was she avoiding him?

Working with her these last weeks he'd come to admire her more and more. She was good at what she did. Very good. If she hadn't been around he doubted that they would have got on top of the outbreak as quickly as they had. Her patience with the affected families, her manner towards the villagers, her determination to speak her faltering Greek to them and the kindness and respect with which she treated young and old alike was very much the Greek ethos. He loved how her forehead furrowed when she was thinking, how her face lit up when she laughed, and most of all the way she was with Crystal. His daughter adored her.

Katherine was almost as perfect in her way as Sophia had been in hers. But she'd be going soon. And the thought of not seeing her again filled him with dismay.

It hit him then. He didn't just like and admire Katherine, he was crazy about her.

So what was he doing here, on his own, kicking his heels when he could be with her?

CHAPTER SEVEN

KATHERINE WAS SITTING on her balcony, watching the sun cast shadows on the sea, when she heard a soft tap on the door. Having come to recognise the sound of Alexander's footsteps, she didn't need to turn around to know it was him. Neither was she really surprised. Deep down she'd known it was only a matter of time before he sought her out.

'Crystal's been looking for you at the taverna these last couple of evenings,' he said softly. 'So was I. And Yia-Yia says she hasn't seen you for a day or two. Are you all right? Not ill or anything?'

The way he was searching her face made her pulse skip a beat.

'I thought I should give company a miss for a while.' Her heart was thumping so hard she was finding it difficult to breathe. 'With everything that has happened, I've fallen behind with my thesis. I'm planning to submit it in the next couple of days.'

He came to sit in the chair next to hers. 'When do you leave?'

'At the end of the month. There's nothing to keep me here longer now the epidemic seems to be under control. I had a phone call from Athens earlier—there's been no more cases reported in the last forty-eight hours. They're pretty confident the outbreak is over.'

'Thank God. If you hadn't got onto it as soon as you did, there could have been more deaths.'

'I was only doing my job. A job I love.'

His expression was unreadable in the light of the moon.

'I never did take you out on the boat, did I?' he said softly.

'No, you didn't,' she agreed. 'But you've been busy. It can't be easy for you, working and being a single father.' God, couldn't she think of anything less inane to say?

'I have Yia-Yia. And Helen when I need her.' He hooked his hands behind his head. 'Although as Helen's getting married in a few weeks it's unlikely that Crystal and I will see as much of her.' He leaned forward. 'I could still take you out on the boat. In fact, we could go later tonight. It's a perfect night for it.'

She didn't think it was possible for her heart to beat any faster but apparently it could.

'You don't have to take me, you know,' she said stiffly.

He looked taken aback. 'Of course I don't have to take you. Why would you think that?' His eyes locked on hers. 'It's not just Crystal who's missed you, I've missed spending time with you too,' he said softly. 'I like being with you. Haven't you realised that by now?' He stood and reached out a hand for hers.

Her heart beating a tattoo against her ribs, she allowed him to pull her to her feet. For a moment she swayed towards him, driven by a need to feel his arms around her. At the last moment she stopped herself and took a step back. Hadn't she told herself she wouldn't make a fool of herself?

He looked bemused, as well he might. How could he

know what was inside her head when she barely did? However, he didn't let go of her hand.

'We should wait until Crystal's asleep, though,' he continued, 'otherwise she'll insist on coming too. If I say no, I wouldn't put it past her to launch a boat of her own and come after us.'

Katherine had to laugh, even if it sounded shaky. 'No one can say she's not your daughter.'

'No.' His expression grew more serious. 'I could do with having you on my own for a bit. My daughter has taken such a liking to you, it's difficult to prise her from your side.'

Her heart catapulted inside her chest.

Why was she worrying about the future? It felt right that he was here, and why not sleep with him if he asked? And she was certain he would ask. She would be leaving soon and although there was no chance of a future for them, why resist snatching a few days of happiness? He need never know her secret. What mattered was here and now and if she could be with him, even for a short while, why not? She'd have plenty time to lick her wounds—to regret what could have been—when she left here. She surprised herself. Greece had changed so much about her.

'We should make the most of what time you have left,' he said, as if reading her mind. 'I could take some leave. We could spend it together.'

'And Crystal? Isn't she expecting to spend time with you?'

'Of course. And she will. I thought the three of us could do some stuff.' He searched her face. 'I know having my daughter around, adorable though she is, puts a spanner in the works, but happily she does go to sleep in the evenings. You do like her, don't you? She's definitely taken a shine to you.'

She wanted to ask him whether he liked to be with her because of Crystal because, much as she was coming to love the little girl, she needed him to want to be with her. But she wouldn't ask him. And what if he said yes? What if he asked her to stay permanently? What would she do then? At the very least she would have to admit that there was a very large part of her life she was keeping secret from him. Perhaps the time to tell him was now, before they got in any deeper. But if she did, what would he say? How would he react?

And what was she thinking anyway? Even if he did ask her to stay, she wouldn't. She couldn't. How could she take on the care of a child after what she'd done? However, didn't he deserve the truth from her, whether she stayed or not?

She was being given a glimpse of a life she might have. A chance to break free from the strait-jacket of the one she'd imposed on herself with its rules, self-denial, hard work and determination. Could she forgive herself—allow herself the joy of loving and being loved? Even for a short while.

He misinterpreted her silence and stood. 'I'll see you about then?'

'What time do you want me to meet you?'

His expression lightened. 'About ten?'

'I'll be there.'

When she arrived at the bay he was leaning against the boat, wearing a black T-shirt and dark jeans with fisherman's boots. He looks a bit like a pirate, she thought, especially with the five o'clock shadow darkening his jaw. He whistled appreciatively when he saw her. She'd been like a cat on a hot tin roof all evening. After discarding several outfits, she'd finally settled on a pair of faded denim shorts and a cheesecloth embroidered blouse she'd purchased in the village. Underneath she wore a lacy bra with matching panties. She'd shaved her legs and moisturised all over.

She couldn't remember the last time she'd felt so nervous and was ready long before she was due to meet him. Unable to change the habits of a lifetime, she'd packed a small bag with a cardigan in the unlikely event it was chilly on the water, and at the last minute had added some fresh fruit and olives, a bottle of wine, a corkscrew and two glasses. It was always better to be prepared.

'Hello,' she whispered. Feeling inexplicably like a naughty child, she suppressed the desire to giggle.

'You don't have to whisper, you know,' he said with a grin. 'It's not as if we're ten years old and stealing a boat.'

'Sorry,' she said in a normal voice. 'Whispering just seemed to go with the moment.'

The boat was in the water, where it drifted gently in the waves, and he was holding on to the rope to stop it being pushed out to sea. 'Why don't you climb in?' he suggested.

She slipped off her sandals and stepped into the sea, shivering as the waves lapped around her ankles, then her calves and above her knees. As her skin adjusted to the temperature, the cool water felt delicious against her overheated skin.

But once she'd reached the boat she stood dumbfounded. How was she supposed to get in? As if reading her mind, Alexander, still holding the rope but gathering it in towards him, waded over until he was standing next to her. Suddenly she felt a pair of strong hands circle her waist and then she was off her feet and he was holding her in his arms. Even in the warmth of the evening air she was conscious of the heat radiating from his body and the clean, fresh scent of him.

He laughed down at her. 'Good thing you weigh nothing.' A slight exaggeration, she thought—she wasn't the smallest of women—but then she was being dropped gently into the boat. A few seconds later Alexander sprang in alongside her. Tentatively she took a seat at the back. He picked up an oar and pushed them away from the shore, before coiling the rope into a neat round and placing it on the bottom of the boat. 'Sit in the front if you like,' he said. 'No, not now!' he added as she stood, making the boat wobble. 'Wait until we're a bit further out. Unless you want us to both end up in the water?'

Feeling a little foolish, she sat back down as Alexander started rowing. The moon was so bright she could see the muscles of his arms bunching with every pull of the oar.

'Are we going to fish?' she asked.

'If you like. But later. I want to show you something first.'

A comfortable silence fell, punctuated only by the creak of the boat against the oars and the lapping of the sea. Katherine trailed her hand in the water.

'Watch out for sharks,' he cautioned.

She pulled her hand out of the water as if she'd had an electric shock. But when she looked at him she saw, from his grin, that he'd been teasing her.

Her skin tingled and she grinned back at him. How she loved this man!

'So, what is it you want to show me?'

'I'm afraid you're going to have to wait and see.' He refused to say any more so she let herself relax, gasping with delight as a shooting star sped across the sky before falling towards the black depths of the ocean. It was if she had been transported into a different world. Happiness surged through her. Everything about being here—being with Alexander—made her feel more alive than she'd ever felt before. As if the person she was when she was with him was a different, more together version of herself on one hand and a wilder, more interesting, version on the other.

It must have been so hard for her mother to leave here when she married. Britain was a colder, greyer place than the one she'd left. Although the way the villagers lived, almost on top of each other and constantly visiting each other's homes, had taken Katherine time to get used to, and she could see how someone used to living in such close proximity with their neighbours, always having someone to call on for support, would struggle to adapt in a strange country with an entirely different culture. Her mother had loved her father very much and, as she'd told Katherine often, she would rather have been with Dad in hell than without him.

A wave of sadness threatened to swamp her mood. At least she was here. In the country her mother had once called home, she felt nearer to her than she'd felt since she'd died.

'You okay?'

Alexander's voice jerked her back to the present. 'Yes. Why?'

'It's just that you looked sad there for a moment.'

She forced a smile. 'Just thinking about my mother and wishing she'd been able come back even once before she died.'

In the distance the tiny lights from other boats bobbed on the sea. Beyond them dark shapes of small islands broke up the horizon.

'Perhaps *you'll* come back—or stay?' he said softly.

Her pulse upped another notch. Was he asking her to?

'I have my work. But, yes, I think will. What about you? Do you think you might ever return to the UK?' She held her breath as she waited for his answer.

'To visit my mother certainly. But I couldn't leave Greece permanently. I couldn't take Crystal away from her grandmother. At least, not until she's older.'

Her earlier happiness dimmed. She could understand him not wanting to separate Crystal from her great-grandmother, not until she was older anyway, but if he felt about Katherine the way she felt about him, wouldn't he want to be with her? Wouldn't he ask her outright to stay?

'Why,' he continued, 'do we always regret what might have been instead of being grateful for the life we have?'

Her heart thudded a tattoo against her chest. She wanted to ask him what he meant. Was he referring to her? What might have been? Or was he talking about his wife?

'Do you regret coming back here?' she asked instead.

'Not at all. It was the right decision for Crystal. Anyway, the UK was too—' He stopped suddenly. 'Too cold,' he finished. She was sure that wasn't what he had been about to say. In unguarded moments his sadness mirrored her own. Even after two years he was still grieving for his wife. But he should find some comfort in the knowledge he had found love—a great love, she suspected—and she envied him for it. More, she envied the woman who had been the recipient.

They lapsed into silence again. Just when she was beginning to wonder where exactly he was taking her, an island with a small bay came into view.

'Is this the place you wanted to show me?' she asked.

'Greece has many beautiful islands, but this is one I like to come to whenever I take out the boat. Not least because no one ever comes here. The only other place I like more is Cape Sounion.'

'Where's that?'

'You mean you don't know? You must have heard of the temple of Poseidon. It's where Byron used to go to write his poetry. I'll take you one day.'

His assumption that they would be spending more time together sent a ripple of happiness through her. She'd waited how many years to find someone like him and she'd had to come to a remote part of Greece to do so. If only she had an inkling of how he felt about her. If only he could love her the way he had loved, and probably still loved, his wife; if only she could make him understand why she'd done what she had, they might have a chance of a future together.

But he would never understand. She was certain of that.

He jumped out of the boat, holding its rope, and held out his arms. She let him swing her into them. As his arms tightened around her she closed her eyes, wanting to savour every last moment. He carried her ashore before standing her gently on her feet.

'So, what's so special about this island?' she asked, when he returned from pulling the boat out of the water. 'You've just told me Greece has hundreds of beautiful islands.'

'Legend has it that a Spartan soldier brought a Trojan princess here when he captured her. I have no evidence that this is the exact place,' he said, holding his hands up as if to ward off her protests, 'but he described it as an island not far from my village whose beauty was only dimmed by the beauty of his wife.' His voice dropped to a murmur. 'He believed if he kept her here, safe, nothing bad would ever happen to her and they could live out the rest of their lives together and in peace.'

'And did they? In your story?' It might only be a legend but she really wanted to know.

His gaze returned to hers, the tone of his voice almost dismissive. 'No. In time he got bored. He missed the excitement and prestige that came with being in the Greek army.'

'What happened?'

'When he was away, fighting in some war or another, his enemies found her here. They captured her and intended to make her a consort. She guessed what they planned so when they weren't watching her, she escaped and ran to the cliff. She threw herself into the sea.'

'Oh, no! And what happened to her lover?'

'As soon as he came back and discovered what had happened, he went mad with grief and guilt. He drowned himself so he could be with her in death.'

Katherine shivered. 'That's so sad.'

He reached for her hand. 'What do you think he should have done? Was he not wrong to bring her here where she was alone and unprotected?' His eyes bored into hers as if her answer really mattered. 'Don't you think he deserved what happened?'

'Well, first of all,' she began cautiously, her reaction was her choice. I don't think she would have agreed to come and live here with him if she hadn't wanted to. She must have known he was trying to protect her the best way he knew how. In the end he was wrong, but that doesn't mean he didn't do what he did for the right reasons. Didn't you say earlier that there is no point regretting what might have been?'

She knew she was talking as much about her own situation as this mythical couple's. 'It's easy to look back on our lives and see what we did wrong, what we should have done—but at the time we can only make the best decision we can in the circumstances.'

'Is that what you really believe? I can't imagine you have much to regret.'

This conversation was getting too close to the bone for comfort. Perhaps it was time to tell him about Poppy. But fear held her back. She couldn't bear it if he judged her or, worse, rejected her. She forced a smile. 'Why do you like the island so much if it has such a sad story attached to it?'

He poured her some wine and passed the glass to her. The touch of his fingertips brushing against hers sent hot sparks up her arm. 'In a way, I guess it is sad. But legend has it that the gods took pity on them and turned them into dolphins. I like to think of them out in the ocean to-gether—always.'

Her heart twisted. So she'd been right. He was still in love with his wife.

He stepped forward and took her face between his hands. 'I don't know why no man has captured you yet. What is wrong with English men?'

'Perhaps it is me,' she said, then could have kicked her-self. It was difficult to think straight with him being so close. 'I mean, being too picky.'

He laughed down at her, his teeth white in the dark. 'You should be picky,' he said. He tangled his hands in her hair and, with his thumbs under her cheek bones, raised her face to his. 'You are so beautiful. So perfect.'

No, she thought wildly. *Don't think that!* He mustn't think she was perfect. He'd only be disappointed.

He lowered his head and brought his mouth down on hers and then she couldn't think any more. This was what she'd been imagining almost from the moment she'd first set eyes on him and it was everything she'd dreamed it would be. As his kisses deepened she clung to him, almost dizzy with desire.

When he moved away she gave a little gasp of disappointment. But he lifted her in his arms and carried her over to a soft patch of grass where he laid her down.

'Are you sure?' he asked as she gazed up at him.

'Sure?' She almost laughed. She pulled him down to her. 'What took you so long?' she murmured against his lips.

Later, they lay wrapped in each other's arms, gazing up at the stars. She'd never felt so peaceful, so thoroughly made love to. He'd been demanding, gentle and teasing and had touched her in ways she couldn't remember being touched before, until she'd cried out with her need to have him inside her. She blushed as she remembered how she'd dug her fingertips into his back, how she'd called out to him as wave upon wave of pleasure had rocked her body.

But she didn't really care. This wanton, this woman he'd unleashed, was a revelation to her and she never wanted to go back to the one she'd been before. She smiled to herself. This was what sex should be like.

The moonlight shone on his naked body. It was every bit as she'd imagined—better than any of the Greek statues she'd seen. No wonder she hadn't been able to stop thinking about how he would feel under her hands. A smile curved her lips and she laughed with sheer joy.

He propped himself on his elbow and gazed down at her. Instinctively she reached for her blouse to cover her nakedness, but as she moved her hand he caught it in his fingers. 'Don't,' he murmured. 'I don't think I could ever get enough of just looking at you.'

The new wanton Katherine revelled in the desire she saw in his eyes.

She reached up to him and wrapped her arms around his neck.

As the horizon turned pink and apricot they lay in each other's arms, looking up at the star-sprinkled sky, their hands entwined. 'There's something I need to tell you,' he said softly.

Oh, God, here it was. *This was wonderful but...*

'Remember I told you that I was training to be a surgeon when Sophia died,' he continued.

'Yes.'

'And I said I was working all the time?'

She wasn't sure where this was going. 'I know how competitive the speciality can be.'

'When Sophia fell pregnant with Crystal I was so happy. And so was she. If at times I caught her looking wistful I just put it down to her being homesick for Greece. It suited me to believe that's all it was. Looking back, I think she knew it was the end of her dream to become a concert pianist.

'I was determined to make it in surgery, but you know how it is—the competition is fierce, especially for the top positions, and only the best job in the most prestigious hospital would do me. I had it all planned out. I would qualify for a consultant post then I would apply to the Mayo Clinic in America and do some further training there. I'd already sat my board exams when I was a resident in my final year at med school so getting a post wouldn't be an issue as long as I stayed focussed.

'Sophia backed me all the way. She said she could play

her music anywhere. I knew that wasn't necessarily true—not if she wanted to play professionally—but I chose not to listen to that particular voice. I was a selfish bastard back then—completely focussed on what I wanted to achieve. I told myself I was doing it for all of us, for me, for Sophia—and for the baby on the way.

'What I chose to forget was that she'd already put her career on hold for me. A musician's career is, if anything, more competitive than medicine—they have such a short time to "make it" and she'd already jeopardised her chances by coming with me to the UK. But, as I said, I planned to make it up to her. One day when I'd got to where I needed to go, I would slow down, let my career take a back seat and let her enjoy the limelight for a while.

'We both wanted a family and I told myself that by the time I had reached the top, the children would be of an age to allow her time for herself. There was always going to be more than one child. We both wanted at least three. Call me clever, huh? If I'd done the math I would have realised that if everything went to plan she would have been thirty three by the time the youngest was born. I thought it was simple. We'd have children. Sophia would stay at home until the youngest was six weeks or so and then we'd employ a nanny. And Sophia went along with it. Until Crystal was born. Then she could no more see herself putting any child of hers into a nursery than she could have left them home alone. She loved being a mother. If she found it boring she never said so and I never asked.

'She always made friends easily and the house was always filled—at least so I heard as I was rarely home long enough to see for myself. It was as if she'd gathered around her friends to be the family she'd left behind in Greece. I told myself she was happy. But when I thought about it later, I couldn't remember the last time she'd played the piano. At the time I told myself that that was good—that she wasn't really driven enough to make it as a concert pianist. Why is everything so much more obvious in hindsight?'

Katherine rolled over so she could see his face. 'We all see things differently later, don't we?' she murmured, although every word he'd said about Sophia cut her like a blade.

'I never stopped loving her. She was my best friend, my lover, the mother of my child, but I stopped seeing her—really seeing her.'

The sadness in his eyes twisted her heart.

'She deserved more than I gave her. Perhaps I didn't love her enough. If I had I wouldn't have put my needs so far above hers.'

'She was lucky to be loved the way you loved her. She would have known she was deeply loved,' Katherine whispered.

'I'm glad you told me about her.' And she was. She wanted to know everything about him. Even if hearing about how much he'd loved Sophia hurt.

'I had to. You have to know why I'm not sure I can ever promise more than what we have here tonight. I care too much about you not to tell you the truth about myself. And there's more…'

She stopped his words with her fingertips. The here and now was all they had. After what he'd told her, how could she ever tell him about Poppy? And not telling him meant they could never have more than what they had now. 'Let's not think about the past,' she said. 'Let's only think about now.' She moved her hand from his lips and taking his head between her palms lowered herself on top of him.

* * *

When they returned to the village she led him by the hand up the path and into her home. Her heart was beating so fast she couldn't speak.

He kicked the door closed behind him. '*Agapi- mou*,' he breathed into her neck. 'I want you. I need you.'

She stepped into his arms feeling as if, at last, she'd come home—even if only for a while.

They spent every day of the next week with each other, until Alexander's leave was over. Crystal came to the house often. If Katherine was working, the child would take the colouring book she'd brought with her and lay it on the table next to Katherine's papers, and quietly, her tongue caught in the corner of her mouth, use her crayons to colour in, stopping periodically to admire her work or to study Katherine from the corner of her eye, waiting patiently until Katherine stopped what she was doing to admire her efforts. Increasingly, Katherine would find herself, at Yia-Yia's invitation, at the family home, pitching in to make olive tapenade or some other Greek dish. Then, instead of sitting and looking out at the beach, they'd retire to the bench at the front of the house and sit in silence, enjoying the heat of the sun and letting the ebb and flow of village life happen around them. Katherine's rusty Greek was improving by leaps and bounds and she and Alexander's grandmother were able to communicate reasonably well.

She'd also become confident enough with her Greek to stop to chat with the other villagers when she was passing through the square. Soon small gifts of ripe tomatoes and zucchini, enormous squashes and bunches of fat grapes still on the vine appeared on her doorstep, and before long she had more plump olives than she could hope ever to eat

and more bottles of home-made olive oil than she knew
what to do with.

She often thought of her mother. It was as if she'd
planned this, knowing that Greece would weave its magic
around her and that Katherine would discover what she
had missed out on in life. It was, Katherine realised, her
mother's final gift to her and one she wanted to savour. As
it had done during the epidemic, her thesis lay largely ignored—dotting the 'i's and crossing the 't's didn't seem as
important as they once had—although Katherine knew she
would never submit it until it was as perfect as she could
make it. Greece hadn't turned her into a complete sloth.

But she *was* less than perfect here. She no longer blow-
dried her hair every morning before twirling it into a
tight bun. Instead she wore it lose around her shoulders
or twisted carelessly into a ponytail, no longer caring if it
frizzed a little around the edges. She felt freer without the
tights, the buttoned-to-the-neck shirts, tailored trousers
and sensible shoes she'd worn when she'd first arrived.
Now it was bare-shouldered sundresses, skimpy shorts
and strappy T-shirts. She'd even repainted her nails in the
same blood red as Crystal had—leaving Crystal's handi-
work would have been a step too far! With Alexander back
at work, she saw little of him during the day, but most evenings they drank cold beer and nibbled olives and fresh
figs, spoke about work and history while Crystal played
in the square. He made her laugh with his amusing stories
of the villagers and his patients and although her skin still
fizzed every time he looked at her, she was able to relax in
his company in a way that she hadn't done with anyone,
apart from Sally, in years.

It was, Katherine thought, the happiest time of her life.
For once, nothing was asked of her, nothing demanded,

no one expected anything of her. Sometimes Crystal came with them and sometimes they went on their own. He took her to Cape Souinon and she could see straight away why he loved it. The ruins of the temple of Poseidon looked out towards the sea and she could easily imagine Lord Byron sitting with his back against one of the pillars, writing poetry.

Often they spent the day on the beach with Crystal, swimming, picnicking and sharing intimate smiles. In the evenings he would call at her house and together they would climb the path to the village square, releasing their hands by unspoken consent moments before they reached it. But it was the nights she longed for most. When his daughter was asleep he'd come to her house and they'd make love, either in her bed or down in the little bay. He'd wake up early and leave her to return to his home so that he'd always be there when Crystal woke up. And every day she fell just a little more in love with him.

She didn't know how she was ever going to say goodbye.

Alexander was whistling as he showered. In a short while he'd be seeing Katherine. It had been a long time, he reflected, since he'd felt this good. Not since Sophia had died.

And it was all down to Katherine. He grinned remembering the night before. How could he ever have thought she was reserved—when it came to making love she was anything but.

Unfortunately his lunchtime date with Katherine was going to be curtailed. He had a patient who needed a home visit. Perhaps Katherine would come with him? He didn't want to waste any of the little time they had left.

But why should she leave?

He stepped out of the shower.

She could come to live with him in Greece. He was certain she would find another job here easily. Or he could find one in England. He quickly dismissed the thought. He couldn't uproot Crystal again. At least not until she was older. Katherine would understand. She knew how important it was for Crystal to be brought up around family.

But would she stay? They would get married of course. The thought brought him up short. Marriage! He almost laughed out loud. He'd been so certain he'd never marry again, but that was before he'd met Katherine. Now he couldn't imagine the rest of his life without her.

Although she hadn't said, he was certain Katherine was in love with him. But enough to marry him? Give up her life in the UK?

There was only one way to find out. 'What do you think, Sophia?' he murmured. 'Do I deserve another chance at happiness?'

CHAPTER EIGHT

KATHERINE WAS PORING over her computer, trying and failing to concentrate on finishing her paper, when there was a knock on the door. No one in the village ever knocked and certainly not Crystal, and although she was expecting Alexander any minute, he always marched in, announcing himself by calling out her name. She quickly saved the file she was working on and went to answer.

When she saw who it was her heart almost stopped beating.

'Poppy?'

Her daughter pushed by her and dropped her rucksack on the floor. 'I'm surprised you know who I am.'

Admittedly, for a brief moment Katherine hadn't. Her daughter had changed so much since the last photo she had seen of her. Gone was her long, golden hair. Gone was the awkward yet beautiful, fresh-faced teenager. In her place was an angry-looking young woman with black spiky hair, kohl-ringed panda eyes and a lip-piercing.

'Of course I know who you are,' Katherine whispered. She'd dreamed of this moment for so long but in her imagination it had taken the form of getting-to-know-you phone calls followed by lunches and shopping trips. In her head, Poppy had been like her as a teenager; demure, well spoken and beautifully mannered. Nothing in her dreams had prepared her for this. But despite her dismay, a warm, happy glow was spreading from her stomach towards her heart.

Poppy flung herself down on the sofa. 'I thought you might be staying in a villa or something. But this place is pokey. I don't see a pool.'

'That's because there isn't one.' She was still stunned. 'But there's an ocean to swim in.'

'Oh, well. I suppose it will have to do. Anything's better than being at home with *them*.'

'Them?'

'Liz and Mike. The people who call themselves my parents.'

Katherine's head was whirling. 'How did you know I was here? Do Liz and Mike know you're with me?'

'I had your email address, remember? I emailed your work address and got an out-of-office reply, so I phoned them and told them I needed to know where you were. I told them it was urgent—a family emergency—and luckily I got through to a receptionist who didn't know you had no family.' The last was said with heavy and pointed emphasis on the 'no'. 'And as for Mum and Dad, no. They don't know I'm here. They don't care where I am!'

'Poppy! They must be out of their minds with worry! You must—'

'All they care about is their new baby. It's Charlie this and Charlie that. God, why did they adopt me if they were going to go and have a baby of their own?'

Mike and Liz had had a baby? Well, it wasn't unheard of for couples who believed themselves infertile to conceive spontaneously when they'd given up all hope of having a child, but Katherine wished Liz had written to tell her.

It had been a long time since she'd heard from Poppy's

adoptive mother. Not since a year ago when Poppy had turned sixteen and Liz had emailed Katherine, telling her that any further contact would be up to Poppy. In the meantime, if Katherine chose to continue writing, not emailing if she didn't mind as Liz couldn't monitor those, she would keep the letters but only pass them on to Poppy when and if she asked.

It hadn't been written to hurt her, although it had. In her heart, Katherine had wanted to argue but in her head she'd agreed. At sixteen Poppy was old enough to decide for herself whether she wanted to stay in touch. Katherine had always hoped that she would decide to—but not like this.

'I didn't know they had another child,' Katherine said. 'That must have been a surprise.'

'They didn't have *another* child. They had a child. I'm not their child. Not any longer. What is it with you lot that you can cast off your children when it suits you?'

'They put you out?' Katherine said, astonished and outraged. 'But that's—'

Poppy stared down at the floor. 'They didn't *exactly* put me out,' she mumbled. 'I mean, they never said in so many words that they wanted me to go—but it was obvious.'

'And they don't know where you are?' Katherine asked, beginning to recover. 'They'll be frantic You need to let your parents—'

'They're not my parents!'

'According to the law, they are. They've probably alerted the police. How did you leave without them knowing? *When* did you leave?'

'Yesterday morning. I said I was going to a sleepover at my friend Susan's'

Katherine was aghast. 'You *lied* to them?'

'Well, I could hardly tell them where I was going, could I?'

'If you're so convinced they don't care, why didn't you try it?' Katherine winced at the tone of her own voice. Now she sounded as snarky as her daughter.

Poppy glowered. 'They have to pretend, don't they, that they care? Even if it's all a big, fat act.'

'Of course they care and they need to know where you are. They need to know you're safe.'

'I don't want to talk to them.'

Katherine retrieved her mobile from her bag and held it out. 'Phone them. Now.'

'No.'

Katherine was tempted for a miniscule moment not to phone Liz and Mike. They might phone the police to return Poppy or at the very least insist Katherine put her on the next plane and she couldn't bear not to steal a day or two with her child. Her child! She gave herself a mental shake. Of course she couldn't possibly do that to Mike and Liz.

'You can't stay here unless you do. I'll have to notify the police.'

Poppy got up from the sofa and picked up her rucksack. 'In that case, I'm off. I should have known you wouldn't want me either. Jeez, I'm so stupid. You got rid of me once. Why on earth would you want anything to do with me now? I just thought you might have a little leftover maternal feeling—if not a sense that you owe me something at least.'

Katherine knew she was being manipulated, but even so, she couldn't let Poppy leave. Not now, not like this. If Poppy walked out her life, would she ever get another chance with her again? And under the sullen exterior Katherine glimpsed the lonely, confused child within. It took all her resolve not to march across the room and envelop her daughter in her arms. Somehow, instinctively, she knew that wasn't the way to handle the situation either. Best to remain calm and reasonable. After all, there must be *some* reason for Poppy to have sought her out—even if part of her motive was to hurt her adoptive parents as much as possible. She had to tread carefully.

'Poppy, please. I don't want you to go, that's not what I meant. I can't tell you how...' her heart swelled '...thrilled and delighted I am to see you.' She gestured towards the sofa. 'Please, sit back down. Let me phone your parents, talk to them. I'll ask if you can stay here for a couple of days. It'll give us a chance to talk...'

Katherine held her breath, her heart beating in her throat, while Poppy considered what she'd said. Now that Poppy was here—here! In front of her! she couldn't bear not to grab this chance to talk to her, maybe hold her... even once.

Just when she thought her daughter was going to bolt for the door, she dropped her bag again.

'Okay.'

Relief made her legs weak. 'Great.'

'But I'm not going back. Ever.'

'We'll talk about it later.' Katherine sat down then stood up again. 'Look, why don't you have a shower—freshen up while I phone Liz and Mike? Then I'll make us something to eat, okay?'

Poppy's contemplated her from under her fringe for a few moments before nodding sullenly.

'I could do with a shower,' she admitted. 'I feel as if I've been in a sauna with my clothes on.' Now that she mentioned it, they did have a faint whiff of body odour. 'Then after that I could do with crashing. Is there a spare bedroom?'

'Yes. Let me get you some towels for your shower and check that the bed's made up.'

'Towels would be good, thanks. I don't think I brought one.'

Katherine hid a smile. It seemed that Poppy had forgotten to forget her manners. And as if she'd realised the same thing, the scowl returned with a vengeance. 'No need to make the bed if its not already. I'm so bushed I could sleep in a pig's pen.'

As soon as she heard the shower running, Katherine dug her diary out of her handbag. She could still hardly believe that Poppy was here. And wanting to stay. It was what she'd always wished for, but in her imagination it had been organised in advance and arranged to perfection. Fear, excitement, nerves—a whole tumult of emotions coursed through her. But first things first: she had to let Poppy's parents know she was safe and well. Flicking through the pages until she found Mike and Liz's number, she sat down on the sofa and rested the phone on her lap. Twice she had to stop pressing the numbers her fingers were shaking so much.

'Poppy?' Liz sounded harassed and hopeful when she answered the phone. Katherine could hear an infant crying in the background. That had to be Charlie.

'No, it's Katherine.' It had been years since they'd spoken, all subsequent communication after the adoption having taken place by letter or email. 'But Poppy is here. Don't worry, she's fine.'

'Katherine? You say Poppy's with you? Thank God!' Liz started to cry. Katherine waited until she was able to speak. 'We've been beside ourselves. We didn't even know if she was alive. She just upped and disappeared.

We thought… Oh, God. She's with you? And definitely all right?'

'She's a little travel weary. Nothing a sleep won't put right.' It was clear that whatever Poppy believed, Liz did care about her.

'Where are you?' Liz continued. 'We'll come and get her.'

'I'm in Greece. Working.'

'Greece? Poppy's in Greece?'

'She found me through my work email.' Katherine lowered her voice and glanced behind her to make sure Poppy hadn't suddenly come into the room. However she could still hear the sound of the shower running.

'She did? Mind you, she's a bright girl—almost too bright for her own good. That's why I wanted her to go to university, but she's not been working… I don't know if she's going to pass her A-levels. She's been going out till all hours despite being grounded and refusing to study. She's changed!'

Katherine smiled wryly.

'I gather you've had a baby. She seems upset about that.'

'Charlie? Oh, I know I've been caught up in caring for him. He's such a demanding baby. Not like Poppy at the same age. That doesn't mean we don't care about her, Katherine. We love her. She's our daughter!'

Katherine winced inwardly. As if she needed to be reminded. Liz broke down again.

'Should we come? No, I can't. Not with the baby—I haven't got around to getting a passport for him…Mike's working… I…' Liz said between sobs.

'She can stay with me for as long as she likes.'

'Oh, that would be a relief. She'd be all right with you.'

They finished the phone call with Katherine promising

to keep Liz and Mike informed and also promising to try and convince Poppy to go home if she could. The problem was, Katherine didn't want her to go.

As she waited for Poppy to re-emerge, Katherine quickly laid the patio table and stood back to survey the results. She cocked a critical eye at the little vase of flowers she'd placed in the centre and hesitated. Too much? Definitely. Hastily she snapped it away but now the plain white tablecloth appeared too plain and unwelcoming so she placed the vase back. For God's sake, she was more nervous than on a first date—but this was way more important than that. Even with this little gesture she wanted Poppy to know how much she cared.

Hurrying back to the kitchen, she tossed the big bowl of salad and added a touch more seasoning. Was it too salty now? Did Poppy even like salt? Or figs, for that matter? Fish? Was she vegetarian, a vegan? She knew absolutely nothing about her, nothing. Not one single iota about her likes and dislikes. Well, perhaps a simple lunch was the place to find out.

The sound of the shower finally stopped. Nervously Katherine paced the small living room, preparing herself for Poppy's reappearance. *Keep conversation light and simple. Ask questions without probing. Get her trust.*

When the front door opened and Alexander walked in, Katherine could only stand and stare at him. With Poppy's sudden arrival, she'd completely forgotten they'd arranged to go out for lunch.

He strode into the room and gathered her into his arms, kissing her softly on the lips. 'I've missed you.' His eye caught the laid-out table. 'Oh, are we eating in, then?' He grinned. 'Smart thinking. I have to go and visit a patient later, but I have an hour or two before I need to leave—'

Katherine wriggled out his arms. 'Alexander, some-thing's come up… Could we step outside a minute? There's something I have to tell you.'

He raised an eyebrow. 'Sounds ominous.' He studied her more closely. 'What is it? Something's really upsetting you. Have there been more meningitis cases reported?'

'No. It's not that.' She took him by the arm. 'We can't talk here.'

'Hi. Are you her boyfriend?' Katherine whirled around to find Poppy, wearing only a skimpy towel, draped against the stairpost. When Katherine looked back at Alexander his eyebrows had shot even higher.

'I'm Alexander Dimitriou,' he replied, 'and you are?'

'Hasn't she told you? Well, that doesn't surprise me.' Poppy flounced into the room and sprawled on the sofa, her long thin, legs stretched in front of her. 'I'm Poppy.' She pointed at Katherine. 'And she's my mother. Or should I say the woman who gave birth to me. Not the same thing at all, is it?'

It was one of those moments when the room seemed to take a breath. Behind her scowl, Poppy seemed pretty pleased with herself. Unsurprisingly, Alexander appeared bewil-dered, and as for her, it felt as if her legs were going to give way.

'Would you excuse us for a moment?' she said to Poppy. 'Alexander, could we speak outside for a moment?'

Still looking stunned, he followed her downstairs and out to the patio. She closed the door behind them.

'You have a daughter?' he said.

'Yes.'

'You have a daughter,' he repeated, with a shake of his

head. 'You have a child and you didn't even mention her. Why the hell not?'

'I was going to tell you about her.'

'When?'

Good question. She had no answers right now. At least, none that would make sense to him.

'I didn't know she was coming.'

'Evidently,' he said dryly, folding his arms.

'I probably should have told you before now.'

He continued to hold her gaze. 'Probably. So where has she been all this time? Most women would mention they had a child and if I remember correctly you told me you were childless.'

'Oh, for heaven's sake,' she burst out, immediately on the defensive. 'It's not as if we— I mean…' What the hell *did* she mean? She couldn't think straight. 'It's not as if we made promises…' Damn, that wasn't right either.

His mouth settled into a hard line. 'Fool that I am, I thought we did have something. I thought it was the beginning.'

Had he? He'd never said. But she couldn't think about that now. Not when Poppy was upstairs, waiting for her. She glanced behind her, caught between the need to return to her child and the need to talk to Alexander. Right now her child had to take precedence. Explanations would have to wait.

'Can we talk about this later?' she pleaded. 'I could come down to the bay.'

He shook his head. 'I think you've just made it clear that you don't owe me an explanation and I doubt there is anything…'

Poppy chose that moment to appear from the house, wearing a bikini and a towel slung casually over her shoulder.

'I'm going for a swim,' she said. 'Where's the coolest place to go?'

'Coolest?' Katherine echoed.

'Where the boys hang out. You don't think I'm going to hang out with you all the time, do you?'

'The little bay just below the house is quite safe to swim in as long as you don't go too far out. Actually, perhaps it's better if you wait until I come with you before you go into the water. And if you're sunbathing, put factor thirty on. The sun here is stronger than you think.'

'I'm seventeen, not seven, you know. Besides, don't you think it's a bit late to do the maternal thing?'

Katherine winced. 'I've spoken to your mother. She knows you're with me. She's been worried about you.'

A faint gleam appeared in Poppy's eyes, to be replaced almost immediately by her habitual scowl. 'Serves them right.'

Katherine sneaked a look at Alexander. He looked confused. No wonder. 'Her mother?' She saw the dawning realisation in his eyes.

'Liz wants you to go home. They miss you,' she told Poppy.

'Well, I'm not going.' Poppy pouted. 'I always fancied a holiday in Greece.'

'We need to talk about that.'

'Whatever.' Poppy yawned, exposing her tongue and, to Katherine's horror, another piercing. She hid a shudder.

'I should go,' Alexander said stiffly.

Poppy sauntered past them and towards the bay.

Katherine turned back to Alexander. 'I'll see you later. Or tomorrow. I'll explain everything then—'

'As I said, you don't owe me an explanation. Hadn't you better go after your daughter?'

'I had to give her up,' she said quickly.

'Did you?' he said coldly. And with that, he turned on his heel.

Alexander left Katherine standing on her patio and strode towards his car. He was stunned. How come she'd never mentioned that she had a child? How old was Poppy anyway? At least seventeen. So Katherine must have been around the same age when she'd had her. Had she been too dead set on a career in medicine to contemplate keeping a baby? If so, he'd had a narrow escape. Thank God he'd found out before he'd proposed. He'd never understand how a woman could give up her child.

But what he found harder to forgive was why she hadn't told him about her. He'd been open and honest with Katherine—sharing stuff that he'd never shared with anyone before—and she'd flung his honesty in his face. He'd let himself believe that finally he'd met a woman who matched up to Sophia, but he'd been mistaken. He'd thought she was pretty damn near perfect. What a fool he'd been. What a bloody fool. He'd come damn close to asking this woman—or at least the woman he'd thought she was—to spend the rest of her life with him. How could have believed he'd find someone as true as Sophia?

He wrenched his car door open with such force it banged against its hinges. Damn.

If Katherine thought that the evening would be spent chatting with her daughter she soon found she was mistaken. Every time she went near Poppy she'd pick up her book and walk away, and, after only picking at her supper she'd excused herself and gone to bed, slamming the door behind her. Left alone, and feeling raw, Katherine had pulled out her photograph album and picked out the photo of Poppy that had been taken on the beach.

What would her life have been like if she hadn't relinquished the care of her daughter to someone else? She would have been the one holding her. She would have been the recipient of those ice-cream kisses. It was something she would never know, although she had questioned it then, when her tiny infant had been gently but firmly tugged from her arms, and she wondered more than ever now.

Early the next morning while Poppy was still asleep Katherine sent a text to Alexander asking him to meet her down on the beach around the corner from her house. She didn't want to go to his home and she didn't want him to come to hers. Not when they could be overheard at either. Whatever he said she owed him an explanation.

He replied almost immediately, saying that he'd be there in five minutes. She tied her hair into a ponytail and applied a touch of lipstick and let herself out of the house.

She was sitting on a rock when he appeared. Her heart jerked when she saw the grim expression on his face. What else had she expected? She *had* lied to him.

'I don't have long,' he said, stopping in front of her, his hands thrust into the pockets of his light cotton trousers.

She leaped to her feet, hating the way he towered over her, making her feel a little like a schoolgirl waiting to be told off by the schoolmaster. 'Thank you for coming,' she said stiffly.

'Look,' he said, 'I can see you have a lot going on at the moment. What we had was fun but as you pointed out, it was never going to be anything but short term, was it? You have your life…' he glanced towards her house '…back in Britain and I have mine here.'

He'd clearly made up his mind about them, then. She'd thought that after a night to think things over, he'd at the very least be prepared to listen to what she had to say.

'No,' she said softly. 'I can see that now. I came here to explain but if that's the way you feel...' She didn't wait for a response but, blinking back tears, turned back towards home—and Poppy.

Katherine paused outside her door and waited until she had her emotions under control before going inside. She gasped. It looked as if a tornado had hit it. There were empty cups and plates and a cereal carton scattered over the work surface. A damp towel was in a heap on the floor, along with several magazines. Her daughter's bedroom was in a worse state. Poppy's rucksack lay on her bed, clothes spilling from it, some on the floor. Instinctively Katherine began to pick up, folding the clothes as she went along.

She called out Poppy's name but there was no answer. She quickly searched the small villa and the garden, but there was no sign of her anywhere. Had she decided to go? But where? Back to Liz and Mike? Or somewhere else? It hadn't even crossed her mind that Poppy might up and leave. But if she had, wouldn't she have taken her rucksack? So where was she? Panic ripped through her. What if Poppy had ignored Katherine's warnings and had gone swimming and been dragged out to sea? She should never have left her alone. Underneath that sullen exterior was bound to be a desperately unhappy girl. Katherine had only just got her back and she'd failed her again.

She ran outside but there was no sign of her daughter. However, Alexander was still standing where she'd left him, apparently lost in thought.

She hurried over to him. 'I can't find her,' she said.

'Who? Poppy?'

'She's taken her swimming things but I looked—she's not in the bay.' She spread her arms wide. 'I can't see her anywhere.'

'I'll check the bay on the other side,' Alexander said. He squeezed her shoulder. 'Don't look so worried, she'll be fine.'

He couldn't know that for sure. She ran around to the bigger bay. On the small stretch of beach was another towel and a pair of sunglasses but no sign of Poppy.

She scanned the bay, searching for her, but apart from a couple of boats the sea was empty. A late-morning breeze had whipped it into frothy peaked waves. Had she gone for a swim and gone out too far?

'Where is she?' She grabbed Alexander's arm. 'We've got to find her.' She began tugging off her sandals.

'What the hell are you doing?'

'I'm going to swim out. I need to find her.'

Alexander gripped her by the shoulders. 'Calm down. Think about it. You'd see her if she's out there.' He cupped his hands and called out to one of the boats nearby. The man called back to him.

'He says he hasn't noticed a stranger, and he's been out here since dawn. He'll ask the other boats just to make sure. Come on, let's check the village. She's probably gone in search of a Coke. Someone will have seen her.

Filled with dread, Katherine followed him back up the steps. He stopped a woman and spoke to her in Greek. She shook her head. They asked several more people and they all denied seeing a young stranger. Katherine's panic was threatening to overwhelm her when the village store owner told them, his expression aghast, that, yes, he'd served a girl with short black hair and an earring in her lip. She was, he said, with Alexander's pretty daughter. The last was said with significantly more approval.

Inside Alexander's house, Grandmother was in her habitual place in the kitchen. In the small sitting room Crystal was lying on the sofa with her feet in Poppy's lap as Poppy painted her toenails. The little girl was giggling while Poppy seemed totally oblivious to the stir she'd caused. Katherine sagged with relief.

Then fury overtook her.

'Why the hell didn't you leave a note to say where you were?'

Poppy looked up in surprise. Immediately her face resumed its belligerent look. 'Why should I leave a note? You didn't and it's not as if you've ever known or cared what I do.'

'While you're staying with me, you're my responsibility. For God's sake, I thought you'd drowned. Your towel—all your things—were on the beach.'

Something shifted in Poppy's eyes. If Katherine hadn't known better she would have said it was regret.

'Well, as you can see, I haven't drowned. I went to the beach and came back to your house for a drink and Crystal turned up. She wanted some company.'

'Poppy's painting my toenails! See, Baba, she's made patterns on them.' When the child turned her face towards them, Katherine noticed that Poppy had also given her full make-up.

Alexander placed a restraining hand on Katherine's arm. 'Thanks for spending time with Crystal, Poppy.' He crossed the room and smiled down at his daughter. 'Have you seen my daughter, Crystal? She's a beautiful little girl with a clean, shining face who never needs make-up.'

Crystal glared at him. 'I am your daughter, silly. And I like my face the way Poppy has done it.'

Grandmother muttered something from behind Katherine. When she glanced at her she couldn't be sure whether it was amusement or disapproval on her face.

Alexander scooped Crystal into his arms. 'I think it's time for a wash.'

'But Poppy is going to do my fingernails next. Then we're going to get dressed up and go to the square.'

'Poppy, we need to go,' Katherine said firmly.

'Oh, all right.' She stood up. 'See you tomorrow, Crystal.'

'That woman is not good,' Alexander's grandmother told him when he returned from helping Crystal to dress. 'What kind of woman gives away her child? I am disappointed. I thought I had found the right woman for you.'

So Poppy hadn't wasted any time in telling Crystal and Grandmother her story. 'We shouldn't judge her, Yia-Yia. Not until we know her reasons.' But wasn't what she'd said exactly what he'd been thinking? Katherine clearly wasn't the woman he'd thought she was. No doubt she'd had her reasons for giving her daughter up for adoption—although he couldn't think what they could be. She'd lied about having a child—that's what he couldn't bring himself to forgive. He'd thought he knew her. Now he knew better.

But a few days later his heart kicked against his ribs when he saw her emerge from the village store.

She hurried along the street, a few steps in front of him, and he was appalled to find that the villagers no longer called out to her or smiled in her direction. Since Poppy had arrived the village had been alight with gossip about her and her mother. Word had it that Poppy had been abandoned as a baby—where, no one could say exactly, but it varied between a hospital doorstep and an alleyway, that she had been taken away from Katherine because she had been unfit to look after her, to all sorts of even crazier versions. One of the other rumours he'd heard had involved Poppy running away from adoptive parents who beat her to a mother who hadn't wanted her in the first place. It seemed now that they knew about Poppy and having made up their minds, they had decided to spurn Katherine. Alexander suspected that most of the gossip had originated from Poppy, who no doubt was making the most of the sympathy she was getting from the women in the village.

He'd seen mother and daughter yesterday, sitting on the downstairs patio. Both had been wearing shorts, revealing long brown legs, both barefoot. When they'd turned to look at him, two identical pairs of blue eyes had stared out from porcelain complexions. It was obvious they were closely related, although, given the gap in their ages, they might have been taken for sisters rather than mother and daughter—even with the radically different hairstyles and Poppy's piercing.

Feeling she was being unfairly accused was one thing, re-igniting their aborted love affair quite another. Nevertheless, it was about time the gossip stopped.

Furious with them, or himself—he couldn't be sure which—he called Katherine's name and ran the few steps to catch up with her. He took the shopping bag from her hand. 'Let me carry this for you.'

She looked up at him, defiance shining in her blue eyes. 'I can manage,' she said. 'You don't have to keep the fallen woman company.'

But behind the defiance he could see the hurt and

his chest tightened. No matter what she said, she'd been wounded badly by the villagers' attitude. She'd told him how much she'd loved feeling part of their small community.

'You'll be a seven-day wonder,' he said. 'Then they'll forget all about it.'

'I'm not so sure,' she said. 'But I won't be judged. Not by them—not by anyone.' She looked at him again. He knew she was including him in her statement and she was right. He had been as guilty as the rest of drawing conclusions without having the facts. 'Neither do I need you to stick up for me.'

'I know. You're perfectly able to do that yourself.' He was rewarded by the briefest of smiles.

'How is the prodigal daughter anyway?' he asked. 'I understand she spends a fair bit of time at my house.'

'She seems to get a kick out of being around your grandmother. She's shown her how to make soap from olive oil, how to dry herbs and how to cook. The things she was showing me before I fell out of favour. Don't get me wrong, I'm sure she's wonderfully patient with her and I'm happy Poppy has someone she feels good around.'

'She tells me Poppy is very good at entertaining Crystal. I suspect my grandmother sees a different side to Poppy than you do.'

She smiled sadly. 'I'm trying to get to know her. I'm trying not to nag, just to make her aware that I'm ready to talk whenever she's ready. I thought that she would have begun to unbend towards me a bit, but she seems as angry with me as she was the day she arrived.' Her shoulders sagged and he had to ball his fists to stop himself taking her in his arms.

'Give her time. She hasn't gone home so being here must mean something to her.'

'I don't think I'm anything more than a bolt-hole to her. And in many ways I'm glad just to be that. I took her to Mycenae the other day. I thought doing things together would help us to bond.' She laughed bitterly. 'I was wrong. It was nothing short of a disaster. She managed half an hour before she sulked off back to the car.'

Despite everything, he had to suppress a smile. 'You know the ruins of ancient cities aren't everyone's cup of tea. Especially when they're teens. From what little I know of Poppy she strikes me as more of a beach girl.'

'But I thought she'd be interested—I would have been at her age. I thought we'd have something to talk about at least. Something that was less emotional than our relationship and what's going on with her back home.'

She looked so disappointed he almost reached out for her. Instead, he dug his hands even deeper into his pockets. But was she really so naïve to think that dragging a seventeen-year-old around ruins was the way build a relationship?

'Have you asked her what *she* wants to do?'

'Of course! I'm not a complete idiot.'

'And her answer?'

'Let me use her exact words. "Duh. To chill."'

Alexander hid another smile. She'd mimicked the little he'd heard of Poppy's truculent voice exactly. 'Then just let her to do whatever she wants. If that means hanging around my grandmother's or sunbathing on the balcony or beach, just let her. She'll come to you when she's ready.'

'I've tried. But every time I go near her she gets up and walks away.' Her blue eyes were bewildered.

'Tell you what,' he found himself saying. 'There's some

caves with amazing stalactites and stalagmites not very far from here. And there's a good beach nearby—shallow, so it's great for swimming—so why don't the four of us go there tomorrow?'

'You must have other things you want to do.' But he could tell by the way her eyes lit up that she liked the idea. She looked like a drowning woman being tossed a float. He hadn't planned to suggest a trip together, but the words were out and he couldn't take them back. Not that he wanted to take them back. A day with Katherine was suddenly irresistible.

'Crystal would like nothing better than to spend the day with her new idol—especially if it involves a boat trip in caves followed by a picnic and a swim. No, I promise you that is my daughter's idea of a dream day and so it's mine too. Do you want me to ask Poppy?'

'I'll do it,' she said, taking her shopping from him. Suddenly she stood on tiptoe and kissed him on the cheek. 'Thank you,' she said.

To Katherine's surprise, when she told Poppy the next morning about Alexander's invitation, she seemed keen to go. She disappeared into the shower and returned an hour later dressed and carrying one of Katherine's bags. In the meantime, Katherine had prepared a picnic with some of the fresh bread she'd bought from the village store as soon as it had opened. She'd also made a fig and mozzarella salad, which she'd put in a plastic container. There were olives, cold meat, soft drinks, and crisps too. She hoped Poppy would find at least some of it to her taste. As she made her preparations her head buzzed. Did Alexander's invite mean he was ready to listen to her? Or was he simply sorry for her? Whatever the reason, she had to at least try and make him understand.

Crystal ran into the room ahead of her father. 'We are going to swim. We're going to see magic caves! And you are coming too.'

'Yeah,' Poppy said, sliding a look at Katherine. 'So she says.' Then her daughter's face broke into a wide smile and picked Crystal up. 'Let's get into the car.'

Alexander looked as gorgeous as ever in a pair of faded jeans and a white T-shirt and Katherine's heart gave an uncomfortable thump. She couldn't read the expression in his eyes when they rested on her. Perhaps at a different time they might have had something—perhaps if she'd been a different person... Timing had never been her strong suit.

'Ready?' he asked.

'As I'll ever be.'

Crystal did all the talking as they drove towards the caves. 'I can swim, you know,' she told Poppy proudly. 'Can you?'

'Of course,' Poppy replied. 'I swim for my school.'

Katherine was surprised. But delighted. They had this in common at least. 'I swam for my school too,' she remarked.

'Whatever.'

Katherine shared a look with Alexander. It would take time, it seemed, for Poppy to unbend towards her—if she ever did.

They parked at the top car park and, leaving their bags and the picnic, walked the rest of the way. The sky was a brilliant blue, feathered with the slightest clouds, and the sea was turquoise against the blindingly white shore.

They bought the tickets for the boat trip into the caves and the children were given life jackets to put on. Poppy looked as if she was about to refuse but clearly thought better of it. Katherine was relieved. No doubt if she had refused, Crystal would have too.

The girls clambered into the front of the boat, with Katherine and Alexander squashed together on one of the seats in the stern. She was painfully aware of the familiar scent of the soap he used and the pressure of his leg against hers. She closed her eyes, remembering the feel of his arms around her, the way her body fitted perfectly against his, the way he made her laugh. She shook the images away. They might never be lovers again, but did him being here now mean that at the very least he was still her friend?

As their guide used an oar to push the boat further into the depths of the caves she gasped. Thousands of spectacular stalactites hung from the roof of the cave, which was lit with small lights that danced off the crystal formations like thousands of sparks.

Crystal turned around, eyes wide, her small hands covering her mouth. 'It is a magic cave, Baba. It's like Christmas! Only better!'

Even Poppy seemed stunned by their beauty. She spent the trip with her arm around Crystal's shoulders, pointing out different formations. Katherine had read about them yesterday after Alexander had extended his invitation and was able to tell the girls how they'd been formed as well as a little history of the caves. Poppy asked some questions, appearing to have forgotten that she wasn't speaking to Katherine. Katherine glanced at Alexander and he grinned back. He'd been right. This was the kind of trip to impress a seventeen-year-old—inasmuch as *anything* could impress this particular seventeen-year-old.

Their trip into the caves finished, Alexander returned to the car for their costumes and their picnic, while Katherine and the girls found a spot on the grass, just above the pebbly beach, where they could lay their picnic blanket. As soon as Alexander came back Poppy and Crystal disappeared off to the changing rooms to put on their swimming costumes.

'Aren't you going to swim?' Alexander asked.

'In a bit. What about you?'

'What are the chances of Crystal letting me just lie here?' When he grinned she could almost make herself believe that they were still together.

The girls came out of the changing rooms and ran down into the sea, squealing as the water splashed over their knees.

'She's a good kid,' Alexander said.

'Yes. I believe she is.'

'What happened to her father?'

Katherine sighed. It was a question she'd been waiting for Poppy to ask. 'Ben? Last time I heard, he was married with three children and doing very well as a lawyer.'

'You must have been very young when you had her.'

'I was seventeen. Sixteen when I fell pregnant.'

'You don't have to tell me anything you don't want to. It's none of my business.'

'No,' she said. 'I'd like to. It's not something I've ever spoken to anyone about, but I think I owe it to you to tell you the truth.'

'I don't want you to tell me because you think you owe me, although I would like to understand. It's not so much that you have a child you gave up for adoption, it's the fact you didn't tell me. Hell, Katherine, I bared my soul to you.'

'I know…' She sighed. 'It's just—it's been a secret I've kept for so long, afraid of what people would think if they knew…'

'I can't imagine the Katherine I know caring about what people think.'

'We all care what people think if we're honest—at least, the opinions of those we love and respect.'

'If they love and respect us, then their feelings shouldn't change…' he said slowly. He was quiet for a long time. 'I promise I'll listen this time.'

'It's a long story.'

He nodded in the direction of the girls, who were splashing each other and laughing. 'Looks like they're not going to be out of the water any time soon.'

Seeing Poppy like this reminded Katherine how painfully young her daughter still was and how painfully young she herself had been when she'd fallen pregnant. A child really.

'Remember I told you that I won a scholarship to high school?'

He nodded.

'I was proud and excited to have won it but I was totally unprepared for the reality. Being there terrified me. Most of the rest of the pupils came from well-to-do families—the children of business people, doctors and lawyers. I was desperately shy as it was, and with my second-hand uniform I knew I stuck out. Unsurprisingly perhaps, they wanted nothing to do with me. I pretended I didn't care. At break times I'd take a book and read it. I knew I still had to get top marks if I wanted to be accepted at medical school.

'I was in my second year when I met Ben. I'd been roped in to swim for the school team in the swimming gala—it was the one sport I seemed naturally good at—and he was there. He was a couple of years older than me, as confident as I was shy, as good-looking as I was geeky—but for some reason he seemed to like me.

'We were friends at first. We spent our break times together, usually in the library or just walking around, talking about history and politics—even then he knew he wanted to be a lawyer—stuff that no one else was interested in discussing but that we both loved to debate.

'Being Ben's friend changed everything. I wasn't lonely any more. I now realised there were people just like me who didn't care about clothes and the latest hairstyle. Then when I was in fourth year and he was in sixth year—he already had a place to read law—everything changed and we became boyfriend and girlfriend. He'd come around to my house. By that time Mum and Dad had bought a small restaurant and were working all hours to get it established, but then Dad died suddenly. Mum, as you can imagine, was devastated and so was I. I clung to Ben and eventually the inevitable happened. We slept together.

'It didn't seem wrong—quite the opposite. It seemed a natural progression. We'd talked often about how, when he was a lawyer—famous and defending the poor and downtrodden, of course—and I was a doctor, the very best, of course…' she risked a smile in Alexander's direction, and was reassured to find he was looking at her with the same intent expression he always had when they talked '…saving lives and discovering new treatments and cures, we'd marry and have a family. But then I fell pregnant. Stupid, I know. We did use contraception but with the optimism and ignorance of youth we weren't as careful as we should have been.

'By that time, he was about to leave to start his law degree and I had just sat my A-levels. I expected, rightly as it turned out, to get all As and I was confident I would get a place in medical school.

'To say we were both shellshocked would be an understatement. We talked about getting married, but we couldn't see how. My parents' restaurant was struggling without Dad and barely making enough for Mum to live on, and she'd been recently diagnosed with multiple sclerosis. Ben's parents weren't much better off. There didn't seem any way to have the baby.'

'What about Ben? Didn't he have a say?'

'Terminating the pregnancy was Ben's preferred option.' She looked over to where Crystal and Poppy were splashing each other and her heart stuttered. Thank God she'd never seriously considered it. 'He said he couldn't see a way of supporting me or our baby—he still desperately wanted to be a lawyer—and one night he told me that if I continued with the pregnancy he couldn't be part of either of our lives.

'We broke up. With the pregnancy something had changed between us. It was as if all that had gone on before had just been us play-acting at being a couple. Maybe if we were older… Whatever, I couldn't blame him. I didn't want to marry him, I knew that then—just as I knew I wasn't ready to be a mother. But neither could I bear to terminate the pregnancy. Oh, I thought about it. I even went as far as making an appointment with the hospital, but when it came down to it I just couldn't go through with it. I knew then I had to tell my mother. It was the most difficult conversation I've ever had in my life. I could see her imagining her and Dad's dreams of a better life for me going down the plughole. She lost it and broke down.

'When she'd pulled herself together she said that she would look after the child. It would mean my delaying going to university for a year but we'd manage. Just as we always had. But she was ill—some days I had to help her get dressed—and even then I knew what a diagnosis of

MS meant. I knew she couldn't help take care of a child—not when she would need more and more care herself. I was in a bad way, Alexander. I felt so alone.' She took a shuddering breath.

'I told her that I had decided to have the baby but that I was going to give it up for adoption. I'd done my research, you see. I knew that you could arrange an open adoption. I would get to pick the parents—ones already pre-selected by the adoption agency. My child would always know they were adopted, and although I could never see him or her, I could write care of the adoptive parents and in return they would send me updates. If I couldn't keep the baby myself, it seemed the only—the best—solution.

'My mother tried to argue me out of it—she couldn't imagine how any child of hers could even consider giving their child away, and I think she believed I would change my mind.

'But she was wrong. I refused to imagine it as a baby. Instead, I pored over the biographies of the would-be adoptive parents. The adoption agency did a thorough job. There were photographs, bits of information about their extended families, letters from them. It was heart-breaking, reading their stories. I could almost hear their desperation. They had to advertise themselves to me—they had to make me want to pick them.

'When I read about these couples I knew I was doing the right thing. At least I managed to convince myself that I was. Far better for the child I was carrying to have a home with a couple who would be able to give them the love and attention I couldn't. In the end I picked out one family. They weren't particularly well off—I wasn't so naïve that I thought money was all that important—but they were financially secure. Enough to give my child everything he or she could ever need.

'But more than that, it was them as people who made them shine. They seemed kind, loving and so desperate to have afamily to shower love on. They'd been trying for a baby for several years and were getting close to the age where they'd no longer be able to put themselves forward for adoption. This was, I knew, their final chance of having a child. They also said that they hoped, in time, to adopt an older child, a brother or sister for this one. I liked that. I didn't want my child to grow up, like I did, as an only child. I wanted him or her to have a sibling who would always be there for them. So I picked them. I could have picked any of a dozen couples but I picked them.

'I know you probably can't imagine how anyone could do what I did. But I thought, I really believed I was doing the best thing for her. I insisted on an open adoption—I wouldn't have chosen Mike and Liz if they hadn't agreed to that—because although I couldn't keep Poppy myself I wanted to know that wherever she was in the world she was all right.

'But Mum was right. I hadn't accounted for how I would feel as my pregnancy continued. I began to feel protective of this child growing inside me. I didn't know what to do. I had already committed to giving her up and I knew her prospective parents were longing to welcome her into her family. But even then I thought about changing my mind—even though I knew the grief it would cause them and even though I knew I was too young to bring up a child. I began to persuade myself that with Mum's help we would manage.'

She paused and looked out to sea. 'But then Mum's multiple sclerosis returned with a vengeance. She had to have a wheelchair and she couldn't do even the basics for herself. I wondered if the stress of my pregnancy had made her worse. I felt as if it was all my fault. I didn't know what to do. So in the end I kept to my original decision and gave her up.

'The day I gave birth to her was one of the worst in my life. The labour was easy compared to what came next. They allowed me a few hours alone with her to say my goodbyes. I hadn't realised how difficult it would be. Here was this tiny thing in my arms, looking up at me as if I was the only thing in her world. I felt such an overwhelming love for her it shook me to the core. But how could I go back on my decision then? I was only seventeen. I thought it was unfair to everyone if I did. So I let them take her from me.'

It was only when he leaned across and wiped the tears from her face with the pad of his thumb that she realised she was crying. He waited without saying anything until she'd regained control again.

'I wrote to Liz often and she wrote back, telling me about Poppy's progress and sending photos. I knew when her baby teeth fell out, I knew when she got chickenpox, I saw her in her school uniform on her first day at school. I had more regrets then—seeing the photos of her, watching her grow up, albeit from a distance, made her real in a way she hadn't been before. Of course, by then it was too late to get her back. Mike and Liz were her parents and there was no doubt they loved her and that she loved them.'

He said nothing, just waited until she was ready to continue.

'I sailed through my final year at school and all my exams at medical school. But I worked for it. I hardly went out, hardly joined any clubs or societies, just worked. It all had to be for something, you see? If I'd failed I don't think I could have lived with myself. Mum never spoke of it. It was as if we pretended it hadn't happened. But sometimes I'd see Mum looking at me with such sadness it ripped me in two. I caught her once. About six months after I'd had Poppy. She was in the small bedroom at the front, the one that we kept for visitors. She was kneeling on the floor with a pile of baby clothes in front of her. She was smoothing out each item with her palms, murmuring to herself, before she placed it in a little box. Tears were running down her face. I doubt she even knew she was crying. You see the adoption only became final after six months. I could have changed my mind up until then and, believe me, sometimes I thought I might. But when I thought of the couple who had Poppy, how happy they'd been, I knew I had done the right thing. But I know now that Mum always hoped I would change my mind.

'She didn't see me so I tiptoed away. What was the point in saying anything? Even if I'd wanted to it was too late to change my mind. I had to keep believing I'd done the right thing.

'We never spoke about it. Not once.'

She drew in a shuddering breath. 'By all accounts, she was a happy child. She grew up knowing that she was adopted—that was part of the deal—and I guess it was just something she accepted.

'So many times I wished I could have been there to hold her when she was sick, to hear her laughter, just see her.' She swallowed the lump that had come to her throat. 'But I knew I had given away all my rights. I was just pleased to be allowed into her life—if only in small slices.'

'And have you told her this?'

'I've tried. But every time I raise the topic, she gets up and walks away.'

'Yet she came to find you.'

'I'm not sure she came to find me for the right reasons. When Poppy turned sixteen, Liz said that she would no longer give her my letters unless she asked. She also said that she wouldn't pass on news of Poppy. She thought, at sixteen, Poppy had the right to decide what place, if any, I had in her life. I heard nothing after that. It seemed Poppy had made her decision and I couldn't blame her. I hoped when she was older that she might seek me out.' She laughed shortly. 'I just never imagined it would be now.'

'What made her come to find you?'

'I think it was the new baby. Liz and Mike didn't think they could have children—that's why they decided to adopt. I know they intended to adopt another child, but they never did. About eighteen months ago, Liz fell pregnant—as you know, it can happen long after a couple has given up hope. The child is eight months now. I suspect Poppy's nose has been put out of joint. A baby can be demanding and she's bound to feel a little pushed out. Liz also said she's been bunking off school and her grades have taken a turn for the worse. If she carries on like this then there will be no chance of her getting accepted at university.'

'And that's important to you and to Liz?'

'Yes. Of course. Wouldn't you want the same for Crystal?'

'I want Crystal to be happy. I found out the hard way that success at work isn't the same as having success in life. Nothing is more important than being with your family. Nothing is more important than their happiness. At least to me.'

She felt stung. Somehow she'd hoped that she could make him understand, but it appeared she'd been mistaken. She bent over and undid her sandals. 'I've told you everything. Now I'm going to join the children in the water.'

Alexander watched her tiptoe gingerly into the sea. Her legs had browned in the sun and appeared to go on for ever in the tiny shorts she was wearing. He cursed himself inwardly. She was right. Who was he to judge her? It wasn't as if he had nothing to regret. But he'd wanted her to be perfect—which was rich, given that he was anything but. He still loved her but he needed time to get used to this different version of the Katherine he'd thought he'd known.

'Baba!' Crystal called from the water. 'Come in!' He rolled up the bottoms of his jeans, pulled his T-shirt over his head and went to join them.

It was, Katherine had to admit, despite the tension between her and Poppy and her and Alexander, a happy day—one of the happiest of her life. Despite everything how couldn't it be when she was spending it with the people she loved most? They swam and ate, then swam some more. As the afternoon became cooler, Alexander bought some fish from a boat he swam out to and they built a small fire over which they roasted the fish.

By the time they drove home, Crystal and Poppy were flushed with tiredness and happiness. Poppy had even come to sit next to Katherine when Alexander had taken Crystal away to dry her off and help her change back into her clothes.

'It's cool here,' Poppy said. 'I think I'd like to stay until you go back. If that's all right with you?'

'Of course,' Katherine said, delighted. 'Until I go back

at the end of the month, at any rate. Will you let your mother know?'

'Sure,' Poppy said, and leaned back, hooking her arms behind her head. 'I kind of miss them. Even the crazy baby.'

'They miss you too.' She didn't want to say anything else, frightened of spoiling the fragile truce that had sprung up between them. There would be time to talk in the days to come. At the very least she owed it to Poppy to keep trying to explain why she'd given her up. Maybe Alexander was right. She shouldn't force it. Just tell Poppy she was happy to talk about it and leave it to her to bring it up when she was ready.

Back home, Alexander parked the car in the square and lifted Crystal into his arms. 'Perhaps we could do this again?' he said.

She looked at him. 'Maybe. I'm not sure.' She still felt hurt. They had been friends before they'd become lovers. Didn't that count for anything?

He nodded and, holding his daughter in his arms, turned towards his house. Back home, Poppy also excused herself, saying she had her sleep to catch up on. Katherine suspected that she wanted to phone Liz in privacy and she was glad.

She poured herself a glass of wine and took it out onto the balcony. She'd told Alexander everything. At least now there were no more secrets between them.

She didn't see much of Alexander over the next few days, although Crystal and Poppy continued to visit each other's houses.

Katherine went to call Poppy for supper one day to find

her up to her elbows in flour. 'I just want to finish these baklavas,' she said.

Alexander's grandmother looked at Katherine, shook her head and said something to Crystal in Greek. For one mortifying moment Katherine wondered if she was being told not to visit again, but to her surprise Crystal told her that her grandmother wanted her to come and sit with her outside on the bench by the front door.

Bemused, Katherine did as she asked.

They sat on the bench and Alexander's grandmother reached out and patted her hand. As people passed she kept her hand on Katherine's. Every time one of the villagers passed, her grip would tighten and she'd smile, while calling out a greeting. Many stopped and said a few words to Grandmother and greeted Katherine too, with a 'Hello' and 'How are you?'

So that was what the old lady was up to. Whatever she thought of Katherine's decision to give her child up for adoption, she was, in her own quiet way, telling the other villagers that she supported her. Tears burned behind Katherine's eyes. It was an unexpected, touching gesture from Grandmother and she wondered whether Alexander was behind it.

Speaking of which, he was coming across the square towards them. Katherine's heart leaped. Frightened he would see the desolation in her eyes, she lowered her lids until she was sure she could look at him calmly.

'Oh, hello.' He bent and kissed his grandmother on her cheek. He said something to her in Greek and she laughed. The old lady got to her feet and retreated back inside, leaving her space on the bench for Alexander.

'I think she had an ulterior motive for sitting with me here,' Katherine murmured. 'I suspect she's telling the village to stop shunning me. Did you have anything to do with it?'

'No one tells Grandmother what to do, least of all me,' he said evasively. 'But I need to tell you, I've forgiven you for giving up Poppy. I'm sure you did what you had to and for the best possible motives.'

Katherine leaped to her feet. 'Forgiven me? Forgiven me! How dare you? I wanted your understanding, not your forgiveness. You're right about one thing. I should have told you earlier. That was wrong of me. But if you think I need forgiveness for giving birth to her then you are badly mistaken. And as for giving her away, you make it sound like tossing out so much rubbish. That's not the way I felt. I gave her to two loving, stable parents and it ripped me apart. You just need to spend time with her to know she's a young woman any parent would be proud of.'

Tears burned behind her eyes. She didn't even care that her outburst had garnered a bit of an audience. 'As far as I'm concerned,' she hissed, 'if I never see you again it will be too soon.' She whirled around to find Poppy standing behind her. Her daughter grinned. 'Way to go, Katherine. Way to go!'

Katherine and Poppy talked late into the night after Poppy had witnessed her outburst. It hadn't been an easy conversation—there had been no instant falling into each other's arms, but the tension and angst had begun to ease. There would, Katherine knew, be many more such conversations and bumpy roads but they had made a start. It would take time for them to be totally at ease with one another, but at least they were moving in that direction. And despite the rift between her and Alexander, she was more content than she had been in years.

* * *

'Crystal's great-grandmother isn't well,' Poppy told her a couple of days later. Katherine's heart tumbled inside her chest. She was deeply fond of the old lady but hadn't seen her since she'd made an absolute exhibition of herself by ranting at Alexander in public.

'Do you know what's wrong with her?'

'Crystal says she has a bad cold but she didn't get up this morning.'

If Grandmother had taken to her bed she had to be ill. 'Where is Crystal?'

'I left her at the house. I wanted her to come with me so I could tell you but she wouldn't leave Yia-Yia.'

Katherine snapped the lid of her laptop closed. 'Does Crystal's father know?'

'I don't think so.'

'Come on,' Katherine said, picking up the medical bag she'd brought with her. Luckily she had a whole case of antibiotics left over from the meningitis outbreak. Did Yia-Yia have a chest infection? If she did, it wasn't good. But she shouldn't get ahead of herself. It was possible Grand-mother did have just a cold.

But as soon as she saw her she knew this was no ordi-nary cold. The old woman was flushed and clearly run-ning a temperature.

'Poppy, could you take Crystal to our house, please? Stay there until I come for you. You can go down to the bay if you like but no further. Do you understand?'

Was it possible that the meningitis had come back in an-other form? No, that was unlikely if not impossible. How-ever, until she knew for sure what it was, it was important to keep her away from the others.

For once Poppy didn't argue with her. She took Crystal

by the hand. 'Go fetch your costume. My mum will look after your great-grandmother.'

It was the first time Poppy had called her Mum and a lump came to Katherine's throat. She swallowed hard and made herself focus. She had a job to do.

After listening to Yia-Yia's chest and taking her temperature, which as she'd expected was way too high, Katherine phoned Alexander.

'I'll come straight away,' he said, when she told him.

'I'll give her oral antibiotics,' Katherine said, 'but she could do with them IV to be on the safe side. Do you want me to take her to hospital?'

'Wait until I get there,' he said. 'I'll be thirty minutes.'

While she waited for him to arrive, Katherine wetted a facecloth in cold water and wrung it out, before placing it on Grandmother's forehead. When the old lady tried to push her away she soothed her with a few words in Greek, grateful that it had improved to the point where she could reassure her.

'Alexander is on his way,' she said softly. 'He says you are to lie quietly and let me look after you until he gets here.'

'Crystal? Where is she?'

'Poppy has taken her to my house. Don't worry, she'll make sure she's all right.'

The elderly woman slumped back on her pillows, worryingly too tired to put up a fight.

Alexander must have driven as if the devil himself was behind him as he arrived in twenty minutes instead of the thirty he'd told her. He nodded to Katherine before crouching at his grandmother's side.

'Her pulse is around a hundred and shallow. She's

pyrexial. I've given her antibiotics by mouth. Crystal is with Poppy. I thought it best.'

When Alexander looked up she could see the anguish in his eyes. He took out his stethoscope and Katherine helped Grandmother into a sitting position while Alexander listened to her chest again.

'As I thought. A nasty chest infection. She's probably caught a dose of the flu that's been going around and a secondary infection has set in very fast.'

'Does she need to go to hospital?'

Grandmother plucked at Alexander's sleeve. 'She says she won't go,' he translated. 'She wants to stay in her own home.'

'In that case,' Katherine said, 'that's what's going to happen. We can easily put her on a drip and give her IV antibiotics that way. Poppy and I can help look after her. What do you think?'

'I think it's risky.'

'More risky than admitting her to hospital?'

His shoulders slumped. 'You're right.'

She wished she could put her arms around him and tell him everything would be okay, but nothing in his demeanour suggested he would welcome the overture.

'I'll stay here with your grandmother,' Katherine said, 'while you fetch whatever it is we'll need.'

Later when they had Grandmother on a drip and her breathing was better, Katherine slipped home to ask Poppy to take Crystal back to her father. A short while later she was standing on the balcony when she became aware that Poppy had come to stand beside her. 'Is she going to get better?' she whispered.

'I hope so.' She reached out for her daughter's hand and squeezed it. Poppy didn't pull away. Instead, she leaned into her. Katherine pulled her close. 'We're all going to do everything to make sure she will. But, sweetheart, I think you should go back to Liz and Mike. If flu is going around, I don't want you to get it.'

'But I could have it already and just not be showing the symptoms yet. If I go back I could pass it on to my baby brother.' It was the first time she'd referred to Charlie as her baby brother. 'So I'm staying,' Poppy continued in a tone that sounded much like her own when she wouldn't be argued with. 'I'll help you look after Grandmother and any of the villagers who need help. I can't nurse them but I can cook and run errands.'

Katherine's eyes blurred as she considered her amazing child. 'I'm so proud of you,' she said. 'Did I ever tell you that?'

Poppy grinned back at her. 'And I'm proud of you. Now, shouldn't we get busy?'

'I think it's time I went home,' Poppy said. She'd been a godsend this last two weeks, helping by playing with Crystal while Alexander and Katherine took turns caring for Grandmother. They barely saw each other, the one leaving as the other took over. She'd also helped care for some of the other elderly villagers who'd fallen ill with flu. But Grandmother was much better, as were the others affected. 'I think Mum can do with some help with Charlie.' She looked at Katherine, a small frown between her brows. 'You're okay…' she grinned self-consciously '…but she's still my mum.'

'Of course she is. She's the woman who's cared for you all your life, the woman who nursed you through all your childhood sicknesses. Who was always there for you. Of course she'll always be your mum. But I hope you'll always remember that I love you too. If it helps, think of me as an honorary aunt. Someone who will always be there for you.'

'You know, and I don't mean this to sound horrible, I'm glad you gave me up. I can't imagine anyone except Liz and Mike being my parents. I mean, they get on my nerves sometimes but, you know, they've always been there.'

Katherine winced at the implied rebuke in Poppy's words.

'Would you still have given me away if you had the chance to do it all over again?'

Katherine took her time thinking about her answer. She loved Poppy too much to be anything less than honest.

'I feel so lucky that you are part of my life now—to have been given this second chance to get to know you. And knowing you now, I can't imagine a scenario where I would ever give you up. But back then I didn't know you and I wasn't the person I am now. Remember I was about your age. Half grown up and half still a child. Everything seemed so black and white then.

'I do know that I thought of you almost every day and receiving the updates about you from Liz were the highlight of my year. Wait there. I'd like to show you something.'

She went inside and retrieved the album she always carried with her. She placed it on the patio table. 'Liz sent me a photo of you on every birthday and Christmas. This is you on your first birthday.' She passed a photograph to Poppy. She was standing in front of a birthday cake with a single candle. A hand belonging to someone just out of shot was supporting her and Poppy was grinning into the camera, two small teeth showing. Katherine handed her several more photos. 'Here you are on your first day at school, when you joined the Brownies, your first swimming lesson, your first trip to the beach. Liz sent me a letter with every photograph and sometimes a little souvenir from your life—like this picture you drew when you came back from a holiday in Spain. I wrote to you too.

'I'm not pretending any of that makes up for not bringing you up myself, but I knew you were happy and so I could live with my decision.'

'Why didn't you ever get married?

'The right person never came along. One of the things I promised myself when I gave you up was that I would concentrate on being the best doctor I could be.'

'And you did.' The admiration in her daughter's eyes made her want to cry.

'I'm human, Poppy. You of all people know that. Don't ever think anyone can be perfect.'

'You like Alexander, don't you?' Poppy said out of the blue. 'And I think he likes you too.'

It felt odd discussing her love life, or rather lack of it, with her seventeen-year-old daughter.

'He did once, I think.' She leaned across and wrapped her arms around her child. 'But I've got you now. And that's more than enough for me.'

Two days later, the tickets home were booked and Poppy had gone for a nap, exhausted after a day spent cooking and running errands. Her daughter was truly an amazing young woman.

Katherine had made supper but Poppy hadn't reappeared. She boiled the kettle and made her some of her favourite camomile tea. She loved how she now knew these small details about her child.

Taking the tea with her, she tiptoed into Poppy's bedroom. Her daughter was lying spreadeagled on the bed, the sheets tangled in her long limbs. Once more Katherine sent a silent prayer upwards for whatever had brought her daughter back to her.

But something about the way Poppy's face was screwed up—as if she were in pain—made her cross the room and place a hand on her child's forehead. At the feel of cold sweat alarm shot through her. Poppy had been complaining of a sore stomach the night before but this was something more.

Perhaps she had the same flu that had brought Grandmother and some of the other villagers low? Stamping down on the panic that threatened to overwhelm her, she gently shook her daughter by the shoulder. 'Poppy, wake up.'

Poppy opened her eyes, groaned and closed them again.

Her heart beating a tattoo against her ribs, Katherine knelt by the side of the bed and examined Poppy's limbs. To her horror she saw that her legs were covered with a faint but definite purpuric rash. It was one of the signs of meningitis. Worse, it was a sign that the disease had already taken hold.

Forcing herself to keep calm, she ran back to the sitting room and picked up her mobile. Her hands were shaking so badly she was almost not capable of punching in Alexander's number.

To her relief, he picked up straight away.

'Dr Dimitriou.' The sound of his voice almost made her sink to the floor with relief.

'Alexander. Where are you?'

'At home.' He must have picked up the fear in her voice. 'What is it? Are you all right?

'It's Poppy. I need you to come.'

'I'll be there in a few minutes.'

She went back to Poppy's room and tried to rouse her again but once more, her daughter's eyes only flickered. She needed to get antibiotics into her and soon. Perhaps she should have phoned for an ambulance instead of Alexander. But that would take longer. The ambulance would have to come here—at least an hour—and make its way back. And every moment could make a difference.

She sat on the bed and pulled her child into her arms. 'Hold on, darling, please, hold on.'

Alexander was there in less than five minutes, although it felt like hours. He took the scene in at a glance. Katherine looked over at him, anguish etched in every line of her face.

'She feels unwell and has a purpuric rash. I think she has meningitis. Help us, Alexander.'

Although he wanted nothing more than to take her into his arms, he automatically switched into professional mode. He felt Poppy's pulse. Rapid but still strong. She was clammy to the touch but the night was hot. He inspected her limbs and torso. There was a rash but it didn't quite look like the ones he'd seen on patients suffering from meningitis. However, given the recent outbreak, meningitis was still the most likely diagnosis.

'Let's get her to hospital,' he said, picking Katherine's child up. 'You sit in the back with her and phone ahead to let them know we're on our way.'

For once Katherine didn't complain about the way he

drove. She cradled her child in her arms, murmuring words of love and encouragement.

Later that night Katherine sat by the bed, holding her daughter's hand. Poppy had been started on IV antibiotics and it would be some time before they would know whether they'd caught it in time. Alexander had disappeared. He was going to phone Liz and Mike as soon as he'd spoken to the doctors again.

Was she going to lose her daughter again when she'd just found her? Why hadn't she forced her to leave even if she'd felt confident that there was zero chance of her daughter contracting the disease? Had she let her own desire to have Poppy with her get in the way of what was right for her child?

She murmured a prayer. 'God, if you're there, please don't take my child. I'll do anything—give up everything—if only you won't take her.'

A few moments later she heard a soft footfall behind her and looked up to find Alexander smiling down at her. Why was he smiling? Didn't he know she was in danger of losing her child?

'I have good news,' he whispered. 'Poppy doesn't have meningitis.'

'What do you mean? Of course she must have. The aches and pains, the rash…'

'It's the rash that got me thinking,' he said. 'It's very like a meningococcal one but I noticed it was only on her shins. I remember reading something about an illness that can mimic meningitis so I looked it up. Katherine, Poppy has Henoch-Schönlein purpura, not meningitis. When the kidneys get involved it can be nasty but Poppy's kidneys aren't affected.'

'She doesn't have meningitis?' Katherine could hardly believe it.

'No. She'll feel quite ill for a week or two, but I promise you she's going to be fine.'

Katherine's vision blurred as Alexander wrapped his arms around her. 'It's okay,' he murmured into her hair. 'You can let go now. I promise you, everything is going to be okay.'

'How is Poppy today?' Alexander asked Katherine a couple of days later when he visited them in hospital. She was a different woman from the one bent over Poppy's bedside when she'd thought her child was desperately ill. The worry and fear had left her eyes and the steely determination he knew so well was back.

'She's booked on this afternoon's flight to London. I'm going with her.'

'Of course.'

'Thank you for being here.' She held out her hand and he grasped her long, cool fingers. 'Thank you for recognising she didn't have meningitis.'

'Will you come back?'

She smiled wanly. 'I don't think so.'

'I love you, Katherine.' She needed to know that.

There was no response. She just looked at him with her cool blue eyes. 'Do you?'

'I was a fool, an idiot-think of any noun you like and it could apply to me, but I love you, more than I thought possible to love another woman. Just give me a chance and I'll prove it to you.'

She smiled wanly. 'I'm sorry, Alexander, but it's over.' She shook her head. 'I need to go if we're to catch our plane.'

He wanted to reach out to her but the coldness in her eyes held him back. Now was not the time to convince her to give them another chance.

He pressed her fingers. 'If ever you want to come back, if ever you need me, I'll be here.'

CHAPTER NINE

KATHERINE THRUST HER hands deep into her coat pockets and pulled her collar up. Almost overnight, the leaves had fallen from the trees, carpeting the ground.

In a week's time, Poppy would be coming to stay with her for the October school break. Liz and Mike were dropping her off before heading off to stay with Liz's family in the Cotswolds. After Poppy had a week with her, Katherine would drive her daughter up there and stay for the night, before returning to London.

It was amazing how quickly she'd become part of Poppy's family. As she and Poppy had discussed, she never tried to take Liz's place but instead acted the part of the trusted aunt or wise big sister. Poppy had applied to and was starting medical school the autumn after next should she get the grades she and her teachers expected.

Katherine's feet were beginning to freeze as the cold seeped through her boots, but she was reluctant to return home. The solitude that she'd cherished before she'd gone to Greece—before Poppy and Alexander—now felt disturbingly like loneliness.

The crunch of footsteps came from behind her and she whirled around.

At first she'd thought she dreamed him up.

He was every bit as beautiful as she remembered. His hair was slightly longer and he'd lost weight so that his cheeks were more prominent but laughter still lurked in his eyes.

He was wearing a thick trench coat over a thin jersey and jeans and heavy boots.

They looked at each other for a long moment. 'Katherine,' he murmured, and stepped towards her.

She'd been waiting for him to come to her since she'd left Greece. She'd told herself that he would but she hadn't been sure. Then, as the days had turned into weeks, she'd given up hoping.

What had brought him here now? Her heart hammered against her chest.

'How did you find me?' she whispered.

'You do know that Poppy and Crystal still write to each other? Crystal has been giving me regular updates every time your name is mentioned, which is pretty often, or so I gather.'

But it had taken him all this time to come and find her.

'Is Crystal with you?'

'Of course. I left her at the hotel with Poppy. It was Poppy who told me you'd be here and where to find you.'

'Poppy is in London?'

'She met us at the airport earlier.'

'It sounds as if she's decided to meddle. I think she's frightened I'll stay an old maid and she'll spend her adult years looking after me when I'm an old lady. That's why she asked you to come.'

It was a conversation they'd had as a joke—so why was she repeating it? Why was she babbling?

'Poppy didn't ask me to come, Katherine. I wrote to her and told her I was coming to see you and she asked me to keep it as a surprise.' He stepped towards her, his familiar soapy smell turning her bones to water. 'To be honest, I wasn't sure you'd want to see me.'

She stepped back and he halted where he was. 'How is Grandmother?' she asked.

'Looking forward to seeing you again. I think she's decided that you are already part of her family.'

Already part of the family?

He took hold of her collar and pulled her close. 'I've missed you,' he said into her hair. 'More than I thought possible.'

'You don't sound too pleased about it,' she mumbled.

'I am. I'm not. It depends.'

She placed her hands against his chest and although she wanted nothing more than to go on touching him for ever, to be held by him for ever, she pushed him away. 'Depends on what?'

'On whether you feel the same way.'

'I think you know how I feel.' She took a moment to steady her breathing. 'But I won't be with you and have you disapprove of me—or of what I did. I can't go through life thinking and feeling I have to pay over and over for what I did.' She tried to smile but it came out all wobbly. 'I've spent the last seventeen years of my life feeling as if I don't deserve to be happy. Being in Greece, being with Poppy changed all that for ever. I did what I felt I had to do at the time. That was the person I was back then and I can't change her. I'm not even sure I want to.'

'God, Katherine. Don't you understand what I'm saying? I love you. I love everything about you and that includes the person you were as well as the woman you are now. When I met you I didn't want to fall in love with you. I tried not to but I couldn't help it. So I told myself that

Sophia would want me to be happy, would want me to re-marry, especially someone who obviously cared for Crystal.' He looked at her with anguished eyes. 'I didn't tell you everything about Sophia. I have to tell you the rest so you can try to understand why I did what I did.'

He took her hand and led her across to a bench. 'I was six months away from being able to apply for the job in America. In the meantime I had been offered a consultant post at St George's, even though they knew I was going to America. In fact, they said it was one of the reasons they'd chosen me. While I was away they would employ a locum and my job would be kept open for me. It was a flatter-ing reminder of the esteem in which I was held, but at the time I saw it as nothing less than what I was due—what I had worked for over the years.

'But I didn't want to take my foot off the pedal, although I could have. I had the job I wanted—one that was mine for life. I had the post in America. I had done everything I'd set out to do. Now, if there ever was, it had to be Sophia's time. And I was prepared to shoulder more of the child care—or at least that's what I promised Sophia.

'She had an interview for one of the smaller orchestras. It wasn't the career as a concert pianist she'd hoped for but it would have been a start. I wasn't sure. I didn't know if she'd be expected to travel. And it would only have been for eighteen months. But she was so happy to be given the chance. Nervous too. She started playing the piano, prac-tising as if her life depended on it.

'Every hour that she wasn't looking after Crystal she was practising. Often I'd wake up in the night to hear the sounds of Mozart or Beethoven; I can barely listen to their music now. She was in a frenzy—so sure that this was her last chance. It was only then that I realised how much she'd sacrificed for me. And then she fell pregnant again. It wasn't planned, just one of those things, and that was that. Her chance was over.'

He paused for a long moment.

Katherine held her breath as she waited for him to continue.

'It was December and the winter had already been harsh. I left the house early—sometimes before six—but she always got up to see me off. That morning she'd been complaining of a headache. When I think back she'd been complaining of a headache the night before too. But I didn't take too much notice. I was already thinking of a complicated surgery I had that morning. She said she would take some painkillers and go back to bed for an hour or so. Crystal was staying with my mother for a few days. Sophia was thirty-two weeks by this time so I told her that I thought it was a good idea, kissed her and left.' He passed a hand across his face.

'If I'd stopped to look at her, really look at her, I would have seen the warning signs. I was a doctor, for God's sake. A couple of minutes—that's all it would have taken.'

A chill ran up Katherine's spine as she sensed what was coming.

'The roads were bad. The gritting lorries rarely came down the lane leading to our house so I'd taken the four-by-four. She sometimes drove me to the train station so she would have the use of the car, but because she had a headache she suggested I take it. I would leave it at the train station and catch the train from there. It would mean Sophia being without a car, but she said she wasn't intending to go anywhere anyway. She didn't need anything from the village and if she did, she would call me and I could pick it up on the way home.

'I was just relieved to get the use of the car. I needed to catch the six-thirty train if I was to make it to the hospital in time to see my patient before surgery was scheduled to start.'

Katherine's heart was beating a tattoo against her ribs. She sensed what was coming. 'You don't have to tell me any more,' she said softly.

'I do. I have gone over the day so many times in my head, trying to make it come out a different way, but of course that's impossible. We make these decisions in our lives, sometimes ones made in a split second, like the car driver who reverses without looking or overtakes when he shouldn't.'

'And sometimes we agonise over decisions for months but it doesn't mean that they turn out to be right,' she whispered. 'I, of all people, know that.'

'But you've come to terms with your demons. It's taken me this long to come to terms with mine. You need to know what happened so you can try and understand why I reacted to finding out about Poppy the way I did.'

'Tell me, then,' she said softly.

'Surgery that day went like a dream. I had two on my list—both major cases so I wasn't finished in Theatre until late. My secretary had left a note that Sophia had phoned and I tried to call her back, but there was no answer. I assumed she was in the bath—if I assumed anything. I went to see my post-operative patients and planned to try to get her again after that.

'Typically I got caught up and it wasn't until seven that I remembered I hadn't phoned her. I tried again and it went to voice mail. I still wasn't worried. She could be in the bath or in the garden and not heard the phone. She didn't keep her mobile on her unless she was away from home.

'But I was keen to get home—just to reassure myself. I had this uneasy sense of something not being quite right.

'The train seemed to take for ever. I kept trying to get her on the phone and when she still didn't answer I became more and more worried. I wondered if she'd fallen. There was no one nearby—no neighbours for me to call. Sophia would have known their names but I wouldn't even have recognised any of them.

'It did cross my mind to call the police, but I couldn't think of a good reason. My wife not answering her phone for an hour or two was hardly an emergency.

'I collected the car from the station, cursing the snow and praying that the road wouldn't be completely blocked, but nothing was going my way that night. I could only get as close as the lane leading down to the house before drifting snow made it impossible for me to go any further. There was nothing for it but to walk the rest of the way. All this time I was getting increasingly frantic. What if Sophia had gone outside and something had happened? What if she was caught in a snow drift?

'But I told myself that she was too sensible for that. Why would she need to go outside? By that time I was at the house. It was dark—it would normally be lit up like a Christmas tree. It could be a power cut—they weren't in-frequent where we lived—but I couldn't fool myself any longer about something being seriously wrong.

'I let myself inside and called out for her. No answer. The lights were working so it wasn't a power cut.

'I found her in our bedroom. She had her mobile in her hand. She was unconscious. But she was alive. I could see that she'd been fitting and now I noticed that her ankles, hands and face were puffy.

'Eclampsia. And I'd been too damn into myself and

my career to even notice. But there was no time to berate myself then. If Sophia was to have a chance of surviving I had to get her to hospital and quickly.

'I called 999. They said they would send an ambulance straight away. I told them they wouldn't get any further than my car and that I would meet them there. They said it would take around twenty minutes to get to me, supposing the roads stayed clear. The baby had to be delivered. If I'd had a scalpel with me, so help me God, that's what I would have done.

'She came round briefly, enough to recognise that I was there, but she started fitting again. I waited until she stopped and then I wrapped her in a blanket and carried her to the car. Thankfully the ambulance arrived at almost the same time.

'They delivered our son. But it was too late. For either of them.'

Katherine wrapped her arms around him and held him. What could she say? All she could do for him was let him talk. No wonder he'd been so shocked when he'd found out about Poppy. Sophia had died bringing a child into the world, whereas, it must have seemed to him, she had casually given hers away.

'If it wasn't for Crystal I don't know how I would have got through the next months. In the end it was Helen stepping in that saved us both. As soon as she heard the news she jumped on the first plane. She was with us before night fell. I was like a madman. That I'd lost the woman who was my very heartbeat was bad enough, but the guilt that she might not have died had I been a different man was worse.

'I stopped going to work. I turned down the consultant job at St George's and the one in America—to be fair to them they told me to think it over, to take my time, but I knew I wouldn't take them up. You see, I no longer felt as if I deserved it. I guess, to be honest, I was sunk in self-pity. So far sunk in it I was wallowing.'

'How old was Crystal?'

'She was three. Old enough to miss her mother but not old enough to understand that she would never see her again and definitely not old enough to understand that this man—who she barely knew, remember—hadn't a clue how to look after her. Even if I had, I was so deep in my trough of self-pity I think I was in danger of enjoying it.

'And when Helen came to stay that gave me more opportunity to wallow. Now she was there to take care of Crystal, there was nothing to hold me back. I drank myself almost unconscious most nights. I rarely got out of bed until mid-morning and when I did I couldn't be bothered getting dressed or shaved. Sometimes I didn't even shower until mid-afternoon.

'God knows how long that would have gone on if Helen hadn't called in reinforcements. It was as if the whole of my extended Greek family had taken up residence. Helen, her mother, my mother and my grandmother too—if my grandfather and father had been alive they would have been there also. I'm pretty sure their disapproving ghosts were in the background, cheering them on and wagging their heads at me.

'Those formidable women kissed and hugged me and then marched me off to the shower. My mother threw every last drop of alcohol down the sink and then Helen and Yia-Yia cooked up a storm. They looked after Crystal, but most importantly they made me see it was my job to care for my child. They fed her and dressed her, but after that it was up to me to look after her.

'Do you know, she clung to them the first time I tried

to take my daughter to the park on my own? She gripped the sides of the door when I tried to lift her, so in the end my first trip outside with my daughter since the funeral was with my whole family in tow. It got better after that. I still mourned Sophia but my family made me see that she would have been furious if she'd seen the way I'd gone to pieces. And I knew they were right. I had stolen her dreams from her, and what kind of major creep would I be if I couldn't make a life—a good, loving, caring life—for our daughter?

'The rest, as they say, is history. I sold everything we owned in England and ploughed it into a small practice here in Greece. Then…' he smiled wanly '…I met you. I fought my attraction to you, but I couldn't help it. You were the only woman who had come close to measuring up to Sophia, the only woman I could imagine spending the rest of my life with. But I felt guilty. It seemed a betrayal of Sophia's memory.

'Then I found out about Poppy and it was as if I didn't know you at all. As if the perfect woman I had built up in my mind had disappeared in a breath of wind. I'd put you on a pedestal' you see. I guess we're not so dissimilar, huh? Both of us seemed to feel the need to atone.'

Katherine grimaced. 'I no longer feel I have to atone. As I said, I did what I did and I just have to look at the wonderful young and happy woman Poppy is today to know I made the right decision. I'm sorry I couldn't be perfect for you. But, you know, Alexander, I don't think I want to be perfect.'

'No,' he said softly. 'Of course you don't. You're human. Like us all.'

'So what changed your mind?'

'Nothing changed my mind. When you told me why

you gave Poppy up I realised why you'd felt you'd had no choice. And when I saw you with Poppy I could see how you felt about her. I was coming to beg your forgiveness when Grandmother became unwell. As soon as I was sure she was all right I was coming to ask you to stay—to marry me. That's when you phoned me about Poppy. I knew it wasn't the time to tell you how I felt. Every ounce of your attention was—quite rightly—focussed on your daughter. I knew there would be time later—when she was better.'

He rubbed the back of his neck. 'What I wasn't so sure about was whether you could forgive me. Then when you were about to leave and you looked right through me, I thought I had ruined any chance I had with you.' His Greek accent became more pronounced, as it always did when he was emotional.

She looked him in the eye. 'You said you forgave me! I wasn't looking for forgiveness. Not from you! How could I be with a man who thought I needed his forgiveness?'

'It was a stupid, thoughtless thing to say.'

'It was,' she agreed. 'I needed the man I loved to love me warts and all.'

His eyes burned. 'So you do love me?'

'I think I fell in love with you almost from the moment I set eyes on you. But I was frightened too. I wanted to tell you about Poppy but I just couldn't. At least, not then. I was planning to tell you, but then Poppy turned up. I never wanted you to find out that way.

'Then she became ill and I couldn't think of anything else. I thought I was going to lose her again. I made a pact with myself, with the gods, to anyone I thought might be listening. If they'd let Poppy live I would give you up. I know it's crazy but I was crazy back then.'

'But when she was better, why didn't you write to me?'

'It took a long time for her to recover completely. I couldn't leave her.' She smiled wryly. 'And I was keeping my pact. Then when she was completely better I wanted you to come to me. I needed to know that you wanted me. The woman I am, not the one in your imagination.'

'I would have come sooner, but I was arranging a job here. I've taken a year's sabbatical. I love you. I adore you. I don't want a life without you. I lost Sophia because I put my ambition before her needs. I won't do that to you. God, woman, put me out of my misery. I have to know if you love me—if you will marry me and live with me. If you say yes, I'll spend the rest of my life trying to make you happy.' A gust of wind blew the leaves around his feet. But she needed to be sure. She had to know she wouldn't be second best.

'What about Sophia?' she asked. 'I don't want to spend my life competing with the memory of a woman who was so perfect. Because we both know I'm not. None of us are.'

'You're perfect to me,' he said. When she made to protest he stopped her words with his fingertips. 'I don't want perfection, my love. It's too hard to live up to.' He grinned. 'But you'll do me. What about you? Can you put up with a man who doesn't always appreciate a good thing when he comes across it?'

She smiled back at him, her heart threatening to burst from her chest. 'You know what? I rather think I can.'

EPILOGUE

THE TINY WHITEWASHED church was perched on a small promontory overlooking the sea. Poppy had helped Katherine find the place where she would marry Alexander. And it was perfect.

It was a glorious spring day and even the small breeze that whipped Katherine's dress around her ankles was welcome.

Crystal could barely control her excitement. She'd been hopping from foot to foot all morning, keeping up a constant flow of chatter. Poppy wasn't much better. Although she'd tried to hide it, she was almost as excited and thrilled to have been asked to be Katherine's bridesmaid—to the extent that she'd removed her piercings in honour of the occasion, although Katherine had no doubt they'd be back in place tomorrow. Not that she cared. Poppy could have turned up in a paper bag for all she cared. All that mattered was that she was here today, celebrating what was the happiest day of her mother's life.

She glanced at the girls. Crystal with a basket of rose petals hooked over her elbow and Poppy holding the little girl's hand. Who would have thought a year ago that she would be standing here with her two children, because that's how she saw them. Crystal and Katherine had other mothers—women who would always be an important part of their lives—or, in Crystal's case, an important memory, but they had her too. And she would always be there for them—to hold them when their hearts got broken, to help them achieve their dreams, whatever those might be, to support them when life wasn't so kind and eventually to help them plan their weddings, if that's what they wished. Whatever lives they chose for themselves, she'd be there cheering them on, as she was certain her mother was cheering her on. Mum would be so proud.

Her gaze turned to the man beside her, more Greek god than gladiator in his cream suit and neatly pressed shirt. She'd earned her doctorate and had accepted a job in Athens for a couple of years. She was almost fluent in Greek now. After that? They didn't know, but they'd be deciding together.

She had the future—a wonderful future—to look forward to, and she'd be doing it with Alexander by her side.

* * * * *

RETURN OF
DR IRRESISTIBLE

BY
AMALIE BERLIN

Published in Great Britain 2014
by Mills & Boon, an imprint of Harlequin (UK) Limited,
Eton House, 18-24 Paradise Road, Richmond, Surrey, TW9 1SR

© 2014 Amalie Berlin

ISBN: 978-0-263-90782-7

Printed and bound in Spain
by Blackprint CPI, Barcelona

Dear Reader

I'd love to open this letter with something deep and philosophical that inspired me to write RETURN OF DR IRRESISTIBLE. Or I could go on at length about my fascination with the circus microculture, and about how it doesn't matter because at heart people are people…

But really…? I just wanted to write about the circus! Who *doesn't* like the circus?

My motivation was really that deep at the start. So, naturally, as I had no vested interest in the subject at the outset, writing the book provided me with insights into my own psyche. I should expect that to happen by now, but it's always a surprise when it does.

It doesn't matter if you grew up in the suburbs, in a circus, or in the hills of Appalachia: everyone feels like the weirdo or an outsider at some point. And you always have to step outside your safe zone to grow past that.

Take risks. Be brave. And, for the love of chocolate and fat, and roly-poly puppies, go to the circus whenever you can! :)

Amalie xo

www.amalieberlin.com

Twitter: @AmalieBerlin

Facebook: www.facebook.com/amalie.berlin

Dedication

To my little brother Seth, a great writer whose name
will be on the front of a book before long. He who
read my first book (even though it's a romance) and
promotes my new releases to the point that my secret
identity is no longer secret with my family (doh!).
If I end up on the prayer chain for acts of
text-based naughtiness it's all his fault.

To my editor, Laurie Johnson. She's either very brave
or she's got a heck of a poker face. This was our first
book together and she didn't even hesitate when I
emailed to let her know: 'I WANT TO WRITE A
MEDICAL ROMANCE SET AT THE CIRCUS!
YAY!' Nerves. Of. Steel.

Praise for
Amalie Berlin:

CHAPTER ONE

FOR TEN YEARS Dr. Reece Keightly had been dreading this night.

He'd known it would come to this. Of course he'd known. It was all on his shoulders—the dynasty, the future of the company and the weight of the past. Two centuries of history all ending with him.

The tenth-generation owner of Keightly Circus was the one who would tear it all down. Nice round number, ten. Like Fate had decreed it. Like he was just filling the role assigned to him. Like it wasn't his fault.

Except it was. That's how they'd see it.

Reece took a step forward, shuffling with the crowded line to the ticket booth. The traditional last annual stop of the circus was always Atlanta due to its proximity to where they summered, but it was also the best crowd. The local, hometown circus returning triumphant from a season on the road, played out the last week near home. Traditional, like so many other things with his family's circus. Keightly's prided themselves on tradition.

Due to the coverage given to the impending closing—local television and radio stations had blared the news for weeks—they were enjoying record crowds for the last performances. For Atlantans, parents had been coming with their children for generations. Another tradition that would be violated after this year.

As excited as he was to see the show—and he never lost that excitement—the prospect of seeing people he cared for putting their lives in danger built in him a kind of extreme awareness of the world around him. It slowed things down, pulled him out of himself, and amplified every ounce of fear until it became a physical sensation, the taste of cold metal on the back of his tongue and he couldn't swallow past it.

Excited terror. He almost longed for ignorance, to be just one of the crowd, another random person in line who only knew the fantasy. But Reece knew the horror too.

All around him children giggled and chattered happily. Ahead, inside the massive blue tent, the band tuned up, readying to start the show, and every note amplified the dread eating at him. The sawdust awaited him. A tradition he could do without.

Dwelling on the unpleasant details wouldn't help him deal with them better. Shut it down. He just needed to see this show. One last time, make certain he was making the right decision. Not that he had any real doubts, but two hundred years deserved one last think. One last chance for them to change his mind.

Two people away from the ticket counter, he heard the first slow whistles of the calliope wheezing through the lot. Soon the ancient steam-powered contraption blanketed the area in sound—cheerful music silenced his chaotic thoughts.

He'd always loved the old calliope, but in the wake of those first warbling notes a surge of homesickness slammed into him. Nostalgia so strong it was like overlapping two realities—belonging and alienation, comfort and terror, peace and anger.

He latched on to the last emotion. Anger was better. He could do this—be angry enough to drown out the rest. But he should at least be honest with himself—he wanted to be there if for no other reason than to see her perform. He wanted to see them all, but the promise of Jolie Bohannon in the spotlight would see him through.

He just needed to see the show one more time. Everything would be fine.

Say goodbye.

Purge the sawdust from his blood, and all the rest of it. One last time.

Then he'd take care of everyone. See them settled. And go back to his safe and orderly life. Find a place to build his practice. Buy a home with a foundation beneath it. He could have people relying on him for their health—it's what he'd been raised to do—but not while he had to stand by and watch them put their lives in jeopardy to make people cheer.

Out of the corner of his eye he caught his first glimpse of the steam-powered calliope rolling across the lot. His mother sat at the back, playing the piano-like keyboard that operated the old steam whistles, while Mack Bohannon drove the carriage.

Jolie's family had traveled with Keightly Circus since before the Civil War. They might as well be family for real, and soon there would be a link when his mother married Mack and left Reece as the last Keightly standing.

Not yet ready to be seen, Reece pulled down the brim of his fedora, hunching his shoulders like that would make him stand out less. Keightly men grew tall. Every one well over six feet. But nobody expected him to be here tonight, and he didn't know how they'd react to his presence. He wanted to just be an observer.

He had a right to be angry. Reece harbored no illusions, though—if this were a movie, he'd be wearing black and twirling a weird mustache in the corner. Only villains closed circuses... Even if he was making the right call for the right reasons, something beloved was dying. Making the death of the circus quick rather than letting it limp along on life support was a kindness.

If he wasn't going to take the reins, if he wasn't going to step up as the last Keightly and lead, he had to take care of laying the show to rest. And he would do that. With the respect and honor it deserved.

But first he'd see one last show and say goodbye on his own.

And maybe somewhere along the way he'd find a way of convincing himself he wasn't a monster.

Jolie Bohannon stood at the back of the tent, holding Gordy's leash. The miniature white stallion always had to be held back until it was absolutely time for him to enter the ring. He lived to perform, a feeling she could once have identified with. It was still there—in theory—but she had other important responsibilities to handle now. Like making sure the full-sized mounts and the Bohannon Trickriders didn't accidentally trample Gordy because someone let him off his leash too soon. Calm and orderly, that's how everything and everyone stayed safe.

She listened for the change in the music—everyone in the circus learned to gauge where the performance was by the music—and adjusted Gordy's flashy silver bridle and the wee matching and no less flashy saddle. His costume.

At the first trumpet, she unclipped his harness and

reached for the tent flap, barely getting her hand in before he barreled through the flap and down the causeway. She stepped through in time to see him enter the ring. Darting between the other horses ridden by the Bohannon Trick-riders, he stopped dead center, reared on his back legs to stretch to his tallest—four feet and some change—and whinnied.

One by one, the other horses in the ring bowed to him, the little king. The little clown to end the act, the segment of the horse act that reached out to the children and in the audience, drew them in, and got their minds away from the scary excitement of moments before. Jolie smiled. Gordy could still make her smile.

The show was almost over. One more act and then the finale.

She stepped back outside, listening and watching the bustle of the crew getting ready to change the ring for the next act.

Watching the show was a little too much for her right now. She never let her emotions get out of control. Never. But with the circus closing down for good, emotions she'd long ago buried seemed closer to the surface. The last thing she needed was for something to set her off. Watching the show, getting sentimental and weepy over the last performances? Would interfere with her job. Everyone had a job to do and they'd do it with or without her, but she had to hold up her end. That meant right now she had to stand here and wait while Gordy played the fool and the crew changed the set, but she didn't have to watch the well-oiled machine.

The music stopped suddenly, snapping Jolie's attention back to the present. In a well-oiled machine, the music never stopped for no reason.

A cold feeling crept up over the back of her head. That emotion could never be buried or ignored. But fear could be used.

Cries had barely begun rising from the crowd before Jolie was inside the tent, running toward the ring. There she found her family off their mounts, surrounding something.

Where was Gordy?

She burrowed through and found him lying on his side, all playfulness gone. He thrashed about, repeatedly trying and failing to rise. She didn't have to look hard to see that his front left leg was injured. Not again.

Three of her cousins stepped in to try and get him to his feet, but he bit at them.

"Get out of the way. Call a vet. We need a vet." Her order was loud enough to be heard above the din. Gordy was her responsibility. Her job... But more than that, she loved him. He depended on her to take care of him.

Grabbing her phone from her pocket, she thrust it at her uncle as she moved past, holding on to her calm. Gordy needed orderliness and calm from her. "Whoa, Gordy. It's okay. Whoa..."

He was just scared and in pain. She squatted at his side and, despite his thrashing, got the straps circling his belly unbuckled and the spangled saddle off. Freeing him from the extra weight didn't help him rise on his own, and she needed to see him on his feet.

He wouldn't bite her. He'd never bitten her.

Taking a breath, she leaned in, arms surging for his chest and belly to try and help the small stallion to his feet.

"Jolie, his leg is broken." She heard a deep man's voice, winded but loud. Someone who'd been running too, familiar and unfamiliar even if he said her name. Too busy to question it further, she tried again to lift Gordy. So heavy. Jolie adjusted her arms and tried harder, straining to get the tiny stallion off the ground without putting any pressure on that leg.

He got on his knees, but she wasn't strong enough to get him all the way up. The position put pressure put on his leg and her favorite friend peeled his lips back and bit into her forearm. The shock of the bite hit her almost as sharply as the pain radiating up her arm.

She must have hurt him because it wasn't a quick bite. His jaw clenched and ground slightly, like he was holding back something intent on hurting him. He held on, and so did Jolie.

Someone stepped to the other side of the horse and put his arms around Gordy's middle. "On three." She gritted her teeth, counted, and the excessively large man lifted with her.

This time Gordy's back legs came under him and they got him to his feet, or least to the three good ones. She needed to see him standing, assess how bad the break was. It occurred to her that she should be more freaked out about this.

Veterinary medicine had come a long way since the days when a broken leg had been a death sentence for a horse, but Gordy may as well be living in the Wild West. He had a history of leg problems. Jolie remembered what they'd gone through the last time and what Gordy had gone through. Someone would make that terrible suggestion. Someone would say they should put him down… She needed to keep that from happening.

She also really needed him to stop biting. A few deep breaths and she'd be able to control the pain, but it'd be easier if he'd let go. Having her screaming at him would freak the tiny horse out and he was already afraid.

"Let go now," the man said, pulling her attention back to him over Gordy's pristine white back. She expected to see a vet, or maybe someone who had traveled with the circus in the past…

Ten years had changed his face. Broadened it. Made it more angular. But she knew those eyes—the boy she'd known ten years ago. The boy she'd loved.

Reece wasn't supposed to be there yet. And he probably wasn't supposed to be looking like he was about to throw up.

"I can't let go." Jolie grunted. Speaking took effort. Suddenly everything took effort. Controlling the pain. Controlling her voice. Breathing… "He's got me." And letting go might just mean that he fell again, hurt himself worse, and maybe his teeth would take her flesh with him.

As much as Jolie might normally appreciate the value of distraction to help her control wayward emotions, Reece was the wrong kind of distraction. He just added a new dimension of badness to the waves racing up her arm. She didn't want him there. He wasn't supposed to come until they were all on the farm, where she'd have room to avoid him. He'd stayed gone for ten years so why in the world would he come to see the show now?

Because she didn't want it. But here he was, helping with Gordy and being gigantic. Good lord, he was big.

She could use that to help Gordy.

Get the horse and the show back on their feet.

The throng of people gathered around, children in the audience pressed against the raised outside of the ring, getting as close as they could… The weight of all their emotions pressed into her.

It had to be their emotions she was feeling. She'd mastered her own emotions several years ago, and maintained proper distance from anything hairy, she reminded herself. And she'd regain control of them as soon as she got Gordy out of there and Reece the hell away from her.

First things first. "We have to get him out of here." She needed out of there too.

A single nod and Reece reached for the horse's mouth while she kept him standing. Large, strong hands curled around the snout and lower jaw and he firmly pried the miniature horse's jaws apart, all the while speaking to him gently, making comforting sounds that did nothing to comfort her—but which seemed to do the trick with Gordy.

Or the combination of comfort and brute strength did the trick. Gordy released her bleeding arm and immediately Reece slid his arms under the horse's neck and through his legs to support his chest and hind quarters. Then he did what she'd never seen anyone do before: He picked the horse up.

"Which way?" Strained voice to go with strained muscles, and the look of nausea was still on his face. How had Reece gotten so strong? She thought doctors studied all the time and played golf... Even as small as Gordy was, he was still a horse and weighed a good one hundred and eighty pounds. But Reece carried the miniature horse out of the ring. By himself.

Right. Not the time to think about that. Gordy was hurt. She was hurt. The show had stopped. Children were probably very scared and upset. "This way." She cleared a path and led Reece and his load out the back of the tent, the way she'd come, off toward the stables.

He could carry Gordy to the stable and then go away, let her have her mind back. The stable was Bohannon property, she would just order him out and take care of her horse.

Someone else would step in, get the show moving again, and she didn't care who that task fell to. As long as the vet came soon.

The stable wasn't far, but by the time they reached it, Reece was breathing hard. Maybe harder than she was while desperately trying not to feel nothing—not the pain in her arm, and really not the anger and betrayal bubbling up from that dark place she stuffed all her Reece emotions.

Once in Gordy's stall with the fresh hay she'd put down earlier, Jolie directed, "Lay him in the straw." That was something she could think to say. One step at a time, that's as far ahead as she could make her mind work. It took more effort than it might have otherwise done if she hadn't been bitten and her arm didn't ache to the point she was considering that maybe the bone had fractured...

The rest of her mental capacity was filled to the brim with the echoes of voices reminding her of Gordy's history, the way Mack would undoubtedly react, and all the animals she'd lost over the years. Of everything she'd lost...

Ignoring those voices took effort.

Nothing was going to happen to Gordy. He was practically a sibling. Her first mount when she'd been little more than a toddler herself.

Jolie forced herself to still. Reece gently laid the injured but considerably calmer animal in the bedding. "I think he remembers you," she murmured. Gordy remembered Reece, even if he looked loads different—even if he'd bitten *her*. He remembered Reece enough to go docilely into the straw.

Still not a good enough reason to keep Reece in the stable. She couldn't focus with him there. "Thank you. Go watch the rest of the show." She got in between him and the horse, focusing with all her might on first-aid training for horses.

Reece stood behind her, looking down over her shoulder. "Let me look at your arm."

"It will wait." Gordy might have thrashed himself into a bad intestinal situation…so the next step should be…

Reece's hands closed around her waist, dragging her attention away from what she should be doing. He lifted her to her feet and secured her left arm with his horse-lifting grip locked around her wrist. Fire and ice, his touch was like peppermint, an utterly inexplicable combination of heat and chill that momentarily cut through the fear of losing Gordy and made her think…so many different things. Primarily it reminded her of one thing: He needed to leave. But Gordy needed to stand up more, and she'd failed at lifting him to his feet twice already.

"My arm can wait," she repeated. And it could wait outside his grasp. She twisted her wrist free, ignored the deep ache the motion caused, and pointed to Gordy. "He needs to be on his feet."

"He can rest a moment. You're hurt."

He sounded so sincere, genuinely concerned… Which was crap, of course. "He needs to be on his feet," she repeated, "Resting a moment is the last thing he needs." *Don't look him in the eyes. Don't look him in the eyes.*

"Jolie…"

"Reece…" she replied, and looked him in the eyes. Right. No time to waste. She started moving again, toward the stall door so she could get to the supplies and away from him. Something in his touch, in the fact that he had helped them, and the concern in his eyes made her feel weak, muddied her thinking. Roused emotions she couldn't afford right now.

She knew what needed to happen for Gordy, not him. "You can stay here until I get him in a sling. He needs to be in a sling. And don't think you get to tell me what to do just because you went all strongman and carried my horse to the stable. You don't get to dictate anything in here. The circus might be yours to destroy, but Gordy is a Bohannon, so I'll take your help with him, and then you can get the hell out of my stable."

Not calm. Not calm at all. What had happened to her calm? Her arm. Pain and fear did this to her. That and the weirdness of seeing Reece. But it would all go away again soon enough. Losing Gordy on top of everything else would be a pain she couldn't ignore. Sling. She needed one of the horse slings.

Flipping open the lid of the trunk where various first-aid implements were kept, Jolie dug through, using her injured arm even if every second the ache grew worse. The only sling she knew they had was for the big horses…

"Tell me what you're doing." Reece said, apparently deciding it wasn't worth fighting with her.

Good. She didn't have time to fight.

Reece moved to the side of the trunk. "I'll help you if you tell me what you need."

More Good. Be helpful. The sooner Gordy was on his feet, the sooner Reece could go away. "I didn't see him fall," she said. "I don't know how much he could have jarred his insides when he went down, but I saw him thrashing to get up and that could have twisted his bowel. I don't want him fighting colic while his body needs to be focused on healing his leg. We need a sling. And some way to hang it. I'll work on the sling, you see if you can find a couple of pieces of lumber that will stretch across the top of the stall."

He left immediately. Of course he knew the way. The circus might be somewhere new every week, but it was always set up in the same layout. And that layout hadn't changed in the last ten years. She'd changed. He'd changed—God, had he ever—but the circus was the same.

A few minutes later Reece came back with two especially thick posts thrown over one shoulder and found her crouched in Gordy's stall, stringing together belts and harnesses.

"Lay them across the top. This isn't a proper sling, but it should work until the vet gets here." She stretched the leather across Gordy's chest, noting the labored breathing, and fought down another wave of panic. Once she had it in place over the shoulder she could access, she looked at Reece. "Think you can pick him up again? I need to get this around the other side and I need him on his feet, so I need you just supporting that place where his leg is compromised. Then I'll climb the stall and get it all hitched to the lumber."

He scowled at her. What did that mean? A longer look at her arm told her why he looked so sour, but to his credit he squatted beside Gordy and got him up again, just as she'd asked. Which didn't make up for anything. He would probably pitch some kind of fit when this was over. He was a showman after all. Doctor. Showman. Jerkface.

She'd been upset with him for years, but had thought she'd finally let go of it a few years ago. The strength of her anger at seeing him now surprised her.

Not that she could spare time for reflection. To hell with Reece. She'd help Gordy—they'd help him. He'd survive. Get him up. Get the vet to cast his leg. Take care of him.

Not a detailed plan, but it was as good as she had right now. And when Gordy's leg was in a cast, she'd figure out what the next step was. And then the next. She had a job, and right now Gordy was it.

"Hurry…" Reece said through clamped lips, doing his best to keep his head away from Gordy's mouth, should he get bitey again, but he managed to get the little stallion on his hooves and support his chest.

Jolie ducked around the other side and in a few seconds had threaded the makeshift harness through, clipped the ends together and thrown the long tail up and over the wood.

Good thing they were all pretty much acrobats…and that she was good at jumping. Her small stature made her the perfect size for tossing and flying, but made reaching objects in tall cabinets or shelves difficult. Made hauling herself to the stall top require a hop first.

She grabbed the top of the stall with both hands. Pain shot up her left arm and she let go again. It took a few seconds for the buzzing to subside so she could try again.

"Jolie?"

"I'm okay. It's…probably not broken."

He swore under his breath. Like he cared that much. Like someone who'd cut those he'd supposedly loved out of his life for a decade could care at all, let alone enough to swear.

A burst of anger at the bitter memory gave her the strength she needed to pull herself up on the second attempt. She maneuvered herself between the lumber Reece had slatted across the top of the stall, balanced and reached for the leather dangling over the lumber.

As she worked, she looked down and saw Reece scowling up at her again. "What?"

"Hurry," he said.

"You carried him all the way in there, is supporting one end such a chore now?" She looked down, noticed red on Gordy's white fur and howled, "Is he bleeding?"

"Dammit, Jolie, that's *your* blood."

"Oh." She swallowed back down another wave of hysteria and fastened the belts until the little horse was lifted ever so slightly from the floor.

"Too high," he called. "His front hooves aren't on the ground."

"I think the next notch will put too much weight on his leg, though... This is the best we can do. Maybe we can find a tile or bit of wood, something to slide under his good foot so he can stand but keep the weight off the other."

"After we clean your arm."

Back to the arm. "Later. What happened out there? You saw it, right?" Should she give him a sedative? Could she even do the math right now to figure out the right dose, or find a vein to inject it?

"He hurdled a little leap and just landed badly." He let go of Gordy slowly, letting him test the sling, and she waited to climb down until she was certain she wouldn't have to adjust the buckles.

Reece got to that decision before she did then stood and plucked her off the top of the stall. Picking her up again.

She'd forgotten he did that, just picked her up whenever he wanted to. And now that he was twelve gazillion feet tall, he might be even worse about it.

"Good grief, put me down." Being this close to him made her feel more breathless than she wanted to sound. She wanted to sound angry. Angry was better than fragile and girly.

"I'm helping you down."

She couldn't kick him because he might drop her and she already hurt. Though in a way she was grateful for the pain as having something else to focus on had to help keep her from thinking too hard about the past and just what Reece was there to do. "I climbed up on my own, I could've climbed down without your help too."

"You're hurt, and you're too stubborn to let me take care of you...your wound." He set her in the straw, and when Gordy whinnied and tugged at the sling, he lowered his voice. "It needs to be cleaned at the very least. Animal mouths..."

"I know. But it's waited this long. If I'm going to catch some dreaded horse-bite disease, then I'm pretty sure there is no difference in waiting fifteen minutes to clean it or fifty."

Gordy thrashed about, trying to escape the makeshift sling, causing the lumber above to skid on the stall. Jolie watched the wood move enough to be convinced: Gordy definitely needed a tranquilizer. And she needed a shot of something too. Like whiskey.

"Who's going to take care of him if you're sick?"

"I won't get sick. You're the one who's been looking like you were going to throw up."

He ignored her vomit talk. "This is ridiculous. He is in the sling. There is absolutely nothing else you can do for him until the vet arrives. Come with me to Mom's RV and let me treat it."

"No." She redirected his attention. "I have some sedative but I need some help with the math. You do medicine dosage calculations all the time, right?"

"I don't know the dosage for horses," Reece muttered, but reached up to hold the lumber steady.

"I know the dosage for a big horse and the weight differences, so you should be able to figure out what to give Gordy if I tell you that, right?"

"Fine, then we'll deal with your arm." He looked at her, but direct eye contact did something to her insides and she had enough to worry about.

She looked away, told him the dosage for a full-sized horse and the weight differences, and then left him thinking and holding the lumber to run to her trailer where she had the medication in her fridge. When she came back, he stood there still and immediately told her the number.

Flipping the cap back on the needle, she plunged it into the vial and extracted a slightly smaller amount than Reece had told her. Just to be safe. "You can treat my arm when the vet gets here. Gordy needs me. He needs reassurance. The last thing he needs is to be alone and scared."

"Jolivetta Chriselle Ra—"

"You just stop right there, Dr. Reece I'm-Going-To-Act-Like-The-Boss Keightly." She'd poke him in the chest if her arm didn't hurt so much and she didn't have a needle in the other. "I'm not going anywhere. The vet or someone might come in and get the idea of putting him down if I'm not here to stop them. Now, let go of the wood and hold him still. This medicine isn't great in the muscle—it eats it up. Has to go into the vein."

"Do you want me to do it?" Reece asked. Like she hadn't done this a hundred times before.

"No. I want you to hold Gordy." *And stop being bossy. And stop being around. And stop being...everything else.*

Reece let go of the wood, rubbed a hand over his face like he could wipe off frustration, and slung his arms around Gordy's chest again, his voice gentling a little too. "Why are you so convinced they're going to put him down?"

"He's got leg problems."

"Explain."

"Really bad circulation." Jolie maneuvered to the other side of the horse before adding, "And he's broken that leg before. It was very hard to heal the first time…"

"So it might be kinder if they come to that decision now rather than after—"

"No!" She shouted, causing the horse to flinch. She took a breath and calmed her voice. "It's not going to come to that. Horses can survive broken legs. And the circus is closing anyway! He has time to recuperate."

She went for a vein she had found before, back of the neck, easier to get to and somewhere where she could talk softly and provide comfort. Not that she felt calm and comforting right now. She felt way too much of everything. Worry. Fear. Betrayal. Anger. A disconcerting awareness at Reece's foreign manly scent in the stable… But she channeled worry away for Gordy's benefit and gentled her tone. "We're leaving here and going back to the farm in a few days, and he'll have space to relax and get better. He doesn't need to get better fast so that he can perform."

"It's nothing to do with performing."

"No, it's about taking the easy way out. Gordy's part of the family, and you don't just shoot your family if they get a hangnail." She threaded the needle into the vein, pulled back to make sure blood came into the cartridge, and then injected slowly. "You take care of your family. At least, that's how it's done in my family. You might not be willing to fight for yours, but I am."

The sedation worked almost instantly. She hadn't given Gordy enough to knock him out, but he did stop thrashing and mellowed significantly. With the safety cap back in place, she waved Reece off Gordy's back. "You can go now."

"You know no one is going to put him down if he has a chance to recover." He moved to the door of the stall but didn't leave. "I'm not leaving until you stop acting like a crazy woman and let me get a look at your arm."

If he didn't stop going on about her arm and about Gordy's leg, she might hit him. From the angle she'd have to swing up to hit his chin, and might even be able to knock him out. Providing his jaw was more glass than the granite it looked like. "He has a chance."

"Just wait for the vet." Reece leaned against the jamb.

She slid past him to grab a stool and moved it back into the stall. "I have been taking care of horses forever." Okay, she might be acting crazy—she'd never felt moved to violence before—but Gordy was important. "And I take care of people too. I know what I'm talking about. He can be casted. Sometimes a kind of exoskeleton can be built to support a broken leg. I've read about it, and we have the slings for the big horses. We have one who has a metabolic condition that causes him to get laminitis, and we had to sling him once. This little makeshift sling is taking weight off that leg, and we can get a better one for him set up. It's temporary. So stop preparing me for the worst."

Her throbbing arm needed a break, and so did she. She scooted the stool toward Gordy's head with her feet. He might be sedated but he'd feel her there. She'd comfort him. And maybe she'd absorb a little comfort from keeping near him too. A little comfort would be good right now. "I hope you're not so fast on the plug-pulling for your *people* patients."

CHAPTER TWO

REECE RUBBED HIS HEAD, a headache starting between his brows. This was not how he'd pictured their reunion going. That had gone entirely differently. She'd been wearing something sparkly for starters.

"Hey…" His brain caught up with the situation now that the immediate emergency had passed. "You're not dressed."

"I'm dressed just fine," she bit at him, and then her voice turned honey-sweet as she began to pet Gordy's face and talk to him. "It's going to be okay. I won't let anyone hurt you."

"For the show," he cut in. He'd been waiting at the show the whole time to see her perform, and only now did it register with him that she wasn't dressed for the ring at all. Jeans and a pink T-shirt with a white unicorn and a rainbow coming from its butt, while funny, wasn't per-formance attire. "You haven't performed yet. I figured you'd come at the end, the aerial act maybe, but you're not dressed."

"I don't perform any more."

"Why not?"

"None of your business." Her words were angry, but she kept her tone sweet. Not for him, he realized. She looked back at Gordy and ruffled his ears. The sedative had taken the fight out of the little horse, but her touch and proximity soothed him. Despite the drug, he tilted his head against hers and accepted the comfort.

She had the touch. Reece forgot his irritation for a few seconds, remembering the way she'd sat with his head in her lap after the accident, petting his temples in much the same way she that she petted the horse's face now too.

Two people in one body. In the ring she came alive—so full of energy that even when a trick failed she still held the audience in her hands. And the rest of the time she had that gentle touch that soothed any kind of animal. Even teenage boys. She'd been the only one he'd wanted around him after Dad had died.

The pink T-shirt had a growing spot of red on it where she'd clamped her arm to her side, cradling it protectively against her and using her other arm for Gordy.

"Hurts?"

"Adrenalin is wearing off," she murmured, "but I can wait."

"No doubt." He made a note to ask Mom all the things about Jolie that he'd never let her tell him before, when he had been trying so hard to stay in school and keep Jolie off his mind. Something was up with her, and it wasn't just upset about Gordy's accident. It might even be about more than his reason for being there, and the myriad other reasons she had to be angry with him. Not performing any more wasn't something she'd have decided for the last week of the circus. It was older than his decision to close the show down. How much older, he had no idea.

He was saved from thinking further about what kind of knots Jolie might have worked herself into while he'd been away when Mack Bohannon escorted the vet into the stable and ushered Reece and Jolie out—two too many people for the small stall.

"I know that's not a proper sling." Jolie said, gesturing to the small injured horse from the gate, "but I couldn't think of anything else we could do for him that might keep his digestion working properly and keep weight off that leg. We don't have a sling small enough for him."

"I have one." The vet pulled a backpack off his shoulder and handed it to Mack, Jolie's uncle and head of the Bohannon clan. Ultimately, Gordy's future rested with Mack, who dug into the pack and retrieved the sling then proceeded to help the vet swap it with the makeshift one.

"He's going to be okay. He can heal this," Jolie said to Mack, who looked grim. Not the right look. Not one Reece wanted to see any more than Jolie did. Whatever her protestations, she didn't need to watch the play-by-play.

He reached for her shoulder and tried to pivot her toward the door. "Let's get your arm tended to."

"I'm not leaving yet." Mack looked back at her and she shook her head, her chin lifting, "I'm not leaving. You might need me."

As easy as he'd like to be with Jolie of all people, he'd mistakenly thought perhaps time would have made her somewhat less stubborn. She'd always been this way when it came to Gordy, and Reece had started throwing his weight around to get her to mind him all those years ago when her mother had gotten her back when she'd been taken. That had been the first time his father had ever put him in charge of anyone in the company.

She thought him bossy? Well, she made him bossy.

The vet needed room to work and, knowing very well how hard it was to treat a patient when being hovered over, Reece made his decision. He scooped her legs from under her as his other arm caught across her back, and he carried her out of the stable.

Too stunned to say anything for a few seconds, it took them actually leaving the stables for Jolie's indignation and terror to kick back in. "Reece! Reece, put me down. I need to stay with Gordy."

"You need your arm cleaned and inspected." Reece tightened his arms lest she take a mind to thrash free of his grip. "I'm done talking about it. Mom will have first-aid supplies in her RV."

"No. What if they decide to put him down while I'm gone? He needs an advocate. He needs me there to promise to take care of him. See him through this again. I know he can heal." She twisted, testing his hold, and then locked onto him with a baleful glare. "Please." The word didn't go well with the glare or the tone.

"It won't take long."

"It will take five minutes to walk to your mom's RV. If you must have your way, my trailer is closer!" As the words tumbled out, she realized what would convince him. "I have all the medical supplies anyway, I'm the EMT on staff. And I won't fight you if you go there and we do this fast. Or just let me go do it myself and—"

"You're an EMT?" He stopped walking and looked down at her, his eyes going from hers to her mouth long enough to distract her. Kissing…would be bad.

Don't look at his mouth. "Can't you walk and talk at the same time?" Jolie barked at him, startling his gaze back to hers. "I am an EMT, yes." With the stable now officially out of sight, the firm heat of his big body and the prospect of being alone with Reece began to scare her more than Gordy's plight. One crisis at a time, that's all she could deal with. Not knowing what she might say or how she might react when she got her emotions sorted out? Well, that could cause another crisis. "Put me down and let me clean it myself, or start walking. Don't just stand here while they might be making decisions without me!"

"Didn't you have to leave the circus to attend classes to become and EMT?" What the hell? Why did he care so much about this?

"Do you see my face? This is the face of someone who is freaking out. Put me down or I swear I will belt you with my broken arm...*which isn't broken*..."

Reece scowled, but he started walking again and she almost relaxed. At least she stopped gritting her teeth.

"I took a course over the summer when we were between seasons."

It figured that he'd focus on her dislike of the outside world, like that was important right now. She could do things outside the circus, she just didn't care to. When the circus off-seasoned at Bohannon Farm, as it did every year, it was like living at the circus. The only difference with the summer she'd gone to school had been that she'd had to spend time with a bunch of possibly dangerous weirdos who'd thought mowing the lawn every Saturday, frequenting the mall, and driving an SUV was something to brag about. "My trailer is that way." She pointed with her good arm, and he veered off, following the directions she supplied.

Within two minutes she was inside her cozy little home. "There's supplies in the skinny cabinet above the sink."

Reece put her down in front of the sink and the first thing he did was wash his hands. "Paper towels?"

She gestured to the other side of the counter and then opened the cabinet to start getting out supplies with her good arm, then thought better of it and stuck the bad one under the faucet. It would hurt, but if she was going to have pain she'd either control it or be the one in control of inflicting it.

Number-one rule or dealing with Reece? Don't let him hurt her again. Even if it was that for-her-own-good kind of hurt.

No, especially the for-her-own-good kind of hurt. She'd had enough of that, thank you very much.

"This doesn't look good," he muttered, as he wrapped his hand around her wrist to take control of the flow of water over the wound. In that second she forgot all about her fear for Gordy and about the pain. She even forgot about how angry she was at him for what he was about to do to them all. Skin-to-skin contact was more potent than being carried, especially when it reminded her of how big he'd gotten. Hadn't he supposed to have been full grown when he'd gone off to school? When did men stop getting bigger? Was he still growing? This was ridiculous.

Her chest ached when she looked up at him. "You're too tall. Makes my neck hurt." She pretended that was where the pain was. It was better than give in to the urge to press against him and lean into the strength she'd seen in action. Give in to the urge to keep forgetting the bad things. Soak in the comfort she knew waited in his arms.

Stupid.

That should be rule number two—don't let Reece comfort her ever again.

She pulled her arm from under the water and ripped a fresh paper towel from the roll to blot at it, then applied pressure to staunch the blood that started flowing again. The ache deep in her arm had subsided but it surged back to life when she put pressure on it. If she mentioned that, he'd have her at the emergency room faster than she could say, "Don't put me to sleep, it's just a broken arm." It'd be her front left leg if she were a quadruped, mirroring Gordy's injury. Fate's twisted sense of humor…

He caught her arm again and directed it under the counter light where he could examine the bite. It was well on its way to bruising and there were several ugly punctures and a shallow gash.

"It doesn't need stitches. There are a couple of punctures that I might put a stitch or two into, but if you have butterflies, that can hold for now." He watched her, his voice having lost that edge of irritation as soon as he'd gotten his way. His mouth hadn't got the news that he was less irritated, though. His lips pressed together, hard and cranky. "Probably better anyway, in case an infection does start up—which happens way more often in punctures than cuts, you realize. And the reason we should have gotten this treated faster."

He unfurled his fingers from her arm and her thinking cleared a little. She needed more of that. "You know, I can do the medicine and bandaging. You visit your mom. I need…I need you to go and I can take care of this myself." Him going would help. It had to help.

"I'm almost done." The way he no longer met her eyes said that he felt something at least. It might be a ghost of the connection that they'd once had, but he still felt something.

"I don't care if you're almost done. I want you to be somewhere else. Somewhere I'm not. I will finish up and then go back to the stables. You're messing everything up." Her voice rose as she spoke, reaching to near shrillness at the end. "Because…you're still…"

"You can be calm if you want to be calm." He sure

sounded calm. But then she remembered—he didn't really care about them. This was just Doctor Man, who lived to treat patients. Or something.

"I'm trying to be calm. You could hurry up some. You know I need to get back." Gordy needed her. Focus on that. "Except I forgot that you're good at leaving people waiting." *No, don't focus on that. Gordy. Get it together.*

He gave her a look and snagged her wrist again—no doubt to keep her from getting away. She'd have to climb out the window in her bedroom or squeeze through the one over the sink if she wanted to get out. His big body blocked the tiny kitchenette. And he continued to work at his own pace.

She tried deep breaths to calm down. She really was trying, that was the problem. She'd thought she could always be calm, but right now she couldn't. Her heart hammered against her sternum like the beat of so many hooves in the ring. She could hear it, see it pulsing in her vision, and she knew that wasn't good. Her deep breaths got shallow and fast, outside her control.

Everything was out of control.

"They won't euthanize him while I'm gone, right?" she blurted out. "That's the kind of thing that takes time and preparation, right?" More words tumbled from her lips.

Like he knew anything. Or maybe he did. Maybe he was keeping her there forever for a reason. "They'd wait long enough to let people say goodbye if it came to that, right?"

Right? Right? God, she really did sound crazy. And she'd had a plan for speaking to him on the farm, when the dust had settled after they'd all settled in. Later. In the future.

"Take a deep breath. In through your nose," Reece

said, his voice firm and demanding. He wanted to control everything. Even how she breathed!

"Jolie," he said her name again. "I think you're having a panic attack. Slow down your breathing."

"I'm not panic attacking." Was that even a term? She'd said it wrong. Everything was wrong. That's exactly the kind of inarticulate nonsense that would make him think twice about even considering her request when she got round to making it. And probably everything she'd said and done since she'd seen him again would add to that thinking twice and thrice, and whatever fourth, fifth and sixth were… Sure, no problem, he'd hand over the reins of his birthright to someone who might be a babbling idiot.

Jolie had no proof she could even lead picnic ants in a straight line to the potato salad. She knew she could do it. Or she thought she could. She'd been so sure before he'd got here. Before she'd fallen headlong into that deep place where she stuffed all the emotions that were too hard to put words to.

It would be better if she knew it in some logical manner that came with charts and graphs. Doctors probably loved charts and graphs!

"I can't breathe." She probably had caught some awful horse-bite disease. Everything was wrong. Everything.

He let go of her wrist suddenly and grabbed her hips. Half an accelerated heartbeat later she was sitting on the counter in front of him, gasping for air and shaking all over, helpless against the onslaught of tears that swamped her vision and poured down her cheeks.

Reece cupped her cheeks, tilting her head until he had her gaze. So blue. So steady.

He said something. His thumbs stroked her cheeks, wiping away the tears as they poured down. She had no idea what he was saying, calming sounds. Comforting sounds. And they reached her. The tears slowed along with her breathing, and behind them she felt a stampede of embarrassment. And confusion. What the heck had just happened...?

"That was a panic attack?" her voice rasped, the raw sound causing a few aftershock hiccups.

He nodded, wrapping his arms around her and pulling her to his chest. Warm. Firm. Right where she'd wanted to be.

"I've had some experience with them."

It was hard to imagine anything rattling Reece like this. "They're awful," she mumbled, drained, ashamed, and wantonly breaking rule number two.

"Yes, they are."

She'd stop breaking rule number two in a second, but right now she needed the hug. And with her face hidden by his chest she didn't have to look him in the eye...

When she didn't say anything else, he added, "They're your family, and they love Gordy too. They're not going to make any decisions while you're getting your injury tended to."

"I know. I'm sorry. I don't know why... I don't know what happened. I don't usually act like a crazy person." She swiped her eyes again and pulled away, before she did something even crazier.

It had just been the shock of seeing him again for the first time. But that shock was gone, it couldn't last forever. So it was done. She willed it to be done and she was the one in control of her emotions...not the other way around. Never again. Focus on one big emotion at a time, that was the key to remaining tethered to her sanity. And right now that one big emotion had to be concern for Gordy. He needed her. She could fall apart later.

Forget that the last time she'd been this scared she'd been sixteen and watching Reece drive away into the world alone, and remember how all the faith she'd put in him— all the worry she'd had for him—had meant nothing. In the end he had been just like her father, who, incidentally, had been good at hugging too.

She should remember all that. If Reece was going to consider her request, it wouldn't be because he cared so much about them. She had to find another angle. "You should finish." Because she'd freaked out before they'd got to bandaging.

He nodded, looked at her longer than she was comfortable with him looking, then resumed treatment—dabbing on ointment, placing a couple of rectangles of gauze onto the wound, which he had her hold in place so he could deal with the tape.

"Don't worry about this. You're just wound tight right now. We all are. I'm worried about him too." A couple of rips of tape later and he replaced her fingers with white cloth tape, guaranteed to hold even if she should bleed again and get the whole mess wet. "If it starts feeling hot or hurting more, tell me."

"I know. Antibiotics." She pretended he hadn't said anything about worrying about Gordy. He could turn his worry on and off like a light switch or he didn't really feel anything. Or Doctor Worry was different from the worry of mortal men who couldn't worry and fret over loved ones while ignoring them utterly.

"If I had my kit, I'd start you on them right now," he muttered, and smoothed down the last strip of tape. "You haven't got any bigger, have you?" He squinted at her in a way she could only deem as judgmental.

"I'm big enough. Not everyone aspires to be a giant's stunt double." Sarcasm: Her Refuge. Her voice-activated ten-foot pole for keeping things away, keeping things from getting to her.

"I'm not judging. I was considering your weight for prescription purposes."

"Oh." Okay, so maybe she wasn't totally done being crazy. But it was easier to jump to a negative conclusion than to think that he cared. He was still here to destroy her *everything*. Time to go. She slid off the counter on the other side of him and hurried to the door. "Lock it when you leave." Not waiting for an answer, she took the stairs at a near run.

"Do you want some pain relievers?" he called from behind her. She heard the question as the door swung shut but didn't go back inside to answer him. Pain relievers? Hell, yes, she'd like some. She'd also like some amnesia pills. And she'd like him to take them too and forget the last ten minutes.

Even if the small part of her mind that was currently sane said that no one would put Gordy down without giving her time to say goodbye, she was still more than half-terrified she'd get back to the stables and find him already gone.

Reece stared at the screen door for several seconds, expecting it to open again and for Jolie to come back for some ibuprofen or something. But she didn't.

He shook a couple of pills out, laid them on yet another paper towel and folded it around the pills so he could stick them in his pocket. Before the night was over, someone would need them. Possibly him. If he didn't know better, he'd say that panic attacks were contagious. That he'd somehow given her the one he'd been fighting all evening.

A mess of paper towels and tape littered the counter, so he spent time tidying it up before he left. That was one thing always ground into the circus kids: keep your living area tidy. When it's small, and on wheels, you had to be as tidy and deferential to everyone else as you could be. And you had to be okay with making things work, even if that meant taking a shower with the garden hose behind the RV because you were on a schedule and all the other showers were occupied. You learned to make the best of things. He could control the physical mess he left behind, and the only speculation he could offer to the emotional devastation he knew he'd leave in his wake? He could only hope that they could make the best of it.

It was their nature. It was *her* nature.

Three years age difference between them, but circus kids grew up fast. Especially Jolie. When they'd gotten her back, she'd never really been a normal little kid. Always looking over her shoulder. Always afraid something would go wrong. Children learned behavior, like worrying, and she'd learned it then and learned it well.

He'd spent the last ten years trying not to think about what she'd learned by him leaving.

He still didn't want to think about that, even with it staring him in the face.

His worry for Jolie could cripple him. It certainly would've had him running back home to her that first week away at school if he'd so much as let his mother mention her name. It had been his only survival tactic. The only way for him to stay in school had been to quit Jolie cold turkey.

She might be the same size, but she'd changed in other discouraging ways. He'd probably played a part in that. Thirty minutes in her presence had dredged up more questions than just how she was going to handle him closing down the circus.

The show music had stopped a while ago, so Mom was either at her RV or the mess tent. She always liked to eat with everyone. Keightly Circus really did band together as a family, which was the hardest part of shutting it down. They ate together. Off-seasoned together. Raised their children together. The elderly performers even tended to retire to the same places…

He flipped the lock on the doorknob and stepped out, giving it a good pull. Locked up. As requested. Now to find Mom and get more information.

An hour later, having received the lecture from his mother that Reece had been dodging for a decade, he walked into the stables with two plates and bottles of water.

He found Jolie alone with Gordy, who was now utterly unconscious. A simple cot had been slid into the remaining space in Gordy's stall and Jolie sat on it, her back to the wall and her legs dangling, eyes fixed on the small white stallion. Though by her glazed look, she wasn't really looking at Gordy.

Reece knew only too well that you could stare right into your past if left to your own thoughts long enough. Usually at the memories you least needed to focus on. The ones you'd probably be better off forgetting entirely.

Since he'd stepped foot onto the lot, when he'd had any time alone with his thoughts, he got images of his father's blood, muddying the sawdust and sand in the ring…

"What are you doing? You look sick. Is the food really

that bad?" Jolie's voice cut through his haze. Thinking too hard was contagious too…

"It's fine. I'm fine. Brought dinner. Thought you might be hungry and I'd like to know what the vet said." He nodded toward the cot—it was big enough for both of them to sit on without touching each other, provided it stood the weight. "You mind?"

A suspicious squint answered him, but that was better than the panic earlier. Her green eyes still had that glassy look, like emotion wasn't too far beneath the surface. She was the first to look away, but she held up her good hand for the plate, freeing one of his so he could fish the water bottles from his pockets before he sat. "So?"

"He said front-leg breaks are worse than back, which aside from his circulation issues… I don't really understand." She rested the plate on her thigh, freeing her hands to shuffle the water bottle off to the other side. It must still be hurting. "Not sure if he means that they happen more frequently or if they are harder to splint, harder to heal, harder on the horse, or if it's Gordy-specific…" She gestured to the new harness on Gordy with the toe of her boot. "But that sling is more comfy and it's not bound by notches. They got it perfectly seated. Mack said it's possible he twisted something inside when he fell, so it was good that we got him on his feet so fast. They couldn't feel anything when palpating his belly, but he was out of it by then and couldn't have told them it hurt even if the pain was blistering."

"Prognosis?" He looked at the food, not able to bring himself to take a bite yet. She hadn't either, even if she was using her feet to gesture so her hands could keep hold of her dinner. Well, hand. She wasn't using the injured arm for anything but keeping her water tucked against her thigh.

"Oh…" She breathed the word, her tone confirming the worst, and that she wouldn't agree with it until forced to. "He said it's rough… We would try…"

But.

She didn't actually say it but he still heard it.

He put his bottle down, fished the pills from his pocket and placed them beside her leg. "Anti-inflammatories," he murmured, leaving her to take them or not, and went back to the conversation about Gordy. "So what's the next step?"

"Sit with him. Keep him comfortable. Watch for signs of colic." She took the pills. "And I have both pain medicine and tranquilizers to inject if he gets worse."

"You did really well with the tranquilizer earlier. Hit the vein the first time. Did you take courses on animal care too?"

"No, I learned to care for people, but I've given injections and done blood draws on the horses before. And I read. A lot."

He remembered that. She read anything zoological in nature, didn't matter if it dealt with the horses and dogs that were in the show or wild animals, which had not been in the show since her twice great-grandfather had been mauled by a lion during an act. The circus was always dangerous, but it had got a little less dangerous when they'd got back to their roots and away from the exotic-animal fad popular from the Victorian era.

"Thank you for dinner."

He kept his eyes on the food, but not looking at her didn't keep memories at bay. He made himself eat. It would be a long night, as he had every intention of spending it here at her side. "You're welcome." He looked at her again. Dammit.

The wild auburn curls had been worked into some kind of fancy braid so he could see her clearly even in the dim light of the stable. Still the prettiest girl he'd ever seen in the flesh. Even prettier than when he'd left. She might have cried again since she'd left her trailer—her wide-set green eyes looked bigger, glassy, and heartbroken. There was a little crease between her brows that said she frowned more than she should, and even now, with her expression mostly blank, the shadow of that unhappy crease remained.

"I know it's not the right time for this, but I wanted to apologize," Reece said, feeling his way through the words as he went.

"For leaving us?"

CHAPTER THREE

No. He couldn't apologize for that. "For…" He looked at her again and drew a deep breath. "I mean about the circus. About what I'm here to do. I know it's not what you want, but I want to help you get settled wherever you want to go after Keightly."

"I don't want to go anywhere else," she said.

None of them did. He was the bad guy in this, but for the right reasons. One day she'd see that. "I know you don't."

She put the untouched plate aside and turned on the cot to face him. "Listen. I didn't expect to see you tonight. Actually, I didn't think I'd see you at all until Ginny and Mack's wedding. And what happened to Gordy…I had a plan for how it should go when you came to the farm. What I wanted to say… But it sort of evaporated when I freaked out."

She had a plan? She had pictured him coming back and it didn't involve being a crazy woman? "Don't say you wanted to talk me out of closing."

"I was going to ask you to work with me and change what we do. No more traveling circus, a new future."

That sounded an awful lot like "Please don't close".

"There is no future for Keightly, Jolie. This isn't just about me and what I want to do with my life. It's dangerous. Especially with people getting older, it's getting more dangerous for them. Gordy is an old-timer and—"

"He's not an old-timer," she cut in, the flash of her eyes telling him that the crazy woman might be about to make a reappearance if he didn't watch out. "He's twenty-eight. Miniature horses live much longer than big horses, and we have some big horses on the farm that are over thirty-five. Gordy is firmly middle-aged."

She was still afraid someone was going to announce plans to euthanize the little guy. "Not what I'm getting at."

"Number one, the big-spectacle acts, the ones that are the most dangerous, aren't done by the core troupe any more. We get contracts for the headliners—fliers. We had a Russian bar act a couple years ago. But just because the core group is getting older doesn't mean that they want to give up the life."

"I know they don't want—"

"Number *two*." She held up two fingers, silencing him. "I don't want to keep the circus on the road. I don't even want to keep it a circus."

"Not keep it a circus?" His headache was increasing. "Stop counting lists of supporting...whatever, and tell me what you want to do with Keightly."

"I want to make a circus camp," Jolie said, her voice softening. "At the farm."

"A circus camp."

"The older performers can still teach. I'm proof of that. Just because I don't perform any more doesn't mean I don't know how to do things. I can be the demonstration, they can instruct, and we can make sure to...to..." Her hands flew up, a gesture he knew was meant to summon some word that had temporarily eluded her, and which had always been his cue to finish her thought when her mouth got ahead of her. Not that he could do that any more.

"Circuses are dying." She abandoned that train of thought and started again. "They're dying out. There were probably thousands in North America, now how many are left? How many close every year? How long before these art forms are no longer even remembered? Sooner, if we don't teach them to children and pass on our knowledge. Plus, we're only half an hour from Atlanta, and people love Keightly in this part of Georgia. They'd love to send their children to circus camp in the summer. Physical activity, fun, a day camp while their parents work. And for the rest of the year we could do the circus-school thing for older kids. Like high school and college age, those who are at their most fit and can best handle the rigors."

"Wait." He lifted a hand to rub his forehead, a headache blazing to life dead center behind his eyes. It wasn't exactly asking him to keep things going as they were, and while he appreciated that... "You make good points. All your points are good, but Mom is done with running things. She's said so over and over again and that's why I'm here. But I don't have time to devote to co-running a circus camp. I have a practice to build and run."

"I'm not asking Ginny or you to run anything. I'm offering. I will run it. I can do it. I'm not a little girl any more." It wasn't that she didn't like being told no, she just wouldn't be told no about *this*. Her fingers twitched then drummed against her legs, trying to calm her indignation. "You do whatever it is you want, focus on your practice. Ginny can retire and participate however much or little she wants to."

"My name is on it, this is my equipment, I'll have to take a hand in it. Plus, there's also no way I want to subject children to that kind of danger."

"I wouldn't just welcome them and throw them on the trapeze without a net," Jolie said, and then winced, realizing how badly chosen her words had been for him. "We'd be safe. Start slow. Probably start with simple tumbling for children without any gymnastic experience. And it's not all acrobatics. You know as well as anyone that there are a blue million different disciplines within the circus that don't even approach performance. Including costume design, set designs, tending animals…"

"People like you who don't perform any more."

"Right." She stopped looking him in the eye, shifting her gaze back to the sleeping Gordy.

Because she'd basically told him to stuff it earlier when he'd asked why she hadn't been dressed to perform. He couldn't tell if she didn't want to talk about that or if she just didn't want to talk about it with him. Screw it, he wanted to know! If it was another of his sins, he had to know so he could fix it. "When did you stop?"

"I stopped when you did."

His stomach lurched. "Why?"

She shrugged. "I just did."

"You had to have had a reason. You loved it…"

She shrugged again. "I didn't want to any more."

"Jolie—"

"I still practice, do different things, it's a good way to keep in shape. I don't do the trick-riding, but I figure the rest of the Bohannons have that market cornered anyway."

She didn't cast blame on him, and that was something he should be thankful for. What could he say if she brought up his past sins? And why was he digging into her history and motivations when he really didn't want her digging into his? Because he was an idiot. Because he couldn't know her without wanting to know every single thing about her.

Because he couldn't say no to her, which was why he had stayed as far away as he'd been able to.

And it was because he couldn't say no to her that he had to get out of there now. Bad plan to stay with her. "Are you going to be all right here on your own tonight?"

"Yes. Someone will come and try to relieve me in a few hours." She looked him fully in the eye again, somehow managing to look even smaller on the cot beside the unconscious horse. "Will you at least think about it?"

He knew what he thought about it. He thought—no, he knew—it was a bad idea. No matter how badly she wanted it.

"Please? Give me some time to show you how it can be. After Gordy is stable enough that he doesn't need me round the clock? After we relocate to the farm?"

After her arm healed? After he told her he had a probable buyer for all the equipment?

He stretched to buy a few seconds in the vain hope the right words would appear, present him some way to let her down easily, but his words were as elusive as hers had been. "Okay. I'll wait until we've settled at the farm, see what everyone else thinks about the idea. Weigh the pros and cons…"

She breathed out slowly, in what he could only term as relief, and leaned back against the wall. "Don't take this the wrong way, but could you also stay away from me for a few days?"

"Why?"

She shrugged. "Because if you're around, I'll just keep wanting to ask you to do it, and then—" She stopped suddenly, her cheeks flaring pink. "Well, not *do it*, obviously, because that would be stupid. Obviously." She was repeating herself so she stopped, shook her head, and then tried again. "I wasn't talking about sex. Obviously."

If she said "obviously' again…

"We don't…not sex. I wasn't talking about doing that. Hah." She shook her head. The more she tap-danced around, trying to clarify, the worse it got. "I meant doing… the camp. I would keep asking you to do the camp…" A great sigh came from her and she stopped talking. Finally. Without more obviouslys.

"Sure," he said, working to keep his voice normal. Unaffected. "I can give you space. You should sleep. Mom's got my number if you think the bite's growing infected. I need to go take care of some things anyway." He walked out.

He had important things to do, like locating his backbone before he just said yes to whatever she wanted to keep from letting her—and everyone else—down.

It was like that. The reason he didn't want them in the circus any more? He didn't want any one hurt. Any kind of hurt. But physical hurt—which could kill—had to trump emotional hurt. The emotional hurt just made you feel like you were dying.

They would acclimate to life off the road and outside the circus, he reminded himself yet again. And if they couldn't, he'd help them find new homes. Somewhere he could stop worrying about them. Somewhere someone else would have to take responsibility when luck turned and those death-defying feats could no longer defy.

Since the second his father had died, that responsibility had passed to him, and even when he hadn't actively been with the circus, he'd felt it. Oh, he'd ignored the hell out of it, but now that he could no longer do that he felt the weight of every life in his hands. And it was about damned time he used those hands to shield them.

He was a man now, not a boy to be shushed and ignored.

And really not a horny teenager who kept replaying Jolie's clumsy words: *I'll just keep asking you to do it.*

There had been moments in Jolie's life when the instant she'd done something, she'd regretted it.

Usually, those moments had involved falling off something. When she'd first started learning the wire, she'd had that feeling a lot. It had always gone away as soon as she'd hit the ground.

Since she'd learned to control her emotions, she'd not experienced this level of regret over anything she'd done.

And that feeling had never lasted for three days before.

She couldn't stop worrying about her sudden anxiety-driven freak-out and the way it painted her. More evidence that she was losing her mind. Her practiced, easy, unflappable calm had abandoned her the second she'd seen him, and even though he'd stayed away, as she'd asked, she couldn't shake it.

The very last show had run last night. Jolie had not attended. The show had ended for her the night Gordy had been hurt.

Today she should be doing what she always did—helping load everything with the others—but Mack had come and told her to stick with her charge. Maybe he heard about the freak-out. Maybe it was in deference to her arm. She had no idea.

So she did what she could in the stables, tried to wipe her mind, and tried to ignore the ache in her arm and the worry over how Gordy would fare during the ride to the farm. There could be no sling in the back of the trailer, not with it bumping down the highway and over potholed country roads. He'd have to lie down.

People came and went, carrying out equipment and moving out the other horses.

Jolie disassembled the cot and set it out, then resumed her vigil from a small stool in the stall. That was something she could do. Now, if only she could stop feeling like she'd just made the biggest misstep in history and at any second she was going to fall. No, actually, it was more like at any second she was going to stop falling. A sudden bone-crunching, sixty-to-zero-in-the-blink-of-an-eye method of stopping.

It might just be a relief when it finally happened. The fall was just killing her more slowly.

If she hadn't turned into a crazy person, Reece could've come today and waved his big stupid arms and impressive shoulders around to move Gordy when he needed it. Or lift him up in the horse trailer if his belly started bothering him when they were on the road. The poor little horse was still under the effect of drugs, and she couldn't tell whether his innards were out of sorts or if he was just too out of it to eat enough for any sort of digestive motility. Any time he flicked his ear, she checked for poo, and celebrated even a little bit of the stuff.

She looked behind Gordy again.

"You need help with him in the trailer?" a deep male voice asked, and this time she recognized it instantly.

Great. He would show up while she had her head right down there by the horse's butt.

"I'm not doing anything!" Jolie blurted out, jerking her head back from Gordy's rear quarters, "Just looking for horse poo." Right, because she wanted to remind him that she was inarticulate. She should've said a clinical word. Who in the world over the age of ten said "poo"?

"I didn't ask what you were doing," Reece said, grinning at her for the first time in over a decade.

"Sorry. I'm really tired." And she'd blame that on her acting like a crazy person this time. "What did you say?"

"I asked if you need help with Gordy."

"I do. Yes. Please." Jolie took a deep breath and peeled herself up off the stool. "I'm stressing about getting him home. And about—"

"Whether he's developing colic," Reece filled in, understanding her fecal fixation, thank God. "Have you changed the bandage?"

"Not since yesterday…I think." Maybe. The past three days were a bit of a blur.

He lifted a leather case and gave it a rattle. "Lucky for you I came prepared this time."

"Lucky for me." She glanced at Gordy again and then stepped toward Reece. "Maybe we could do this outside. I think I need a little air before we get crammed into a horse trailer. Wait, that's what you meant, right? Riding with me and Gordy in the trailer?"

"That is what I meant," he confirmed, stepping to the side to let her pass and then following her out into the sunny spring morning.

They always loaded the animals and outbuildings first, mostly because they were done taking them down first. The Bohannons would likely be on the farm before the workers were even done pulling down and packing up the big top that had put food in their bellies for years.

She tried to put that out of her mind. It wasn't the last time she'd see the tent. It'd go up again for his mother's wedding, whatever Reece decided about the camp. She sat at a picnic table and laid her arm on the sun-warmed wood, then let her eyes wander away from whatever he was going to do.

She added a new rule to her growing list intended to help her learn to traverse this new, overly emotional landscape.

Rule number three—focus on one emotion at a time.

Picking one emotion right now was harder than when her terror for Gordy had had her by the throat. Reece's presence made it hard to think. Not having slept much for the past three days also made it hard to think, and she'd already gone two for two with crazy Jolie appearing whenever Reece did.

Made her not want to ask if he'd come to any decision. To talk about something less like emotional napalm.

"Do you remember when I used to ride Gordy?" She felt him flicking at the tape and within a few seconds the bite was exposed, and the open feel made her look.

"I remember." His voice changed, a softening that gave her some small hope that he had something in his heart for their history, their lineage…other than just the horror and tragedy of his father's death.

"It wasn't long before I was too big for him. For a long time I asked when he'd grow up so I could ride him again. I didn't understand he was different from the other horses," she murmured, feeling the familiar burn return to her eyes. Three days of it springing up. Three days of waiting to fall. Three days of insanity. "He can be such a brat sometimes. He bites the other horses all the time. But this was the first time he ever bit me."

Reece almost reached for her hand but pulled back at the last second in favor of the medical supplies. "He didn't mean to."

Jolie swallowed, shifting her gaze away from him again. It took her a while to work up the will to speak and the ability to trust her voice. "I know."

"It's looking good." He shifted them away from the sad topic and back to something he could control. "The punctures at least. Better than I hoped, but there's more bruising than I like. You should get it X-rayed, just to be on the safe side." Reece uncapped a fresh bottle of water and poured some over gauze pads to clean the wound.

"If it's broken it's just a tiny fracture. That might not show up on the films for a couple of weeks. I'll wait a little bit and see how it goes." She continued shifting the topic. "Have you been staying with your mom?"

"No. I have a short-term apartment leased. I haven't been here at all since that first night, though I meant to come back. One of my professors called to advise me about a doctor in the area who is retiring and wants to transition his practice into the hands of another. He set us up to speak and it's actually pretty close to the farm."

"Who's the doctor?"

"Richards."

"Oh, I know him. He's got great peaches, and planted more at his orchard not long ago. Doing something with apples. I kind of zoned out when he was explaining that part." She shook her head. "Something about apple breeding, which sounded weird and not like something I wanted to know. It might forever ruin me on apples."

Reece applied antibiotic ointment then started tearing strips of tape to get ready for bandaging. But he stopped when she mentioned knowing Dr. Richards. "Have you seen him?"

"Granny Bohannon sees him, and I've taken her to the doctor several times. Practically have to hogtie her to get her there, no matter how bad she's feeling," she answered, and when he didn't immediately respond, she prompted, "I haven't seen him for my own health, if that's somehow weighing in on your decision on whether to get in on his practice or whatever. You wouldn't get me grandfathered in as a patient."

"I'm not worried about that," he said, getting the bandage supplies together and finally moving on to the application stage.

Jolie squinted a little. Lying. He was lying. "You *are* worried about that."

"I'm more worried about other things."

"Are you sick?" Jolie looked him in the eye again. "Or are you worried that I'm going to freak out again?"

"Neither."

"You're lying." She resisted the urge to turn his head so he faced her. "You've looked like you're about to puke at least three times since you came back. So either you're sick or I make you sick."

"You don't…" Reece smoothed the tape down with his fingertips and Jolie finally noticed it wasn't just the hand-pat he aborted to avoid touching her, he was working hard not to touch her even while treating her arm. "It's the sawdust."

Sawdust? "Have you developed an allergy?"

"No. I just don't like the sawdust. Haven't been able to stomach the smell since Dad died." His voice was low and sincere, but gruff like he really didn't like admitting this. "The college I attended? The main old academic building where pretty much all the core classes were was remodeled during my first year. I learned to come in through the back door and take the long way to my classes to avoid it."

Jolie felt her stomach bottom out. All the time she'd

spent with him after his father's death and she hadn't picked up on that? He hadn't even looked at her when he'd made this admission, which told her that it was something he felt vulnerable about. Reece still had some of his tells, though she obviously didn't know them as well as she'd always thought she did if this news was such a shock to her.

She'd never met anyone who didn't like the smell of sawdust before. That Keightly Circus used it to the end was a point of pride to them and the deep-rooted circus traditions they'd always tried to preserve while other outfits had grown bigger and more modern.

"So you wouldn't throw up?"

"No. That would have been okay. It was the panic I couldn't handle. Got over the worst of it, no real panic any more. Still makes me queasy, though."

"I'm sorry." She didn't know what else to say, but she did know that he needed some kind of contact—and she just didn't think her over-emotional self could handle him pulling away if she tried to touch him. At least it didn't seem like he was just being difficult any more. "I didn't know."

"I didn't want anyone to know. I still don't," he admitted in a low voice. "Just wanted you to know it wasn't you. But I think you were right about trying to keep some distance right now. It would be easy for things to get confused between us. Taking it slow would be for the best."

"I agree." She pulled her freshly bandaged arm away, stood, and began gathering the refuse. "They've already left with the other horses. We have a trailer to ourselves. We can get him in there and get on the road now if you're ready."

He nodded, gathered his supplies and approached the

truck, where he handed his treatment bag to the driver and asked on his way back to her, "Is he tranquilized?"

"I hate that word. Makes it sound like such a peaceful state, and most everyone or everything I've ever seen tranquilized ended up slack-jawed and drooling." Jolie headed into the stables, Reece behind her. "But to answer your question, yes."

She peeked to make sure he was still out of it, that the poo fairy hadn't shown up while she was outside, and then unhooked the sling as Reece worked his magic muscles and lifted the horse to carry him to the trailer.

"You need to prepare yourself. If he's not doing any better after three days…" Reece began, leading where he knew Jolie didn't want to go. They were sitting in the hay in the trailer, Gordy between them, his head in her lap.

"Don't," Jolie whispered, emotion in her voice pulling at his insides.

"I'm not trying to hurt you."

"No, I know you think you're being practical, delivering the hard doctorly advice and whatever, but I'm not giving up on him while there's hope."

Denial. "Is there hope?"

She'd probably held out hope for him for months. He hoped not, but he didn't know. And he didn't really want to know yet. Her emotional state wasn't the only reason Reece wanted to go slow with her.

"Of course there's hope. He's still alive." She looked at him like he was a monster, but she already had too many weapons to use against him to admit how gutted he would be when Gordy died. Admit how easily she could gut him if she wanted to. She probably didn't know she had any weapons at all, and his only chance was if she continued not to realize it.

"When we get to the farm and we get him situated in his sling, you need to wean him off all the drugs and see how he feels when he's alert."

"He's in pain."

"Yes, he is." Reece gave in to his decision not to touch her and laid his hand over her forearm, where the thin material of her sleeve would keep flesh-to-flesh contact at bay.

It was enough. She looked at him. "He stuck by me when I was in pain." Even with the sleeve barrier, she pulled her arm away. "It was just you, me and Gordy. When I got back. When Mom got me back from that awful group home when Dad left me. Just you and me, and Gordy. And he never left." She looked back at him and resumed petting the sleeping horse. "Dad left. You left. Gordy never left. I won't leave him to the whims of Fate. We're going to fight, and he'll get better."

He didn't know whether she was talking about just Gordy any more, or if she'd included herself in that declaration.

All he knew for sure was that he didn't like being lumped into the same category as her gutless father.

CHAPTER FOUR

REECE DIDN'T LIKE to sort through emotions. He ignored them as best he could until it all became clear without reflection. But nothing regarding Jolie was clear.

Well, nothing except the fact that she could still drive him crazy in every meaning of the word—even when he'd not seen or heard from her for two weeks.

Reece pulled into the long country driveway and reached up to loosen his tie, which seemed to be growing tighter and tighter the closer he got to the farm. The old quote about the road to hell being paved with good intentions rolled around in his head.

The old proverb was embroidered on a pillow in Dr. Richards's office, the practice he'd finalized purchase of in the past two weeks. If Richards didn't take that damned pillow with him when he left, Reece was going to burn it.

The road to hell wasn't paved with anything, let alone intentions. It was a long gravel driveway into the middle of nowhere Georgia.

His mother's wedding would start in about an hour, so here he was, no solution and no idea what he was walking into, or how the temperament of the group would be. All he knew was he'd grown really tired of waiting for a solution to the camp question. Jolie was probably tired of waiting too. If she wanted to open in time for summer, there was definitely a clock on his decision-making process.

The white summer big top had been raised, and Reece pulled up far enough to the side that he wouldn't be disturbing any post-wedding photo ops, and got out. Spring was always a volatile time in the South, and with the weather growing ever hotter, a cold front from the northwest promised something nasty. In the distance he could see black clouds looming, and already the wind had picked up.

He rolled up the windows of his car, grabbed his jacket and wandered into the tent.

No one was inside yet, but flowers and an arch of some sort stood in the ring.

Reece took the opportunity to check for sawdust, and breathed in deeply, braced for the revulsion he expected to follow.

"It's just sand." Jolie's soft voice came from off to the side, refocusing his attention on her.

She sat on the end of the bleacher, her pale auburn curls pinned up on the side by a flower, lots of milky skin on display, a lightly freckled shoulder bared by the filmy pink dress she wore.

No solution there either. The only thing he could think of was: girl next door. "Thank you." It was kind of her to see to that, though she might want to hurt him.

Jolie looked him over, noting the extremely well-cut suit. "You had that tailored? It looks tailored. Your mom will be pleased."

"Does that mean I look good?" Reece wandered over and leaned an elbow on the edge of the bleacher, right by where she sat. His elbow almost touched her thigh, so she slid down the seat a little.

"You look good. If they don't move up the time, though, I imagine no one will look good for it."

"Storm?"

"Storm." She tilted her head toward the entrance he'd come through and added, "I stashed a bucket of gloves, hammers and ropes back there, just in case the wind starts wreaking havoc with the tent." Because even if Reece wasn't going to let her use it, she couldn't just let it fly away in a strong wind.

"Good idea."

"I wasn't sure you'd be here," she murmured, looking back at the ring and decidedly away from him.

"At my mom's wedding?"

"It's been two weeks." She'd made up her mind not to bring up any of the camp business with him today if he came, so she probably shouldn't pick a fight with him because he'd been gone without word again for two weeks. And really it was dumb to be upset about it, and she wouldn't be upset about it if he didn't leave her hanging in limbo again. This time it wasn't about their personal relationship, it was about their possible professional relationship. Which probably meant that it shouldn't actually upset her.

Besides, Reece didn't need her giving him an excuse to abandon everyone again. They were all happy he'd come back, the prodigal son. If she ran him off, they'd forgive her—that's what family did—but it would hurt them and most of Jolie's existence was focused on protecting these people, not unthinkingly hurting them.

So maybe she should take a page out of Reece's book and avoid him.

She stood up, smoothed down the one-shoulder pale pink chiffon dress she'd gotten especially for this wedding, and walked away from him to the stairs so she could walk down. His eyes followed her to the end, and once on the ground she turned in the other direction and walked away from him.

"Do you have something you need to do?" he called after her, sounding confused. Welcome to her world. He left her in a perpetual state of confusion.

Did she have something she needed to do? Not really.

"Yes," she lied, sort of, not looking back at him. Did it count if that thing she needed to do was find somewhere to continue their decade-long tradition of not talking to one another?

She felt him following and stopped to look back. "What are you doing?"

"Helping?" Reece shrugged, like this was perfectly normal.

"The thing I need to do is be alone. It's your mother's wedding, and having us at each other's throats or acting crazy would be bad."

"So let's not act crazy," Reece said, shrugging again. "Truce for a day?"

"Stop shrugging. It just draws attention to your gigantic shoulders," Jolie grumbled. "Truce? Easier said than done."

He reached up and pushed back a stray lock of sandy brown hair, tucking it behind his ear. The rest of his mane stayed caught in a short ponytail at the base of his skull, but that one lock kept breaking free, making her itch to touch it.

"Do you hate me, Jo?"

What?

Right. He wasn't talking about his hair.

"Sometimes," Jolie murmured, refusing to lie about that, even if it wasn't an admission she wanted to make.

"I also don't want to bother you, and I don't want to fight with you…which is kind of a lie because I do want to fight with you. Or actually, I want to yell at you. And maybe kick you in the junk. But that would be bad. Counterproductive. Pathetic. And it's exhausting."

She stopped her random confession because dealing with any sort of feelings meant she might get uncontrollably teary. Something else she'd discovered in the past two weeks. People weren't supposed to cry *before* the wedding. She should save up her tears for the wake to follow.

He reached up and tugged on his tie, loosening it around his neck.

"You're messing it up."

"You said that before. I'm messing everything up. I know. And I don't care. I can't breathe." Reece worked at his collar until the tie was hanging loose and the top button was unfastened.

Jolie closed her eyes and took a deep breath, seeking strength from somewhere.

He stepped over to her, stopping close enough that even with her eyes closed she knew she'd have to crane her neck to look him in the eye. Nothing touched, but she felt heat radiating off him. "I know you said you want to kick me in the junk, but aside from this unexpected violent streak you've developed you look amazing."

"I don't…it's the dress. It's new." She opened her eyes, forcing herself to meet his eyes.

"I thought it was bad manners for anyone to outshine the bride."

"And you haven't even seen the bride yet."

"I know a tough act to follow when I see one." Reece ran the tip of his finger over the pink orchid pinned in her hair and his voice quieted. "I didn't know I wasn't going to come back when I first left."

Every survival instinct in her roared to life, demanding she step back, put some space between them, not look at him…but closed eyes didn't hold tears well, and the fool seemed bound and determined to make her cry. "Please, don't do this now."

"Can we just pretend for today that I haven't been an ass for the past ten years?" A ghost of a smile danced across his lips. "That I'm just the owner's idiot son? Bossy, opinionated, incapable of keeping his hands out of your hair… And you the big-hearted girl-next-door who puts up with me?"

"I never just put up with you," Jolie whispered, looking down and drawing a deep breath. They were having a moment. That needed to stop. She stepped back and put on her best sarcastic tone. "I suffered you."

"Did you?" Reece grinned despite her sour words.

Jolie mustered a smile and nodded. "Totally. Important distinction." And then she drew a breath. "Okay. I'll sit with you. For a little while."

"Just until you feel moved to violence against Samson again?" He turned, offering her his elbow.

Jolie laughed, unable to help herself. "You've named your manly bits? Good Lord, what an ego." But she slipped her hand through the crook of his arm. "Why would you name him after a mobile phone?"

"Samson is the strong dude from the Bible. Not the people who make electronics."

"Duly noted." Jolie tried to resist the urge to remind him how strong Samson *hadn't* been the only time she'd gotten up close and personal with him. And wait a minute, did that make her Delilah? Okay. Weird.

"Well if I start feeling violent toward him, I'll stay until I've carried out whatever instinct is telling me to do."

The wind picked up, buffeting the tent so hard that the thick vinyl thumped like a drum in the cavernous tent interior and saved her from reflecting too hard on the sudden bizarre ramifications of their genitals.

"If they don't hurry, they might end up getting married in Oz." Her hand tingled where it was wrapped around his arm, and even with the not inconsiderable heels she wore, he still towered over her. A feeling crept in with his presence and proximity that she refused to name. It was a stupid feeling, the kind of feeling that led her to all sorts of bad decisions.

They climbed a few rows up and sat, Jolie making sure she left some space between them, and while they waited for everyone else to get there, he talked. Safe topics.

It began with a story about his first day in residency, and how his size had auto-selected him to wrestle some naked, violent drunk down while others had got restraints on the man, and how he'd never been so happy to see insane amounts of body hair. "It was almost like he had on a fur suit, so that's what I pretended. Actually, I was a little envious at his ability to grow hair."

"You're really stuck on that Samson story, aren't you?" Jolie teased, but by the end of the story he had her laughing and, at least for the moment, distracted from all the crap that had piled up between them.

When the bride and groom entered the big top on foot, Jolie sat up straighter. "I thought they were going to ride in."

"Horseback?"

"That had been the plan." She shrugged. "Maybe they

decided—" A crack of thunder stopped her words. Everyone looked up, including Reece.

As if Mother Nature had generously waited for the happy couple to find shelter first, as soon as they made their way to the ring, the sky opened up and rain poured down in such heavy amounts it echoed loudly in the nearly empty tent.

Lightning and thunder arrived, and the winds picked up, rocking the whole thing. Big storms made circus people nervous, but in the spirit of enjoying the wedding, everyone got out of their seats and moved to the outer edge of the ring so they could hear the vows.

Before the pastor had got out the "Dearly Beloved," a whistle cracked through the air and in that instant forty heads turned in unison toward the direction the storm was rolling in from.

One of the anchor cables had come loose.

"Damn." Jolie took off in the direction where she'd stashed supplies and grabbed gloves, a couple of extra spikes and a hammer. A group ran with her, cousins and circus cousins along with Reece, all dragging on gloves and making ready to do whatever was needed to save the tent.

When another cable snapped free, the rest of the wedding party descended on the northwest side of the tent to hold it down.

Like hang-gliding in a hurricane, they worked between gusts to pound the stakes deeper into the earth. While a group worked on what had come free, others split off with hammers to drive in deeper the spikes that were still set, trying to ensure that they did not come free.

By the time they had the tent secure, every member of the wedding party was drenched and exhausted. All except the bride and groom, who were only severely disheveled, having been kept inside the tent working under threat of death or bodily harm.

Once again everyone gathered around the ring, the windblown bride and groom with the pastor the only three dry people under the big top.

Jolie stepped between Reece and Natalie, another cousin. As it became clear that the meager number of attendees couldn't fill the circumference of the center ring, they stepped inside and the circle of people closed ranks.

There was no bride's side or groom's side, they simply clasped hands and witnessed the joining of two lives.

For the first time in ten years Reece's hand opened beside her and she slipped her hand into his—palms crossed, fingers curling around the edges. Not entwined, not as lovers holding hands. As family. Just as Natalie's hand did on her left, minus that exaggerated tingle Reece always evoked.

But she had to ignore that.

Jolie would never have thought herself one to cry at weddings, and she didn't want to be one of those overly emotional people who did. It was just her stupid inner sixteen-year-old who'd dreamed of a Keightly-Bohannon wedding all those years ago.

That would have been different, of course. She could still remember what her ridiculous sixteen-year-old-self had imagined. Naturally, they would have gotten married on the trapeze, with flowers and vines wound around everything, culminating with her leaping into his arms with some ridiculously intricate trick that no one had ever tried before, spontaneously erupting from her in a flash of romantic inspiration... And then Reece would have caught her and kissed her and tossed her back.

Or the other one, where Gordy was the flower girl.

Every fantasy beyond ridiculous. Not at all romantic. Not like this ceremony, no matter what calamity conspired to interrupt it. In the end it simply stripped away any artifice and left the simple beauty and truth of two people who'd waited for each other…and had finally found their way together.

Her throat thickened. Maybe Reece had been right to leave when he had. Maybe she'd spun some fantasy about their relationship too. Maybe he'd known where she hadn't.

And now they were all so wet that maybe no one would notice a couple of tears on her cheeks…

Reece's hand squeezed, letting her know he'd noticed.

She looked up at him, but he did not look back at her. The way his jaw bunched confirmed for her that he wasn't unaffected now. The strange beast stood there, grinding his teeth. She couldn't even tell if he was reacting to his mother marrying or if she was the only one lost in those old thoughts.

And her doubts grew as the ceremony progressed. At the end hands eventually parted to applaud the new Mr. and Mrs. Mack Bohannon, leaving Reece as the last in the Keightly line. Maybe he was thinking about his dad.

Of course he was thinking about his dad…

"Are you all right?" she asked him as Natalie retrieved her camera and began snapping pictures of the newlyweds.

"They're taking pictures," Reece said, shaking his head.

Jolie nodded slowly. "It's a wedding. I think picture-taking has been the tradition as long as there have been photos."

"Yes, but look at everyone."

She looked at herself, at him, and at everyone else. She

saw lots of clothing plastered against bodies, lots of wind-blown hair, and lots of smiles.

But it was definitely out of control.

"You think that the wedding was ruined by the storm." She reached up and turned his head until he was looking at his mom. "Do they look unhappy?"

"No." He wrapped his hand around her wrist and pulled her hand from his cheek. Without warning, he walked to the seats, grabbed his jacket and walked back. A second later he'd wrapped it around her and now busily buttoned it up, like that would keep the exceedingly oversized thing on her. "They look happy," he said when her arms were in the sleeves and he'd gotten her as warm as he could. "But it should have been better."

"It was pretty amazing the way it was."

"The tent almost blew away. We're all soaked. Her flowers are all broken."

"And her heart is full." She shook her head. He couldn't focus on anything but the parts that were outside his control. "How about me? Do I look happy? Or am I just putting up a good front?" She smiled, though it was a guarded thing. She wasn't going to make this easy on him.

Reece looked at her over the space of several increasing heartbeats. "You were crying earlier."

He caught her arm again and his hands, big and much warmer than hers, closed around hers to warm it.

"I'm okay. A little cold, though, so thank you for the jacket."

"I know you're cold." He chuckled then said, "I'm pretty sure everyone knows that. It was a public service that I put that jacket on you."

"Public service?"

He looked at her now hidden chest, a glimmer of that old flirty light in his eyes.

"I'm sure your cold perkiness was making your male cousins uncomfortable."

Nipples. He was thinking about breasts, even though she didn't have a lot going on in that department. And that wasn't unappreciated. Except for the old rule that predated Reece, and which she should make rule number four, so she didn't forget that it applied to Reece as much as to other men.

She didn't need a man in her life. Better to be alone than with someone who would leave you anyway when he left the circus and the life. A variation on the rule ground into her head by her mother: don't marry a man not part of the circus—he'll only break your heart and abduct your daughter when he leaves.

Only there was no circus now, and she hadn't really revisited that rule.

She glanced over her shoulder to make sure no one was looking at them.

When she looked back, his hand was at the side of her head, fiddling with the hair clip. He untangled it from the bits the wind had yanked free of the clip before dumping gallons of water on her and unwound the coil of curls. "The mess really is bothering you."

"I like it down."

"Even when it's all wet?"

"Especially when it's all wet…"

Her scalp tingled and the hooded quality of his eyes when he looked at her made everything else tingle too.

Damn rule number four. Their truce was in effect until tomorrow, and why couldn't that truce include all the other bad feelings she wanted a night off from?

Flirting, holding hands, kissing…all good feelings. Feelings she might like to try out again.

Giving in to impulse, Jolie stepped between his legs, where he perched on the side of the ring, and leaned up to press her lips to his stubbled cheek.

"What are you doing?" It didn't come out as a question so much as a gruff and somewhat alarmed statement, but his arms went around her nevertheless.

"Pretending you haven't been an ass for ten years." She slid her arms beneath his and turned her head to rest her cheek in the hollow of his shoulder.

His chin came down to rest atop her head, but his body didn't relax.

"You're warm."

"No, I'm not."

Jolie ran her hands up his spine, over the wet material, which thankfully was thin enough to have started drying. With a slow, drawn-out sigh Reece relaxed against her.

"I think they're doing the cake thing," he murmured into her hair, and Jolie turned her head to look, unwilling to pull back yet.

"I think they're in a hurry to get on to the wake and then on to their honeymoon."

"The wake?"

Jolie leaned back and looked at him, her brows pinched. "Yes…"

"For?"

"Keightly Circus? Did you really think we wouldn't have a wake for it?"

"But this is a wedding."

"And your mom and Mack wanted to celebrate a new beginning while we toasted the past. This is how they met, you know. It's balancing something sad with something good."

"They're moving the flower— What are they doing?" Reece's scowl forced her to pull back so she could see and explain to him properly what was going on.

"They're changing the set for the show."

"Performing…"

"I know you've been gone a while, but think. What do we usually do at a wake?" She wrapped his arms around her middle and stepped back until her back fully pressed into his chest.

What do they do at wakes? "Talk…about people. Drink some toasts…"

"And we give tributes." She shook his arm.

"It's been a long time since you checked on Gordy." He did not want to attend the wake. Not telling him was a dirty trick. Dirty. And if it weren't his mother's wedding day, he'd leave and let her riddle out the enigma of how he felt about this.

"No. Gordy's much better, which you would know if you hadn't stayed away entirely for two weeks." She turned in his arms and laid her hands on his chest. This felt good. Jolie felt right. A wake did not.

"Are you okay? No one's mad at you, if that's what you're worried about."

"I'm fine." The look she gave him said she knew better.

"You're nervous. Your hand is sweaty."

"It's fine. Let's sit." Reece let go and started walking, but Jolie caught his hand before he got too far. Surprise caused him to stop and look at her.

She squeezed his hand. "Don't look so grim."

There had better be actual drinks involved in these

toasts. Something to let him turn this off. He let her go ahead of him up the bleachers, and followed.

In the first row someone had set out a line of framed photos. It only took a glance to establish who they were—people Keightly had lost over the years. Some he remembered, some only the older members of the group remembered.

Grandpa. Uncle. Cousin… The wakes he'd attended.

Dad. The wake he'd skipped.

This wake was sounding worse and worse all the time. Mechanically, he sat beside her.

"You'll wish you'd stayed," she whispered, accurately reading his mind. But she still kept her voice low, keeping his discomfort private, like she'd apparently kept the sawdust business private.

"The executioner doesn't usually attend the funeral."

"No one thinks of you that way. They love you, Reece."

She took his hand again, and he ignored the warning in his head that told him he shouldn't be touching her so much. Her hand felt good. Small, but strong. That touch. If this evening was going to go the way he thought it would, he'd need that touch to get him through.

"And as weird as you may feel right now, it's your family too. Everyone wants you here. Well, maybe not everyone—you don't seem to want you here. But everyone else does."

"Even you?"

Jolie nodded, but the sadness never far from her eyes filled in what that nod didn't. She didn't want to want him there. She'd told him to stay away, after all, and he had no doubt that however bothered by everything he was, she was just as affected. He just didn't know whether that was a good thing or a bad thing. All he knew was that it was impossible to ignore.

The lights went down and she scooted a little closer to him. He switched her hand to his other and wrapped the closest around her shoulders. Maybe he could enjoy this part of the wake. Not the performing, because the knot in his gut had already started twisting. But being alone with Jolie in the dark, allowed to smell her hair... That could get him through this.

From somewhere behind the bleachers a spotlight popped on and focused on the ring. A white sheet hung on a frame—makeshift projection screen—and Granny Bohannon strolled up to the still blank screen. He'd always called her Granny, even if she wasn't his grandmother. A heart of gold and a mouth like a sailor in a small, spunky package. The Bohannon women all seemed to be as small as the Keightly men were large. "If Granny's the presenter for the evening, things are already looking up," Reece murmured, wanting her to enjoy things and not worry about his reaction. And it was true. Granny made everything either fun or utterly inappropriate. Usually both.

"She's been organizing the kids for this for weeks," Jolie whispered.

A slide appeared, one he recognized as the oldest in the collection. A very serious-looking performer without a smile. Once they'd gotten a good look at the picture, another spotlight came on, illuminating one of the kids in a replica of the old costume from the photo. The sandy-haired teen tried to juggle and ended up chasing the balls around the ring while Granny narrated...in language that almost made Reece blush.

He couldn't stop the smile that followed. "Start with the clowns," he murmured to Jolie, who patted his arm again. They all loved to laugh. It was the best way to start off the wake. History, memories, and laughter. People he didn't know, people he did know, and some he wished he knew better.

The first non-clown performer to enter the ring had Reece tensing again. He squeezed her shoulders just a little too tight, not hurting her but making the turmoil he was feeling clear. Luckily, there was no rhyme or reason to the format of the wake. People had been preparing acts, tributes to the old acts from the past, compiling stories to tell and writing toasts. They took pride in every aspect, but there was no schedule or program.

Ten years ago, not equipped to know how to help him, Jolie now realized she'd failed to pick up on all his signals. Failed to help him through his father's death, or even recognize the kind of thoughts he'd been having. She'd thought she'd had him figured out, but if she had then he wouldn't be suffering now.

She'd lost her father too or, well, she'd been lost by her father, but the result had been similar. And she'd gotten over it. That's the only way to make it in life, get through the bad things until stuff got good again.

The sawdust had been a revelation. While she'd seen Reece's personality shift after his dad died, she'd always thought of it as being anger—that was the only emotion he'd ever allowed her to see until he'd made that unexpected sawdust confession.

The bright spotlights reflected off the sand and created a low glow in seats. Enough that she could see the muscle of his jaw bunching and the unnatural rise of his shoulders. But his biggest tell was the look of extreme concentration on his face. He didn't even seem aware that she was scrutinizing him.

Only an idiot wouldn't know he'd been in pain when his dad had died, but she just hadn't picked up on how traumatized he'd been until now.

"If I tell you a secret, do you promise not to tell anyone?" Jolie touched his hand again, trying to draw his attention from the ring.

"No," he replied, keeping tones low. "Maybe later." Because he was concentrating.

"No one is going to be hurt."

"Burns," Reece muttered. "Juggling seven clubs is just as impressive without fire or added danger."

"From a technical aspect, but it's not as exciting."

The look he gave her confirmed what she'd thought: He was escaping back into anger.

Armed with what she'd picked up this evening, Jolie now felt the need to protect Reece. To help him. Her own anger was still there, and still righteous—he had been an idiot to cut them all out of his life as he had done. And since he'd done it once, she had no doubt that he'd do it again, pack them all off at his earliest convenience. But she understood him a little better.

Her father leaving her had driven deep the need to stay within the safety of the circus, and his father dying had driven into Reece the idea that there was no safety at the circus.

Evening turned to night, then to morning. There were toasts, stories, and tributes. And no one got hurt. Reece met a new stepbrother, a fifteen-year-old boy called Anthony who'd come to Bohannon Farm as a ward of the state, part of their program to foster troubled kids. He endeared himself to Reece the instant he introduced himself and asked Reece and Jolie to come with him outside, and immediately bowed out with a slug to Reece's arm and a murmured, "You owe me."

"Did you put him up to that?" Jolie squinted at him, but mostly just looked amused.

Reece shook his head, smiling at Anthony's retreating back. "I did not. But I'm glad he picked up on my desire to escape." He offered a hand to Jolie and when she took it, he started walking toward the trailers.

They walked as close as they could, giving up hand-holding in favor of arms around each other. Before they even made it to the footpath leading to Jolie's trailer, they both knew where they were going. The question in Reece's mind was about whether or not she knew why he wanted to go there.

When she stepped up onto her stairs and turned to face him, the way she looked at his mouth for a few seconds before looking him in the eye was invitation enough.

He slipped his arms around her waist and closed his mouth over hers, kissing her with the longing he'd never lost.

Her soft lips parted in an instant, welcoming his tongue into her mouth.

The hands on his back squeezed, fingers pressing into the flesh in a way that caused a riot of goose-bumps and driving chills under the now dry material. No one else tasted like Jolie. No one else kissed like her either. She'd hold the kiss as long as he did, lack of oxygen be damned. When his heart had sped up to the point that he needed air, he broke the kiss but kept her close enough for them to fight for the same air with big shuddering breaths.

"This is a bad idea," Jolie whispered, swallowing and licking her kiss-swollen lips.

Reece shook his head. "Good idea."

"Bad idea. Bad bad…" She kissed him this time, releasing her hold on him to get at the jacket buttons and shed the bulky material that kept them apart. Freed from it, she pressed tight against him, the gauzy material of her dress leaving very little to his vivid imagination. God, he wanted to feel her. Everywhere.

CHAPTER FIVE

SHE PUSHED HER tongue into his mouth and he barely stifled a groan.

The groan made her pull away, or something did. She felt for the door behind her, flipping the latch and stepping to the side so she could swing the door open. "I don't know whether to invite you in."

"Invite me in. I…am a great guest." He grabbed his jacket and stepped up onto the stairs, which forced her up the remaining couple into the trailer.

"What I mean is I have rules. See, mostly I had one rule, but now I have four. I think. I might have five. Because…" She licked her lips and he closed the door, but couldn't take his eyes off the little pink tongue tracing her lips.

"I like rules." Reece would have said he liked anything at that point. The unfocused look of her eyes as she stared at his mouth made the words mostly meaningless anyway.

He dropped his jacket in the floor, wrapped his arms around her waist and lifted her against him.

No hesitation, she kissed him again, whatever she'd been trying to say. All heat, and deep kisses that made him question whether he'd have another episode like the last time they'd got heated.

The edge of the couch cushions touched the backs of his legs and Reece sat, arranging her legs to straddle his thighs as he leaned back, keeping her close so she could have no doubt how much he wanted her.

"I have rules." She tried again, winding her fingers in his hair and pulling to keep his head tugged back.

He couldn't tell whether the look in her eyes was the heat between them or an impending panic attack. The glazed sexiness was gone. "What rules?"

"Rules about men," she panted, shaking her head.

Freaking out was a sign to stop kissing her.

"I'm not sleeping with you." She blurted the words out before running them through her one-emotion-at-a-time rule. Lust was having a showdown with fear, and she couldn't decide which one to go with. Fear won for control of her mouth at that second.

"Okay." He reached up to pull her hands from his hair then carefully lifted her from his lap and placed her beside him on the couch. "Do you want me to leave?"

"I don't know." She could see both reactions as equally compelling.

Reece shifted, winced, and settled into the cushions again.

"Are you in pain?"

"I'm fine." He took a deep breath and looked at her. "I'd really like to know what you're thinking, though, because a minute ago…we were on the same wavelength. Then you started to panic."

"I'm still soggy."

Reece nodded. "So you want to change before we talk?"

It would give her a chance to think about what she could say to him, what information she was willing to part with… "Yes."

He gestured to the other end of the trailer. "I'll wait."

"Do you want to change too? I don't have much that would fit you, but you could go back to the RV and change."

"I'm not leaving. I want to talk and make sure you're all right. I'm making the most of our truce."

Jolie headed for the other side of the trailer and stripped down to her underwear with her back to him. There wasn't much privacy in the small living space, and she twisted to see if he was looking.

Of course he was looking. "Close your eyes."

"I've seen it all before."

"Do you really want to go there with me? I hear that rodeo riders can last at least eight seconds."

Reece winced.

That zinger had been a decade in the making. He looked away and she went back to changing. With clean underthings and her fluffy pink robe on, she wandered back to the couch, turned on a space heater on the way and sat down, feeling somewhat warmer if not more in control. She may not have changed that much since he'd last seen her, but he'd changed. It really wasn't fair.

"What's with the pink? You seem to wear it a lot now."

"I like pink. It's a myth that redheads can't wear pink." He looked large and out of place on her sofa. And something else, uncomfortable maybe. Angry? No, his jaw wasn't bunching, but he had that look of concentration again.

He looked her over and added, "You turn pink easier than you used to."

"One of the many ways I'm an enigma," she mumbled, and tried to remember why she'd stopped kissing him.

"Tell me your rule about men."

The color in his cheeks rose a little. "So you mean you don't date."

"I don't date," Jolie confirmed.

"How long has that been going on?"

She sighed. "Long enough. I don't need to date. And, honestly, there have been slim pickings with the circus. We have guest artistes. Mom married one and is now travelling with a new circus family. But I haven't wanted to have to move on with a troupe when they left. So, no, I don't date. Though I am starting to see that I could now. I mean, if there is no need to be on the road any more then there isn't that obstacle when you're getting into a relationship. I don't really need anyone who is in the life any more." She didn't date, but right now she also didn't know how to get control of her mouth. He hadn't asked for all this information. "I'm not signing up for dating sites or whatever. I'm okay with not dating."

"You're not convincing me." He stretched back, keeping those blue eyes fixed on her. "No one who wants to be alone kisses the way you kissed me." He tilted his head in the direction of the big top. "You might be able to sell that line to someone else, but I have a very long memory."

It felt weird to talk about this. She'd gone so long without talking to anyone about these intimate details of her attempted love life, but Dr. Long Memory begged to be reminded. "Then you should remember how the sex went with us."

"I remember. Believe me. It's a dent in my ego that I'm the worst sex you ever had." The way she looked away from him and turned just a little pinker, a little guiltier meant something. "The only sex you ever had?"

She cleared her throat, shifting and straightening her robe so it kept her well covered. "That's not your business."

"The hell it's not if I put you off sex for life," Reece muttered, angrier than he rationally should be to hear those words. He certainly didn't want to hear that she'd been with, well, anyone else. But hearing that she'd been with no one since him…was worse. "You have no appetite for it?"

"I have a fine appetite, I just don't need a man to help me…with that."

"With orgasms, you mean." He tried to keep his mind blank, because this conversation had suddenly taken a new interesting turn and his mind summoned appropriate visuals.

"With orgasms," she confirmed with a grunt, waving a hand. "I don't need help. I can do it myself."

Definitely a mental image he could spend months contemplating…but not if he wanted to get anything else done. "There's m-more to it than that." He stammered, trying to find his cool. He'd had the idea that this conversation would help him understand her, and maybe help her somehow. Not break him.

"I have a toy and I'm not ashamed to say it."

More…fantastic mental images. Images that completely robbed him of words.

"So, however much better orgasms are with a penis, it's covered?"

Stop picturing. Stop, stop, stop.

He leaned forward, turned off the heater, and sat back again. He'd had a point to make… "Okay, but it's still different with someone."

"It's close enough. It can't be all that different." She squirmed around at the other end of the couch, growing pinker by the second, despite her claims. "The mechanics are all covered!"

"Oh, Jolie…you're either fooling yourself or trying to torture me." Maybe both.

The shake of her head that followed was slow, less certain than all this my-orgasms-are-acceptable-as-is talk had been.

"So you're saying that hypothetically, if someone else controlled the vibrator…"

"It doesn't vibrate." She waved a hand.

"So it's…"

"A kind of squishy penis thing."

Reece rubbed his face, trying to relax his brows before she gave him another headache. "So, hypothetically, by your definition if I controlled the…toy, it would be no different for you than doing it yourself." He should be trying to get this out of his mind, not grilling her about it. Only someone stupid would have this fight with her, but he needed her to know he was *right*. What kind of grown woman didn't understand this basic truth? The kind he'd broken.

"Right."

"Fibber. Please, tell me you don't really think that. You're just getting some payback because of how…awful I was the first time we…"

"If I was torturing you, I'd say, 'Here, hold my happy playtime-penis while I have an orgasm.' And afterward push you out the door. But that would be mean to you and meaningless to me."

"Fine."

"What?"

"Get your play…time…penis. Your whatever. Get it."

Jolie laughed, a breathy laugh that said she was picturing things now. "You're joking."

"No, I'm calling your bluff. You're just messing with me."

"Reece…"

"Say it, you're just—"

"I'm not messing with you! But sleeping together is a bad idea."

"You're right, I'm definitely not getting laid tonight. I don't have condoms with me, and unless you are lying about that rule against men in your life, you don't have them either."

"I don't have them."

"Then get your toy."

"Because you've seen it all before?"

"Because I've seen it, and you deserve to see me suffer after you know exactly what it means." A good man, knowing how she responded to dares, wouldn't dare her sexually. But he wasn't feeling like a good man right now. He was feeling like a very frustrated man who had to open her beautiful damned eyes. And maybe vindicate himself a little along the way.

"Is this what they taught you in Playing Doctor School? Because—"

"Hell, no. There will be nothing clinical about this. And I'm still of the mind that it would be insanely hot, but if you want to turn me off the idea fast, keep up the doctor talk. Makes it smarmy and unappea…less appealing."

Jolie watched his face, and then she pointedly looked at his groin. Yeah, he might just suffer from this if she agreed to it. "So you are swearing you won't try to have sex with me."

"I promise you, I will behave myself."

She considered a moment. Pros and cons. Pro: she would get to make him suffer. He'd taken her virginity and then promptly freaked out, had got out of there and run away—like to another freaking state and never came back. Making him suffer and give her an orgasm? That sounded vaguely like justice. Pervy poetic justice…if she didn't have some kind of performance issue. Did women get those? And he would have nothing and suffer and... she wasn't sleeping with him. No matter what he said... and he could be made to want something really bad and not have it. *Like her camp.*

Cons: he might break his promise. He did have a record of broken promises, and he was right about there being no condoms in the house. Which could mean that there might be a little Bohannon in her future. Which actually wouldn't be a con. She loved kids. She just didn't love the idea of being abandoned by a lover or husband or a whatever Reece was.

Too many emotions to think about, especially when the big one that kept distracting her was the idea of more kissing... One emotion at a time.

"Fine. But you should know that I have no good and honorable motives. And no matter how much you want to have sex after, I'm not going to do it. I'm not going to touch your penis. I'm not going to kiss it or anything else. And oral sex seems dangerous. I'm not doing it."

"I wouldn't ask. This is all about me proving I'm right." He stood up, grabbed her off the couch, and marched the short distance toward the bedroom. "But you're going to have to explain the 'dangerous' comment later."

"I know how that thing goes off willy-nilly, like an unstable grenade. And if it's by my face...I would really have to insist on some kind of protective eyewear. Goggles."

"That was one time," Reece muttered, and now had the mental image of her with goggles on, and it was still sexy to him. God, he should put a halt to this nonsense.

"You really have to stop picking me up and carting me around. You're not a caveman. Didn't they teach you any vocabulary at doctor school?"

"Medical school," he corrected again, since he was pretty sure she was calling it doctor school now to annoy him. "I know a lot of big words. You don't want to play Scrabble with me. I dominate."

"I imagine if your opponent gets the letters you want, you just pick them up and move them where you want them to go."

"Don't you?" He put her down at the foot of the bed and began shedding clothes. Probably looked like he wanted to get this over with, and he kind of did…but it was more eagerness. She'd made him stop looking earlier. "Why are you just sitting there? Get the toy. Does it have a name?"

"No. Of course not." She gestured to the bedside table while looking him over. He wouldn't stop her. The point of this completely insane idea was to show her that sex was better with a partner, not a toy.

The way she looked up at him was an encouragement until she said, "Leave the boxers on."

Getting undressed was a little harder for Jolie. Reece stripped without a shred of hesitation, but she couldn't match that. Her boldness almost abandoned her as she reached for her panties and stopped to look at him.

This wasn't the sort of thing she'd ever have pictured herself doing on a dare. But if she was honest, that wasn't all this was. She had his taste still on her lips, and the memory of his warm hand in hers. The idea of being flesh to flesh with him—of feeling the length of his big body melding against hers—awakened a need inside her she'd not felt in a long time.

And she knew he was right there with her. His pupils dilated, his mouth was open, and there was a color on his cheeks she would have called exertion in any other circumstances…they all added up to the same thing. It may have been ten years, his face might have changed, matured, but she could still recognize want in him. He still wanted her. Logically, she knew he'd probably shared that look with a number of other women since he'd left her. And tomorrow she'd no doubt remember that…but right now he wanted her. Not anyone else. She deserved a night of that. Whether or not he deserved to suffer, she couldn't really say.

"Come here." He held out one hand and when she took it and sat on the bed, topless beside him, he guided her mouth back to his.

Something else to think about tomorrow, when she'd probably regret this. Right now she was stuck in some loop of not believing him, wondering if he was right, wanting him to be right, and then wondering if she'd regret finding out.

His breath came fast, and her heart sped up in tandem. Probably some primitive warning system she'd also regret ignoring.

She shut it down. The way his hands gripped and squeezed, greedy for the feel of her, that peculiar trembling low in her belly…all shouted a little louder than that warning system.

They stretched out on the bed, and when the hair on his chest teased her flesh, she was surprised to find her breasts beginning to ache. Kissing had been a great deal calmer when they'd first started doing it. And by the time they'd got around to it affecting her breasts, eager hands had been involved, and sometimes his mouth. But he hadn't even touched them yet, and her body was already responding.

She slid her hands to his head and curled her fingers in his longish sandy locks, pulling his head away. Air, she needed air. Her heart was beating too hard and too fast.

As soon as their lips parted she took several great shud-dering breaths, all the while staring into eyes as blue as a stormy sea.

He would break his promise. That's what Reece did. The muscles in his arms and back strained and shook with restraint, but it wouldn't last. He'd at least try to break his promise. For the first time she was fairly certain she'd let him.

She closed her eyes, trying to calm down, trying to still her hips and belly, which alternated between writh-ing into the mattress and quivering. The sensation of his warm hand tracking up the inside her thigh got her eyes open again. "That's not Mr. Happy."

He grinned as she spilled the name of her toy. "I'll get you for the lie later." His smile faded and he just watched her eyes. "Just want to make sure…you're ready."

A tremor of anticipation started deep inside her, and every whiffled breath confirmed for him before his long fingers found her sex and gave a long stroke.

Pleasure lanced through her, and somewhere in the back of her mind Jolie was aware she was supposed to compare this with pleasure she'd had on her own. But thinking was entirely too much effort.

Reece's look of concentration returned, and with it high, tight breaths. If her horses ground their teeth like he was doing, she'd bit them. Okay, yes, he was suffering. She couldn't even take any pleasure in that because the terrible need coiled in her felt like suffering too. It had never been this intense, even compared to how awful it had been that one other time they'd started to make love and he'd…had issues and bailed immediately afterward.

He licked his lips, withdrew his had hand from between her legs, and the fingers that had stroked her went into his mouth, shocking every other thought from her mind. She became aware that he was proceeding with the imitation penis when she felt it gliding, seeking her entry.

His eyes devoured her. She knew before he'd even slid the toy home that it was going to be the best orgasm she'd ever had. No doubt lingered that one waited for her. But she was supposed to do her part too…and slid a hand toward her sex.

Reece let go of the toy, grabbed and pinned her hands above her head.

"What are you—?"

"I'm the one who gets to." He crossed her arms at the wrists and held them with one hand, the other sliding back to the toy and beginning to move it. In and out, slow then fast, twisting and straight, adjusting the angle by the sounds every lick of pleasure ripped from her. But it wasn't enough. Just a pathetic substitute for what she desperately wanted. She wanted to feel the heat of him between her legs, feel the muscles on his back flex as he moved inside her…and she wanted him to feel. Pleasure. And whatever that dark current passing between them even now was… she knew it'd be more.

"Take it away." She panted the words, unable to move her hands and do it herself. The distress in her voice must have reached him. He stopped, breathing as hard as she, and shook his head, confused.

"I want you. I don't want it. I want you." She nodded, backing up her shameless, desperate words.

Reece closed his eyes, shook his head and began slowly working it within her again. "I promised." His hand still held hers, wound together now more than pinned. He opened his eyes and watched her. "I can feel you shaking. Don't fight it. You need it. I need it."

Then he whispered, "I will never break another promise to you, Jolie, no matter what it costs me."

It wasn't true… She'd never be that important to anyone. But the fantasy of it pushed her over the edge. When her climax came, her body bucked, but she kept her head still and her eyes locked to his. He knew she didn't believe him. She could see it in the frown that flashed through his eyes. No barriers existed between them right now.

She'd have expected him to gloat, but there wasn't even a hint of victory in his tortured gaze. He said nothing to taunt her, no *I told you so.*

He simply withdrew the toy, his hand shaking as he laid it behind him on the bed, and dragged her whatever fraction of an inch she was away from him—not satisfied until their flesh melded and his arms held her. Burying his face in her hair and his nose in the nape of her neck, he shuddered and sighed.

Stiff and unyielding, his erection pressed against the cleft of her butt, but he did nothing to relieve himself. Just held her while both their hearts tried to slow back down.

Jolie was the first one to crack. However much she wanted to punish him for the past decade, now she just wanted him to feel what she'd felt. "I could touch you…"

"No. I told you. I'm not going to break any more promises to you. Not now, not ever." He shuddered again, but apparently deciding that he couldn't stay tucked against her warmth he released her and rolled to his back and then to a sitting position at the foot of the bed and reached for his pants.

"You're leaving?"

"I'm removing myself from temptation." He tugged the pants on as he stood, and wrested them over the…impressive tent in his tight boxers.

She hadn't taken the time to admire him before, but he really had stayed in magnificent form in his time away from the circus. "You were right," she whispered, unable to keep from an honorable answer when he was suffering to keep from breaking promises.

"We can talk about that tomorrow." He pulled his shirt on, in a hurry to get out of there, but he did pause to look at her. "Are you okay?" He smiled, a tired, forced grin if she'd ever seen one.

Jolie nodded, pulling the sheet over herself as much for him as for her.

Reece stepped around the bed, bent down and kissed her on the head, then made his way to the door. It closed and she scooted into the warm spot he'd left on her bed and pulled the blankets over her to keep what little of his heat remained.

She should try to figure out what this meant before they talked about it. But if he remained true to form, he'd beat feet and she'd see him when he came to sell the equipment to some buyer.

Knocking at the door and the sound of his name being called in a frantic manner pulled Reece from fitful sleep. He stumbled out of bed and to the door, then wrenched it open to find Granny Bohannon there, looking wild-eyed.

"Get your doctor things. One of my boys got hurt."

It had been a few months since his last ER rotation, but he shook his sleepiness out and focused. "Hurt how?"

"Fell, got his arm bent around bad somehow. Don't know if it's broke, but we can't hardly get him on his feet. Dammit. I told him to stay the hell off the equipment, but he listens about as good as my fifth husband. And he was the deafest son of a…"

Another bone injury? Reece left Granny cussing at the door, crammed his feet into his shoes, grabbed the bag he'd brought with him for the exams he planned on offering today, and took off out the door behind her. She'd already climbed onto a four-wheeler and gunned the engine, leaving him the seat behind. And she hadn't stopped complaining in a vocabulary blue enough to make high-school boys jealous.

And just what his ego needed: to hold onto a tiny ninety-year-old woman to keep from being dumped off the back of an ATV. He stuck his arm through the handle on his bag and reached behind himself to grab a metal rack in the hope it would save him from an unexpected head injury.

They bounced over the uneven ground, which turned out to be as good as coffee when trying to wake up from staying up all night, staring down the gullet of the beast from your past that kept trying to swallow you whole, and then volunteering for more sexual frustration than he could have imagined before Jolie and her toy...

It didn't take long to reach the barn, it just felt like it. Reece got off when Granny rolled the vehicle to a stop, and followed an especially sober-looking teen into the barn where several people were gathered around boy of about fifteen, leaning against a post, his face ashen from pain.

Jolie knelt beside the boy, helping hold his arm to his chest for stability. So they had gone to her first? Seemed they weren't entirely ready to take what he was offering yet, but at least they had when Jolie presumably hadn't been able to help.

She looked at him long enough to confirm where her thoughts were too. The blush just added to his awareness and difficulty in focusing.

"His shoulder is dislocated," she announced, keeping

the arm held in place and shifting her gaze back to the kid. "Anterior dislocation of the humerus."

Reece stooped beside the boy. "How can you tell?" he asked, but a quick examination confirmed Jolie's diagnosis.

"Well, it's in front of where it's supposed to be. Probably hit it on the back as he fell because the ball is in front of the socket." Jolie pointed to a bump that shouldn't have been there. "If it were worse, like a sprain or a break, there'd probably be lots of swelling and bruising by now." She reached up to push her hair back from her face, looking back at Sam and offering the teen a tight smile.

"Good instincts."

"I've had some experience with this type of injury," she murmured, deflecting the praise.

"You've had a dislocated shoulder?"

She nodded but didn't look at him. Because the circus life was dangerous, no matter how much she'd like to pretend otherwise. Right. He could deal with this later.

"Bet that hurts." He shifted his attention to the boy, whose breathing sped up as Reece pulled his arm from the protective fold across his chest and began moving it slightly. Scared, anticipating pain.

Jolie moved around and knelt on the other side of the kid. "Look at me, Sam. Hurts like crazy, I know. And it's about to hurt a lot more for just like…a few seconds. Imagine you're putting all that pain into a ball, and we're going to kick it away. That kick is going to hurt…but then it's going to be gone. Yeah, it's really going to suck, but after it's going to feel so much better. You need to relax and do what Reece says to make that happen. Can you do that?"

So much for his usual plan, which was to say, "You might feel some discomfort…"

"I'll try," the kid said.

"Just keep looking at me," Jolie said, one hand on the boy's cheek to keep him face to face with her.

The muscles liked to spasm when the bones were out of the socket like this, and he'd only ever set an anterior dislocation once, but he remembered how to do it. With the boy sitting there on the dirt floor, his gaze fixed on Jolie's, Reece slowly lifted and rotated the arm, drawing a scream from the kid but causing the head of the humerus to reseat itself.

Jolie winced, but the scream—like the pain—passed fast, as she had promised. Just not before the boy had jerked away from her, leaned to the side and thrown up his breakfast. Or lunch. It was later than Reece had thought when Granny had come banging on his door.

"Breathe, Sam. It's all over." She leaned away from the vomit and stood pretty quickly.

Granny held out a bottle of water to Reece. He smiled at her, uncapped it and handed to the boy. "It's okay, Sam. Natural reaction to extreme pain." He wrapped an arm around the boy's middle and hauled him back from the barf, then pressed the water bottle into his hand. "Drink this. It'll help."

A few seconds later, while they all stared at the kid, the color started coming back to his face.

"Feel better?" Reece asked.

A nod, and he held the water to Jolie so he could use his hands to stand up. Not wanting him to use his newly reduced arm, Reece slung an arm around his waist and helped him stand. "Bet the next time Granny says don't climb on the equipment…"

"I won't," Sam filled in, then muttered, "I'd really like to lay down."

"I'll go fetch the golf cart," Granny announced, and pointed to a chair. "Sit. I'll be right back."

Sam obeyed.

"If you have a sling at the house, or some material we can fake one with, that'd be good too, Granny," Reece called after her.

She waved. He hoped that meant she understood.

Jolie hovered around the kid, and Reece gave them both the necessary aftercare instructions. He couldn't trust the kid to remember, but Jolie really did have a head for this stuff, terminology or no.

"You're good with the kids," he commented, and soon Granny returned with a sling and got them all onto the golf cart for a ride to the big house. Sam sat in the front, and he and Jolie sat in the back with their legs dangling off the vehicle—hers dangled better. He had to work to keep his feet off the ground.

She reached behind him and slid a box from behind him to behind her, allowing him to scoot back enough to keep his feet from banging on the ground.

"I like the kids," Jolie answered finally. "They've been kicked around by the outside world too. It helps them to be here with us."

She really didn't like the outside world.

"But you probably see that kind of thing all the time," Jolie said, hopping off the back of the cart as Granny rolled it to a stop. "You can get callous about that kind of thing. Probably doesn't bother you much any more, right? You see it every day, you get used to it."

She smelled good. His libido, never really normal since the night before, kicked in—memories of her squirming beneath his touch and the disheveled bed steeped in her sweet scent... He couldn't think, and she was probably saying something important to him. Reece stood and turned to grab his bag, and in doing so he saw several of the company members waiting on the big wraparound porch.

"We're here to see the doctor," someone said, taking Reece's attention off Jolie. He counted…eight new patients waiting.

"Got a place set up inside. Used to be a laundry room before we set up the laundry in the pole barn there," Granny announced, but she stuck by the kid, pointed to some building, and gestured for Reece to follow her inside.

When he looked back to tell Jolie he wanted to talk to her later, she was already far enough away that he'd have had to shout for her to hear him.

Later. He'd find her later. Right now he had a family to take care of, and for the first time since he'd come back into their lives, Reece felt like he was doing his job.

A good feeling that would have to hold him through being the village hard-ass again later when he told Jolie no to the camp idea and wrecked the connections they'd reforged yesterday and last night.

But a truce could only last so long.

CHAPTER SIX

AFTER THE LONG task of compiling medical histories for the last generation of performers, and with the extensive list of their profession-related health problems in mind, Reece went in search of Jolie. He still had a couple to see after they got done with the day's chores, but there was a break he could take advantage of now.

If the wake had given him any doubts about his decision, the twisted spines and cartilage-free joints shared by every performer he'd seen so far shored up those doubts.

He found Jolie by following the music to the big top, where she was perched on a wire strung between two portable stands, not exactly a high wire but a good ten feet off the ground.

The leather slippers she wore he recognized from seeing other wire dancers, but the hand guards protecting her palms were new to him.

A slow, sultry guitar solo blared from hidden speakers, but the music paused as she slid her front foot forward on the wire. She looked toward the player, lost her balance and fell.

Reece started forward, and had run several yards down the causeway when he realized she wasn't on the ground—or on the mats below. Thank God she had mats down.

Ever nimble in reflexes, she'd managed to catch the wire

on the way and was now pulling herself back up. Maybe that's what the hand guards were for. The thing bowed and stretched some where her hands put pressure, but she managed to get back on it and onto her feet.

With a few quick, bouncing steps she ran the length of the wire to one of the towers, bent over, grabbed a remote, started the song over again, and approached the wire again.

It was a routine. She was practicing a routine…what other reason would she have for starting the music over? The mats and his curiosity gave him the strength to stand and watch her, when otherwise all he wanted to do was make her get down onto solid ground where she couldn't fall to her death.

Her moves started slow and sinuous, the kind of moves he'd expect in a belly dance or a strip tease. Sexy didn't fly in American circuses, but if she could move like that, she might pull it off. Maybe in Vegas…not that she belonged in Vegas.

Reece stuck to the shadows to keep from interrupting her, but he did stand out enough to look around and see if anyone else was watching.

Just when his thoughts started to scrape bottom, the music picked up and she began a series of heart-stopping leaps, feet high off and back low on the wire. Within the space of a few notes she'd gone from siren on the high wire to something that he'd expect to see in gymnastics. Some combination of beam and bar that at once thrilled and terrified him.

If she fell she'd land on the mats. He repeated the mantra every time his heart stopped.

Now he understood what the hand guards were for—to protect her palms when she swung on that wire. Not just safety gear should she fall.

She let go of the wire three times during different spins and angles. The final one she didn't catch but used it to dismount, and he had never been so thankful for mats in his life.

Another new experience: being both terrified and turned on at the same time. And neither of those reactions did he particularly want to admit to.

The only thing he could admit to right now? She was still a performer—as much as pained him to admit it. She had to want to, no one kept in that kind of conditioning if they didn't want to.

Well, no one but him. He didn't want to perform, but he still wanted to be in the kind of shape he'd have been if he hadn't left. It was part of the life...just how he'd been raised, to value the peak of human performance that highly. If she didn't have an actual routine choreographed with music, he might be able to believe that was her reason too. But it felt more like something else he'd broken when he'd left.

Maybe her wish for the camp was a way to try and satisfy that need. Even believing herself alone in the big top, she smiled. She glowed, though the siren-like quality to her performance was new.

"I thought you'd have interrupted," Jolie said, unwrapping the guards from her wrists and turning to look toward where Reece skulked in the shadows. "Really didn't expect to get to the releases."

"I didn't think you saw me." Reece stepped out of the shadows and immediately took a seat on the raised outside edge of the ring. "The music pause makes you stumble, but you go jumping and leaping and don't get dizzy? Makes no sense."

"I don't know why. I think I have an inner-ear condition."

Reece focused then, brows pinched.

"I'm kidding." Jolie laughed, hanging the guards over one of the rungs on the tripod ladders up to the wire. "I really don't know the answer. I couldn't at first, but I was convinced it was possible…so I just kept trying. Eventually it got easier."

"I read something about ballet dancers training their brains to ignore the inner-ear signals of dizziness. Maybe it's something like that," Reece said, but he still looked a little freaked out. And tense. "Speaking of conditions, how's your arm?"

"Smooth segue." Jolie stopped beside him and sat. "A little sore but manageable."

"You should get it X-rayed." He reached for her arm and ran the pad of his thumb over the remnants of the bite, a gentle touch that sent a wash of goose-bumps up her arm and down over her chest. Her breasts reacted, small as they were, and she suddenly became hyper-aware of the leotard stretched across the sensitive peaks.

He noticed. And then he made a point of looking at the wire. "The dance…the act? Very sexy. When you weren't flipping around, scaring the hell out of me."

"I had the mats down for safety. And I toned down the sexiness a lot. It's hard to play with those emotions for no one."

"I wouldn't say no one. You knew I was here."

"I also knew you'd freak if I performed for you, and what might that do to my concentration?" She grinned and drew her arm back from his inspecting gaze. "You look like you have something on your mind."

Reece nodded, a smile saved for her. "I do. I'm just

blown away a little." He looked at her mouth just long enough to prepare her. "And I decided there was something else I'd rather do than talk."

Jolie swallowed just before his mouth came down on hers and his arms went around her, lifting her from the seat as he stood and covering the short distance to lay her on the oversized mats beneath her wire, pinning her and rousing her recently super-charged passion.

Kissing could happen without promises to stay forever. He wouldn't stay forever, she knew that. He'd leave her again, and them having kissed or having gone to bed together wouldn't matter to him at all when he made the decision to go.

She wouldn't let it go too far. She would stop before her brain entirely turned into hormone pudding.

In a little while…

Nap time. Some people might think the smell of the stables to be the sort of thing you didn't want to sleep with, but Jolie disagreed. None of the horses were allowed to trample in their filth. The stalls were kept clean and as fresh as could be. The strongest scent was the hay, except for right after the horses came in sweaty. There was that odor too. But as hot as it had gotten this week, no one was up to getting themselves or the horses sweaty. Least of all her.

So, naturally, someone would be walking around in the stable, interrupting her nap time. Jolie knew who it was before she opened her eyes. "Reece." She lifted the sleep mask she liked for her stable napping and looked at the massive man looking down at her from the head of her cot. "Seriously, when did you get so big? Big as a horse. I could ride you." She paused, pulled her mask off and sat up, like that would make her not say stupid things. "Okay, that came out wrong."

He smiled. "I could throw you over my shoulder. I know how you like being carried around."

"Oh, yeah, every woman wants her butt in the air for the world to see." She swung her legs off the edge of the cot and reached for her boots. "What can I do for you?"

Reece tilted his head behind him to the many full-sized mounts in their stalls. "Thought we could go for a ride."

"You're here in the middle of the week. That's a new one for you. Sounds like something more than a horse-back ride."

He nodded. "We should talk."

It was her turn to nod. "And you think we'll talk better on horseback? Because that seems like a distraction, some kind of sleight of hand to try and distract me from something that you don't want to say."

"Not entirely wrong, but it would also be nice to get out in the fresh air." Reece stepped back from the stall and held the door for her. "I also wanted to check on Gordy." The small horse was sleeping again. "Did you stop his tranquilizers?"

When Jolie stepped out of the stall, he went back in and squatted down to look at the cast holding the horse's leg in place.

This stall was bigger than the ones in the traveling stable, but Reece took up enough room for her to give him the space. She stayed in the doorway watching him. "I stopped his tranquilizers. But he still has some pain medicine and I occasionally give him a mild sedative just to keep him mellow. I don't know if he actually needs them, his mood is pretty good, but I imagine it keeps him from trying to walk around too much. Every now and then he kicks his back legs and tries to buck out of the sling, but the one the vet brought is good. He gives up pretty quick."

"Still on poop vigil?"

"Nope, his belly is doing just fine. The kids are cleaning the stall frequently. Especially since they keep sneaking him apples."

"I was going to ask you about the kids. How many are there?" Reece backed out of the stall and closed the door, taking over in his bossy manner.

Since she had pointed out his reason for asking her to go for a ride, he was now using another method to distract her. "Seven." She cleared her throat and dropped her hands to her hips, planting herself in his path.

"I don't want to go riding. I'm tired. I'm sore. It's hot. I'm borderline cranky. And I'm pretty sure you came here to tell me something I don't want to hear, which I guess I should be grateful for—the fact that you're willing to at least tell me bad news in person."

"Jo…" He stopped her tirade with one syllable, and when she stood staring at him, waiting for him to spit it out, he sighed and gestured her to a bench.

"I don't want to sit. Is that how they taught you to break the bad news to people in doctor school?"

"Medical school," Reece corrected, an edge coming into his voice that said the cool look he wore was more fragile than he'd like it to be. "I want you to sit down so you don't feel like I'm looming over you. I want to talk to you, not intimidate you. That's easier if we're closer to eye level."

"I don't think that's going to help us see eye to eye."

"Stop." He reached for her, like he was going to pick her up and put her on the bench, but then caught himself and drew back again. Old habits did die hard. "Fine. I'll sit. You can stand."

Jolie folded her arms over her chest and looked at him, a little more irritated that his sitting did make him look less intimidating. "I'll stand." And those few inches she had on him in height then would help…

"I am not able to support your camp idea," he said without further preamble. Right to the heart of his decision. "It's not safe. I understand why you want to do it, and I appreciate you wanting to keep Keightly intact, take care of everyone, but it's not the way."

"Because you don't think I can do it."

"I honestly don't know if you could do it, but that isn't why I've come to this conclusion." He frowned, wearing the serious expression she assumed was supposed to show how tortured he was about these hard decisions he had to come to for the greater good…and the idiots who couldn't take care of themselves. "You might manage it just fine, though I have doubts considering how you avoid leaving the safety of the farm. But the real issue is the danger. Someone would get hurt. Add to that what a waste of your talent it would be."

Talent. Right. This was about what was best for her. The man was a walking contradiction. "I'm sorry, is this that thing you do to break bad news to people by saying something good with the something bad so that they don't feel like the bad thing is as bad?"

"No." Reece leaned against the wall behind the bench, watching her in a way that made the height difference no longer matter. "You want to be performing."

"I don't want to be performing," Jolie grunted. "I want to be here, with my family. I want to take care of them. I want to preserve our traditions and our way of life. We can do that here without being on the road." Okay, she did enjoy performing, but that wasn't the biggest part of her life. They were. Even if Reece didn't care about any of that any more.

"You aren't being honest with yourself. You haven't seen yourself perform. You glow. It was always your dream. Didn't change, did it?"

"It changed. I was sixteen. It's not my dream any more. My dream…" What was her dream? The camp. And, well… "My dream is for everything to stay the way it was. But that isn't going to happen. So now my dream is doing the best that I can for everyone. And the camp is a good idea. No, it's a great idea. You think everyone is just going to settle down and retire, but that's not who these people are. They want to do this, but they're going to listen to what you say and not put up a fuss. Because when they look at you they see Henry Keightly, the boss, a man who everyone loved and respected, and who did everything for this family. I look at you and I see…broken promises and control issues."

"Broken promises?" Reece scowled, his own arms crossing now so that they stared over their arms at one another. "You see more than that. What word have I broken lately?"

"Having a good track record for a couple of weeks doesn't wipe out the bad one you've had for a decade. I'm not stupid, I know that you are here now and you'll act fully present and connected to everyone, but as soon as you decide to go somewhere else, you'll go without a backward glance. I remember that part of you very well. Do you want me to tell you what it was like? Because I can tell you—in excruciating detail—just how long it took me to give up on you."

He didn't say anything, but his nostrils flared and his lips compressed. Nothing to say? Well, she had plenty!

"You haven't been willing to have any of us in your life until you thought you could come in here and control us, unless we do what you say we can't be part of your life. That's how it is. That's probably why you became a doctor, so people would pay you to tell them what to do."

"That's not true." Reece spoke quietly, and she remembered that voice. She got louder and louder the angrier she got, but Reece got quieter. "I'm buying a practice fifteen minutes from here and making this place my home."

"And everyone here is going to listen to your orders. Except me. So, what's the solution? Get me to go find some other circus to join, because obviously I should be performing! Should I be offended that you're worried about the safety of everyone but me, who obviously should be performing?"

"Jolie, I'm trying to take care of everyone and do right by them. And doing right by you doesn't fit into the plan of what's right for everyone else. You're different. And stop saying 'obviously'. I hate it when you say that, like anything about you is obvious. Ever."

"I'm just so darned different…"

"Stop," he ordered again, then changed direction on her. "You know how much all the equipment is worth? I have a buyer. It will endow the farm for a long time, take care of the animals, and the people who take care of the animals will have a wage. It's a lot of money."

"The camp would bring in money too, and allow everyone here to hold onto their pride rather than being put out to pasture."

"You're not thinking clearly. You're just too emotional about this. No one is putting anyone out to pasture." He gritted his teeth—that muscle in the corner of his jaw bunching in time with her rapid heartbeat. "Your dream is for everything to stay like it was? That way you don't have to go out into the world and be part of it. You want this camp so you can still be in the life without actually being in the life. No ties outside the circus. No learning to get along with regular people."

"Are you joking? I'm talking about inviting strangers into my home on a daily basis, forever. I'm talking about pulling back the curtain and showing children that the magic isn't magic. That they can do great things if they work at it, no matter what anyone out there says about them." She knew that world very well, and she knew exactly why she had to stay away from it. "I'm going to do this, no matter what you say."

"Are you?" He stood up again. Sitting no longer worked for him. Or he had decided he needed to be more intimidating to make her agree.

Jolie squinted, not feeling intimidated so much as empowered by finally getting to have the fight with him that she should have had years ago. She stormed up to him, stepped to the side, and then right up onto the bench he'd vacated, forcing him to turn around to keep that intimidating stare. Unfortunately, that also put him in primo chest-poking range, and she was fired up enough that her index finger was already rod-straight and itching to jab him in his impressive torso.

"I know what I'm doing this week. Going to the bank! They give business loans and I'm smart enough to figure out how to get one for this. Though, honestly, with all the supporters we have, if the loan is troublesome I am certain I could finance the camp by contacting a few of Keightly's former supporters. Then I'll buy the equipment from someone lest prone to tyranny than you are. It won't have the Keightly name but the Bohannons are known too. I can keep the Keightly name off everything so your family legacy isn't sullied by my ineptitude. It would have been good for advertising, and to have the iconic tent for the children to perform in, but there are trapeze schools who set up outside, and the free-standing rigging isn't all that expensive."

He didn't flinch from her bench, and to his credit he didn't grab her and put her back on the ground either. He stood his ground, arms still crossed, though his thumbs stuck out in that annoying he-man manner that made her want to bend them backwards.

"So you're just going to stick a sign up by the highway and hope people come? You know if you really want to do this you will have to go to schools to introduce the idea, talk to parents at activities and athletics centers and let people know what's going on. Get insurance for everything—"

"I'm not a shut-in, Reece. I do go out when I need to. I speak the language and everything! I may not like it out there, but I can do it. You act like I'm asking you for charity. I'm offering you the chance to honor two hundred years of history in a venture that *makes money*. Not just uses it up."

"You don't understand how much responsibility this is. And, yes, it might make great wads of money, but this equipment is mine and even if I do nothing for this camp besides supply equipment, at the end of the day it's my responsibility if anyone gets hurt." His voice rose. Finally she'd struck a nerve.

"Fine, then it's settled. I'll get the equipment somewhere else. Go ahead and sell off the big top."

He loosed a loud groan of frustration and turned to walk away from her, enough to presumably give him room to get hold of his hands if they reached out to grab her again. "You remember how it was when Dad died. You remember how awful it was. I know you do. For God's sake, Gordy's hurt because he's a working animal. And we've had a number of really close calls with other performers in the past. Some who were injured badly enough they couldn't perform any more. You don't want to saddle children with that, Jolie. You ignore the danger. Have you seen how many of them have back and bad joint problems?"

"I'm not ignoring the danger, I'm just not going to be crippled by it."

"No, you let yourself be crippled by other things."

She took a breath and forced herself to stop for a few seconds, think about what he was saying. Was that an acknowledgment that he was crippled by the fear of other people dying like his dad had? "You want me to say I have abandonment issues? Fine. I do. I also don't want to go out there and get a job in an office and have a house with a white picket fence, live in a subdivision where it is supposed to look like a community but where everyone's interaction ends at their property line."

"What's so bad about it?"

"Loneliness is a sickness, Reece. People medicate it with materialism and they forget the things that are important."

"There are worse things than being alone."

Her face suddenly felt cold and she knew the angry red face she'd worked up had abandoned her. Jolie could hardly believe he'd just said that to her. "No, there isn't." She'd never say to him that there were worse things than watching your dad die in a horrific accident. Her throat constricted, but it was the burning in her eyes that demanded she summon her anger again. Anger was better than tears. "If you think telling me all the ways that it's too hard for me will do anything but make me more resolved than ever, then you've done a really good job of forgetting everything you ever knew about me. But thank you for reminding me for the thing I forgot about you."

"What's that? That I'm always right?"

"No, that it's stupid to get into bed with Reece Keightly, because the sting lasts longer than he does!"

Done with this conversation, with hoping that he'd do the right thing, Jolie stepped down and stormed toward the door.

"What are you doing?"

"Leaving!" she answered, but didn't turn round. She just raised her voice to make sure he could hear her. Strategic yelling. "I'd think that would be something you'd recognize when you saw it."

Reece watched Jolie leave, the wind knocked out of him as effectively as a punch to the solar plexus. He took a few steps back and sat on the bench again.

Because it turned out that shaming himself for taking her virginity in that way was one thing, and having her say it out loud were wildly different things.

Jolie had more reason than anyone in the world to hold grudges against him, but she still kept trying to be kind and generous with him. She had taken care of the sawdust for him. Had put down the mats below her wire so he'd be more at ease. Tried to preserve his family history and the Keightly dynasty...but there was still a wound there.

A big one.

She was right to question his staying power.

She was also right that he was a control freak. Letting her buy the equipment and do this without his support—or his input—with his people... At least if he let her use the Keightly equipment and the name, he could keep some constraints on what was taught at the camp. Establish a curriculum that would minimize the possibility that she'd have massive future regrets. Make sure he did the physicals so that the kids were all healthy enough to participate...

He groaned, and then got up and went into Gordy's stall to sit with the little horse, who was actually awake and eating. He did look better. He'd been ready to give up on the little stallion in those first days, but Jolie had stuck it out. She didn't let go of anything she loved without a fight. Which made him wonder: had she ever actually let go of him? He'd denied her the fight. Denied her the closure.

He should go back to his apartment and get ready for work tomorrow. This week and next, Dr. Richards was overseeing him treating his patients. There was no contractual clause demanding that, but Richards wanted that extra bit of reassurance that his people would be in good hands, and Reece could understand that. He felt the same way and wanted Richards to be at ease with the transition and the future care of his people.

Even if the core company no longer bore the Keightly stamp in any form, even if they lived on the Bohannon farm, he'd consider every one of them to be his people until the very end.

"I'm here to see Reece."

Reece knew that voice. He followed Richards into the exam room, and smiled as soon as he saw the patient. "Anthony, this is Dr Richards, he built this practice."

Anthony introduced himself as Reece's brother, extending his hand. When Richards appeared confused, Reece jumped in and explained about how Anthony had come to be his new stepbrother.

"Could I just see Reece? I have a problem that I would rather…"

"Certainly." Richards nodded and left the room.

When the door closed, Reece rolled a stool over to where Anthony sat and joined him. "Are you worried about Granny? Or are you here for yourself?" Please, don't let the girlfriend be pregnant… Jolie already gave him too much Bohannon drama to deal with.

"I'm here for me." Anthony took a deep breath. "I didn't want to tell Mack and Ginny. Didn't want to tell anyone really. But now I think I have to."

"Well, whatever you say to me as a doctor, I will keep in confidence." Reece maybe shouldn't see his own stepbrother as a patient, but he'd do it this once to find out what was wrong, if nothing else.

"I'm diabetic. Type II. I used to be pretty big, you know, chubby…when I was a kid, before you guys took me in, and then I got diabetes. But as I got older, I lost weight, it got better. I didn't have to take medicine for it any more, so I didn't think I needed to tell anyone about it." His knees bounced in the seat and he looked down a lot.

Reece took the hint to help him out. "But something has changed?"

"I've been using Granny Bohannon's meter to check my blood sugar every day. She knows about my diabetes, but I didn't want to tell anyone else. I didn't think it was important any more."

He could read between the lines: Anthony thought Mack wouldn't adopt him if he knew he had an illness. Reece understood hiding weaknesses. He nudged the kid's foot with his own, making him look at him. "He would have still adopted you. Mack and my mom? They're not like that. You don't need to worry about that."

"Medicine is always expensive. I don't want to be expensive."

Reece would hug him if he knew him better, and if he didn't also know that fifteen was not a hugging age for boys unless it was with someone you had a thing for. Reece resisted the urge. "Anthony? Don't worry about that. It's not always expensive and, besides, you're part of the family. You came here today for a reason, so you tell me what's going on, we'll get it sorted out."

Anthony nodded, still slouching, still looking uncomfortable. "Jolie caught me testing yesterday. And she's in town today, across the street, but she dropped me off here because she said you would help me. I think it's not in control as much again. I have been getting higher blood-sugar numbers when I check it." He sighed, like every word he managed was another nail in his coffin.

"Listen, I don't know what you've gone through in your life before you came to us, but I want to. Like you said, we're brothers now. Brothers look out for one another. So when I tell you not to worry about this, that the only reaction that Mack and Mom are going to have is concern for you, you can believe me. Jolie didn't lie to you about me helping, and I'm not going to lie to you either." Reece wrote some notes on the chart, giving Anthony some space. "We're going to do a little bloodwork and then get a plan formed, figure out how to get this fully under control. Maybe you've just been doing something different, maybe you could do something different, maybe you need some medicine to help you out. There are a bunch of options, and none of them are a good reason to be upset."

Anthony nodded and sat up a little straighter, rolling

up his sleeve, ready for the blood draw. "There might be a reason…"

"What sort of reason?"

"My girlfriend likes to bake…"

Reece laughed. "You think that might be the reason?" A shake of his head and he stood up. "It's not easy to find a girl you like who wants to bake for you. She pretty?"

"She's real pretty,," Anthony confirmed, pulling out his phone and turning it on.

Pretty girl picture, front and center. "Oh, yeah, hard to turn down sweets from her. Give me a second." Reece stepped out long enough to request some supplies, and then sat with Anthony again while they waited. "So the bank is across the street. Is that where Jolie is?"

"She's getting a loan to buy the circus stuff from you for the camp. I can't wait. It's going to be awesome. I'm working out upper body now. Jolie said catchers have to be strong in the upper body."

Catchers. Right, Reece's part of the act they'd been working on before he left. He was going to have to pay a visit to the bank… "I hate to make you wait, but the nurse is going to have to come do the blood draw, and then it will take a few minutes to get the preliminary results. I'm going to step over to the bank and check on Jolie."

"You think she's freaking out?" Anthony asked. "She's been running around all morning, but she gets that look when she goes to town."

Funny that he could be so observant about other people but not confident enough to trust those skills when it came to his place in the family. "I'll just be a couple of minutes…"

CHAPTER SEVEN

JOLIE TREATED ERRANDS like a marathon. In order to get all her business in The World done and over with in one day, she'd happily run herself to the point of exhaustion. Today she'd even kept Anthony home from school and managed to get out in the early morning, get meetings done, get back home to pick Anthony up and drop him at Reece's office, and now she'd check "Bank' off her list. As soon as the loan officer got back from wherever he'd gone to.

She wasn't entirely certain what would happen at the meeting, whether or not he would just discuss options with her or whether he'd have her filling out paperwork. Dealing with banks for the circus and the farm had always been the business of Ginny and Mack. No wonder they'd gravitated to each other. They both had to deal with bureaucracy, and while they might not enjoy it, they were at least competent. Another thing she didn't want Reece to be right about.

He'd said she couldn't go out into the world and get students for the camp. It would be the biggest lie of her life if she tried to say that he was wrong about her not wanting to go out into the world at all. But having him say she couldn't was either a dare or forbidding her to, and both possibilities roused in her the wrong reaction. However ridiculous or immature, shining a spotlight on her weakness made her want to prove him wrong.

But it was more than that. She wanted to prove to herself that she could do this. No matter how good her reasons for wanting to stay safely inside the circus life, those reasons were now a road block that kept her from reaching her next destination.

The door opened and Jolie turned in her seat to look at the man walking in.

"Miss Bohannon, I'm Matt Carmichael. There's a man in the lobby asking for you. He didn't give his name but he said that you would know who he is."

"I know who he is," Jolie said. She didn't need to look and see who it was, but stood and offered a hand to the loan officer in his pigeon-grey suit and overly starched white button-down. "He can wait where he is." She shook his hand and then pointedly closed the door and returned to her seat. Let him watch her, the big jerky know-it-all. "I'm not entirely certain what the meeting is for. I've never applied for any sort of loan before, but with the amount of information about loans and the whole process online, I just wanted to talk to someone face to face. Thank you for agreeing to see me on such short notice."

"You're welcome…"

Before he could continue the door swung open and Reece marched in. "I need to speak with Miss Bohannon for a moment."

"Sir, I really must ask that you wait in the lobby."

"It's okay," Jolie said, sighing and standing. "We'll be quick, Mr. Carmichael. Sorry about this."

He was remarkably okay with the situation, and closed the door behind him when he left.

Reece waited until the man was across the lobby, well

out of earshot, before he said, "You're going to get in over your head if you get a loan and try to do everything at once. I know you're angry but everything I said yesterday is still valid. You need to figure out if you have a market before—"

"Do you think this is my first stop of the day?" Jolie kept her voice low, not wanting to get into another shouting match with Reece in public, especially at the place where she hoped to get money to finance the operation Reece was trying to shut down. Him rousing her to make an ass of herself in front of everyone would be a great way to set her up to wreck everything herself.

"I've been to the elementary school, the middle school and the high school this morning. I have phone numbers for different athletics teachers and coaches, I have been to the little dance academy and spoken with the owner about putting up advertising on her bulletin board and whether she'd support having me speak to a couple of her classes to get a feel for things."

She looked out the door, caught Carmichael watching her, and the look he gave asked if she wanted to be rescued. Funny that the suit could be her safety net. A quick shake of her head had Reece turning to look at Carmichael too. His look was much less friendly, she expected.

"You did all that today?"

"Not that I have to justify myself to you, because we both know you're not going to support my decision and you're not going to work with me." Jolie tried to affect a cool tone. She was getting a teensy bit better at dealing with the emotional onslaught, but she could really stand to be totally better at it by now. "Your only purpose here is sabotage. So consider me onto you."

Reece shook his head. "Think whatever you like, I'm trying to protect you."

"I haven't had your protection for the past ten years, and I don't need it now," Jolie reminded him, just in case he'd forgotten she was harboring a grudge and had a damned good reason to do so.

"You just don't want to admit it. If you wanted to claim normalcy, you wouldn't be so stressed about being in public. But have you seen yourself? You only uncross your arms when you have to, and then right back they go. You're trying to do too much too fast."

"Only when you're around," Jolie said, but whether it was true or not she really didn't know. She uncrossed her arms. "Just go. I have a meeting to attend. Though if you want me to think you're on my side, you could tell me what the bid you had for the equipment was. You know, since I should know what I'm getting into financially."

He answered without a second's hesitation. "Just over two million for everything. Both of the big tops, the climate control, the seating, all the sleeper cars the crew live in, the trailers the performers don't own, the actual—"

"So much," Jolie muttered, her astonishment wiping out her anger in a flash. She'd thought she'd been thorough in thinking through the details of starting the camp, in considering the money she'd need... And she had for the rigging and the seats, but the climate control hadn't occurred to her. The sleeper rails weren't necessary for them because this year she only wanted a day camp, but if they went to a sleep-away camp later, there would have to be some kind of facilities for sleeping. Her idea of details and the actual details? Not exactly the same.

He looked smug, and considering how clueless she might actually be, Jolie couldn't blame him for looking smug. But was that all she saw on his features? No. No, he looked greedy too. Two million dollars was a lot of money. "That's the real reason, isn't it? You talk a good game about the difficulty of travelling circuses in this day and age, about the danger to the people you supposedly care about, but at the end of the day you're looking for a fat paycheck."

"Stop it." Reece reached over and grabbed her elbow, giving it a shake. "You know me better than that."

When had she crossed her arms again? "No, I don't. I thought I knew you, but I've had ten years to come to grips with the fact that I never really did. And I'm so stupid… I let flirting, old memories, and *hormones* make me forget that basic truth about you. It's all about Reece. Everything is about you."

Such an idiot. Didn't she ever learn? He may have been Reece when he'd left, but he was Dr. Keightly now.

Reece had to work to keep the frustration from his voice. What did he have to do to make her willing to give him the benefit of the doubt? Even as he asked himself the question, he knew the answer: he had to say yes to the damned camp. So he'd just have to keep dealing with her issues until she gave up, because the camp couldn't happen.

"No matter how badly I behaved in the past, I'm here now. I want to absolve myself by doing what is best by everyone. I'm not your enemy." He let go of her elbow and stepped to the door. Making sure his voice was low, he added, "How many people have been injured in training? More than in the performances. Training is the most dangerous time. When did your shoulder get dislocated? Training, right?"

"No, Reece. Not during training. You don't remember, do you?"

He had been around when it had happened? Reece scoured his memory. She'd fallen a few times, but never to any great harm. "When?"

"Never mind," she muttered, nodding toward the door. "Just go back to work or something."

Through the glass, he could see the suit approaching. He'd said what he'd come to say. She'd either listen or she wouldn't. Time to go. "We'll talk more about this later." He stepped out into the lobby.

Jolie called after him in tones anyone who didn't know her would think were sweet, "Thank you for letting me know, Dr. Keightly." Reece knew better. That was the Jolie equivalent of *Screw you, Reece*.

He passed the loan officer, who stepped back into his office, and for a second he considered throwing Jolie over his shoulder again and dragging her out of the bank. But he couldn't do that, not without it affecting his new practice across the street. "Don't sign anything, Jolivetta!" he yelled instead, even if he knew she probably would.

"Are you all right?" the bank official asked Jolie as he stepped inside.

Reece stopped and looked back, half expecting Jolie to say something about how unreasonable he was.

"I'm fine. I'd still like to speak with you about the loan, though the amount has gone down significantly." The door swung shut, keeping him from hearing anything else, so Reece continued out of the bank.

That could have gone much better…

Glad he'd taken a late lunch, Reece came back into Richards's practice, soon to be his practice, and let himself into the administrative area.

All the gray suddenly bothered him. His head hurt.

Tension headache, and he didn't need medical school to diagnose that one with how tight his forehead had stayed bunched since the fight with Jolie.

That had been in color. Not like these gray walls. Pale gray floor. Darker gray baseboards and furnishings. He was losing his damned mind—a color bothered him this much?

Finding the door to Richards's office standing open and the room empty, Reece walked in and closed the door. Thank God. He just needed to sit and close his eyes for a few minutes. Close out the monochrome.

More gray. The same thing happened at his apartment, just with a different color. Beige. Beige, beige, beige.

But the farm had color. Green fields and trees. Red and white barns. Pale yellow farmhouses. Blue Keightly logo everywhere.

Red hair. Pink clothes. Jolie.

He had to find some kind of alternative to her camp idea. With the farm being Bohannon property, he couldn't throw her off and tell her to go and find a job.

He could bring her into the office as some kind of office worker maybe. Somewhere he could monitor her, help her if she started to freak out. A couple of hours a week, just to get her used to it.

Except she would be angry with him for even suggesting it. Probably bring Gordy into the office just to prove a point to him. He rubbed at the tension between his brows.

She'd looked nervous at the bank, but most people who were going to talk loans looked nervous. It was just across the street from the practice, he still had some time. He could go back and see how she was handling it. But dropping in once had been enough, considering how that had gone. She might try and beat him to death with a check-book if he showed up again.

If she was going to go ahead with the camp without him, God only knew how far in over her head she'd get. Not that she wasn't smart, but she had the kind of creative mind that tilted when presented with math and schedules. He was sure she could handle the simple accounting of taking tuition and setting up paychecks for the performers—all she had to do was get the forms on that from his mother—but the overheads would never occur to her. The light bill, water bill, the cost per day for lunches and snacks. Insurance. Inspectors.

He closed the door and dropped onto the couch. The judgy pillow he hated—the one with the eye-searing embroidered flowers and travel advice about the road to hell—rested at the far end of the couch, setting his teeth on edge. He wouldn't let a piece of gaudy fabric change his plans. Taking care of everyone wasn't about having good intentions. It was his responsibility.

The practice was also his responsibility.

When he'd told her he didn't have time, it hadn't been entirely true. He'd considered the amount of time he would be spending to set up a new practice, but the deal with Richards took away a great deal of that. Sure, he had the patients themselves, but he didn't have to worry about all the other stuff it took to set up a brand-new practice. Or deal with the time and money issues that came while establishing a patient base.

He could help her run a camp if he wanted to.

He just wasn't sure he wanted to.

Teaching would be less dangerous for her on a daily basis for her. And with the amount of safety gear available, it could be reasonably safe for the kids. Some things. Not the trapeze though.

A knock on the door roused him from his chair in the dark.

Richards was back. Patients to see.

Time to stop sitting in the dark and do what *he* had been put on this earth for. He couldn't control her any more than he could control Fate. All he could do was try to steer her in the right direction. That would be easier if she trusted him at least a little.

"Dr. Reece Keightly." Reece introduced himself, extending his hand to the first patient in the office the following Wednesday morning. "Dr. Richards is ill today. Have you been informed about my buying the practice, Mrs. Nolan?"

The woman, who looked every ounce the perky soccer mom, shook his hand and smiled. "I have. Nice to meet you. You're one of the circus people, aren't you?"

That had never happened to Reece before he'd decided to settle here. In Nashville, where he'd gone to school, no one had known he was "one of the circus people." "Yes, ma'am. My family have owned Keightly Circus since the early 1800s."

"So you're the one that closed it?"

He hadn't expected that either. "I am." He hooked the stool from below the counter and sat, facing his new patient. "What am I seeing you for today?"

"I actually came because you're here. My daughter Briona? She's thirteen and such a talented gymnast, but two weeks ago her coach told her our Olympic ambitions were a pipe dream. Said that no matter how hard she practices, she's not capable of that level of performance. And she's just crushed. Doesn't want to train any more, even though she loves it. I've just been beside myself, trying to figure out how to help her get through this, and my sister told me there was going to be a circus camp this year on that horse farm outside town. I know how people will be interested, and that space will be limited…but since you're going to be our doctor now, I thought…"

It took him a minute to recover from his surprise. "Actually, it's not certain that there will be a camp yet, Mrs. Nolan. It's not going to be run by the Keightly family, if it even comes to fruition. Jolie Bohannon, whose family traveled with the Keightly Circus for generations, has been researching whether or not it's viable for the area and it's… she's not certain at all that it's going to happen yet." He looked at the chart, noticed that the nurse had taken vitals and left the reason for the visit blank. "So you don't actually need to be seen for anything related to your health?"

"Well, no. Not today. I'm in good health. We're all in good health, except for how sad my daughter is about her Olympic dream." The Gymnast Mom, not Soccer Mom, smiled at him. "But could you give me contact information for Miss Bohannon? I'd really like to speak with her. Maybe I can help her arrange the camp, if that's part of what is making her hesitate on the decision. I'm a party planner, but I think those same skills could be useful in… It's not going to be an equestrian camp, right? It's a circus camp. Like with juggling and tumbling and maybe trapeze?"

Everyone loved the trapeze. Except him these past ten years.

"You give me your information and I'll pass it to her," Reece cut in, really not having expected this for his first patient flying solo. "And where did you hear about this again?"

"My sister runs the gymnastics studio. That's where

Briona, my daughter, got started in gymnastics. Then she moved on pretty quickly when it became clear she could use a private coach. I just want her to have something else to be excited about, and see other possibilities. The performers for circuses are on those TV talent shows, and in Vegas, and all sorts of places. She'd really like—"

Reece waved his hand, smiling at her to hide his irritation. "I'm sure she would enjoy a circus school, but you should know it is dangerous, especially the trapeze. If I were Jolie, I wouldn't offer trapeze at all the first year. That's the major barrier to the camp now, trying to decide how much could be done safely for all children who might want to come, not just those who could be Olympians."

"Oh, I'm sure that can be worked out. Gymnastics is dangerous too, but you just have to try and do it the safest way possible. And I did some research online. There aren't any in the South, but there are a couple of circus schools in New England and on the west coast. And they all look really wonderful."

Nodding, he stood and held out his hand. "I'll pass on your interest, Mrs. Nolan. Just leave your contact information with the receptionist, and I'll move along to the next patient. Wouldn't want to get behind and have Dr. Richards think the new guy can't cut it."

She laughed and stood, shaking his hand longer than he'd actually have liked.

The ghost of Keightly Circus was haunting his practice. Great. He'd thought it was possible that people in the area would put the name association together, but he hadn't expected them to seek him out when this was Jolie's project. It had also never occurred to him to check out what the other circus schools or camps—if there even were any camps—offered.

On Thursday, he was asked about the camp by three more patients.

Friday, his receptionist fielded calls all damned day. They all wanted to know two things. When did it start? How much did it cost?

Richards officially bowed out on Friday. He made himself available by phone in the case of emergency for the following week, but the practice was now Reece's.

He had to talk to Jolie before the practice became her answering service.

"We're going to have a helluva time keeping the kids off the trapeze at night," Granny said, watching the many cousins working to erect the rigging overhead.

"I thought you had them under lock and key when it got dark," Jolie said, kicking back and propping her feet on the raised edge of the ring. Paperwork surrounded her—loan papers, licensing papers, insurance papers, examples of curricula from the few other schools and camps around the country, and an article she'd printed about the ins and outs of starting a summer camp—all stacked in piles of hand-cramping and head-exploding glory.

Choking up the grip on her ink pen, she bent over the clipboard on her lap, writing yet more letters on blank lines and filling in tiny boxes. The paperwork was going to break her.

"The side of the lock that needs a key is on the outside, not the inside," Granny muttered. "And the biggest rascal is Anthony. He's a Bohannon now, and we love him, but that boy has been a little wild since Mack and Ginny went off on their honeymoon."

A tingle at the back of her head had Jolie first lifting her hand to check that a bug wasn't crawling on her neck.

No bug. A ponytail pretending to be a rat's nest, half out of the band and tangled, but no bug.

She looked up.

"Reece," Jolie breathed, surprised to see him there.

"No, Reece didn't do anything." Granny shook her head. "But maybe we should have him talk to Anthony. They're brothers now."

"Afternoon, Granny." Reece stepped around the edge of the aisle and walked up, kissing Granny on the cheek. "I'll talk to Anthony. We're getting to know one another, and I'm happy to lend a hand." He looked at all the paperwork and then back at Jolie. "What's all this?"

"Well, I'm gonna leave you two to your damned fight," Granny announced, just before shuffling off. "Got to get dinner on the table, get all these kids fed." Anyone under fifty was a kid to Granny.

"I'll come and help when I get done with Reece," Jolie called after her, her eyes on Reece, who now had his eyes on the rigging installation currently going on. "They're all using safety gear, and always do. Just in case you're worried."

"I'll count on seeing you when you're done. Knowing you two, that should be some time in October..." Granny shook her head and headed away before she really interrupted.

"I'm not worried," he murmured, and then sat down, eyes fixed on the paperwork again, prompting Jolie to answer.

"Loan papers and license papers and other papers." Spreadsheets. Advice from the principals of each school she'd visited. Lots and lots of papers. "We decided that since no one had come to haul off the equipment yet, and no one had told us to take the big top down, we were going to set it all up for inspectors."

"For the camp?" Reece took a seat on the edge of the ring, his voice too calm to be comforting.

"Yes. Everything needs to be inspected before the insurance people can provide good estimates." Was this the kind of calm that preceded an epic eruption? After their big fight the other night, she'd spent about as much time wanting to see him as not wanting to see him. More proof that Reece made her stupid.

"I see. When are the inspectors coming?"

"Tomorrow."

"On a Sunday? Guess I'll be sticking around, then." He picked up a pile of papers and moved them one row down, where more papers awaited her, and took a seat at Jolie's side when a space was made. "I'd like to be here for it."

Heat. The man radiated heat, which made the way the arm nearest him react so weirdly. Goose-bumps rose. Jolie casually wrapped a hand over her arm and rubbed it. Maybe he wouldn't notice. "Why?"

"I have a compromise to offer." He looked down at her arm, but didn't comment.

"I didn't think your expansive doctor vocabulary included that word."

"There you go, doubting my mastery of the English language again." He smiled and Jolie felt herself laughing a little in return.

"Thrill me. Or prove that you don't actually know what that word means. I'm still open to that being the outcome of this conversation, regardless of what you might dub compromise."

"One year. Trial period." He said the words slowly and

then put his arm around her shoulders, sliding her the last remaining inches toward him. "Better?"

Definitely better. And worse. "Better how?"

"You're cold."

"Oh." Jolie nodded, mustering a smile in return to cover the lie. She wasn't exactly cold, but her body would probably just love to react more when pressed against his gloriously muscled torso. "Go on, you sound like you have other qualifications."

He nodded, and with the thoughtful way he looked at her, the way he looked at her mouth, she almost lost the thread of the conversation with the urge that came to kiss him. Memories of his mouth on her flesh, of giving her pleasure over to him and the promise he'd kept and those words that still sent chills through her: *I'll never break another promise to you.* She so wanted to believe him.

She moistened her lips, quite willing to throw the paperwork down and kiss him breathless, right there in front of everyone. Dumb. Dumb, dumb, dumb.

"Qualifications," Reece said, clearing his throat, breaking the connection as he looked back up at the rigging being installed. "You're going to be doing most of the work but I want veto power."

He could switch it off. That must mean that most people could switch this kind of thing off. Probably how he'd kept his cool with her and Mr. Happy. Unfortunately, Jolie's emotions still ran wild in his presence. She dug her fingernails into her thigh, a sharp sensation to override the firm heat and heady male scent wrapping around her. Kind of worked. Sort of. She managed to repeat some words back. "Veto power on what?"

"Curriculum. Number of kids you'll take on the first summer. Length of term. And I want all physicals to go through my practice." He unwrapped his arm and scooted a couple inches away, enough room to put his arm between them and gesture upward. "You're setting up the trapeze rigging and net, so you obviously intend on having an aerial component. I want to be the one who does the physicals to determine fitness level for the more advanced—"

Him breaking contact did wonders to clear her head. Terms. She should think about terms. "Wait. So your idea of the compromise is that with your limitations, I get what? To buy the equipment from you? Use the name? What?"

"You have a knot in your hair."

"I know..." she muttered, frowning at his change of direction. Knowing Reece, if she didn't fix it, he'd start trying to get the band out and that would mean touching again. She needed to be able to think. Jolie reached up to start working on the lopsided curly mass. "Go on."

"You get everything. The big tops. The equipment. The mess tent. The safety gear. The name. Costumes. Lady Calliope. Everything."

Everything? Even the calliope? She managed to drag the band from her hair and dragged the locks over her shoulder to begin combing the tangles out with her fingers, and turned so she could see his face better. "Why?" He was hiding something, Jolie just couldn't figure out what.

"For starters, my practice has turned into an answering service for 'When is the circus camp opening?' calls." Reece watched her working on her hair, pensive frown in place, words slow, the fingers of his right hand unconsciously moving, sliding against one another, and she realized he wasn't lying so much as distracted. By her hair. "Second, if you're going to do it, I want a hand in it."

Jolie got most of the auburn riot under control and stopped touching it, returning him the favor of helping clear his mind…in theory. "You said you didn't. You said you didn't want the responsibility." She tossed the lot back over her shoulder, helping more.

He looked back at the installation, allowing her to study his profile. Still thoughtful. "I'll feel responsible no matter what. Even if you go in entirely the opposite direction. Because it is my decision to close Keightly down that made you make alternative plans. But if you use my equipment, at least you can't have too much of a fit if I make demands and set an uncompromising safety standard."

"I never would have had a fit about that, Reece. I'm not sure when you think I turned into a diva…"

"Divas perform. You don't. So you can't be a diva."

"Why does that bother you so much?" Like a dog with a bone…

CHAPTER EIGHT

"WHY DON'T YOU PERFORM?"

"I told you. I just don't want to any more."

He shook his head, going silent as he watched the Bohannons zip-lining back down to the ground, the last of the rigging in place.

"I figured I wouldn't see you again until the buyers came to take everything away. That's kind of your thing. Show up after being gone, upset plans…"

"I'm not going anywhere." Reece looked fleetingly frustrated, but turned away from her before she could figure out what had caused it. "I told you. The practice is fully mine now—"

"You say that, but you do disappear after every bump? Though this time it's only been a few days. I suppose that's improvement."

"I've been working. You haven't come to my apartment ever, so don't make it sound like I'm the only one who can make the offer."

Okay, so he had a point there. "I guess I didn't know I could. Or I never considered it because when you go, you're gone in my mind." She frowned, feeling a twinge of guilt. "Do you want me to come visit your apartment?"

"Honestly, Jo, I don't know."

Over the past month she'd done more soul searching

than she was comfortable with. But recognizing problems didn't mean she knew how to fix them. She'd just started to embrace the idea that maybe she should tell him the realizations. At least then maybe she wouldn't come off as a crazy person. Not everything. She could seem messed up—there probably wasn't any way to avoid that anyhow, but she would like to draw the line before she got certifiable or psycho.

"The whole thing…after the wedding? That freaked you out, right? That's why you don't know whether you want me around, or is it just not wanting to get too tangled up with me? You don't have to say you'll partner with me over the camp as a way to keep anything relationshippy from happening. I told you before, I can take care of my own—"

"No!" he shouted, cutting her off. "Don't say that again." He stood up, rubbing his upper lip in that way that shouted discomfort louder than his shouty voice did. "That's not the reason."

"Fine!" Okay, so she made him feel uncomfortable. That whole business in her trailer had been his idea, or maybe it had been hers? Whatever—it had made him feel uncomfortable. What was she supposed to do with that? Ignore it? That's how she had worked before she'd become the Most Emo Chick in Circusville. She missed that skill, her calm. Her missing serenity…

As he didn't want to talk about it, she put it aside and asked, "Do you want to put the camp stuff in a contract? I know you like to be official and you're putting off a big sale in order to give us a shot at this."

"Not within the company," Reece said. He exhaled roughly, and held out a hand to her. Handshakes still meant something to him at least. Jolie looked at it and then at his face. Business arrangement. Leave all that bad sex and good sex and all the past and everything else out of it. Just focus on the deal and the future, which would be a business arrangement. Not a sexy business arrangement. She'd file all that under "Weddings Make Her Dumber".

She put her hand into his to shake, but she didn't shake it yet. "Say you promise not to sabotage things." And it wasn't underhanded for her to test how serious he was with the promise.

"I don't sabotage things."

She lifted a brow. "Don't even imply that you're direct all the time."

He caught her meaning because he frowned. "Fine. I promise not to sabotage things."

His promises shouldn't mean so much, not with their history, but if he really meant to never break a promise to her... Her heart squeezed and she gave his hand the fastest shake in the world then pulled away to start gathering up her paperwork. "I'll work on getting you figures and if you want to be here for the inspection tomorrow, you will need to just hang out because I don't know exactly when he's arriving. In the afternoon some time. Also, don't forget about talking to Anthony. I think he's got a girlfriend in town. He's on the phone or the computer all hours of the night. Worrying Granny to death. Generally being fifteen."

"You're not happy that I changed my mind?"

"Of course I am. We can do it the right way now, keep the name, and be everything the community would like us to be. Have the iconic tent."

If she looked at him, she'd say the wrong thing. Like admit that whole week after the wedding she'd been thinking about throwing her rules about men out the window and giving him a chance to redeem himself in a full-contact way that involved no toys... And then he'd gone again and she'd decided that he was a massive jerk and she didn't want to do anything with him. But now he was here, and she wanted to again, but not if he was going to keep looking like he couldn't get away from her fast enough.

"I don't believe you."

"That's okay. We're business associates now. It's not your business to see to my happiness. Just a partnership for the camp."

She felt his hand on her chin before she saw him moving closer.

"I'm not shunning you or anything. I'm just trying to be a good guy. Make the right decisions for the right reasons, which usually comes easier to me."

"I don't know what that means." Jolie sighed, wrapping her hand over his in the hope of steering his grip away from her chin.

"Means I'm avoiding certain subjects because that's not coming easily to me with you."

Right. She pushed his hand away, tired of this suddenly. "I don't know what that means either."

Reece leaned down, not letting her get far. The kiss he claimed was slow, hot and full of want. "Means I want you, and I know it's a bad idea. But I'm having a damned hard time caring about whether it's good or bad." He didn't lean back, staying so close that she could feel his lips brush lightly against hers as he spoke, and the scent of his aftershave enveloped her.

"Why is it a bad idea?" Glad she had not yet picked up her sheaf of papers, she let her fingers find his shirt and curl into the material at the waist. "Because you're thinking of running off and becoming a lawyer or something now that you've got the doctor thing done?"

He kissed her again then straightened back up, but kept

his arms around her waist, his voice as gentle as if he were talking to a skittish horse. "I'm not the one who's going to be leaving, honey."

"I'm certainly not going to be leaving." Jolie blurted the words out and then sorted through his implication. "Are you back on that performing thing again?"

"I found you working on an act, but you don't perform. With this camp? You're going to have to. And when this summer is over, you're going to remember how much you love it, and you're going to want to go back on the road with a new circus."

So rational, like a flowchart. She knew doctors would like charts.

"So your big plan to get rid of me is…say yes to the circus camp, so that at the end of a trial season I'll be bored with it. It doesn't matter whether it's a success or not, you think I'm just going to do all this work to build something and then leave because I want to wear Spandex and walk on a wire."

When she put it like that, it did sound kind of like an ass move. Reece shrugged, unfolding his arms so he could rest his hands on her hips, the better to keep her from getting away from him. "I'm not going to lie and say I like it, but I know how miserable you'd be at a desk job."

Jolie reached up and pushed her hair back from her face. "This is not a desk job." A breeze in the nearly empty tent caught at the curls and ruffled them, so they shined like bright copper where the light reflected. He kept his hands on her hips to keep from putting them in her hair.

"You know, maybe you should give me these little snippets of what's going on inside your head more often." Her angry voice alerted him to the depth of the problem. He looked back at her face. "They make me less inclined to think that I'm the problem, because I tend to do that, you know—blame myself. I always think I'm the problem. But when you think I'm a problem, it just makes me mad."

"I don't think you're a problem." Reece hooked a finger in her a belt loop on her jeans as she twirled out of his grasp and dragged her back to him until her back was to his front and he could get his arms around her waist and hold her still. "I think you have a problem. A problem I contributed to when I left. Maybe a problem I caused. If you're missing out on what you want to do because of me… God, Jolie. You need to move on from that. You need to move on from this. Performing is a young business, but you're still young enough to do it. But time won't stand still forever. In ten years…"

"I don't want to move on from this. I don't think this is something bad that needs moving on from. How else can I possibly get that through to you? And how can you continually degrade me for my fear of the outside world, use it as a reason to say no to the camp, and then encourage me to continue the lifestyle that you believe I've just been trying to use to hide from the rest of the world?" She shoved at his forearms and Reece let go, starting to feel a little of her anger himself.

He sat back down, ready to let her get away if she was so determined to flee. "I don't degrade you. I'm just trying to make you think about your future. And you have this huge stumbling block, blinders that don't let you see there is a whole world of opportunity out there for you."

Grabbing the papers, she began stacking them in crisscross fashion, more orderly than he'd have expected from her.

"You can't have it both ways. Either this camp is in

the life, or it's not. If it is, why do I need to go anywhere else? If it isn't, why should you want me to go somewhere else?" She shook her head, straightening and looking him dead in the eye, hurt evident in hers. "Everything I need is here. I don't need to go anywhere else."

He was so tired of hurting her. "Why did you build a routine?"

"I'm just playing when I do that." The way she looked down confirmed that she was holding something back.

"You're not being honest with yourself. I want more for you."

"Still. About. You. You don't even see it. They always say that you fall for a man just like your father. Well, call me a cliché. That's exactly what I did."

He was also damned tired of her holding his going away to college over his head. "You have to forgive me for going to school at some point, Jolie."

Movement in the corner of his eye told him they were no longer alone, though he'd thought that everyone had finished with the rigging and left a while ago. But maybe the shouting had drawn someone back.

"I don't need to forgive you for going to school." She walked to the end of the row and down to the ground and back until she was in front of him, if much smaller now from his higher position. "I was upset when you left for a number of reasons. I was afraid something would happen to you out there. That someone would hurt you. That you'd be alone and no one would be there to help you. The fact that I missed you—that I was afraid you would forget me—was secondary. I was terrified *for you*. But I never begrudged you your education."

More tears in her eyes, and the high color on her cheeks matched the high way she held her head. Reece didn't know what to say. Confessing how much he'd missed her would only make her angrier, so he said nothing.

"For the record, I'm proud of what you've accomplished. Everyone here is proud of you for that. Proud enough that I keep forgetting that despite the fact that you want to be the good guy, as you put it, you still cut us out of your life without any warning. You never looked back, and I definitely feel a grudge about that. That was your choice, and you're back here now, wanting to be the good guy? Well, *you'll* have to forgive *me* if I expect you to be the one who leaves. Again. As soon as you can."

"You're right. I did all that. Nothing I can say will change it."

She reached up and swiped her eyes then started walking again. He watched until she rounded the bleachers and walked out of sight.

A couple of seconds later he saw movement again and looked up.

Anthony.

"So, we're brothers now, right?"

Reece nodded. "We're brothers now."

Anthony took the bleachers at a quick climb and sat at a manly distance from him. "I heard you guys fighting. You okay?"

"Not sure what I am. Aside from an ass." And not sure he should be the one getting comforted by the kid who needed a big brother to lean on, not the other way around.

"She was crying." And Anthony had been torn between which one of them to comfort. Reece would probably have chosen to stay away from the weeping woman too.

"I've probably made her cry more than anyone in the

world." He leaned his elbows on his knees. "Even her ass-hole father."

"I don't know which one her dad is. Hard to keep track of them all, just a sea of red hair."

Reece grinned at the teenager, fleeting though it was. It was hard to hold a grin right now. "Her dad wasn't a Bohannon. Her mom is Mack's sister. Seven brothers, one sister that generation. Jolie's dad wasn't born in the life. He tried it, married into the family, but it didn't go very well. Hard on people to suddenly start living on the road."

"So he left?"

"He…" Reece started to explain and then paused, uncertain how much weight his words carried and whether he should share. But Anthony was family now. Thanks to Mom marrying into the Bohannons, there was now an actual link to the Bohannons that went deeper than simply decades of tradition and traveling together. Besides that, everyone knew the story. Not like it was a secret that could ever be kept…so even though he might not want to be the one telling the story, he did want Anthony to open up to him. He should lead by example. "Her dad left when she was five. But he didn't just leave. He took her with him."

"Like kidnapping?"

"Yeah." Reece tried not to picture the broken little girl who'd been brought back home. "Got all the way from Florida to Chicago before he decided he didn't want her. So he gave her a note with contact information for the farm, dumped her in front of a police station, told her to go inside, and left her there so he wouldn't get arrested."

Anthony looked back in the direction Jolie had left. He'd been with the family a couple of years. Jolie's oddities were probably beginning to make a lot of sense to him.

"What happened to her?"

"I don't know exactly. I know they had to fight to get her back. There's an assumption of something negative about the lives of circus families. If not abuse then at the very least dysfunction. I have never asked but, straddling both worlds now, I can speculate about what happened. Social workers, attorneys, questions about why her father stole his child from her mother only to abandon her far away? Very suspicious." Reece shrugged, dismayed at the lack of details he really had about such a big event in her life.

Anthony looked around the tent, and Reece couldn't read past the scowl the young man wore. Either he was just angry or he was really trying to work through what Reece had told him. "But wouldn't she have to look abused for them to think that?"

"She was a wild little thing before. Fearless. And clumsy. I've never seen a picture of her where she didn't have some kind of bruises or scrapes. Put it with the other questions…and they put her into a group home for a week or something, until it was sorted out. By the time we got her back…she was different."

Terrified all the time. Wouldn't let go of his hand, even when she'd had to go to the bathroom. Reece could remember standing with one arm in the bathroom stall and the rest of his body outside the door, giving her the most privacy he could because she wouldn't even let go of his hand to go to the bathroom. Just the one good hand, the other had been in that pink sling.

Oh, hell. That had been for her shoulder…not her arm.

"And then you left her too," Anthony filled in, pulling Reece's attention back with a simple statement that ate through his gut.

Reece nodded. And she'd been afraid someone would hurt him. He really was an asshole.

Anthony shook off the scowl on his face, leaned forward to punch Reece in the leg. "Tell her you're sorry, man."

"It's not that simple." Such a good-natured kid. Impossible not to like him. And if Reece ever doubted how much he'd missed his family, being presented with a kid brother intent on taking care of *him*...there was just no way he was leaving again.

"Sure it is. You're sorry." Anthony mustered a smile, shrugging. "Whatever reasons you had for what you did don't matter. You're sorry. Tell her. That's why she talks so much."

"What do you mean?"

"I don't know Jolie real well, but I watch people. She talks when she's confused, trying to work stuff out." He tapped the side of his head. "And she used to be a lot quieter. Actually, she used to be a lot calmer too. She's been riled up since you got back."

"You watch people, eh?"

"I'm going to be a writer, I pay attention."

"What are you going to write?" Reece asked.

"Deep stuff; it'll blow your mind."

Reece laughed finally and stood up. "I don't doubt it." Presented with a fist, Reece bumped his against it and tilted his head. "Granny won't save dinner if you're not there."

"She'll save food for me. I'm her favorite."

And Reece's favorite too, but he cupped the back of the kid's neck and gave him a light shove toward the exit. "Fine, she won't save me any. And if I'm going to talk to Jolie again, I'd better fortify myself."

And he was supposed to talk to the kid about...something. "Don't stay up so late on the phone with your girlfriend. You might be Granny's favorite, but she'll still chew you up in the foulest language you ever heard if you don't do what she says."

"I mind."

"Two words, man: Manure duty."

A sexy blues instrumental didn't go with the horrific bureaucratic forms in Jolie's lap. But what really could go with this kind of insanity? Funeral-home music maybe.

She switched to a new stack of papers, just for something else to look at. Tuition schedules. She'd based them on the idea of paying back loans. Now she wasn't sure how to do it—just change the destination of the monthly payment to Reece as a wage? It was his equipment, and even if he was going to endow the farm with the money, he should be the one to actually do with it what he would.

Talking to him was unavoidable.

Jolie didn't know what was worse—trying to make it through a single conversation with him without being overwhelmed by some emotion or another, or the hours of introspection afterwards when she relived—

A loud knock on the door rattled her trailer, startling her. She yelped and the very next second Reece had the door open and was standing on her entrance stairs.

"You cried out."

"You almost banged a hole in the door."

He came more fully inside, closed the door and stepped around her piles of paper to sit on the couch.

"Oh, come on in, Reece. Sure. Have a seat. Pay no attention…" Now where was she going to run away to? Maybe she should start talking about all the men she was going to sleep with now that he'd made Mr. Happy seem like Mr. Crappy, Lame and Boring…

"If I'd asked, you might have said no. And I'm here to apologize."

Apologize? She slowly lowered the pages to peer at him over the edge. "For what?"

"Everything."

"Everything?" Well, that cleared it right up.

He nodded, looking her in the eye and then shrugging. "I'm sorry."

Her stomach twisted and she crawled over the papers and onto the couch beside him, turned sideways to face him but stayed far enough away to avoid touching him. "Care to expand on what 'everything' means?"

"For hurting you."

"For not calling? Not writing? For disappearing for ten years?"

He kept eye contact, but the wince told her his apology didn't extend that far. "I had to cut off all contact with you."

Either he just didn't get it or he was trying to get out of actually admitting what had happened…and maybe what had driven him to it. "Why?"

"Because…I just had to." Definitely didn't want to admit anything.

"Were you in the witness protection program?"

He made another face. "No."

"A coma?"

"Jo…"

"Did you get abducted by aliens?"

"Jolie…"

"I know, you were a secret agent and—"

"You've made your point."

She shook her head. "Your turn."

"Nothing I can say will give you any kind of peace.

But that doesn't mean I'm not sorry. I want to make things right with you."

"You can't make things right with me without an explanation. If you just want to say you're sorry and have me forgive you...okay. I will stop bringing it up. I won't ask any more. I'll forgive you, and I'll try to forget. Maybe we can even be friends someday... But you can't make it right without telling me the truth. You can't leave this big hole and make it right, even if what you have to say hurts. I deserve an explanation."

"I would have quit school and come back the instant you asked me to," Reece muttered. "I didn't know any other way to stay in school than to just...try to forget you."

The words hurt, but they really shouldn't surprise her. She needed to hear them, she just couldn't look at him while he said them. "Did it work?"

"No."

That was something. Jolie slumped back against the arm of the couch as she listened, her hand going to the fringe of the throw draped across the back, something to play with, something to focus on, something to keep her calm as she listened.

"It wasn't my plan when I left. But before we even got to the campus...I knew I couldn't come back. If I didn't stay away, nothing would ever change. And then someone else would die because that's the nature of the business. And maybe some death would happen that I could have prevented if I'd stuck to my convictions...and I'd have borne more responsibility because I didn't know how to make everyone listen to me. Keightly became my responsibility the instant my father died, and he taught me to protect. But I was nineteen. I couldn't protect anyone."

The truth rang in his voice and reflected in the sadness in his eyes, and she knew how his father's death had hit him. She'd seen him change but hadn't known how to help him. It was the truth to him. He couldn't know she wouldn't have asked him to give up his schooling.

"What are you thinking?"

What was she thinking? "I don't know. Wishing I'd known, I guess. It took me a long time to give up on you." She abandoned the fringe and swiped her cheeks when she realized she'd started crying again. "By the time I accepted that you weren't coming back…I think I was numb. It didn't hurt that much then. I was calm. And I've been having a hard time getting my calm back since you got here. Really would like to get that back. When I'm happy, I'm happier. When I'm sad, I'm sadder. Like…everything is catching up. It's too much. I hate it." Of course her tissues were all the way on the other side of him. She took a wobbly breath and then crawled forward, leaning over him to cram her hand into the tissue box. "And now I'm out of tissues!"

Which just made her want to cry more.

"Stay here." He stopped her before she could lean back, turned her and when she sat across his thighs he wrapped his arms around her.

"I'm sorry. I keep crying, and I don't mean to. Is this a panic attack too?" She pressed her eyes against the side of his neck, her face hot all over.

"You don't have to be sorry." Reece stretched out as much as he could on the sofa, keeping her on top of him, her face hidden in his neck. His voice was gentle. "I think this is something else."

"I'm crazy."

"You're not crazy. Just let it happen. I'm not going anywhere."

More breaking rule number two. Too overwhelmed to

fight it, she relaxed against him and cried long past the point when she even knew what she was crying about, but he never wavered. Never tried to get out from under her.

"Your shirt's all wet." She lifted her head and looked at him. "Do you still want to be in business with a crazy chick?"

"You think this is news? I knew you were nuts the minute I saw your crazy hair. But do you feel better?"

She nodded and he kneaded the back of her head and tugged her forward to press his lips to her forehead.

"I forgive you even if you're an idiot."

He tilted his head until it was his forehead against hers. "Thank you."

"I'm going to get off you before I attack you. I do have one grudge left, but I think we've probably dug deep enough for one night, don't you?"

"What is it?"

She climbed off, fetched a paper towel from the kitchen and blew her nose. "You made Mr. Happy seem very lame."

He laughed as he rolled to his feet. "I'm trying very hard not to ever say those words, turn them into innuendo, or hit on you…"

"The runny nose is a real turn-off." She blew her nose again. "And the red puffy eyes."

"Not so much." He tilted his head toward the bedroom. "I could sleep, though. If you didn't mind me staying. I'd really like…"

"So you can be here for the inspectors?"

"No. I could stay at the RV and be here for the inspectors." He looked her in the eye and smiled. "You want more confessions? Okay, I just want to stay. You got up before I got done holding onto you."

A nod was all she could pull off. Sometimes words

meant too much. A nod didn't amount to promises. When morning came, she reminded herself, everything might look different.

No promises tonight. She didn't want him to fail any tests right now.

CHAPTER NINE

HEAT AT HER back and all around her, Jolie shifted in the bed, aware first of the heat and then the source of it. Reece, at her back, warm breath in her hair.

She grabbed the blanket that was over both of them and tossed it back behind him, as smoothly as she could to avoid waking him, leaving them both covered only in a sheet. She wanted a few minutes to enjoy his presence before things got hard again. They always seemed to get hard again when they each had so many issues bubbling beneath the surface.

The early morning sun hit the windows above their heads, making the pale yellow curtains glow gold. She shifted around in his arms, suddenly struck by an intense need to look at him.

His shoulder-length hair, always tied back from his face, was loose and a sandy lock draped across his forehead. Golden eyelashes fanned his cheeks, hiding those blue eyes she loved.

Carefully, she linked her fingers with his and scooted in until her forehead rested against the two days of beard scruff on his neck. His scent mingled with hers, and her bed became a strange and wonderful place. Full and safe.

She wanted this. She wanted him. For however long it lasted. If she prepared herself for the end before they got started, maybe it wouldn't be so bad when he left. He might stay until the end of the summer, seeing as that's when he was sure she was going to leave. Facing up to the fact that he was wrong might make him leave again.

That wasn't what she needed to think about this morning, it would only lead to dark places, and she had a warm, glowing bedroom and a golden man holding her. Not the time for dark places.

Jolie tilted her head and pressed her lips to his neck—a couple of slow, lingering kisses to encourage him to wake.

He smiled. She didn't see it, but she felt his jaw move against her temple and she leaned up to look at him.

"Morning," he said, stretching until his feet hung over the bottom edge of her bed.

Jolie grinned back and kissed his chin, then his cheek.

When he'd got that pesky stretching out of the way, Reece grabbed her and rolled onto his back so she rested atop him again. Her legs fell to either side of his hips, but that was all the rearranging she had time for. His hands moved to her hair and tugged her head down until their lips met. His tongue stroked hers and his arousal roared to life between her legs, but the cotton pajama shorts she slept in and his boxers kept any accidents at bay. Which meant she could practice moving against him, find out what made him moan.

The last time he'd been in her bed he'd turned her beliefs upside down and had taken no relief for himself. Now she wanted to see that kind of need in his eyes, to make him tremble and shake.

She wanted some kind of reassurance that she could be good enough for him. If he wanted her half as badly as she wanted him, that would be good enough for most people. It was a good starting place…

She knew how to move, the long sinuous rolls of her spine and her hips, until she rode the ridge of his erection through the cloth.

"Jo…" He groaned her name against her lips. "I don't have condoms."

She pulled back, and he relaxed his hold on her hair to let her, but only until she could look him in the eye. She smiled. "I got some the day after we played with Mr. Happy."

"Oh, thank God."

The relief in his voice made her smile. "I would have thought…"

"I've been trying to be the good guy."

"The good guy gets condoms."

"Temptation." He shook his head then rolled them again until she was beneath him. He rose to his knees, suddenly very interested in getting her clothes off.

No slow seduction.

Good. His need gave her confidence.

He dragged her shorts and panties down with one go. Jolie tugged the shirt over her head then reached for his boxers. "I'm tempted to make you stand up so I can properly see wha—"

His boxers were already down and her words died in her throat. "Good God, I'm throwing away Mr. Happy."

This time he laughed, then leaned into her again, pulling her legs around his hips as he claimed her mouth once more.

Reece lifted up enough to give himself a grand view of her beneath him. Her auburn curls spread across the yellow pillowcase, her milky skin and freckles, and the palest, pinkest, most pert…

"I want to be on top," Jolie panted, pulling his gaze back to her rapidly pinkening face.

"You haven't really done this before." No. Don't refer to the other time.

Her brows pinched and she reached up, rubbing her hands over his chest, making him inclined to do whatever she wanted. Because nothing had ever felt more right and it wasn't rocket science.

His inner caveman screamed that she'd been given to him. His father had given her to him to take care of. She was his. Always had been his. Always would be his. Jolie, his Jolie. He kissed her again.

"I was doing it right when we were clothed...wasn't I?" The question rumbled against his lips between kisses.

She wanted to be in control, which might be another test. And she might need reassurance. "You were perfect."

She'd accused him of being a control freak a couple of times, and then there was the method of their last tryst when he'd controlled the toy... It would be great if he could just act, stop second-guessing, but she was wrong—he wasn't a control freak. Reece grabbed her hips and rolled again. "Okay, if you change your mind..."

"I won't." She sat up and the gloriously slick heat ground against him. Every ounce of him wanted to flip her back over, take her, drive himself into her until she knew she belonged to him. Until he got his reason back. Until that hold she had over him was at least a little weaker...

But he'd always need to protect her. "Where are the condoms?"

She leaned to the side, fished around in the drawer, grabbed her toy and tossed it across the room, then found what she was looking for.

And if she wanted control of the condom, it would have

to wait for next time. Reece plucked it from her fingers, tore the foil and slid her down his thighs until he got the thing on.

Sitting up, he grabbed her and dragged her back to him, unable to abide all that air between them. He eased into her. All he had to do was last longer than a few seconds and he'd do better than the other time...but he wanted her shaking and moaning for him, not that damned toy.

After a few tentative, experimental shifts and grinds against him, she found a natural rhythm that made him sweat. Reece grabbed her hips, trying to hold onto some semblance of control. If he didn't...he'd disappoint her again.

"Don't... You liked it," Jolie gasped as he slowed her down. "I want you to like it...a lot."

"I do." He gritted his teeth, tugging her back down with him as he lay back in the bed.

Kissing could always distract her, and he thrust his tongue into her mouth, hands tangling in her hair again. Every rock of her hips got him a little closer to a poor showing. She deserved the best, this was practically her first time as he'd ruined the actual first time.

When he felt his orgasm building at a speed that left him in little doubt that if she kept moving another few seconds he'd be lost, Reece gave in to his need for her orgasm and flipped them again, pulling out before he got there.

The hurt look on her face knocked the wind out of him. "Why? Why did you do that?"

"Jo. I need to... I need... I need to make you come."

Jolie felt him shaking where he knelt between her legs. That and the tortured light in his eyes soothed her. This wasn't because he didn't want her. It was his control issues. Even telling her he needed anything was kind of a milestone.

She nodded, and he crawled back over her, his kiss gentling this time as he began a sensual onslaught that wiped out her ability to worry.

Only golden light today. No dark places.

Once all the details had been finalized and the nightmare days of form-filling were past, completing the actual physical needs for starting the camp were a breeze. If you counted out the conversation both Jolie and Reece were avoiding. An impending showdown over the trapeze.

First day today, and Reece was going to come for the day, but he hadn't stayed with her last night. The first night in the past couple weeks he hadn't. It had taken a while to get to the bedroom, but once they had, neither had been eager to leave it.

It was better for both of them and their fledgling relationship to try and work together in things.

He'd needed an evening to himself and she'd given it to him.

She needed to be reassured regularly that he wasn't going anywhere, and he gave that to her. Any time she got nervous, so, like…every day.

Reece needed to run the physicals for the kids with exacting demands and limits, and she knew why he needed it…so it was no hardship for her to help. Over two weekends leading up to the opening they'd held an open clinic for the campers and he'd put them through the wringer. Health checks. Endurance trials. Games designed to test speed and reaction times. A little over the top for the kids who were going to be working with choreography, costume and set design...but she hung in there.

Jolie finished getting dressed for opening day in a T-shirt identifying her as an instructor and the equipment she'd need for her tightrope class. Along with a few other miscellaneous bits and pieces she'd need for demonstrations with the older instructors and their classes.

During the past two weeks Reece had also started working with Anthony on the monkey bars, starting slowly with the basics of how to be a catcher—a position they both hoped Reece could eventually hand off to Anthony. He decidedly did not want to get on the trapeze. Jolie didn't think he was afraid so much as he had developed an intense loathing for flying after his father had died. And that was the talk they had been avoiding.

When they'd been working to get her into his family's troupe in their teens, it had taken Reece three months to learn to just catch her with any kind of consistency. Three months of leaping and falling before they'd found the rhythm, learned to time their swings and he could catch her eight times of ten. And when they'd begun throwing tricks, it had taken another several months before each one was better than it was worse.

Anthony would not be ready to catch until maybe the end of the season. Having him in the show planned for the end was a possibility, but the other aerialists needed to practice their tricks with someone who could catch them the rest of the time. She had to have that talk with Reece.

Later.

After no one died on their first day.

With breakfast done, and a full hour before the kids were due to start arriving, Jolie wandered into the big top and found Reece alone on a zip-line, hanging from the canopy as he inspected the rigging. Again. She really shouldn't be surprised by now. This was the third time she'd caught him inspecting the equipment. A socket wrench in hand, he methodically made his way around every part of the connection before him, and then carefully maneuvered himself further down.

Safety Man did not like risks of any kind. And while this was something Jolie could appreciate, she did not want him up there when the parents and kids started arriving. She grabbed one of the megaphones and—once he'd anchored himself again—lifted it to her mouth. "Reece Keightly, you had an inspector here. And now you're quadruple-checking to make sure it's good?"

He shot a thumbs-up at her.

"Twenty minutes and I'm coming up after you. You promised— no sabotaging the camp! Scaring the parents counts as sabotage."

"Almost done!" he bellowed back down.

Jolie sighed, put the bellowing apparatus down, and headed toward her class area. Most of the seating had been cleared out of the big top to make more room for the different classes to work in the tent at once. Having been a one-ring circus meant that they'd never shared space before.

Kicking off her shoes, she put on the soft-soled leather slippers Angela had made for her ages ago, and which the costuming maven had duplicated for her five students from impressions made during registration.

She limbered up and climbed onto the low wire with the rodless umbrella in hand she preferred for balance. And by the time she'd run the length of the wire a few times, Reece came strolling toward her.

Not knowing any other way to approach the question

on her mind, she blurted it out. "Anthony isn't going to be ready to catch when they are ready to start learning to fly."

"I know." He watched her. "Do that little hopping thing. Where you change your feet. What's that called?"

"I don't know terms. It's a ballet thing, but I couldn't keep the language in my head. I tried. Just…didn't work." And it looked more impressive than it actually was, one of the easier things she did. She gave the little hop he'd requested, back and forth a few times, and found him smiling at her when she stopped and took the second needed to restore her balance. "Good to see you smiling. Happens so infrequently in the tent."

He stepped over and took her free hand, and she made the little hop onto the mats. "Are you ready for this?"

"I'm excited. But we still need to talk about the trapeze."

"We don't need to talk about it. I know what I have to do. I promised to be a good…whatever I am, and I will do what is needed. But the sooner I can get Anthony up and running on it…"

She leaned up, wrapping an arm around his neck and urging him down. "Kiss me. Make it count because we can't be kissing when the kids are here." And they still had a few minutes before the Big Excitement began for her, and the Big Scary began for him.

Having made a promise to never break a promise to her gave Jolie a great big stick to hold over Reece's head. Especially as he'd also promised not to sabotage the camp. Had given his stamp of approval on the squad selected for the aerial act. And now he had to do what he absolutely did not want to do. Get on the trapeze.

He looked at a sea of faces, all forty children cleared to attend, that wanted to see the trapeze demonstration.

The ones selected for the aerial troupe had been practicing swinging out and letting go of the bar all week, since the opening, safety lines controlling their falls to the net. Reece was supposed to catch Jolie, that's what they hadn't seen. That's what he'd be doing for them until Anthony was ready. Which, naturally, meant he had even more responsibility on his shoulders should one of them get hurt.

While Jolie talked to the kids, explaining what he did to all the non-aerialists who'd just stayed late with their parents to watch, he hooked himself to the safety harness. He hadn't used one to climb the ladder since he'd started flying at eight, but teaching them the safest way possible was important. He hooked into the lines and climbed rapidly to the platform above. Practice swings at ground level had been set up for them to practice hanging, mats beneath and spotters. He'd even used one to make his body remember what the hell it was doing, but he needed a few minutes above ground to get used to everything again.

Just like riding a bike, and possibly just like falling off one.

He unhooked the safety lines and the swing, tuned out whatever was going on with the audience below and stepped off the platform.

Suspended from the bar by his hands, he pulled into the swing. It had been easier to achieve the biggest swing when he'd been fifty pounds lighter.

All he heard was the blood pounding in his ears. Jolie might not get dizzy any more, but he'd been grounded a while. It took effort to remember how to do everything he was supposed to do.

At the height of his swing—as high as he was willing to push it for demonstration—he flipped himself and hooked his legs on the bar. He was the catcher. He wouldn't be doing tricks, he wouldn't be dropping, unless it would hold two hundred but not three when he caught Jolie…and they fell into the net and he crushed her to death. Would blood look the same in sand as it had in the sawdust?

Closing his eyes, he let the swing take him.

It wasn't going to get better. He could do it, but the thrill was well and truly gone.

Reece opened his eyes, pulled up on the swing to a sitting position and gave Jolie the thumbs-up.

She repeated his procedure, wrapping a belt around her middle and hooking safety lines before she climbed to the platform. But she switched things up when she also hooked her megaphone to the belt and carried it aloft.

"So what we're going to do…" She began explaining the mechanics of a simple hand-off. Both hanging by their knees, clasping hands in the middle, and her letting go. The first thing Reece was willing to teach the kids.

He waited on the swing, which now only swung a little. He'd have to work to get it going again when the time came. She talked longer than he'd expected, long enough that the kids were getting antsy before she put the megaphone down and looked at him.

"Scared?" he mouthed at her, standing on the swing but not starting the swing until he was sure she wanted to do this.

She shook her head, unhooked the swing and held it with one hand while holding onto the platform supports with the other. "Ready."

Her pale face said she was lying. Right. Something to make her promise later…to tell him the damned truth even when she didn't want to admit to something. He frowned and looked down at the small audience. If it were anything but a knee hang, he'd call it off. But they were about the safest thing that could be done on the trapeze.

Soon his swing was at height and he lowered himself back to the bar. When he reached the right distance from his platform, he yelled, "Hep!" And she took off. When they met in the middle, she turned over to hook her knees on the bar. When he reached the platform, he did the same.

When they met in the middle again, he caught her wrists, she released the bar, and they swung free. She smiled, but there was no ease in her grin and none of the light that he had always seen when she performed. She really was struggling. "Okay?" he asked, and she nodded. They wouldn't get to talk again until he had caught her.

"Rusty," she assured him and then nodded. "Let go."

Reece hated this part. When they got to the middle, he had to force his hands to unlock and she fell to the net. Normally there would be a partner on the platform to swing out to her again, enabling her return to the platform, but they were a two-person show today. He stayed upside down, watching as she flattened out and bounced a couple of times in the center of the net.

Perfect. Safe. Everything was okay. He rose back up to a sitting position, letting the blood drain back out of his throbbing head.

She exited the net as she'd taught the children, hooked back into the safety and climbed back toward the platform. But by the time she got there she was a little rosier in the cheek. Enough to convince him that she was okay to go again.

As Reece stood and got the swing going again, she explained what they were going to do with the megaphone. And then she explained some more. At least three times she started to put the megaphone down, only to stop and add something unnecessary to her explanation. The third time she put it down she very nearly reached for it again, but changed her mind and reached for the swing hook instead, which she used to retrieve her swing.

They were definitely having a talk when this was over.

By the time she got the swing back, the hook stashed, and had given the lying nod that said she was ready, Reece had his swing high enough. At the height of the swing he slid back to the bar and on his mark called for her to go.

One each, swinging forward and back, and by the time they met in the middle, they were synchronized to catch the trick.

Reece reached, and Jolie let go of the bar, but she didn't reach for him until she'd already fallen out of his reach. His hands closed on air, his stomach lurched, and he watched her flatten and fall onto the net.

He pulled himself back above the bar before he threw up, and watched her exit the net and stop to say something to the kids before she repeated her procedure to get back up to the platform and get ready. She didn't look at him, just announced she was ready and waited.

Reece didn't start swinging until she looked at him.

"What's wrong?" No mouthing anything now, he yelled across to her, regardless of whether or not everyone would hear. This was her camp, she was the one who had insisted on an aerial component, and she had blown that catch.

"Nothing. Just rusty," she yelled back, scowling at him and adding a quick jerk of her head intended to get him moving again.

Reece took a couple of deep breaths, stood, and started the swing going again.

Once more she released the bar and Reece's hands made contact with her arms this time, sliding all the way down to the wrists, where they should lock, but before he could complete the action she jerked her arms free and fell once more to the net.

She'd rather fall than have him catch her?

Reece pulled back up and watched her bounce and then move off the net and march for the other end again. Not again. No.

Before she could get herself secured and climb, Reece swung to the middle of the net and hopped off the bar, letting himself fall into the net below.

He got down and headed for the kids. "Sorry, guys. We're done for the evening. Jolie's getting over a vertigo thing. She thought she was ready, and she wanted to do this for you guys, but her inner ear isn't co-operating." When he got many confused looks in return, he pointed to his ear and explained, "Squiggly bits deep inside your ear that control balance. We'll see you all Monday and the trick will be demonstrated before any of the kids go up on the bar."

Everyone was very understanding of that, except Jolie, who stood out of the way, yanking on the hand guards she wore to try and unbuckle the straps that held them in place. He left the group and walked up to her, his nausea almost a memory now that his feet were on the ground.

"What was that?" He took one of her hands and unfastened the buckles giving her fits.

"I don't know."

"You always say that when you don't want to admit something." He pulled the guard off and held his hand out for her other hand, which she placed in his. "So you can reach your hand into mine. Just maybe not when there's danger involved? Did you think I'd fling you off the net or something?"

CHAPTER TEN

JOLIE SHOOK HER HEAD. "I really don't know what happened."

"All you had to do was close your hands around my wrists." The guard came off in his hands, and she tried to pull her hand back, but his hand clamped down and held her in place.

"I know." Why hadn't she grabbed onto him? They were together now. In a relationship. Having mind-blowing sex, working together...practically living together, and she couldn't make herself reach for him. "I'm sorry."

Reece shook his head, and she noticed that he was pale. "Are you sick?"

"Yes. Yes, Jo. Not catching you? I almost hurled on your head. Twice. You did fine on the knee-hang. I don't get it."

"I don't know. I don't get it either."

"You need to think about it."

"I don't want to."

"Yes, I know, that is how you got through the past ten years, but you have to stop ignoring problems. If we're going to be together, if we're going to try and make this work, as we said we were going to, you have to find some way to trust me."

"I do trust you."

"No, honey, you don't trust me. If you trusted me, you

wouldn't have ripped your arms from my grasp and let yourself fall, instead of relying on me."

Jolie sucked in a breath. She wanted to argue with him, but what good would that do? She'd said she'd forgiven him, and she had…but maybe it would never matter how many promises he kept. Maybe she was too messed up to trust anyone.

"Is it me, or is it everyone?"

She looked up at his quietly spoken question and then stepped in to wrap her arms around his waist. "What do you mean?"

"Do you just not trust me, or do you not trust anyone?"

"I trust you. I do. You've been great. You didn't want to catch but you tried. And I know you've been working with Anthony since he wants to catch for the end of season show. You've been great." She laid her forehead against the center of his chest and mumbled, "I'm reaching now. See?" She shook her arms around his waist. He gave in to the hint and wrapped his arms around her.

"No camp stuff tomorrow. We're going out."

"I have things—"

"Hey…" He waited for her to look up at him and said, "You can do them on Sunday. Tomorrow we're going out."

"Like riding?"

"No. Like out into the world. Date. We're going out, you and me. Not on errands. Not to get groceries or go to the bank. We're going out. Dress casual, wear comfortable walking shoes." He leaned down and kissed her and, as always, she melted into him and her anxiety started to do the same. Before she could get lost in it, he lifted his head and put her back from him. "I'll pick you up at ten. Wear one of your camp shirts."

"You're not staying with me?"

"Not tonight."

He was mad. Which…she couldn't blame him for.

"Ten," he said again, then turned and headed out, leaving her to stare at the trapeze and, eventually, to clean up and shut everything down.

Going out into the world to spend time? Definitely a punishment for not reaching for him.

At least she didn't have to wear heels for it.

"Where are we going?"

Reece looked over at Jolie. That had been the third time she'd asked since he'd wrangled her into his SUV forty minutes ago.

"You say you trust me, but you can't take it that I won't tell you. It's a surprise." Reece shook his head. "If you were paying attention to the highway signs, instead of just sulking and staring at the blur, you'd have figured it out by now." Yesterday had been one of his buttons, but he'd got on the trapeze for her. She could go on a date with him in a public place for him.

"I don't like surprises. And I'm not sulking. I'm listing the reasons that everything is going to be okay." She crossed her arms and frowned but sat up a little straighter and focused immediately on the massive approaching sign. "The zoo?"

"The zoo."

"There will be a lot of people there."

"That's why I wanted you to wear your camp shirt." He looked at the matching Keightly Circus Camp T-shirt he was wearing. "So this is like a business outing too. Good for the camp. Lots of people will be here with their kids, and Keightly has been in the news a lot lately with the circus closing and now with the camp up and running. Have you been here before?"

"No," Jolie admitted, climbing out of the car and pausing to adjust everything, including the hang of her T-shirt so that it looked perfect.

When he offered his hand to her, she had to stop and wipe her hands on her shorts before she took it. Sweaty palms. But no panic attack yet. With the new information she'd given him about her out-of-control emotions since his return, he didn't know whether to expect another panic attack or not. Whether her anxiety at being out in the world would be increased in his presence or decreased, he had no idea.

"It'll be okay." He closed his hand around hers, and then thought better of it and linked their fingers. More secure hold. Maybe the little things would help her. "And you're going to like the zoo. Lots of animals... And we're going to go straight to the kids' area. I don't know what it's called. There's a petting zoo and other things there. So lots of kids. Lots of animals. You can pet a camel or... something else that doesn't bite."

Petting zoos, an idea Reece could get behind. They weeded out the dangerous animals.

She nodded but looked less convinced than he was, and stayed close as he walked them through the ticket booth to the park. Maybe his presence did help her.

It would be great if he could find some simple way to fix his problem with the trapeze.

For the first hour of their visit Jolie stuck to Reece like glue. They wandered through the petting zoo, they ventured out to the see the monkeys, and when she wanted to go back to the child area, he didn't put up a fuss or make her feel bad about it.

Camels, llamas and sheep, and Jolie liked the sheep best. Domesticated animals trumped exotic ones. They could be trained and didn't often eat their owners. But watching the kids with the animals was the best of all. Their glee was an easy emotion for her to identify with and wrap herself in.

And when her eyes skimmed over a little boy of about five, wandering alone with tears in his eyes, she knew that emotion too. Releasing Reece's hand for the first time since they'd arrived, she walked over to the little boy and touched his shoulder. "Are you looking for your mom?"

As soon as she asked the question he started to cry. Most kids outgrew her by the sixth grade, but she was still taller than a five-year-old, and if she'd learned anything from Reece and their fights it was the importance of minimizing your height when someone was already scared or upset.

She squatted, keeping eye contact, and spoke in her gentlest voice. Soon she had his name, the identity of who he'd been with, and at least a small measure of his confidence. She'd always liked kids. "Don't worry, Drew. We'll find your daddy."

He nodded, swiping his eyes with the back of his hand.

"Do you remember what color shirt your daddy was wearing?"

She felt Reece approaching, and the little boy suddenly taking her hand confirmed it. "It's okay. That's Reece. He's my friend. He'll help us find your dad. What color is his shirt?" she asked again, giving the boy's hand a jiggle until he connected with her gaze again.

"White."

Great. A man in a white shirt. That wouldn't help.

"Don't be scared. Everything is going to be okay." She

looked around, but seeing over the crowd was as hopeless for her as it was for the little boy. And Reece didn't know who he was looking for any more than she did.

Surely no one would abandon their kid at a zoo. That wouldn't happen. Who would pay the ticket price and walk through cameras and be on security footage when they abandoned their kid? No one. People who abandoned their children worked to retain anonymity. "He's got to be looking too. Do you see anyone looking?" she asked Reece.

Reece glanced around but shook his head and asked Drew, who still held Jolie's hand, "What's your dad's name?"

"Will you put him on your shoulders?" Jolie redirected.

"My shoulders?"

It took a dose of convincing for both Reece and Drew to agree to the maneuver, but soon Reece had Drew on his shoulders and standing. It took less than a minute before the worried father cut through the crowd and relieved Reece of his tow-headed shoulder-growth. After many thanks, Reece steered her to the cotton-candy stand and got her a fluffy pink treat.

A shaded bench nearby? Even better. She hurried to it and sat, then offered a pinch of the wispy spun sugar to Reece.

"You told me that I have to think about…emotions and things?"

"I asked you to think about them," Reece corrected, but popped the candy into his mouth.

She ignored the semantics and forced herself to look Reece in the eye. "That's what I feel like when I'm…in big public places like this."

"Like Drew?"

"Like I'm lost…or like whoever I'm with will leave me

there and I'll be by myself and I won't know what to do. Which sounds really stupid now that I say it out loud."

"Jolie, you had that happen. Well, you had worse. It's not stupid. It's wrong, but it's not stupid." He took another pinch of the cotton candy and held it to her mouth. She took it and while the fruity fuzz dissolved on her tongue he added, "You knew what to do to help Drew. Some outside-the-box thinking but it got the job done. I would probably have just taken him to the office and got the park people involved with finding his father. But, you know, what you did was better. You got Drew involved. He found his own dad. I doubt that he'll even remember this when he grows up. It's not going to leave a scar."

She got the implication. Drew wouldn't have a scar like hers. Referring to it directly felt like one of those things that would rouse emotions. Instead, she returned the favor and held a puff of the candy up to his mouth. He took it and then kissed her fingertips and looped his arm around her shoulders to pull her in close while the sugar dissolved.

"What other situations do you think might scare you? If I left you here and went home, what would you do?"

"Get a taxi, go home and kick you in the—"

He stopped her before she actually said the words by laying a hand over her mouth. "So you could handle that. What other situations do you get worried about in public places?" He slid his hand down to the side of her neck, where he could play with her hair and stroke her skin at the same time.

She lost the small amount of emotion that had come with her realization about her public fear, replaced by the warm, tingly feeling on her skin that came any time he played with her hair. "I...feel like I might not know what

I'm supposed to do, and I'll do something wrong. Get into trouble, or make everyone hate me."

"That one I understand. I had it the first couple of years at school. But after I figured out the right comeback for some dude getting in my face and calling me a 'circus freak,' it stopped having any power over me. Different doesn't mean bad. Different is just different." And in a quieter voice he asked, "What did you do that was wrong when you were in the home?"

He would have to put that together. "I...drank out of the garden hose. I didn't know any of the cartoons the other kids knew. I kept asking where their horses were, and where we were going next... Different to kids is bad. Not just to them. It was all different than what I understood, and that confused me and upset me. A lot."

"How did you get your shoulder dislocated?" he asked, his voice so deceptively quiet that she almost missed that he'd linked it with her group home ordeal...

"You remembered..."

"Pink sling," he confirmed with two words.

What could she say about that? She still didn't know why it had happened. "I guess I made Mrs. Barch mad."

"Mrs. Barch?"

"She ran the home. But hated kids, near as I could tell." So naturally she'd made kids her career...

"What did you do to make her mad?" His hand slid into her hair, distracting her a little...probably distracting himself.

"I don't know. I know I say that when I don't want to talk about something, but I honestly don't know. I climbed onto the counter to reach the phone on the wall and the next I knew she jerked me down by the arm. I threw up on her. It really hurt. She sent me to bed for being bad. A couple of days later…Mom and Mack got there. The social worker gave them grief, I guess. Kids whose families aren't in the circus don't get abducted, I guess. But the instant Mom saw my arm, the social worker lady realized she'd put me with someone who'd do that…and then left it dislocated for days without taking me to the emergency room. She'd have gotten into trouble.

"So she sent me with Mom, and they were so glad to have me back they didn't file any complaints." It had taken Jolie most of her life to riddle out exactly what had happened with the social worker, the things you missed when you're little…

Reece scowled so hard Jolie was suddenly more than half-afraid he'd tell her to stop being dramatic or something else that made it her fault. But he let go of her hair, wrapped his arm around her shoulders and pulled her snugly against his side. The kiss he pressed to her temple lasted and lasted, and when he eventually spoke it was against her skin. "I should have asked what happened."

"You were eight." Jolie knew she might never learn to navigate the outside world but maybe she could learn to navigate this man. "You took good care of me. Everyone did. But you and Gordy especially."

He made a sound so contrary that Jolie tugged his head to hers to kiss him and subtly shift the conversation. "Thank you for going along with the shoulder thing. You know I was about a heartbeat away from climbing onto your shoulders."

"You know better than to think I couldn't have picked you up," he joked, but his voice said he was still upset.

"Oh, no I'm sure Strong Man could have, but Safety Man—you remember the other side of your personality? He would not have been very happy if I had. I didn't have any spotters, no safety gear on… What if you dropped me?"

"That's not how it goes and you know it." Reece goosed her ribs, and when she was giggling he stood, picked her up and tossed her over his shoulder.

She laughed and hit him on the butt. "Dirty! My defenses were down!" He didn't put her down, just started walking. "You know when you do these things in public, wearing that T-shirt, you're representing Keightly…" Right across the pavilion…in full view of the adults, who squinted, and the children, who laughed…off they went to the exit.

Jolie braced one arm against his back to hold herself up and waved her cotton candy at the kids they passed with the other so no one would be alarmed, and dropped the sugary stuff into a trashcan as they passed it. "Hey, Hercules, where are we going?"

"Home."

Thank God. And if he knew what was good for him, it had better be for sex.

The trapeze didn't smell like sawdust, but it had the same effect on Reece. He had thought the more he got up on the thing, the better he would do with it, but he still always felt on the edge of panic the whole time. His grim glowers even kind of scared the girls in the troupe. He needed to work on that but taking on one more thing seemed too much right now.

Every evening during the week, before the kids were picked up, Reece came and worked with them on the trapeze. The first two weeks of flying with a catcher, they'd all learned the knee-hang and how to fly back onto the swing when another girl swung out to meet them.

It took another two weeks for Reece's body to re-learn the ins and outs of the whole dangerous business, and for the old muscle memory to adjust to his new, bigger body. Only then did he feel comfortable adding the simple toss to their routine. The extra hour he spent teaching Anthony to catch in the evenings helped. Anthony taking the role was the light at the end of Reece's trapeze tunnel...

Two weeks later Reece added the simple toss to their routine. Things were going well.

With Reece's rigorous physicals and safety standards and Jolie's strict behavior policies it meant that at the re-hearsal for the end-of-summer finale show they only had light injuries. The worst had come in the form of a scissor incident in costuming, and it had been when Reece hadn't been around and had only required a couple of stitches.

"How are you doing?" Jolie asked as he stretched his arms and shoulders, preparing to climb the ladder up to the platform.

He turned round so she could push his arm up from the back, stretching his shoulders better. "I'm fine. Have you decided if you're going to do anything during the finale?"

"I don't really want to. I don't want to show up the kids. They've been working hard all summer." She moved to the other arm, repeating the stretch he preferred.

He nodded, looking no less grim as he took to the ladder to get on with today's rehearsal.

Jolie moved off to the stands and took a seat, eyes fixed on the group above. They didn't need her direction today. She simply waited for Reece to climb on the screen and then pressed "Play' on the music that would accompany the aerial act.

The kids had gone for a haunted-circus theme, and

every piece of music sounded like a deranged calliope, taking to the minor keys. While she really liked the theme the kids had put together all summer for the show, today, with Reece's mood, it put her on edge.

Anthony was the best at the knee-hang, but he really wanted Reece to be proud of him, Jolie could tell. He also was a little too confident for her liking. Two days ago Jolie had caught Anthony and his girlfriend, Tara, on the trapeze one evening after the camp was closed, practicing together. She'd put a stop to it. But she hadn't told Reece. He was so on edge about the trapeze already.

Reece got his swing where it needed to be, found his mark, and called, "Hep!" which got the first flyer launching on the swing.

He'd started self-medicating with anti-nausea medicine about three weeks ago, and he had been a little late taking them today because of a small emergency at the office. He wasn't sure he'd taken it in time to get the full effect, but the symptoms when he was in the air never started until he'd been at it for a few tricks and had had time to work himself into a mental lather.

It was psychosomatic, and he knew that Jolie would understand—she had waded through a few panic attacks this spring—but he didn't want her to know. It felt like breaking a promise to her if his mind was making him unable to complete the trapeze position he'd agreed to.

The first flier flew from the bar to his hands. Like always, she looked up at him nervously, like he was going to fling her off the swing. The three girls in the troupe always looked at him nervously. The only one who took every flight with extreme glee and confidence was Anthony— the fourth flier, it was a necessary part of learning to catch.

It would let the kids down if Reece couldn't catch. And the camp. Anthony just wasn't ready to do the catching yet but he got his shot earlier with the knee-hangs. He and Tara had worked that trick out very well during classes.

They each got a shot with the same tricks. The girls went, and when it was Anthony's turn Reece marked his swing and yelled, "Hep!" but noticed when he swung back toward his new younger brother that he was standing on the bar.

"Anthony!" he yelled. A combination of his lateness in taking the anti-nausea and vertigo pills and the surprise trick combined to rob him of the ability to say anything else. Anthony launched up at the wrong time, executed a perfect forward somersault, but when the timing was off, it didn't matter how perfect the trick was.

He was close. Reece stretched for Anthony's hands and only got one of them, throwing his swing off balance so that it swung on the diagonal.

Anthony seemed to understand only when their hands were slipping how dangerous what he'd done had been, and let go to let the net catch him.

The wrong point in the swing. The wrong time. Reece could do nothing but watch Anthony fall and pray he hit the net. They learned to fall properly the first day.

Anthony bounced once at the edge and then flew off into the ring.

Jolie had her phone out, dialing 911, before Anthony even let go of Reece's hand. But it all happened so fast. She ran with the phone to her ear, and gave report and instructions as she fell at Anthony's side.

"He's breathing," she called to Reece. And he, ever the protector, unfolded from the swing and fell to the net as soon as it was safe to do so, taking the fastest route down so he could get to them.

Breathing, but unconscious. She dared not move him, but reached to check his pulse, and breathed a tiny bit easier when she found a strong beat with her fingertips.

Reece knelt beside the unconscious teen and began checking for injuries. "More broken legs." His voice rasped. "Looks like the left tibia. Simple."

Jolie didn't even need to look at him to know how he was doing. His skin had turned ashen, but his hands were steady. This had to be like a nightmare for him.

Anthony started to wake up, and Reece found his voice. "*Do not move*, Anthony. You could have a neck or spine injury. I know you're in pain, but be still." And then added to Jolie, "Brace his head with your knees. Don't let him turn it."

He moved on from the obvious bones to Anthony's abdomen, prodding lightly as he watched the kid's face. "You tell me if this hurts, okay?" Jolie watched as well, as Reece's hands moved around Anthony's belly. At the left side, under the ribs, he pressed and Anthony cried out.

Reece stopped pressing, folded one of Anthony's arms up for Jolie to reach and said in tones so level and steady that her hair stood on end, "Keep an eye on his pulse. I need your phone."

"My pocket." She pressed Anthony's wrist, finding the pulse and counting the beats as she alternated between looking at her watch and watching Anthony's face.

Reece walked a short distance away and called, she assumed, 911 again. She heard the "words possible splenic rupture' and noticed that Anthony's pulse rate was increasing.

"Reece? His pulse is speeding up…a little."

He hung up and came back over. "How much?"

"What's happening?" Anthony asked, his voice breathy, scared.

Jolie answered Reece, frowning, "It's gone up from one-eighteen to one-twenty-five." And then said to the youngest Bohannon, "Do you hear the ambulance? Don't worry. Everything is going to be okay. The ambulance is here and we'll get you to the hospital and patched up. But you need to stay calm, okay?"

The paramedics stepped in, and with Reece's help got Anthony loaded onto a backboard and into the ambulance.

"Go with him," Jolie said to Reece, knowing he would be of assistance. "I'll be right behind you."

She should have told Reece that she'd found them practicing. Tara had gotten the message that she could be kicked out of the camp and not allowed back next year for the stunt with the trapeze, but Anthony had had something to prove. And he'd wanted to impress Reece more than anyone. If she'd told Reece, he could have gotten through to Anthony.

This was her fault.

But Reece would blame himself.

Six hours later Reece had yet to speak to Jolie. She moved along beside him through the hospital, everywhere she could go. He was a doctor so they let him into Recovery to see Anthony when he came out of surgery. And he left Jolie in the waiting room with every single person who lived at the farm—even Granny and the brood of young wild things she fostered.

He just couldn't think about her right now or how she'd take it when he told her the camp was done. No more. No show. No next season. Anthony could have died. But, really, any of them could have died. It didn't matter how safe they played it, when it came time for that last show, the safety gear came off. And he'd fallen for it—the idea that these were safe tricks. That this was fine. He should have been listening to his gut when every time he'd got into the swing, he'd almost thrown up.

Reece stayed back with Anthony as they removed the tube in his throat and Reece got to talk to him.

"You know I'm going to kick your ass when you get better," Reece said, taking Anthony's hand and leaning over the bed so he could look him in the eye.

Anthony smiled, and Reece relaxed.

"I thought you'd catch me."

Reece shook his head, but he was so relieved he couldn't do anything but rib him. "I would have if you had told me what you were going to do. But you're lucky. Your spleen ruptured, but they got it out clean. You survived a ruptured spleen, which is fairly badass. You also have a broken leg, and it's a simple fracture. Granny wanted them to put you in a pink cast with flowers, but I intervened. That old lady is so upset she's forgotten how to swear."

"Sign of the apocalypse, isn't it?"

"Sources say." Reece grinned and then did something that probably would have horrified the kid if he wasn't drugged, and especially if chicks were watching. He dropped a kiss on Anthony's head. "We want you around until you're old enough to cuss like Granny Bohannon. You don't need to impress anyone, you already have. And if you don't believe how many people love you, when they wheel you to your room, I want you to look at the waiting room."

Anthony's eyes squeezed shut and a couple of tears slipped out, but he nodded. "Thanks, Reece."

Reece squeezed his hand.

"If you tell anyone I cried, I'm going to tell them you kissed me."

Reece smirked and let go. "All right, Spleeny." He made his farewells before the recovery nurses kicked him out, and went out to speak with the family.

Later that evening, when the hospital administration made it clear that visiting hours were over, Jolie waited for everyone to exit Anthony's room and then went to speak with him. Luckily, she found him in one of his post-surgery lucid phases and took his hand. "We're going to head home, but Granny is going to be here bright and early in the morning to sit with you. Do you want one of us to stay here with you tonight?"

Anthony smiled a little and shook his head. "I'm okay. Could you call Tara for me?"

"She's been here, honey," Jolie told him, grinning. "And her parents just dragged her home a few minutes ago. But you were sleeping. She knows you're going to be okay. She'll probably bring you something she baked tomorrow…and yell at you."

"Doesn't do any good," he muttered.

Jolie knew precisely what he was talking about: her yelling at him. "Well, it would have been better if you hadn't needed to learn the hard way, but you came through it. Everyone's going to be fine."

"Reece isn't. He's…very upset still."

"Reece learned his lesson the hard way once already." Again she wished she'd just told him about Anthony and Tara. It was her fault really that Anthony was hurt. She was too lenient…or maybe not intimidating enough. Something. She should have handled something differently.

"His dad," Anthony filled in.

"His dad."

"No one will tell me how it happened."

No one liked to talk about it. Jolie didn't like to talk about it, but maybe if she had used it to scare him the other day this wouldn't have happened. Not talking about things wasn't working out for her on so many levels.

"It was equipment malfunction, a Russian swing. His dad was flying on that one. They take two fliers to get the swing moving fast and high enough, and then the front person lets go and kind of…catapults really fast and far to the catcher. Much further than regular catches." She tried to explain gently and quickly, knowing he needed his rest.

Anthony squeezed her hand. "Something broke?"

"Reece was the additional power on the swing. He wasn't supposed to fly, just be at the back to get it going, and he's really good at that. Has a powerful swing." She had to stop and focus on something to keep the mental images away. "Whoever installed it the last time hadn't done a good job. One of the bolts had stripped and as there were a number of other bolts, he'd just figured he'd change it the next time it was set up."

"Did it break?" Anthony asked, the horror in his voice pulling her attention back to his bruised face.

She nodded. "Before his dad jumped, the swing came loose…at the worst time…and they both pitched off it at a really bad angle, moving fast. It looked like they were both going to miss the net, but somehow only Henry missed it. Reece hit it. I think Henry pushed him or flung him off course somehow. He had the air knocked out of him but his dad hit the rigging and then the ground. He didn't die instantly. There was so much blood…and the EMTs didn't get there in time." Which was why Jolie had studied emergency medicine and was a certified EMT.

It had been so long since she'd even let herself remember it…

"So he checks the rigging every day," Anthony supplied.

"I don't know how to make him stop or even if I should try," Jolie confirmed. "Anyway, he's not mad at you, but he might ride you when you get out of this antiseptic-smelling lock-up, but it's just because he's feeling really protective of you."

Anthony nodded. She squeezed his hand again. "We all are. Now sleep. I'm sure Granny will bring you something in the morning to keep you amused. Or maybe she'll make you write 'I will not pull unexpected tricks on the trapeze' one thousand times. Either way, rest." She leaned up and in to reach his cheek, kissed it, and then went to find Reece.

Jolie walked with Reece to the garage. "We should talk about this…" she said, hurrying to keep up with his longer stride. She wanted to hold his hand, but he had them crammed into his pockets.

"When we get back to the farm."

He knew. He knew and he thought she was an utter failure as a camp director.

The trip home felt like a drive to her execution.

Jolie just wasn't sure whether it was the end of them or the end of the camp.

CHAPTER ELEVEN

JOLIE STOPPED THE car and Reece climbed out and set off for the big top. "Reece, you don't need to go back in there right now."

"I have to," Reece bit out, not looking back at her. "I'm taking down the trapeze."

She ran to cover the distance being eaten up by his long stride and grabbed his hand. "I already locked up the ladders. No one can get up to there without getting the ladders unlocked."

He scowled but stopped and looked back at her. "I'll check. Go to your trailer and wait."

As much as she wanted to make him stop and listen to her, talk to her, just be with her until she knew he was okay, Jolie let go of his hand and did as he requested.

She almost hoped Anthony had told him then at least he'd place the blame on her—where it belonged—not blame himself.

After she reached the trailer and got inside, she stepped back out where she could best see the tent and waited for Reece to arrive.

And when he still hadn't come half an hour later she sat on the stairs and waited.

The good news was that she could now unequivocally say that she had control of her emotions again. Calm. She'd managed to stay calm through the whole thing. Right now she was worried but able to keep the panic at bay.

She folded her arms on her knees and laid her head down, giving him the time he needed despite her natural inclination to run after him.

Reece had to admire Jolie's simple solution to lock up the ladders. She'd climbed them and pulled the tail of the rope ladder up behind her. They draped over the platforms, where no one could get to them without extreme effort and construction ladders locked up in the pole barn.

Checking her solution had taken about a minute, and then he spent the next forty minutes throwing up.

Jolie had gone to her trailer, as he'd asked. He saw she was sitting on the stairs with her head on her knees, waiting for him. Hearing his approach, she lifted her head. "You look like hell."

"Yeah. I need a drink," Reece muttered.

She stood, heading into her home to get him a glass of water. "Or did you mean booze?"

He took the glass and drank it all. When it was empty and his mouth was a little improved, he looked at her. "The camp is over, Jo. No finale show. No camp next year. I'm going to call up the buyer from this spring and see if his offer is still on the table."

The calm with which she took his ruling seemed off. She held out a hand for the glass and took it back to the kitchen. "Are you okay?"

"I'm... No." He may as well tell her. "I've been—"

"It was my fault that he did that," she said quietly, stopping him in his tracks.

Reece turned and sat on the couch, taking up entirely

too much room in the small home when he stood around in it. "What do you mean?"

"I caught him and Tara on the trapeze the other evening, and I chewed them both out." Her voice was level, no tears in sight, though she looked haunted by guilt, and there was a small tell about how upset it had made her in the way she kept holding her own hands. "I got through to Tara, but I guess I didn't get through to Anthony. And I didn't tell you because I didn't want you to be upset. I thought I'd handled it…but I hadn't. If it had come from you, he would have listened."

"He might have," Reece said, but shrugged. "Hard to say. It was probably a matter of time. And, really, we're lucky it was family. If it had been one of the kids, they could have sued."

She finally moved to the couch and sat beside him. "Next year—"

"There won't be a next year, Jolie." He needed to stand. She was too close and when she was close he wanted to please and protect her, physically and emotionally. Best she stayed outside arm's reach. "This life is too dangerous. And you're not performing because of it as I thought you would. You teach, and your students are doing great on the wire, but you're not performing except those times you practice your routine, which I thought you were going to perform at the finale, but you said no. So what's the point?"

He turned back to look at her on the couch, silent and frowning. Was it because she worried about him or she was trying to work out how to make him do what she wanted? He didn't know.

"Where does this leave us?"

She probably wouldn't want to wait for a solution to appear, or like the solution he had in mind. "I love you, Jo.

But there's no future for us if you're on the road, and there's no happiness for you if you're not in the life. And I don't even know if I could handle it if you were performing. We tried to preserve the life with the camp, but it can't work. So you tell me, what's the solution? Do you want to come and work at my practice? Make appointments and sit all day at a desk? Good Lord, you're like the ultimate riddle."

"Once again, I am a problem to be solved."

"Stop saying that."

Naturally, he would wait until he could couch it in break-up words before he said "I love you' the first time.

"Sounds like you have made up your mind."

"I have to protect you." He said the words softly, but they may as well have been shouted.

Jolie shook her head. "I'm not your responsibility."

"Yes, you are my responsibility." He laughed, a short, mirthless sound. "And I know how stupid that sounds when I say it out loud, but I'm supposed to protect you. I'm still on that job."

"The job your dad gave you when I was five?" What could she say to that? He'd all but admitted it was insane.

He plowed his hand through his hair. "Yes."

"Is that why you love me? Because I'm your responsibility to take care of?"

"No. That's why I try so hard not to love you. Makes it that much harder to take care of you properly when every time you're sad it's a lance through my chest." He stepped to the door, ready to escape. "I have a list of owners who are looking for a wire act. I'll send it over tomorrow. Email."

"You've been…you've been headhunting a job for me?" She didn't know whether to cry or scream.

"I was just getting a feel for whether there was a market."

"How long? Recently? All summer? When did you take this little task on your shoulders?" She rubbed between her brows. Some of that old numbness began seeping in and she let it. "You know what? Never mind. I don't want either of us to say anything else. Something we might regret. We'll talk again when we have clear heads."

"My head is clear, honey."

"Are you blaming yourself?"

"I'm blaming everyone. You. Me. Anthony. The people in his past who made that kid feel like even when he was part of a family he had to keep working to make them love him. And I'm blaming the lure of the big top and the thrill of flying." He opened the door and stepped out. "I'll talk to you soon."

At least that would be different this time. He didn't want to hurt her, but he would be man enough to put it to her straight before he left her.

Reece drove his car through the grass to park on the far side of the big top, and he didn't care who didn't like it. There was a trail of dust streaking across the flat Georgia landscape where he'd raced down the long dusty drive. At least driving on the grass wouldn't make life difficult for any asthmatics on the farm.

He wouldn't have had to do this if the whole area hadn't been packed with cars and fans—spectators, he imagined.

Jolie had called that morning and left a message that the season finale recital of Keightly Circus Camp would be going ahead, and had then refused to answer any of his calls when he rang her back.

Inside the tent, all the seating had been installed and

it was packed to the gills with people. He saw all manner of dressed performers below the stands, which traditionally served as the backstage area for performers about to come out.

It wasn't a haunted circus. It was a zombie circus.

But no matter how cute it was, it could not go on. "Anyone seen Miss Jolie?" he asked, making the circuit around the tent via that backstage portion. Children pointed in the direction he traveled, and he eventually found her counting heads. Without saying anything to alert the kids, he grabbed her elbow and steered her out of the tent, where he might possibly choke her to death. "Call it off."

"Reece, just listen. There is no trapeze act. These kids have worked too hard to miss their finale. However, all the safety equipment is being used. And you're just going to have to trust me. I know I screwed up with Anthony, but don't take it out on the kids. They need this. They deserve it."

He looked toward the flap and a bizarre little grey-skinned hobo clown smiled at him. And waved. Reece waved back at the little boy then looked at Jolie. "You should have told me."

"Yes. I should have. There's a lot of things I should have told you. And when you said you loved me, even though you said it under duress, I should have believed you."

"You didn't believe me?"

"Not until later." She touched his face and then pressed her thumb between his brows and gave the muscle a little rub. It actually felt good, forcing his brow to relax. "I promise we've taken every precaution that's possible. I know you'll approve of what we've done. It's more camp than circus now. And the only way someone's going to get hurt is if a meteor falls. No trapeze. Please, Reece. Just go and watch the show. I saved you a seat by Granny." She turned to head for the tent again.

"What about the aerialists?"

"They have a new act." She stopped before entering. "And they've worked like crazy the past week to get it ready. It's not on the trapeze. And it doesn't even need a net. Okay?"

He was holding up the show. Reece sighed and walked inside. Once again he'd failed to say no to Jolie. Finding Granny easily enough, he took a seat and tried to relax. Mouth like a sailor and a heart of gold, she laid a weathered hand over his and gave him a comforting pat. "Don't worry, everything's gonna be okay."

"I hope so."

He must have looked sick because she let go of his hand, reached for her purse and put it in his lap. "But if you have to throw up, there's a barf bag in there. I stole it from the hospital." When he didn't say anything, she added, "Them zombies are disgusting."

Over the next two hours he watched the most ridiculously cute zombie-clown parody since the *Thriller* video that he had to laugh. They always started with the clowns.

Then came jugglers with fake bones, balls painted with skulls, sticks modeled like femurs…

Stiff-legged acrobats, who shuffled around before breaking into feats of creepy, contorted tumbling.

And toward the end an oddly placed fashion show where the kid designers talked about the costuming. While the little zombie fashion show was going on, the crew went about in the background, setting something up.

Thick mats went down. Cables suspended from the rigging high above were brought down to dangle and large steel hoops were attached to the ends. Set in the wide shape of a square, so all around the tent everyone would have a good view.

Then he saw his aerialists, minus Anthony, walking out in single file, dressed all in black with gauzy fabric tatters hanging everywhere. While the rest of the show had pre-recorded music with it, he heard the first strains of the calliope as the girls took their positions in the hoops. Mack drove the calliope into the ring with his mother at the keyboard, playing what he could only call music of a haunted carousel.

The stage hands got the hoops spinning. He'd made sure all the trapeze troupe had been gymnasts…except Anthony. Give a gymnast a big spinning hoop to play with? They probably liked it just as well as the trapeze, and at only three feet from thick mats Jolie was right, it would be a miracle if they found a way to hurt themselves badly.

They found artistic ways to arrange themselves within the hoops, each move slowing or increasing the speed of the spin. It was flashy and graceful, and a little bit creepy with the calliope. And as he watched, he forgot the horror that always darkened his circus experience.

Jolie had done it. They'd got off to a rocky start but next year there would be a waiting list a mile long to come to the camp. At the end she made a short speech, giving recognition to all of the former Keightly Circus performers and especially to him, who…

He could fill in that blank. Reece, who had made her beg and plead to be allowed to try it. Reece, who treated her like an incompetent child. Reece, who left for long stretches of time because he couldn't control everyone.

Not that she said any of that. He waved his hand at the applause and circulated through the crowd of parents and performers, giving his congratulations. Then he went to Jolie's trailer to wait for her. She'd left the door unlocked, as usual, so when she finally got back she found him sitting on her stairs with a glass of tea in his hand. The problem was, no matter how long he'd sat there, he didn't know what to say to her. His feelings were all still scrambled in his head.

"You were right. I didn't see anything there that…wasn't amazing. And the kids deserved their shot to do the show. I hope someone taped the zombie clown *Thriller* dance."

Jolie smiled and came to a stop in front of the stairs, just far away that he couldn't touch her without standing up. "Oh, don't worry, we have the whole thing on tape. It might be one of a kind. Collector's edition."

"About that…" Reece licked his lips. "About next year…"

"Wait. I want to talk about us. Can we talk about us first?" She stepped closer, her courage faltering a little. He'd been smiling at the circus. He'd enjoyed it. She should have stuck with that topic. She could handle that topic…

Reece tilted his head back toward the living room. "Do you want to come inside to do this?"

"No. With you on the stairs, we're closer to the same eye level right now. The height changes inside, nothing that tall for you to sit on," Jolie babbled, then paused, took a breath to find her center again and started over. "I have a speech. And if we go moving around, I might forget it. Or forget how it starts."

"You have a speech?" Reece reached behind him to set the glass of tea inside then focused on her. "I'm ready."

"You said I didn't trust you, and you were right. I didn't. I wanted to, and I tried. I knew you were trying. But it just wasn't coming together for me. When I got on the trapeze with you that day, I couldn't bring myself to reach for you. When we did the knee-hang, it was different. I never had to let go of the bar until you had hold of me securely. But when we did the toss and I had to let go of the bar, I couldn't take your hands, even when they were a sure thing. Not because I thought I would fall, I thought it was possible that you would drop me. And just that possibility seemed so much worse than me deciding to fall on my own. It doesn't make a lot of sense."

Reece waved a hand. "It does. That was about being in control, even if the decision you made was one that could have hurt you. I understand that need for control. Believe me." He was very calm. If that meant he didn't care, he was going to have to reject her twice, because she wasn't going to stop.

"I don't even know when I started to trust you. It wasn't like there was a light-bulb moment when I thought, Everything's okay, I can trust Reece now. He hasn't broken his promises or whatever. The whole summer, and even when we got back from the hospital and…well, we broke up, right? I expected it. I had been waiting for it the whole summer. And then you had that list, and it seemed like you had been expecting it too." She felt tears burning her eyes and had to stop talking for a moment to breathe.

"I could be a total psycho and ask you to get on the trapeze to prove to you that I trust you, but I don't need to do that. I already reached for you…today. I knew you would be mad about the show, but I knew you would come. I know you'll always come, Reece. I know it. Even if you…" Her voice cracked and she squeaked the rest in the most undignified fashion while swiping her cheeks. "Even if you don't want me any more."

He stood, took two steps toward her, reached out, and his hands didn't close. "Are you done with your speech?"

She nodded.

His arms surged around her waist and he picked her up, carried her inside, his mouth on hers before the door closed, and her pants were off before they got to the bed.

Ten minutes later Reece rolled onto his back, dragging her with him. "Sorry. I meant to last and last..."

"It was longer than five seconds," she teased, smiling.

He groaned, "I'm never going to live that one down, am I?"

She scooted up closer so she could tuck her nose beneath his chin. "You do every time. I just like to make sure you don't lose the magic." And then she pulled back to look him in the eye. "And you had it at the show tonight, didn't you? Not the sexy magic, but...you felt it, didn't you?"

"I forgot where I was, who I was...and why I had left. That's the first time that's happened. Yes." He pushed her hair back from her face. "I felt the magic. If you want the camp next year, I'm good with that. I think if you run it like you have done this year—"

"Without the trapeze," Jolie cut in.

He smiled, looking relieved. "Without the trapeze. The hoops were wonderful. I'd rather you stay away from the silk aerialists, though. That's more dangerous than trapeze."

"I agree." She kissed him again and said, "We don't have to make any decisions. I don't want to travel, but I did find out that I can get an agent to arrange corporate gigs and big parties, short-term travel if I do feel like performing. But, honestly, the idea of having a pasture to ride in every day, maybe get a miniature mare and breed them? One day build a house with a foundation? That idea's starting to grow on me. I still don't think I could handle suburbia but…I can handle not traveling. I can make a life, a happy life, outside The Life."

"You work on building a life outside The Life, I'll work on making sure it's happy." Reece didn't propose, but it was as good as she needed.

She sat up, straddling his groin, and gave a slow wiggle. "I owe you an 'I love you.' I'll see if I can find one lying about if you can last longer than ten minutes this time."

"If I can't, I'm sure we can find Mr. Happy around here somewhere…" he said, rolling her over and kissing her breathless.

Strides may have been made today, but the man still liked to be in charge.

And that was okay. Jolie knew she had all the time in the world to break him of it.

* * * * *

MILLS & BOON®

Fancy some more Mills & Boon books?

Well, good news!

We're giving you

15% OFF

your next eBook or paperback book purchase
on the Mills & Boon website.

So hurry, visit the website today and type **GIFT15**
in at the checkout for your exclusive 15% discount.

www.millsandboon.co.uk/gift15

MILLS & BOON®

Why shop at millsandboon.co.uk?

Each year, thousands of romance readers find their perfect read at millsandboon.co.uk. That's because we're passionate about bringing you the very best romantic fiction. Here are some of the advantages of shopping at www.millsandboon.co.uk:

* **Get new books first**—you'll be able to buy your favourite books one month before they hit the shops

* **Get exclusive discounts**—you'll also be able to buy our specially created monthly collections, with up to 50% off the RRP

* **Find your favourite authors**—latest news, interviews and new releases for all your favourite authors and series on our website, plus ideas for what to try next

* **Join in**—once you've bought your favourite books, don't forget to register with us to rate, review and join in the discussions

Visit **www.millsandboon.co.uk**
for all this and more today!